FINDING MYSELF

The Final Book In The Chaos Series

BY

VICTORIA J. BROWN

Print ISBN 978-1-912175-84-0

Also By Victoria J. Brown

See how it all began for Kat in the first two books in the
Chaos series :
Holding Myself
Losing Myself

PRAISE FOR HOLDING MYSELF

"Holding Myself is ultimately a life-affirming read with recognisable, real-life moments full of warmth and compassion." **Laura Bambrey - Laura Bambrey Books**

"...a lovely book with some unexpected occurrences and an ending that has left me wanting the next book sooner rather than later!" **Alison Daughtrey-Drew - Ali-The Dragon Slayer**

"Victoria J. Brown has a wonderfully enchanting writing style and the narrative just flows so perfectly, enveloping you in Kats life right from the first page, that it's impossible to put down." **Joanne Robertson - My Chestnut Reading Tree**

"A wonderful story of hope, love and new beginnings!" **Rachel Broughton - Rae Reads**

"The characters were well rounded and believable and I cared what happened to them, always a good sign." **Amazon Reviewer**

"Having really enjoyed this book I find it hard to believe that this is Victoria J. Brown's first novel as the writing just flows and the style is very accomplished." **Julie Ryan - All Thinks Bookie**

PRAISE FOR LOSING MYSELF

"I loved all the twists and turns in the book and can't wait for the 3rd to come." **Amazon Reviewer**

"'Losing Myself' is an emotional, thought-provoking, and touching novel about real life situations, as well as real life emotions." **Kaisha Holloway - The Writing Garnet**

"I adored this book, I thought that the writing style was beautiful and I didn't want the story to end." **Donna Maguire - Donnas Book Blog**

"A thoroughly enjoyable read, with emotion, friendship and dilemma's galore..." **Alexina Golding - Bookstormer**

"Victoria writes with warmth and compassion that means you feel really invested in the characters and their outcome. Very easy to read and highly enjoyable." **Alison Daughtrey-Drew - Ali - The Dragon Slayer**

"Losing Myself is a must read for fans of Holding Myself. It is an endearing read that will fill you full of different emotions and leave you wanting more." **Sarah Hardy - By The Letter Book Reviews**

To my gorgeous girls, Alexia and Gabriella
My world

PROLOGUE

The two bundles were wrapped in white blankets, an additional pink knitted one covering their tiny bodies. The small white wooden crib had been placed in the corner of the room. Max had delivered many of their things before we arrived home. Apparently, it had been a mad rush to gather all their belongings: 'A few trips back and forth,' Marianne had told me. I was grateful Max and Marianne had worked together to sort out all the girls' things, knowing I wouldn't have had the energy to do it.

A traditional Christmas hadn't really taken place for any of us. Four days of understanding this new chapter in my life, four days of staring at these two little people I was now responsible for.

Two little people who couldn't survive without me. Such a scary thought.

The whole experience (not the birth) had been quite euphoric but at the same time overwhelming and quite surreal. I'd spent most of the time, since they had emerged in their innocence into this huge world, trying to believe they were mine.

Suzy cuddled me as I let the tears fall, a helpless sensation sweeping over my body. A mixture of emotions kept whipping its way through me, from joy to shock to absolute terror.

'It's the baby blues.' Suzy stroked my hair. I let her softness take me, as I melted into her, needing someone to take away the vulnerability. 'You'll be fine in a few days; happens to most women a few days after giving birth.'

'I feel so rubbish,' I sobbed. 'They deserve so much better than me. I'm going to be rubbish at this. I don't know what I'm doing.'

'Now, look at me.' She placed her hands firmly on my upper arms, pulling back, forcing me to meet her blue eyes, her petite pretty face firmly staring back at me. This made me feel worse. I knew I looked horrendous. I'd not even looked in the mirror this morning, because I couldn't bear the reflection. 'You are an amazing person. A strong woman. If I could choose a Mum I'd pick you. The girls are so lucky.' Her kind words triggered another avalanche of tears.

She cuddled me close for about five minutes. We didn't talk as she let me release this build-up of emotion. I knew I had to be strong, but didn't have the power to control the outburst.

Once I'd calmed, Suzy obviously wanted to distract me, as she stood up to admire my babies.

My babies: I was still trying to get use to saying that.

'They are gorgeous.' She smiled adoringly – and I thought I saw a yearning in her own eyes.

'I know,' I choked. 'So, did you get anything nice off Lawrence for Christmas?' I asked, feeling the need to change the subject. Wanting to push away the knot that had grown from my stomach to my chest. The knot that I couldn't get rid of.

'Well …' she smiled, her eyes aflame as they always were when she spoke of Lawrence. She sat back down beside me, her grin full of elation as she held out her hand to show me a diamond sparkling upon a platinum ring.

Guilt joined the array of emotions that were swamping me. How had I not noticed? The clear-cut crystal reflected from the Christmas tree lights in vibrant flashing colours.

'Oh my God,' I whispered. I threw my arms around her, hugging her close, not wanting to let her go.

'I know,' Suzy laughed. 'It was such a shock.'

'I'm not shocked: he's smitten!'

'He's so lovely.' Suzy studied the ring, examining the jewel as if she'd just seen it for the first time (as I imagined she'd done many times over the last few days).

'Why didn't you tell me?'

'You had so much going on here.' She shook her head, but her eyes still focused on the twinkling jewel. 'I wanted to tell you to your face.'

'I'm so pleased for you.' The words got caught up with the tears that followed as I hugged her again.

'Thank you.'

'So come on, what's the plan?' I needed her to know that through the emotional imbalance I was experiencing I *was* really pleased for her.

'We've been talking and … the thing is, we didn't really want a long engagement.' She bit her lip. 'We were planning for about April time.'

'April?' April was only four months away.

'Yeah, I know it sounds really soon but we don't see the point in waiting around. This is what we want. It seems pointless holding off for another year or longer, and there's an Ironman tournament around then that would fit perfectly with our plans.' She was talking quickly, as if she had to justify their decision.

'Ironman Tournament?' I laughed.

She smiled. 'I know, we must be mad, but the one we want to do is in May, in Texas, so we thought we could travel around for a bit the week before, then after the contest have a holiday for a week somewhere else in America.'

'I love the sound of the holiday part.'

'I also wanted to ask if you would be my chief bridesmaid.' She was staring at me eagerly.

'Of course, thank you.' We'd been through so much in our lifetime and I wanted her to know how special she was, how pleased I was her life was falling into place.

'There is one other thing,' she said, biting her lip.

'What?'

'Lawrence is asking Joe and Max to be his best men.'

'*Two* best men?'

'He didn't want to upset either of them, so he thought it best to ask them both.' I nodded at her explanation. 'Are you okay with this?'

'*Me?*' Hoping I sounded surprised, 'Yeah, of course,' I shrugged away the dread that was rising inside me. 'Why shouldn't I be?'

'Well, you know—'

'It's fine, can't really expect anything else.' I paused. 'As long as you're not inviting Gina.'

'Erm …'

'I'm joking.' I laughed at her predicament, stroking her arm. I *was* joking, but how nice would it have been for her to tell me there was no way Gina was coming.

'Oh honestly, I don't want them there, but you know he's Lawrence's best friend and Max probably won't do it if—'

'Calm down, it was a joke. I totally understand.'

'Are sure you're okay with it?'

'I'll be fine, don't you worry about me.' Once again I tried to mask the turmoil that was sweeping through me.

'Well, you know you can bring a guest.'

'But I'd take you!' I laughed, as she gave a sad smile. 'I'll be fine, seriously.' I put my hand over her hand that sported the radiant diamond. 'I promise.'

An hour later, as her car drove away, guilt engulfed me. I let out another storm of tears. I was happy for Suzy. I wasn't jealous: that wasn't it. I wasn't crying because she had such a wonderful life. There just felt like there was something missing from mine.

As I stared at my two babies, I knew I had to be strong for them. Protect them.

But how was I supposed to do that?

I had no idea where to start.

1

8 weeks later

'I'd really appreciate it if you could ask Libby to meet her friends somewhere else.' Clare was direct.

'What do you mean?' I felt my forehead crease, as I changed Poppy's nappy. Her lip quivered as the cold air hit her soft skin, and she gave a small whine. Securing the nappy and placing her tiny legs inside her suit, I still felt amazed that I'd mastered the fine art of nappy wrapping.

'Well, yesterday one of my customers was very perplexed about the hooded gentleman who was hanging around outside.'

'How do you know Libby had anything to do with him?' I tried to sound casual, but a warning bell was ringing in my head. One of the reasons Libby had come to live with me in Great Ayton – apart from giving Marianne the freedom to move in with Derek – was to get her away from her undesirable associates. And as far as I knew, she didn't have any friends over this way.

'I went outside to ask if I could help but Libby was talking to him near the entrance to the flat.'

'So she can't have friends near the front door now.'

'I'm not saying that,' Clare said quickly, obviously realising I was getting irritable. I knew it wasn't with her though. 'He seemed …' She paused as if trying to find the words to explain what seemed to have mortified her. '… odd.'

'He looked odd because he had his hood up?' I knew I was being slightly unreasonable, but I wanted her to be wrong. I wanted this to be innocent. Simply a friend of Libby's.

'No, but he looked …' She paused again.

'What?'

'I don't know …' A stutter caught in her throat. She was probably wishing she'd not bought this up with me. 'He looked … homeless.'

I lifted Poppy up from the changing mat, still trying to hide my fear from Clare. Not meeting her eye as my stomach turned uneasily. 'Kids these days, they always look scruffy.' I forced my voice to sound light as I placed Poppy into her cot.

'He wasn't a kid,' she said. Of course, he wasn't. Neither was Libby, but it made me feel better to still think of her as a child. 'He was in his forties at least.'

But Libby's doing so well, I wanted to shout, trying not to hear what a small voice was telling me.

'Are you okay?' Clare asked, my silence obviously perturbing her. 'You've gone a bit pale.' She knew nothing about Libby's problems, her condition; yes, I was still referring to it as a condition.

'I'm fine.' I licked my dry lips. 'I'll have a word with her.'

'Kathryn, are you sure you're alright?' Clare's hand was on my back.

'I'm fine.' I nodded. Feeling suddenly claustrophobic, I wished she would remove herself from my personal space.

'You don't look good.'

'I'm fine … as I said I'll talk to Libby.'

I wanted to scream about how weak and tired I felt. How I simply wanted a good night's sleep. Just one would do; one night of unbroken sleep would be heaven. It would be paradise. I wanted to beg for her help with Libby because I didn't have the energy to help her myself, although I'd promised I would.

'Okay. If you need anything, I'm only downstairs, remember,' Clare said lightly; but every word, I knew, was sincere.

She left the flat through my secret door that would take her back to the salon. I was still trying to get used to her being downstairs. Her constant barging into my home was starting to become unnerving. Often accompanied by a customer, it was unsettling to wonder who would appear next. She'd opened the hair salon only a week ago, but she'd had loads of bookings. I'd let her have my database and she'd contacted them all. Her new business was big news in the neighbourhood of tiny villages. A blend of gossip and Chinese whispers led to her salon being quite busy in the first week, with customers eager to see the changes she'd made to my old place; my old sanctuary.

My flat, at one stage, had felt like the safest place on earth; a protected shelter that was mine. Now it was Clare's. Although she'd offered the babies and me the flat, I'd thought she would respect my privacy, that I would fall straight back into the cosiness that this small haven had once offered. But I'd forgotten one major thing – it was no longer mine. Furthermore, I didn't feel I could complain or air my grievances, as I wasn't contributing to the rent. I would continue to live in this goldfish bowl until I figured out what I could do about it. At the moment, moving house, which at one stage I would have found an exciting challenge, was just another forgotten item on my 'to-do' list: because it didn't involve feeding, burping, rocking, washing and sterilising.

I picked Rosie up from the cot as Poppy happily gazed at the mobile that hung above it. Rosie was a precious baby. Obviously, my love was given equally to her and Poppy; but Rosie was so much more fragile.

Switched onto autopilot, the mode that had become my life, I changed Rosie's nappy. As always, her change was before her feed, as it would only come back up if I laid her straight down afterwards. I'd often wondered about cot deaths, as sometimes it would take Rosie ten minutes after her feed to have mini-convulsions as the milky liquid caught in her throat. I read somewhere that many babies were sick, but because they were only consuming liquid it would stream from their mouths. This wasn't the case with Rosie;

our little routine of propping her up with endless cushions had become the norm.

As she snuggled in my arms, sucking hungrily on her bottle, I tried to block out the implications of what Clare had told me, forcing myself to breathe through the fear.

Libby was coping; we'd enrolled her on a programme, so she was getting all the help she needed for her condition. She was fine.

I'd know if she wasn't.

Wouldn't I?

2

No-one tells you how hard it is. Other parents try, with their frivolous comments: 'Your life will never be the same again, but it's so worth it.' They'd make it sound enlightening, as if those without children were missing out on some special, secret ingredient that would make life so wonderfully happy in a fairy-tale kind of way. I'd listened intently when my customers had told me the joy that children bring, how lovely having a new-born in the house was, how children are the light of our life; and to be honest, I believed this. I felt it. When I looked at these two wonderful beings that had entered my life, I truly felt a love that I couldn't describe. I was their shell. I had to protect them. I knew, even from the short period of time they'd been in my life, I would die for them.

But if this was the case, why was it that Poppy and Rosie had reached eight weeks and I felt like a bag of shite?

I'm sorry to be so blatant. I wish I could fluff it up a little, tell you I felt tired, even shattered; but it was worse than that. A misty fog of haziness surrounded me all the time. I had the ability to perform tasks with my eyes shut, or actually catch a few minutes sleep standing up. The ability to have coherent conversations and digest information was a skill I no longer possessed. I remembered how customers would graciously tell me, 'You need to get as much sleep before the babies arrive; sleepless nights are part and parcel of the baby world.' I didn't think for one second they actually meant it. I thought they meant I'd have less hours' sleep than I was used to.

Not no sleep at all.

Clare had asked me several times, 'Are you sure you're okay, Kathryn?' Her head at an angle, she studied me as if I was a museum exhibit or she was a dog trying to understand this 'thing' in front of her. 'You look peaky,' she'd tell me.

Peaky. There are a variety of synonyms for 'peaky', but the one I love most is 'emaciated'. So, Clare meant, without saying the words, that I looked withered, scraggy and gaunt. 'I haven't any make-up on,' I'd tell her, not the fact that I'd had three hours' sleep in the last seventy-two hours. Every time I give this answer she would peer at me in pity, as if knowing full well that a bit of blusher will not bring me back to life.

If Poppy had been my only child (don't get me wrong, I'm not for one minute saying I wished Rosie wasn't there) it wouldn't have been so hard. Poppy was a dream, textbook baby, feeding every four hours when she was born; and now, at eight weeks, I would dream-feed her at about 11 p.m. and sometimes she wouldn't wake until 7 a.m. That sounds bliss, doesn't it? Though, to be honest before they came I wasn't prepared for the prospect of rising at 7 a.m. every morning to feed another person before myself. But compared to Poppy (and I won't live my life comparing my children) Rosie was difficult. I knew something was wrong, but it was trying to get someone to listen to me that was the problem. My health visitor had been helpful in referring me to the doctors, it was the process after which had become frustrating.

She'd struggled from day one with feeding; even breastfeeding seemed like the most horrendous task. Rosie had been distraught. It didn't take long to move her onto formula, but even then, she would projectile-vomit the whole lot at me. I'd discovered various ways to wind a baby. Rosie struggled to bring up her burps, not like Poppy who would let it go at both ends and often smile to herself, as if she was proud of her efforts.

Poppy would deliver me delightful nappies. I'm not sure you need to know the variation of colours, sizes and textures, but nothing prepares you for some of the scenes you have to deal with. Gloves, mask and hairnet would be used in any other circumstance that involved such contaminated substances. Warnings of pollution would be exhibited for the public: *Please beware.*

But Rosie was different. Poor Rosie, she would scream in pain, daily constipation a battle as her little legs would drive to her stomach, her little face distorted. When finally, she could release some of the agony she would produce pellets; similar to a rabbit, although a rabbit could have performed better.

'Sounds like colic,' one of Clare's customers had told me when Clare had made one of her unexpected visits into the flat.

'Max was the same. I think she's allergic to milk.' Clare told me the same thing every day, but no-one listened when I suggested it.

'You girls never had this type of problem,' June had told me.

'Is this your first child?' the patronising doctor had asked me when I'd landed at the doctors a week after Rosie was born. I nodded, feeling ashamed; protesting that Rosie was a twin and Poppy had no signs of such discomfort. I sound as if I'm making excuses for my child, who years ago would have been classed as a 'whiny baby' or a 'sickly baby'. But even the health visitor expressed her concerns. The doctor had told me to visit the hospital, as new-born babies with these problems needed to be checked by a paediatrician.

At the hospital, the doctor had said accusingly, 'So you're a first-time Mum.' Shamefully again, telling him that I knew something was wrong because Poppy was so settled. 'All babies are different.' There was no room for argument, his words were final, daring me to challenge him. However, he had suggested we stay overnight, so they could see how she fed, slept and behaved. We were still living at Marianne's house at the time, so Poppy stayed curled in the softness of her crib as I watched Rosie's every breath throughout the night. They'd laid her on her back, which she couldn't manage, especially after a feed. She struggled to catch her breath at times, a small noise rising from her throat that made her sound as if she was choking.

'It sounds like Laryngomalacia,' the doctor had informed me, as if he was telling me that Rosie had a common cold. My thoughts whirled at top speed: was this dangerous? Would she need an operation? Would she survive? Obviously noting my concerned expression, he sighed loudly and added, 'It's also referred to as a floppy larynx.' And that term made it clearer!

'It's quite common, but Rosie seems to have the signs. The noisy breathing, which you've told us gets worse when she's agitated, plus difficulty feeding, vomiting her food: they are generally related,' the nurse accompanying the doctor, who'd left his bedside manner at his bedside, explained to me. Still I was none the wiser. What the hell were they talking about? The nurse said it meant there was a part of the nervous system that gives tone to the airway that wasn't developed properly but it would do so, usually by the age of two years.

'Plus, we'll prescribe Gaviscon, which should help with the reflux.'

'Reflux?'

'Acid reflux,' the doctor told me, scribbling on his clipboard, refusing to make eye contact with this neurotic mother who'd brought her child to hospital for such trivial reasons. But I was told to come, I wanted to shout at him. After he'd scribbled the note, he left me with the nurse, advising me to go and see my doctor if there were any more problems. Standard words, I expect.

The nurse was lovely as she explained about the acid reflux. 'Many babies suffer from reflux but when it starts to cause discomfort, as it is doing for Rosie, medication should help.'

I came away from the hospital, feeling useless (being a mother wasn't my forte, but we knew this before the girls arrived) but pleased that I might make progress with Rosie.

But there was no progress.

She still cried endlessly into the early hours of the morning, spewed her milk after every feed and showed constant distress. I tried everything to help her. The best thing was laying her on her front, but then I was petrified that she would die. Sounds ridiculous, doesn't it? The strict advice and guidelines were to lay your baby on their back, but that was impossible for Rosie. So, I would lay with her on my front, spread across my bed, pillows surrounding us, every movement she made making me flinch. Music also helped. I would stroll around the lounge, my hands around her armpits, my fingers embracing her tiny face, securing her floppy head, enabling her little body to feel the release of any pressure. Her little head would nod effortlessly, dozing off as her tiny lips pursed together in pure relaxation and my bingo wings loving this exercise.

It was in the first two weeks of them being born that Libby and I moved back to the flat. I'd needed some space. I'd have rather Libby stayed with Marianne, but I felt so guilty that Marianne had already placed her life on hold for us. She needed to move on, or out. Derek was desperate for her to live with him, so it seemed natural Libby moved in with me. It made sense to take her away from the place where the drugs were so easily available. She still attended her programme once a week. If I couldn't take her, she would get the bus. It had been so hard, though; harder than I'd thought it would be. She'd not been much help at Marianne's, but I thought if she could see I didn't have Marianne helping me she would step in.

But she didn't.

She'd hold one of the girls while I would see to the other, but there was no offer of helping with feeds, and there was no way she was going anywhere near one of those 'contaminated nappies'. Her words, not mine. As for getting up in the middle of the night when Rosie was testing those lungs at full force, I often thought Libby must be deaf. But it came about she was sleeping with earplugs in. I had thought about using them myself, but I couldn't leave Rosie to scream. I just wanted to make it better for her, to help her pain go away. Sometimes when the girls were in tune with each other, their squeals beating out their demands Libby would ignore them. Strange, but in a way, I was pleased that selfish Libby was back, but frustrated that she could be so selfish.

The thing is, I would forget Libby was ill. My lack of sleep, time and patience seemed to keep her to the back of my mind. I knew it would take time for her to get better, but I hadn't appreciated the intensity of her emotions – or lack of them. Libby was in her own world, her own bubble; but then, she'd always been that way. She had counsellors, mentors and doctors helping her. Who the hell did I have? Who the hell did I have when I wanted to close my eyes for a minute, even a second, without some small, precious being demanding my attention? But had my inability to explore outside my own box driven Libby to the dark place she should be staying away from?

I told myself this hooded *gentleman*, who Clare said had visited Libby, could be a mentor or a friend from the programme. Should I chat with her? Her counsellors? Her doctor? Follow her? Oh God, here we go again. I wasn't sure I had the energy to pursue this line of questioning. I barely had the strength to pull myself from my bed (if I'd even had chance to go to bed in the first place), let alone pull Libby from the poisoned, black world she'd polluted herself with.

I had to think carefully about my next step. It could help us move forward … or … it could have my already shambolic life falling apart around me.

3

'We've booked Lampford Hall.' The impact of Max's words came hurtling at me, in the same way they had on New Year's Day when he'd rung to tell me their news. I wondered if he noticed I'd stopped breathing. The uncomfortable silence forced him to speak. 'Gina thinks it's perfect for what we want.'

'Do *you* not think any more?' It was a cheap shot.

'I think it's a great idea. Imagine the memories for the girls. It's not booked for another two years and Gina would love them to be flower girls.'

'Great.' I turned away from him. I hated the way he thought it was okay to play happy families with our babies, with another woman. Now he and Gina were planning to marry in the place where my own memories were secure and peaceful, warmly tucked away; memories which would now be tarnished. I would no longer be able to think about the last day with my mum without thinking about their wedding.

'It's such a lovely place.'

'I know.' I continued to fold the pile of towels, bibs and muslins, staring at him with the contempt I so deeply felt.

'You look tired … you're not ill, are you?'

'I'm fine, Max.' I tried not to bite, keep hold of the thoughts that swam through my mind every time he told me I looked tired. I wanted to ask him, where was he at two in the morning? Where was he when Rosie was screaming? Where was he when she needed to go to the doctor's? Where was he when we'd been to the hospital?

Not with us.

And he wondered why I looked so tired.

'If you're not coping—'

'I haven't said I'm not coping. It's obviously hard work.'

'I'm sorry.' He held up his hands and walked towards me. 'But if you're struggling, though, why don't you let me help you?'

'I'm not struggling.'

'Let me have the girls overnight.'

'Rosie is too ill, she's up most of the night screaming.'

'Have you been to the doctor's again?'

'Of course, I have. Do you think I want her to be in pain?'

'Why don't I take Poppy for the night?' He was beside me. I was back to folding the fabrics that had become part of my everyday life, a bit different from the bright pink towels I would wash daily from the salon.

I could feel his breath. I wondered how at one stage in my life I would have wanted him so badly, I would have undone his shirt, run my hands down his well-defined chest, when all I wanted to do now was remove him from my space.

'You can't have Poppy without Rosie.' I turned away from him, moving across the minute kitchen towards the sink where the bottles had piled up.

'Don't you think you're being silly?'

'No, I don't.' I bit my tongue before I struck him with my heated words, as I calmly told him, 'They are twins, Max. They are comforted by each other, plus I'm not having you and Gina form a great relationship with one and not the other.'

'I can see I'm not going to get anywhere with you today.' He sighed loudly and walked towards the bedroom where the girls were sleeping in their cot.

I wanted to tell him to get out; that this was my room, my personal space, how dare he? But that would have been ridiculous. I could hear him chatting to them, although they were asleep, mumbling about how he would see them very soon for cuddles. His words melted my heart although I wanted to lash out at him. I quickly swallowed the lump in my throat and blinked away the tears that were threatening.

'I'll call you later to arrange the weekend,' he said as he walked down the stairs back to his 'normal' life. He wouldn't call me later, it was an expression he'd become accustomed to using, meaning he may text me to see how the girls were, but generally that would be in a day or so.

As always when he left, I felt irritated. I was exploding inside at the way in which he would saunter into the flat as if he owned it, as if he belonged, making judgments about me as *his* life continued along the same path. He would argue that his life had changed, things were hard for him now – but all I could hear was blah, blah, blah … He'd chosen the way he wanted to go, and I had little patience for his choice.

He was building a new life with Gina now.

*

Max was involved in the girls' lives. We had a casual agreement that he would call in several times in the week after work, but he would take them every other weekend; only for the Saturday or Sunday, there were no overnight stays. More fool you, I can hear you say. But knowing Rosie would be bleating out her sobs all night was too unsettling. I couldn't imagine Gina pacing the floors with her like I did, or Max soothing her pain in the way that I could. There was also that niggling feeling that had knitted its web: I didn't want them playing happy families with my babies. I didn't like to think of them cooing over my girls, tickling them, trying to make them smile. I also couldn't imagine that they would feel the rush of love that would fill me every time they smiled, giggled or simply moved.

The problem was, I couldn't ever imagine letting them stay with Max and Gina overnight. I hadn't aired these thoughts to anyone but Suzy. I'd told Max I would allow them to stay when Rosie was over her problems, but I knew I didn't want them to stay until they could walk and talk. Better still, when they could vote, when they were capable of making adult decisions or when they'd left home. It's hard to explain. I didn't see them as a possession, they weren't a commodity for me to tease Max with, but the anxiety I'd felt about becoming a mother before they arrived had folded back on itself. It was as if no-one was capable of taking care of my babies in the way that I could. I wasn't being conceited, but I felt this overwhelming urge to smother them with my love; the love that no-one else could possibly feel as strongly as I did. Not even Max. I would think about the customers who had told me that losing a child was far worse than losing a parent, how I'd been scared at the prospect of hurting as much as I had when Mum died. But this suffocating need to ensure they were okay was intense, beyond what I could have ever imagined.

*

'Can you believe Lampford Hall?' I told Suzy into the handset, needing to offload quickly before the girls woke up. 'Of all the places. I just can't believe it, Suzy, the one memory I have of Mum. They must hate me so much.'

'I'm sure it's nothing to do with you.' Suzy was always the optimist.

'I think Gina purposely wanted it there. If they had any kind of decency, they would have booked somewhere else.'

'I totally agree with you. Do you want Lawrence to have a word with Max?'

'No!' I breathed deeply, forcing myself not to take my irritation out on Suzy. 'That's all I need. Imagine Gina if she knows how upset I am! I couldn't face Max. My memories are tarnished now anyway, just knowing they've been around the hall. To be honest, I didn't even know they held weddings there.'

'I think they've opened it up since Lord Lampford, died,' Suzy explained, her trivia knowledge once again coming to the fore.

'Anyway, sod them,' I said, diverting my thoughts. 'Are you still up for doing your invitations on Saturday?'

'Yes, definitely.' Suzy suddenly sounded harassed. 'I'm so far behind with it all. I have no idea how I'm going to get it all done in time.'

'You'll be fine, stop stressing, we'll go through it all on Saturday.'

She took a deep relaxing breath, 'I'll pop round before Saturday to see the girls.'

'Great.' I actually meant it. In the midst of other unwanted visitors, I would definitely appreciate Suzy being there.

As we said our goodbyes, I smiled at my friend's ability to be so organised, but the downside was that she collapsed if something wasn't going to plan. She'd been so methodical with her wedding arrangements that I knew this was last-minute nerves: there was nothing she hadn't covered.

As I pulled myself from the sofa, practically dragging my body to the kitchen, every bone ached, even hurt in some places. My neck was tense, my shoulders felt as if they were reaching my ears. I consciously forced them down, stretching my neck to the side, as I prepared two bottles of milk. I pushed away the tears, swallowed my frustration and pulled myself into the numbness of the routine I endured every few hours. The part of me that could block out emotional turmoil, the ability to focus on the task at hand, was still deep within me.

I went into the bedroom, the warm bottles in my hands, ready to tackle the task of feeding, a task, which was now part of my life, in the same way conducting a facial or nail treatment, had once been.

As I set about my routine, I wondered what Max was doing? And as always, I fought away the bitterness. He'd be relaxing with Gina in their cosy life. I very much doubt his thoughts would be on me.

So, I had to stop wasting my thoughts on him. He wasn't worth it.

4

'Morning.' Jane my health visitor smiled warmly when I greeted her at the bottom of the stairs; stairs that had become the bane of my life since the girls had arrived. On Jane's last visit, she'd asked if I'd attended my six-week check at the doctors. Of course, I had, I'd replied cautiously. Her line of questioning probed into postnatal depression; had I spoken to the doctor about how I was feeling?

I'd told her, 'I'm understandably worn out, but I'm not depressed. I've seen depression, I lived with my dad's depression long enough to know I'm not depressed.'

'Depression can show itself in many different ways. It doesn't have to be the same for everyone.'

I'd thought about Libby; how she'd hidden her depression with her jokes and vibrant personality. 'I'm not depressed.' I was firm, daring her to challenge me. Irritated, restless, knackered, but not depressed.

'You should sleep when Max has the babies.' I'd heard this from Clare, Marianne and Suzy.

But I *couldn't* sleep.

I would work my way through the flat, tidying, cleaning, sorting out the girl's clothes, all the things I tried to do when they were with me, but which were generally impossible. The thing was, if I didn't keep busy when they weren't around me I felt I would crash; burn to the ground like a bundle of ashes.

It was strange how things had changed, how I'd been an independent, confident woman. The world at my feet, I'd not relied on anyone, I'd never needed the security of another person. I'd wait in a bar for Suzy, I'd attend a new meeting without knowing anyone else in the room, I was happy in my own skin, not over-confident in a showy way, but comfortable with who I was. Now, I felt strange if I wasn't in possession of a pram, a car seat or a baby huddled into my arms. If I didn't have my props with me to make me feel as if I was performing my part in the play, the play of life, I felt nervous, slightly anxious. I'd never felt the need for props before. I hadn't felt the urge for the crutches that were supporting me through each day, in the way I did now.

'So, how are you feeling?' Jane sat opposite me, elbows on her legs, her hands stretched towards me, her body language open, giving me all the signs to trust her with my every thought.

'I'm fine,' I said. I could feel her eyes upon me as I watched Poppy in her bouncy chair, while Rosie sat up in her pushchair: she hated the movement of the musical chair. We must have looked, to anyone who didn't know us, as the perfect picture of happiness. I appeared organised, my babies were content. Jane knew better, though. Poppy and Rosie were eight weeks old; she should have signed me off weeks ago, but she insisted every time she left that she would come back and see me. I thought it was because she liked me, I was her new friend, but this obviously wasn't true: she wasn't paid to be my friend.

'Have you thought any more about the new mums group?' She'd changed the subject onto another one I wanted to avoid.

'I'm not sure it's my thing.' I'd shrugged. The thought of meeting lots of Mums who were successfully breastfeeding, had their babies in a great routine and were getting more sleep than me (which wasn't hard) made nausea run through my body like an unsettled river.

'It will be good for you ... you'll be in an environment where other women have new-borns and you can discuss any worries you have. There'll always be someone there who feels the same.'

'But I feel fine.'

'It's good to be around other women who have just had new babies. Talking about your experiences can help the process.'

'I'll think about it,' I told her, holding back on telling her that I'd thought about it and I wasn't going.

'Great,' she smiled, convinced or not, I didn't ask. She turned to face Rosie, who was mesmerised by the brightly coloured teddies that hung from the mobile above her pram. 'How's little Rosie?'

'She's still not right.' Here was a subject I really needed to talk to her about. Forget me, I could sort myself out once Rosie was sorted out. 'Nothing's changed. She's obviously in pain. I've been doing some research and I've found this list of symptoms for babies with a milk allergy and Rosie has quite a few of them.'

'Really? Do you have the list?' Jane asked. I handed over the list that included skin rash, continuous crying, inconsolable for long periods of time, low weight gain, gassiness, respiratory problems and abdominal cramps; but my main concern was blood in her stools. You'd think if this was happening to a baby the doctors would be examining the poor little soul, but no, I was told it wasn't really anything to worry about. If it was happening every time she filled her nappy, they would take it more seriously.

Then we both jumped as the secret door that connected to the salon suddenly opened and Clare entered the flat. Jane stared at Clare, who swept into the room as if she was stepping onto a London stage.

'Oh, I'm sorry, I didn't realise you had company.'

That's because you didn't ask, I thought.

Abruptly, the bedroom door then opened, and Libby's bed-head appeared, her limp, tired body, dressed in checked pyjamas, following on behind. She was so pasty white, she could have passed for a ghostly spirit gliding into the room. She didn't acknowledge any of us as she walked to the kitchen part of the open-plan apartment, poured herself a glass of milk, then walked back.

I realised everyone had stopped talking. They had been watching Libby as if she'd stepped out from beyond the grave. I was pleased Clare didn't ask her about her hooded friend, as I'd not had the chance to. Avoidance: I'm sure that's what Libby's counsellors would have called it.

'My sister,' I explained to Jane who seemed bewildered by Libby's entrance, as by Clare's. 'This is Clare, the girls' grandmother.'

'Grandma.' Clare held out her hand and Jane took it politely. You'd think Clare would have left once she realised I had company, especially from the medical arena. It was obvious Jane was in the profession. Although she didn't wear a uniform, her smart dress, huge badge, which hung around her neck and array of papers that bulged from her leather bag, were more than an indication.

'And you are?' Clare asked directly.

Embarrassed I put my head into my hands, pretending to rub my tired eyes.

'Jane … I'm Kat's health visitor,' Jane said politely.

'Oh, fantastic. Has Kathryn told you all about Rosie's illness? My Maxwell had all these problems. He couldn't have cows' milk, so it's obvious it's the same thing. You'd think the doctors would help sort this out.'

'Kathryn has found this list, so hopefully—'

'What list?' Clare, intrigued, put out her hand obviously expecting Jane to give it to her, and to my surprise Jane did. Meeting my gaze, she gave me a small but warm smile, as if understanding that all that was happening around us was the reason I was so fraught. Don't get me wrong, Clare and I had built quite a strong relationship, but to be honest it was becoming weaker every day. Clare had no respect for my privacy; she wouldn't knock before entering, she would bring up customers with their hair in mid-treatment; it was a constant reminder that this wasn't my home. I appreciated Clare's help, and she stuck to her offer of not charging me rent, but it didn't justify her constant interference.

'I told you it was this,' she said, after quickly scanning the sheet. 'What do we do now?'

'I'm going to make an appointment with the doctor. Let's see if we can get this sorted once and for all,' Jane told us both, making a point of addressing me more than Clare, who was watching her intently.

'It's about time something was done, it's gone on far too long. It's disgusting behaviour from the doctors, this poor girl—'

'I think Jane knows, Clare, and it's not her fault.' I was harsher than I intended, causing Jane to eye me discreetly.

'Oh, I know. I'm sorry, I wasn't blaming you; but poor Kathryn has had to cope with so much.'

'Don't worry. Let's see if we can get this sorted.' Jane smiled as she picked up her mobile phone. She spoke politely to the receptionist who answered, explaining that she needed an appointment as soon as possible. She scribbled on her notepad and asked me, 'Can you get there now?'

'Now!' But what about feeding, changing, sleeping ...? 'I better get sorted then.' Of course, I could get there now. Oh God, where to start.

*

I found myself there in half an hour. Clare helped by taking Poppy downstairs into the salon. So, although I hated the way she randomly invaded my space, I had to appreciate the convenience of her babysitting services. I wasn't keen on Poppy being in the salon, but Clare hadn't committed to becoming a hairdresser: she'd hired professionals to help carry the business forward. I knew she would be able to concentrate on Poppy while I was out. I also knew she was using Poppy as a tool to impress the customers; everyone loved a new baby. She was the perfect doting grandmother in their eyes. Someone as nice as Clare who was devoted to family must be a great person to be around. It was great for business.

The waiting room was quiet. Five people sat rigidly, their expressions sullen as if someone had died. The receptionist didn't speak, but stared at me as if it was my duty to talk first.

'My health visitor has just called to make me an appointment for my baby, Rosie Neasham.' I thought by the mention of a baby she would have softened her approach ... but there was nothing.

'Name of your health visitor?' She raised her eyebrows.

'Jane.'

'Jane ...' she scowled at me obviously waiting for more information.

This was worse than an interrogation at the police station. Not that I'd ever experienced such an event, but still ...

'Does she have a surname?' Her insolent tone and roll of the eyes conveyed disdain for her job; or for me. She might as well have asked me if I was stupid.

'Thompson, I think.' Hoping that was true.

'Take a seat.'

'Who am I seeing?'

'Dr Knowles.' She didn't look at me as I walked away from the desk, irritated that she thought it appropriate to treat people with such rudeness. If she'd worked for me, I'd have sacked her. Then reality hit me forcefully: I no longer had anyone working for me. This happened often, and every single time the same sense of loss enveloped me.

I'd seen Dr Knowles before, but he'd not been helpful. With a tap of his pen, a crossed leg and a deliberate stare, he'd made me feel like a disturbed first-time Mum who needed to 'Calm down'. Calm down!'

I rocked Rosie's car seat with my foot. She was so small the straps barely surrounded her tiny body. Her head, which was minuscule compared to the pink snowsuit that encased her, rested gently on the soft padding of the seat. Her little eyelids fluttered. I was pleased she was restful in her own world. My foot was automatically rocking the chair in the hope she wouldn't awake and make a scene. I hated feeding her outside the home, because I was never sure what response I would get. If I could place her upwards in her pushchair it wasn't so bad, but otherwise it was horrendous. I couldn't bear the stares.

'Rosie Neasham.' The ignorant receptionist's jaded tones had an elderly man opposite me rolling his eyes and shaking his head.

'Youth of today,' he said, his throat raspy.

I smiled, picking up the seat, which was heavy with or without Rosie's extra pounds. 'Come here, pet.'

The old man, slowly lifted himself from his seat, his aged body not allowing him to be as fast as he probably once was. In fact, as he opened the door that led into the doctors' corridor, I wanted to say, 'There's no need, thank you,' but that would have been rude. He pulled on the handle, forcing the door towards him. Seeing that he'd gone red in the face with the effort, I showed my appreciation and let him sit back down before he had a heart attack. Suddenly I'd become helpless to some people, even the elderly who should need *my* help. It was worse when I ventured out with both the girls; people would fly from all angles to try and take over.

I knocked gently on the door. A deep voice called me to enter. The doctor sat proudly in his chair, his thin, white hair combed across his scalp, his dark eyes daring me to complain about my baby.

'Miss Neasham.' He welcomed me sternly. 'Come and take a seat.' I did as I was told, placing Rosie at my feet. 'What can I do for you today?'

'Well … the thing is …' I found myself stuttering, his firmness making me uncomfortable. 'I've told you about the problems my baby has.'

'And you've told many others too.' He raised an eyebrow.

I could feel my cheeks burn slightly, my face flushed. 'But, I know something isn't right. I think she may have a milk allergy.'

'A milk allergy?' He stared at me. 'And what, might I ask, has brought you to this conclusion?'

'This list.' I pulled the screwed-up piece of paper from my bag. A scraggy wet-wipe had attached itself, leaving its grimy signature on the list. This probably helped to confirm his opinion of me.

He scanned it quickly, his taut expression not softening; but he nodded, which I knew counted for something. 'You'll have to take her back to the hospital, and take this list with you.'

'What?' Was he kidding me? 'Why back to the hospital?'

'As I explained in your previous appointment, she's under a year old so we prefer that she's seen by a paediatrician.'

I didn't argue; there was no point. 'Will they know I'm coming?'

'Yes, I'll call them now. Can you get there this afternoon?'

I nodded as thoughts of feeding, winding and changing that needed to be done, whirled through my mind, before I even contemplated going to the hospital. Nothing was simple any more. Everything was like a military operation. God forbid if we went in the middle of feed time: the babies' vocal cords would be demonstrated to one and all. If I left it too long after one feed, guaranteed they'd wake up before the next.

He confirmed with the hospital that we'd be there in about two hours. He probably assumed that should give me enough time to get both the girls sorted; I hoped Clare could continue her babysitting duties. It was times like this I wanted to call on Max; not because I wanted him, but because this should be *his* responsibility too.

'I'd like you to come back and see me next week,' he said.

'Why?'

'I see from your notes you missed your six-week check.'

'I'm sorry.' I felt like a chastised child, as I remembered the posters on the walls in the waiting room exclaiming what missed appointments cost the NHS. I also wondered if Jane would find out I'd lied; or did she already know I'd not attended the appointment? 'I'll come … but I'm fine,' I added.

'Good, we can discuss things a bit more next week,' he said, a little softer than his original abrupt manner.

Discuss what? There was nothing to discuss. I was simply exhausted, but if someone could help Rosie, they would be helping me. If I didn't have to wear my carpet thin, night after night, if I had a partner to share the load, or even my mum to take over so I could sleep.

Sleep. That was it, that's what I needed. Sleep.

I'd come back next week, I'd show him I was fine. I knew he wanted to talk to me about post-natal depression, but I didn't want to talk to him about it. I didn't want to talk to *anyone* about it.

Actually, I didn't really want to talk to anyone about anything.

5

'So, who was he?' I asked Libby as she made a tuna sandwich for herself, not meeting my eye.

'Who?'

'The guy who came to see you the other day.'

'What guy?'

'You know what guy.' I stared at her. Her blasé approach to my questioning set alarm bells ringing.

'How do you know about him?' she asked after about a twenty-second pause that felt like five minutes.

'Clare saw him.'

'Bloody hell, it's like living in a fucking jail in here.'

'Well … who was he?' I ignored her not-so-unusual outburst.

'Neville.' She didn't look at me.

'Neville?' Would someone with the name Neville be taking drugs? Was it wrong of me to assume not?

'He's from the programme.'

'Why has he come all the way out here to see you?'

'He's been struggling.'

'Doesn't he have a mentor?'

'Yes, but he's on holiday.' She suddenly threw down the knife. It bounced across the wooden kitchen surface, clattering against the ceramic breadbin. 'What is this, Kat, twenty fucking questions?'

'No, I'm worried that's all.'

'You mean you don't trust me.'

'Of course I trust you.'

*

The next day I rang the programme.

I spoke with her counsellor, and expressed my concerns about Libby's inward-looking personality and extreme character traits. Apparently, this was normal; it was what happened throughout the process.

'No two days are the same,' she jovially told me, 'plus, I hear you have two babies in the house. Maybe this is her coping mechanism.'

So, it was my fault.

I'd fought so hard to ensure I didn't blame myself. I'd attended counselling sessions with Libby, had it drilled into me that it wasn't my fault: and now, in one sentence, I'd been made to feel responsible for Libby's dysfunctional behaviour.

I put the phone down, acknowledging that they didn't think I was helping Libby enough. But I'd been trying to let her have her own space, ignoring the fact that her depression was polluting the air like heavy black clouds in the same way Dad's used to.

Maybe I was expecting too much. I wanted the old Libby back, the selfish, funny sister I so deeply missed. There were the odd moments: a genuine smile, a funny joke or a sarcastic comment. But there was no aura, no light in her eyes, her body functioning in the way it was made to, but with no soul underneath.

In some ways I felt the same. My candle had lost its flame, my fire had diminished. We were living in a cube, a box full of essential items that would help us take daily steps. We didn't really need to venture outside of the box. The walls of the flat had become layers of protection. It was supposed to be safe inside, until others imposed their own views when they weren't needed. Maybe Libby couldn't handle the comings and goings: if it wasn't Clare calling in, it would be Marianne bringing nappies, bread or milk; or Max would call to play the doting father.

There wasn't a day that passed without a visitor. Maybe I should restrict visiting times; a rota of some kind. Maybe it wasn't Libby that needed the peace; maybe it was me.

Perhaps I was envious of Libby, hiding away in her bedroom for hours on end. Perhaps I wished I could join her or swap places. She obviously had a wish to hibernate. Wouldn't I hide if the girls weren't mine? Probably!

Neville's story could be legitimate. He could be struggling, although I found it hard to believe Libby was his saving grace. But was this her speciality; helping others in her position.

Who was I kidding?

Something was amiss. I needed to watch Libby closely. Maybe call on Marianne for help, attend a meeting with Libby; anything that would give me more insight into her thoughts and feelings – because I was so wrapped up in my own, I had no idea what was going on in Libby's world.

6

The river was flowing gently, ripples bubbling around embedded rocks, spreading serenity around the village. The peaceful air was soothing, as the birds sang their tuneful songs. In the crispness of the cold air, Suzy pushed the pram slowly along the pebbly path, the slight, jolting motion helping Rosie and Poppy to sleep longer.

'So, you're happy with the outcome?' she asked quietly.

My arm was wrapped in hers as we walked slowly. 'It's only been two days, but so far so good.' I shrugged. 'I couldn't believe how easy it all was.'

'I can't believe it's been so hard for them to believe you.'

'I walked into the hospital, ready for a fight, and the doctor told me, quite simply, they'd sort out some prescriptions. She didn't look like a doctor, though; she was far too young.'

'You sound old.'

'She was about our age; short, trendy hair—'

'Ooohhh, I love how you describe us as young,' Suzy laughed.

'You know what I mean.' I swatted her playfully. 'She must have studied her arse off to get in that position at such a young age.'

'Maybe she just looked young for her age.'

'Like us.'

'Of course.' Suzy winked. 'So, is it rice or soya milk?' I loved that Suzy had some knowledge of a subject that she would probably never need.

'Rice milk. She's taking it so much better than she has any other milk. She's still a little unsettled, but apparently it could take a while to work.'

'How long?'

'Jane said—'

'The health visitor?'

'Yes, she said that if it *has* been an allergy then she'll be sore inside, and it could take a week or so for the rawness and swelling to go down.'

'Poor little thing.'

I nodded, agreeing with Suzy. I hadn't wanted to come out for a walk, but she'd insisted. She'd pulled me from the sofa, and I mean literally: almost yanked my arms from their sockets and ordered me to get my coat. I'd wanted to cry. I couldn't think of anything worse. I wanted to stay huddled between the soft cushions, in my safe cocoon. She'd sorted the girls into their tiny snowsuits, eased their dainty, fragile heads into cotton hats and covered their long fingers with oversized mittens.

I hadn't left the flat in two days, which wasn't a problem – I'd still seen people. There was Clare with her random visits, and in fact Henry had made a surprise appearance too. Marianne had brought some more baby clothes. I'd not told her my concerns about Libby, mainly because I didn't want her to worry. It could be nothing.

'So, I've got my list of potential people to invite.'

'Great.'

'Are you sure you can still help me on Saturday?'

'I'm positive.'

'Why don't you get some sleep in the morning, after Max picks the girls up, and then we'll—'

'No, it's fine. I can't sleep when they're not there.'

'Why don't you try?'

'I can't.'

'Have you talked to a doctor about how you're feeling?' Suzy asked tentatively.

'I'm fine, I don't need to talk to a doctor ...' There was a short silence between us, as we continued to step slowly over the bumpy path. 'Dr Knowles wants me to go back and see him,' I admitted. I felt guilty that I was so abrupt with Suzy, but I hated all the fuss.

'Maybe that's a good thing.' Suzy spoke softly as she raised her eyebrows. 'I think you should let him know all your thoughts.'

'You do? Even the ones that torture me about ending it all?'

'Kat!' She stopped in her tracks, her hands clenched around the black rubber that secured the metal frame of the pram.

'I'm joking.' I smiled, although my heart was telling a different story.

'You need to tell him how you're feeling.' Her eyes pierced through me, full of sadness and … was it pity?

I didn't want to be pitied.

'I will.' I smiled brightly, hopefully conveying that she was being slightly dramatic.

We walked a little further, silence stretching between us. We always kept away from Melanie's salon; the hurt still festered deep within me. Melanie had gone back to Mandy after offering to come back to me. She'd obviously been keeping her options open. Even though we were now at the far end of the village where the locals walked their dogs, and there were no shops for anyone to venture to, I felt slightly uneasy that I might bump into Melanie and Mandy. They were like ghostly presences that were all around me. Even a walk to the shops that didn't even involve passing their prestigious salon would have my nerves on edge.

'So, any more thoughts on going to that new mum's group?' Suzy interrupted my thoughts as I breathed in the cold frosty air, enjoying its chilly freshness.

'I don't want to go.' I wished I'd never told Suzy about it. This was the third time she'd interrogated me about the group that, quite frankly, filled me with dread.

'Kat, you need some friends who are in the same boat as you.'

'I doubt anyone will be in the same boat as me.'

'They'll all have babies.'

'But they are bound to have husbands.'

'You could be completely wrong.'

'What if I'm completely spot on, and I feel worse then I feel now?'

'Come on, Kat, no-one is going to judge you because you're single.'

'Probably not, but I don't want to take that chance.'

'What if I come to the first one with you? I won't come inside.'

'You're being very forceful about this. Are you wanting me to find some new friends, so I won't bother you as much with my messy life?' I jested.

'No, not at all! But I think it will do you good to be around other new mums.' Suzy stopped walking and turned to me, taking hold of my arms, urging me to face her. 'I'm worried about you, Kat.'

'Don't be silly.' I didn't want to have this conversation. 'There's nothing wrong with me!'

'You need to be around people you can share your sleepless nights with.'

'Fine, I'll go.' I wasn't sure I would, but I needed her to stop talking about it.

'Really, you'll go?' She seemed excited. Did it mean that much to her? Was I honestly that bad?

'If it means that much to you … I'll go.'

'It does.' She smiled. Anxiety pierced through me. I knew I couldn't let her down. I didn't want her worrying about me. She had enough going on with all her wedding arrangements. If I went for one session, half a session, maybe … ten minutes … at least she couldn't say I hadn't tried.

We walked slowly back to the flat. I was pleased she'd forced me outside for a walk. Previously, leaving the warmth of the cosy flat had seemed such a chore, and even a walk in the picturesque village had started to feel like an imposition. I really should push myself to come out alone, to feel the soft breeze, to allow the crisp air into my lungs, filling them with freshness instead of the staleness created by the dry central heating.

It was easier having someone help me into the flat. I would normally carry both the girls upstairs at the same time, not wanting to leave one stranded alone on the street. Not that I should be worried in such a quiet village, but you could never be too sure who was hanging around. I would place them safely in their cot or on the play mat, then run back down the stairs, and at top speed fold away the pram. Now, Suzy took both the girls as I folded down the pram, putting it in its regular place behind the front door at the bottom of the stairs. How easy life was with an extra pair of hands!

'Oh God, Kat.'

'What?' Suzy's fraught tones had me chasing up the stairs behind her, each step echoing throughout the building.

'Shit!'

I knelt down next to Libby. Her arms were spread across the soft cushions on the sofa, one leg hanging off the edge. 'Libby,' I said her name softly, my fear ascending to hysteria. Her breathing was slow and laboured, her body floppy. My fingers upon her wrist detected a faint pulse. Her eyes rolled, her mouth was slightly open.

I pulled my phone from my pocket, dialling the number I'd hoped I'd never have to call for my sister.

As I told the operator I needed an ambulance, the tears that were trapped inside of me suddenly flowed.

7

I'd thought she was getting better. They'd told me her isolation was normal. Secluding herself from the rest of the world was her way of dealing with things. I'd wondered if the programme was working for her. When I'd broached the subject, she'd told me it was helping. I was satisfied with her explanation because I was too tired to comprehend the whole situation: if she thought it was helping, who was I to interfere? I had Poppy and Rosie taking over my life; every hour, minute, second was devoted to them. I needed Libby to be getting the support she needed, the support I couldn't give her.

When Libby had admitted her problem, we'd scraped through Christmas, we'd put on our brave faces. Although the girls were only days old, I'd sat through her initial doctor's appointment. He'd been lovely. I wasn't sure what I'd expected, but I hadn't imagined that he would be so understanding. I'd not shown Libby my fear that he would judge us, because I didn't want to worry her. But he hadn't; well, if he had, he'd hidden it pretty well. He'd told Libby about the damage she was doing to her body, but his gentle kindness was non-judgmental. He didn't say it wasn't her fault, but his expression made it perfectly clear that he didn't blame her, that he completely understood.

I didn't blame her either … but I didn't understand.

I had tried, but I couldn't comprehend why she would do this to herself, especially when we'd seen what alcohol had done to Dad. I wanted to help her. I so wanted her to get better, back to the selfish Libby we all knew and loved; but as for understanding her condition – that was a step too far. The doctor had explained about a programme, Marcoway, but it was a self-referral scheme, so he couldn't refer her. I was surprised at the restrictions on the doctor, but didn't say so. We'd made an appointment, and I'd accompanied her to the first assessment. It was an enlightening experience, as nurses, doctors and counsellors, who understood, surrounded us. They really wanted to help Libby. It was a passion of theirs to ensure she took the best steps forward.

I'd allowed myself to fall into a sense of false security: these people were so good, there was no way Libby could be taking anything because they would know about it. Not that I was blaming them, but this explanation helped ease my own guilt slightly.

When I'd found her, slumped lifelessly, after I tripped over the empty vodka bottle, I found her prescribed sleeping tablets container empty, as were three boxes of paracetamols. I'd handed the evidence to the paramedic, who had quickly taken note of the items.

The young lady doctor of Indian descent was direct, and didn't seem at all shocked by Libby's actions. 'Gastric lavage.' The words hung in the air, the same words that had described Dad's stomach-pumping process. 'She will be given oxygen and fluids to ensure her body is kept stable.'

'Is she awake?' Marianne asked

'Not yet, but you may go in and see her.'

As she showed us into ICU, my heart felt as if someone had stuck a pin in it; deflated and shrivelled, unable to take any more hurt. Images of Dad flashed vividly as Libby's limp and skinny body lay before us. Her skin was ashen, her thin features so fragile under the mask that surrounded her nose and mouth. She looked so delicate and young. She could easily have been mistaken for a child under the mass of tubes. Avoiding the drips that stretched from her slight limbs, I held her bony fingers, her thin hands cold beneath mine. I felt Marianne's hand upon my shoulder.

'Oh, Lib.' I swallowed back the familiar lump. 'Why?'

8

'Instead of forking out that sort of money, why doesn't she come and live in Devon with me for a while?' June had made the surprise six-and-half-hour trip overnight.

'But there will be counsellors and specialists who can help her.'

Marianne had not been pleased to see June when she'd arrived back at the flat this morning. We'd intended to visit Libby while Clare minded the girls, but June's unexpected appearance had upset plans.

Poor Suzy had done a great job yesterday when I'd rushed out to go with Libby. She'd been thrown in at the deep end as I'd shouted instructions from each step of the staircase, on the heels of the paramedics who'd carried Libby out on a stretcher.

'But in Devon she won't have the bad influences she has around here. I could help her enrol on a programme.'

'You're underestimating her illness. She needs some professional help in a restricted environment.' Marianne was clearly tense, sending waves of unease around the flat.

'But it's a lot of money.'

'I'm happy to pay,' Marianne said firmly.

'Marianne, we can't keep taking your money. Don't you think you've spent enough?' I shook my head in despair.

'I agree with Kat, it's a waste of money.'

'I didn't say it's waste of money.' I tried not to sound provoked, but June was riling me. 'I think rehab would be great, but if there was an alternative ...' I sat down on the sofa, rubbing my hands over my face, tiredness leaving a stale furriness in my mouth. 'I want her well more than anything, but Libby has wasted so much money, it's unfair to use any more of your savings.'

'I agree. I can help her if she lives with me,' June said.

'What do you know about alcoholism and depression?' Marianne asked her, her demeanour cold as she faced up to my aunty.

'I'm not saying … I'm not … but when—'

'Look, June, it's a good idea,' I interrupted her as she fumbled to answer, stopping her before she had chance to mention Dad. 'But Libby needs proper help. You can't deal with her withdrawal and her mood swings. We've seen it here and it's awful. It's not fair on Libby either if there is the option of her receiving intensive treatment.'

'I agree.' Marianne added defiantly. A stirring from the bedroom gave me an excuse to duck out of the conversation. I left the two hostile women as I ventured into my bedroom to see who had woken first for a feed. Poppy was blinking slowly, trying to focus her tiny blue eyes as she chewed at her little fist. I lifted the small bundle from the cosy cot. She raised her legs towards her chest. Her long arms stretched towards my face as she comfortably let my embrace take her. I delighted in her warm smell, her soft skin upon my lips as I kissed her cheek.

I made my way back into the lounge where Marianne and June were sitting at opposite ends of the sofa. I half-expected them to be in the midst of an argument, but the silence was quite eerie. June stood as I entered, walking quickly towards me, her smile reaching her eyes as she held out her arms.

'Oh, let me see her,' she enthused as she took Poppy. 'Oh, she could be *you* when you were a baby.'

'Everyone thinks both the girls are more like Max,' I told her, aware that Marianne was sitting quietly, not able to contribute to the conversation, which made me feel guilty. I wondered if June was purposely rubbing in the fact she was a blood relative, gloating that she'd been around in the beginning.

'No. She's your double. They *both* are.' She must be deliberately provoking Marianne, as the girls looked nothing like each other. Poppy was more Max's side than Rosie; but both had Max's features more than mine. June didn't take her eyes off Poppy, as I walked into the kitchen to make a bottle.

Suddenly, Clare entered the flat via the secret door. Both Marianne and June turned to see who was invading our space.

'Oh hello, ladies, I wasn't aware Kathryn had company.'

'I'm just leaving.' Marianne stood up from her seat, smiling at me but ignoring both the other women. 'I'll go and see Libby now. Why don't you call in and see her later?'

'Are you going back to see Libby again tonight?' I whispered as I poured powder into one of the bottles. I hadn't told Clare what was happening, and had no intention of doing so. I didn't need my private life integrating into village gossip any more than it already had over the last year.

'I can do, or I can mind the girls,' Marianne said.

'*I* can mind the girls,' June offered quickly, interrupting our conversation.

'I can babysit,' Clare contributed. 'I was hoping to show them off.'

'It's hard not to,' Marianne agreed.

'I know, so many of Kathryn's customers have been in this week and have asked to see the babies. Poor Kathryn must be sick of me traipsing in here.' There was my opportunity to say something, but once again, I let it pass.

'How could you not show these gorgeous girls off?' June said, undoubtedly desperate to be part of this motherly gang.

'Hello, you.' Clare tickled Poppy's cheek and rattled off some other baby talk.

This was hell; these three women fighting for attention, needing to be top dog with the babies and me. Although Marianne and Clare hadn't exactly become best friends, they understood and respected each other. I wasn't sure what June would bring to the dynamic.

'I'll call you.' Marianne leaned towards me to kiss my cheek. Her soft touch was tender on my skin, as she whispered, 'I meant what I said. I'll pay for Libby to get better.'

She moved towards Poppy. I hoped I'd imagined June pulling Poppy close as Marianne kissed the baby's forehead. She then headed into the bedroom to say her goodbyes to Rosie and then quietly left.

I couldn't bear the tension if June was to stay. Marianne had been such a big help I didn't want her to feel she was being excluded. I needed to keep her close.

'So, do you need me to babysit later?' Clare asked.

'I can do it,' June offered as Clare folded her arms.

'Why don't you come with me?' I suggested to June.

'Oh yes, I could do that,' June agreed as Clare's features softened.

'So what time would you like me?' Clare's chest seemed to grow as if she'd won first prize.

'Four o'clock?'

'Excellent,' she agreed, before disappearing through our secret door back to her new life. I was pleased she hadn't asked where we were going; although that conversation would probably come later.

June helped me to feed, wind and change both the girls: waking Rosie for a feed seemed the best idea, keeping the girls in tune with each other made life a little bit easier. June and I analysed Libby's addiction. We were following the same pattern as Dad. We needed to get her the proper help that Dad had always fought against.

I was trying not to be angry with Libby, but it was hard to comprehend her actions when there were so many others worse off than her. So many others with problems that Libby would never have to face, so many people with difficulties that Libby would never have to comprehend. Whereas unforeseeable circumstances hit so many other families, my sister had *chosen* to wreck herself; she'd had a choice. She'd decided it was all too much, and I couldn't help but feel disappointed, no matter how much I understood that it was an illness.

But maybe it wasn't her I was disappointed in … maybe it was me.

'How would you feel if I stayed here with you?' June was walking around the room, Poppy hanging over her shoulder as she rubbed her back. 'Only for a few weeks, help you out.'

'If you want to … of course.' I was unsure how I felt about it. I was so used to my own routine, I didn't think I could cope with her. I really wanted an extra pair of hands, but I was also desperate for personal space rather than people encroaching.

'I could help out with night feeds and all the other bits.'

'There's not much space, Libby will be back in a few days.' My conscience pricking, wishing that I didn't have one, I added, 'But we could set you up a blow-up bed until Libby goes away.'

'Are you sure about her going away?'

'I don't think we have a choice.'

'You do … she could come and live with me. Don't let Marianne push you into this.'

'I'm not. Marianne is right; Libby needs proper medical help.'

'But what about when she comes out?'

'What do you mean?' I studied her. Her vibrant attire, her perfectly styled hair, completely made-over face, her stylish elegance: all were out of place in the cluttered messy flat.

'When she's received her treatment, I mean. How long do they keep them in those rehab places? Four weeks? Four months? Will she *ever* be allowed out? Some of the mental institutions don't let people back out. When your dad was inside I was worried sick he wouldn't—'

'She'll be fine.' I didn't exactly know what was involved in residential alcohol and drug rehabilitation, but when June mentioned Dad my hackles rose. I felt torn between wanting to be loyal to Mum and wanting to understand her sister. I didn't know if it was rehab Libby needed, or purely a quiet place to stay for a while. Either way, she would get this help somewhere professional.

There was a slight silence between us as she seemed to falter, obviously thrown off course by my sudden sharpness. 'Maybe she could live with me once she's released.'

Released? She made it sound as if Libby was going to jail.

But perhaps it *was* like prison.

What were we doing? Poor Libby. Could I do this to her? I needed to calm down. We couldn't do anything unless Libby consented.

'It's really quiet where I live, and she'd have a fresh start,' June persisted.

'Do you mean for ever?'

'For as long as she likes.'

'I thought you were planning on coming back to live this way.'

'I am, but I can't sell or rent the house out, so I'm happy to take it off the market to help Libby.'

'Let's get her sorted first and see where we go from there.'

'So … in the meantime I'll stop with you.'

'Yeah, fine,' I nodded. I was pleased that Rosie was starting to settle so much better with her new milk, although if she hadn't maybe June would have only stayed the one night when she realised how bad things really were.

We both fed the girls, who sucked the milk from the bottles as if they might never receive another. Both had their eyes shut, pure bliss enveloping them. My spirits lifted at this picture of perfection. Once again, a mixture of normality and complete disarray surrounded me.

Often, as in this moment, I didn't feel as if I was actually here. My body moved, and my voice spoke when necessary, but my mind felt in another place: inside a box, an empty box, but outside the box there was crashing, smashing, screaming and shouting. I didn't want to come outside of the box, because then I would have to deal with that noise.

If I could continue to shut out the world, maybe everything would fall into place and I could be left alone; on my own, in silence.

9

Max held up his hand in a casual wave as he drove slowly away. Depression engulfed me as it always did when he took the girls. Flatness and lethargy would work its way through my body, but the inability to sit still would irritate me like an itchy rash.

'Did they get off okay?' June sat on the sofa, yesterday's newspaper spread open next to her. Her silky dressing gown showed her bare white leg that was crossed over the other knee; a kitten-heeled slipper displaying a row of feathers and diamantes sparkled as her leg slowly moved up and down.

'Yes,' I said, walking towards my bedroom. 'Will you be alright on your own today?' I shouted from inside the room that felt so empty without my babies.

'I'll be fine. I might have breakfast in the café near the bridge. It looks nice in there.'

'It's lovely.'

'I'll have a wander around the shops. Is it cold outside?'

'Quite nippy,' I said distractedly, coming out from my room, pulling on my coat. A check-list running through my mind of things I had to do today.

'So, you're going to see Libby now?' June acknowledged, as if reading my thoughts.

'Yes, then I'm going to help Suzy with her invitations.'

'And, what time is Max bringing the girls back?'

'About four, maybe five.'

'Do you not have a definite time?'

'I used to tell him four, but then Rosie would bring her milk back up or one of them would fill their nappy, so they were always running late, which caused arguments. So, I've told him if he aims for four, he'll definitely make it by five.' Exasperated that I had to explain myself to her. I searched for the spare keys in the kitchen drawer that contained all the bits I kept in case one day I needed them.

'Oh, I see.' I could feel her gaze upon me, questions probably running through her mind at top speed. 'You're coping amazingly.'

'I don't have a choice.' I was sharper than I'd wanted to be. Plus, I didn't think I was handling anything; automatic was a great place to be, switching off was a wonderful technique.

'I am here, if you need me to do anything.'

'Thanks.' My problem was I knew I wouldn't accept her help. There was this internal mini-fight going on – in one corner there was the need to feel I was doing the best job for my babies, so no-one could ever tell me I was a bad mother. In the other corner was the selfish part of me who wanted my old life back. The guilt I felt about this internal battle was the reason I kept functioning: I knew that it wasn't the babies' fault; they hadn't asked to be brought into this crazy world, this dysfunctional mess.

So, I couldn't let them down.

*

The hospital was still the dismal place I'd remembered it to be when Dad was here. When we'd arrived with the ambulance I'd taken little notice of my surroundings as they'd rushed us through the corridors, doctors and nurses on our heels.

Walking through the corridors to ward nine, I wondered if this was a ward for people with addiction problems or mental health issues, if there was such a ward. Would she be lying in bed next to another drug addict? I figured probably not.

I hoped no-one had checked her notes. I imagined some nosey visitor reading her records like a story. Yes, I was embarrassed. I realise that sounds appalling. She would be judged by anyone reading about her personal life. Had I picked up someone else's hospital notes, would *I* have judged them? Of course: who wouldn't? I would have also analysed anyone coming to visit. So, I knew I, too, would be considered carefully. If not by visitors, then by the doctors, the nurses, the cleaning staff; they would be studying me as if I was a feeder, an enabler. They would think it was my fault she'd taken the overdose, it was my fault she had enclosed herself inside her tiny world and shut me out.

My body felt as if it would overheat, the blood rushing from the pit of my stomach, reaching my neck. I could feel blotches breaking out over my skin, redness forming across my face, driving through me as if someone was pouring hot water onto my already heated body. My steps began to slow as heaviness weighed upon my feet. It took everything in my power to keep walking, pushing my legs forward as if they were wading through thick snow. I was determined that I would not turn around.

I would not leave Libby here alone.

I, too, would be judged with her.

Libby was in a room with three other beds, but only one was occupied. An older man sat by the side of an elderly woman who lay on the bed facing him. Their hands were clasped together. He glanced at me but took little notice. Had he read her notes? He looked as if he would probably have had a heart attack if he knew what my little sister had been up to.

Libby was lying on her side facing away from me. A chair was in front of her. I made my way around the metal frame of the bed, pleased to see her eyes were open.

'Hi, you. How are you feeling?' She didn't even glance at me, let alone respond. So, it was going to be like that, was it? 'Look, we obviously need to talk about this.' I tried to sound gentle, but still no response. In fact, it was only the blinking that confirmed she wasn't dead.

Her dark hair now reaching past her shoulders hung lifelessly around her pasty cheeks. She looked so much better with a shorter cut. Even before she started messing around with drugs she had petite features, and a chin-length elegant bob always looked classy on her. But elegant and classy were no longer words I could use to describe Libby. It was funny because Clare had offered to give us both free haircuts. I was hoping she'd meant one of her staff would do it. I'd joked with Libby about it: 'You can brave Clare's scissor-hands first. I'll follow.' I'd expected a witty reply back, but a quick upturn of her mouth was all I'd received.

'Marianne and I have been talking and we wondered how you'd feel about going into a rehabilitation place.' I'd told Marianne I'd try and have a chat with Libby about how she'd feel about it. Bit hard when it's a one-way conversation, reminding me of the days I would try to talk to Dad.

But when Libby didn't answer, I wondered if I was asking too soon. But then, how long should I wait before I broached the subject? I continued, hoping she could see I wanted to help her. 'The programme obviously isn't working. I'm not sure which step to take next, Lib.' I was so desperate for her to tell me if this was a good idea or not, fearful that she would think not, though I'd decided she would probably be okay with the plan; especially when I thought back to our conversation at Christmas, when she'd been despairingly fraught.

It was my fault she had done this: she'd begged me not to let her do it again. As she stared out towards the window, where the only view was the grey clouds, a tear fell down her thin, bony cheeks.

I leant forward quickly to wipe away her suffering. 'Please don't cry, Lib, talk to me.' My throat thickened, the love I felt for her welling up while the mixed emotions of anger and disappointment simmered. She closed her eyes and I debated whether to leave. 'We're here for you, Libby.'

'It didn't work.' Her husky whisper just reached me, and another tear fell.

'Everything is going to be fine. We'll get you all the help you need.' I rubbed her thin arm, not too hard, worried I'd break her.

*

Suzy had the silver ribbon, the glue, the diamantes, the card, the printed inserts of the invitations and the silver envelopes all arranged perfectly in a line across her coffee table. She explained the process to me, how the ribbons would secure the insert and how the diamantes would border the cut-out heart on the front of the card. 'Less is more,' she told me as we sat opposite each other. I didn't have the heart to tell her this looked more rather than less!

'Where is Max taking the girls today?' she asked as we started our mini-production line.

'Don't know.'

'Didn't you ask?'

'I hate asking.' I shrugged like a rebellious teenager. 'I find it hard enough with them playing happy families as it is.'

'S'pose,' she agreed.

'Aw, Suzy, these diamantes are really awkward,' I commented, as one got stuck to my finger and as I tried to shake it off, about ten fell on the floor.

'Don't worry there's plenty of sparkles if we lose any.' She grinned, obviously enjoying this part of her wedding planning.

To be honest, so was I. It was therapeutic; not just the monotonous rhythm we'd created quite quickly, but also sitting with my best friend.

I'd unravelled all my thoughts about Libby as soon as I'd walked through the door. And I had no energy left to talk about Max. Whenever I talked about Max having the babies, Gina would pop into my head, her innocent face smiling sweetly in the background; and that infuriated me. I couldn't get over Gina. I *would* one day. I knew I would have to, unless I wanted to end up rocking back and forth in a chair, which at the moment seemed possible.

'Do you need any help?' Lawrence's long, lean figure appeared in the room.

'Don't you dare touch a thing!' Suzy fired at him, a smile emerging.

'Aw, spoilsport.' He leaned down to kiss her forehead, in the way Max used to kiss mine … I hadn't really noticed when he'd stopped kissing my lips, and when he'd moved upwards towards my hairline. But I knew by the glint in both their eyes, their kisses actually meant something: forehead, lips or mid-air there was no doubt they were totally in-love.

'How's Kat?' Lawrence asked me.

'I'm fine.'

'How's your sister?' His sad expression showed his concern.

'I'm sure she'll be fine when we get her some more help.' I focused on placing the diamante I had on the tip of my finger in the correct position.

'I hope so.' There was a silence; only ten seconds, but it was noticeable. 'So, babe, have you sorted things with your mum and dad.' He turned to Suzy.

'Not really.' Suzy sighed dramatically.

'I've told you I'll talk to them.' He sat on the edge of the sofa close to her, his hand on her shoulder.

'It's okay, I'll sort it, one way or another.' She held his hand, strained her head upwards, their eyes meeting as he leaned forward, kissing her gently on the lips.

'If they don't sort themselves soon, I'll have to get involved.' He lifted himself up, and as he left the room, he said, 'I'll leave you lovely ladies to it.'

'What's wrong?' I asked, when he'd gone. Suzy shook her head, screwing her nose and shrugged as if brushing away the problem. 'Come on Suz, what's happened?'

'Oh, honestly, it's nothing. I haven't said anything because you've got so much going on. It seems pitiful compared to your problems.'

'Come on, Suzy, that's what friends are for. I need a break from my own bloody life most of the time,' I forced a laugh. I knew she was trying to protect me, but still I couldn't help but feel slightly hurt that she felt she couldn't come to me.

'Mum won't come to the wedding if Dad is bringing his *floozie*.' She used the word her mum would use to describe her father's girlfriends. Since they'd split up, nearly twenty years ago, her father had introduced Suzy to over seventeen women. These seventeen women were the ones Suzy was allowed to know about: the ladies he was serious about, the ladies he wanted Suzy to be friends with. All were in their late twenties or early thirties, and obviously as we'd grown up, this had become increasingly uncomfortable for Suzy. But his latest, who was thirty-five, had been on the scene for six months. Believe me, this was a record in her father's books.

'Do you have to invite her?'

'He has given a load of money towards the wedding. He's practically paid for the whole lot … and he won't come if I don't invite her. It's a mess.'

'Oh, Suz, I'm sorry.' It was unlike Suzy to be so chewed up. It was unfair that this important event in her life was being overshadowed.

'Apparently weddings always cause a family row,' she laughed.

'So, I was told many a time in the salon.' I smiled. 'Would you like me to talk to her?'

'I don't think anyone talking to her will do any good.'

'I don't mind if you want me to try,' I offered, undecided how I would start that conversation, but I really wanted to help.

'Thank you, but I'll sort it. I'm sure.' If she felt as unconvinced as she looked, I knew she was really struggling.

I felt terrible for her. I really wanted to jump in my car, head that way and tell her mum to stop being so silly. There were more important things in life. How could she put such pressure on Suzy? I wanted to say all the things that Suzy had probably already said … but I thought coming from someone like me who *couldn't* have her mother at her wedding, it might hit home harder.

*

As I drove away from Suzy's, the thirty invitations perfectly sealed, a diamante adding the finished touch, it took all my energy and focus not to drive to her mum's.

The flat was empty when I arrived home. No note from June, pure stillness. I sat on the sofa, closing my eyes wanting to escape for five minutes before my life was sent full-force back into pandemonium. I'm not sure I even got two minutes' peace before the doorbell shrieked through the tiny space, ricocheting off the walls of the combined living-and-kitchen area.

'Oh, bloody hell, here we go.' I smiled to myself. Although the tiredness was overwhelming, I was so pleased to have the girls back. I felt as if I'd lost a limb when they weren't with me. It was hard to fathom how I'd lived my life without them, although I so desperately wanted to claw back some of that time. Every day that passed, those memories went deeper into the pit.

Max stood there holding both the car seats. He looked troubled and his complexion pastier than normal.

'Have they worn you out?'

I took Rosie's seat from him. Then I noticed a small, but dark and slightly swollen bruise on her forehead. 'What the hell happened?'

My heart started to race, beating so fast I thought it would burst from my chest. My hands shaking, I ran up the stairs with Rosie in the car seat, desperate to hold her in my arms.

'It was an accident.' Max was frantic as he followed me. I placed her down, undoing the lock to release the straps, pulling her into my arms. She didn't wake as I held her tightly, rubbing my fingers across the tiny, but protruding mark above her left eye.

'I was changing her, I promise I only turned away for a second, and then next thing I knew she was on the floor.'

'Where the hell were you changing her?'

'On the kitchen top, it was—'

'On the kitchen top?' I rocked Rosie in my arms. 'What the hell is wrong with the floor?'

'She's fine ... we took her to the hospital.'

'You took her to the hospital but didn't ring me?'

'I didn't want to worry you. Gina said we needed to take her; any babies under a year old that suffer a head injury would need an X-ray.'

I could have thrown up. Head injury? X-ray?

'I can't believe this, Max.' I practically spat the words at him. 'Get their stuff from the car and then please leave.'

'It was an accident, Kat. She's been checked. She's fine.'

'Please go.'

'I'm sorry.' He ran down the stairs out into the cold. I stroked Rosie's head as I heard him open the front door. He must have placed their bags at the bottom of the stairs, as the door closed again. Seconds later I heard his car start and drive off into the distance.

How could he let this happen? How could he be so stupid?

I found it hard enough when the girls were with them, but never because I believed him and Gina to be irresponsible. Gina was a nurse for God's sake: it never occurred to me that an accident could happen.

I sat next to Poppy's seat, her tiny body snuggled in the chair that still looked far too big for her, and let my tears fall. The love that washed over me, the panic I'd felt when I noticed the mark, was overwhelming.

The room seemed to close in on me as I held Rosie close and rocked Poppy's seat, as I tried to understand the terror that was enveloping me.

10

'So, have you been feeling down over the past few months?'

'No more than I'd expect to feel when I'm not getting any sleep.'

'During the past few months have you had pleasure taking part in things that would normally make you happy?'

'Not really.' I was trying to be as honest as possible. A year ago, I'd have been so excited to help Suzy with her invitations. Although I did help, it was for her benefit, really, as the whole event felt like a chore. But I knew it was nothing to do with Suzy; I blamed my tiredness; my inability to focus on any task at hand.

'Have you been able to laugh and see the funny side of things?'

'There is no funny side to anything at the moment.'

Dr Knowles glanced at me, nodding, then noted something down on the scripted questions he had in front of him. 'Is there anything you should maybe be enjoying, or be excited about, and you're not feeling that joy?'

'My friend's wedding.' It slipped out. I wanted to push it back in, feeling guilty for acknowledging such thoughts. But he didn't ask me any further questions on the subject, he just nodded again.

'Are you anxious and worried for no good reason, or feeling panicky and scared?'

'Mmm … I am quite worried about many things, but generally there is a reason.' I didn't finish with: my sister will probably be attending a mental health/drug rehab, my ex-partner has left me alone with two babies, I've lost my business … would you say these are not good enough reasons to be anxious and stressed?

'Do you blame yourself when things go wrong, although they probably aren't your fault?'

'But things that are going wrong *are* my fault.'

'How's that?' Diverting away from the fixed questions, he studied me intently.

'Well, my sister obviously has issues that must relate to our upbringing, or me trying to help raise her. My partner left me for someone else, so I obviously failed there. The girl who took all my clients was often left in my salon, on her own, so she thought it best to leave me; so that's my fault because I didn't look after her. Plus, Rosie's allergy, which is getting better now, could have something to do with me not breastfeeding for long enough; or maybe I didn't do something when I was pregnant that I should have done.' I bit my lip, feeling as if I'd unloaded a whole load of crap at his door.

The difference was, he'd forget about it when I left. I'd still have it weighing on my shoulders.

'But can you see that all of this is circumstantial? All these people have choices; their decisions were not based on your actions.'

'I get that, but still, if I wasn't here none of this stuff would be happening.'

He frowned at me. I can't even figure myself out, so there was no point him even thinking about it. 'Let's move to the next question. Do you feel sad and miserable?'

'Mmm … sometimes …' I didn't really want to answer. Sometimes, was better than, always. It was like admitting defeat. Yes, I'm so goddamn down, it hurts to be awake. He nodded as if understanding, though I hadn't spoken the words aloud.

'Are you so unhappy that you're having trouble sleeping?'

'I wish.' I let out a small laugh that surprised me. 'I'm having trouble sleeping because I have two babies.'

'Do you find yourself crying?'

'Yes.'

'Do you find yourself crying for no reason?'

'I always have a reason.' I wanted to tell him I cried daily. I cried at least twice a day, often around five times a day. But there was always a reason. I was tired. I was alone. I was lost in a world that was closing in on me. I cried endlessly, but it was always for a reason.

He moved his pen around the page, nodding his head slightly as if he was counting. Still nodding, as if his thoughts were confirmed: 'You are showing signs of post-natal depression.' Really? God help me, if I'd answered completely truthfully, St John's would be receiving my admission forms. 'So, we have a few options. I can prescribe some medication that could take three or four weeks to lift that cloud, and we can look at putting you forward for counselling. Or you could do one or the other. But we do recommend counselling.'

I expressed my concerns about medication; considering Dad and Libby's addiction issues, I was worried that I too would get hooked. A family trait I could do without. He told me this would be highly unlikely with post-natal depression. He talked about chemical imbalances in my brain, how I would stay on the medication for six months to a year, then we could look at weaning me off them.

I didn't want to talk to a counsellor. I couldn't analyse my life any more than I already had over the last year. I couldn't pick my life to pieces any more. I wanted a boost, a lift, not to go over past details and blame whoever or whatever. I needed to move on.

I walked away from the doctor feeling as if a heavier weight had been placed upon me. The pain between my shoulder blades felt on fire. The girls were sleeping soundly in the double pushchair; Poppy's chair lying flat and Rosie's lifted slightly. Although, Rosie had been so much better with the rice milk, it was early days and I was still paranoid she would rocket her insides at me, it still happened but not as often.

I wished I was in there with them, wrapped up warm, sleeping through the next few years, or for ever.

I thought about the last question he'd asked me before I'd left. 'Has the thought of harming yourself occurred to you?'

'No,' I'd told him straight. I was too much of a wimp to harm myself. Now, if he'd asked me, 'Have you had thoughts about dying?' then the answer would have been, yes.

Yes. I have hoped that I wouldn't wake up.

I often wondered how long it would take for my pain to end. Maybe there was a way I could end it, without physically hurting myself. I couldn't see what the future would bring; how things could get any better.

I didn't really want a future.

I hoped many a time when I placed my head on the pillow that my mum would come and rescue me. As these thoughts swam around in my mind, I let the second batch of tears of the day fall.

How could I think these thoughts?

How could I feel this way when I wouldn't have wished my own mother's absence on anyone?

All I knew was, my girls would be better off without me.

11

Libby was sitting in the front, Marianne in the back. I was focused on not getting lost and getting us there before lunch, although they'd not given us a specific time. We'd been driving for an hour and we still had half an hour to go, or so the map I'd printed off indicated.

Marianne and Derek had researched the best rehabilitation centres and phoned a few of them across the country. 'It doesn't matter how far we have to travel, she needs the best care available,' Marianne had told me as she explained about Pondergate Park. 'Not only do they focus on mental health and drugs, it has the most amazing facilities, they are surrounded by woodland, there are yoga classes and other activities, Derek and I believe she'll receive the best care there.'

'How does Derek *really* feel about this?' I'd asked tentatively.

'Derek is fine, he just wants Libby to get the help she deserves.'

Deserves. I'd considered that word, wondering what constituted Libby as deserving of help. Probably that she was one of God's children, but I didn't want to get into that conversation.

'But what about the money?' I asked.

'Don't you worry about that.' Marianne's tone was soft but undeniably firm.

Derek had wanted to come along today to 'talk to the counsellors about his experience in the drug world'. I was glad Marianne had talked him out of it, as I was sceptical about what benefit he would bring except to talk about himself. And using his term 'the drug world,' unsettled me. I wanted Libby to get help for her depression, as much as for her addictions.

As we crossed the Scottish border, Libby continued to look out of the window. She'd not spoken a word on the seventy-mile trip. But she'd not spoken a word in over a week; since she'd tried to commit suicide.

Yes. She'd admitted she didn't want to be here. She wanted it all to end.

But that was all she said. I'd tried to talk to her further about it, but she would look away from me, a blank expression covering her fragile face. She was trapped inside her own mind; this was the only way we could release her. Quite honestly, it was the only way we knew how.

I'd spoken to her counsellor from Marcoway, who'd agreed that if we could support Libby through this avenue then she would recommend it. Support … pay for it, she meant. I was worried about the amount of money Marianne had spent on Libby's condition. Unless she had some kind of endless pit or a magic jar that produced shiny coins, which I doubt she did, this couldn't go on for ever. I couldn't even think about how we could start paying her back. I say 'we' because I still felt that Libby was my responsibility.

We drove past acres of muddy, unkempt fields, homed sheep, cows and horses. Trees clung together as their bare branches interlinked, dancing gently in the wind. Libby was glued to the bright scenery, but it was highly unlikely that she'd taken in its beauty. Marianne was also staring at the variety of browns, greens, yellows and reds that we passed by. The amazing array of colours that were on display was remarkable. The surroundings were a sight that we took for granted, not relishing the splendour that bordered our daily lives.

Marianne helped with directions as she helped steer us to the place that would become Libby's home for the next six weeks. There was an option that she could have stayed for four weeks, but Marianne said, 'A few extra weeks will help to make sure she's better.' I couldn't help but agree, even though the tension that filled the car felt as if we were throwing her to the lions. Libby needed to be around people who understood her, people she could relate to.

The entrance was hidden between two thick bushes; a small plaque stated it was Pondergate Park. If Marianne hadn't been telling me in a high-pitch panic, 'It's left here somewhere,' I would have driven straight passed it. I turned the car slowly into the opening. We were suddenly between excessively high bushes and concealed from any form of life for about ten metres, before a heavy metal gate prevented us from trespassing. A metal speaker gleamed at us, daring us to make our presence known. The natural light that seemed to peer sheepishly from behind the gates beckoned us forward, but my head was shouting at me to reverse. *Take her home. Keep her safe.*

But this was safe, this was the safest place she could ever wish to be.

I released my window and pressed the button on the metal speaker. A loud ringing noise echoed into the air.

'Hello, Pondergate Park. How can we help?'

'Hi, I'm Libby Neasham's sister, she's due to be—'

'Oh, yes. Wonderful. Please drive through the gates and follow the road to the house.' A thunderous clang vibrated through the car as the gates were automatically released. We drove through as if we were taking a magical step through time. A whole new world hidden behind acres of woodland area, the fairy tale that Libby would have loved when she was a child.

Pity this was more of a horror story.

An old, prestigious manor house stood proudly across the park. A smooth, winding road that seemed to flawlessly join with the grass verge led the way to the magnificent home. It reminded me of Lampford Hall. As soon as those thoughts entered, so did thoughts of Max and Gina. I'd calmed since our last meeting. June had told me that Mum had tripped with Libby when she was a baby, sending her flying across the room. Luckily Libby had landed on the sofa.

The girls had gone to Max's while I took Libby to her new home, although I'd not explained any of this to Max. I hoped the girls were safe. Dramatic, I know, but I couldn't help it.

We drew closer to the home, accompanied by Marianne's commentary on how wonderful the surroundings were, how Libby would be so settled here; talking about her in the third person.

As we reached a gravelled area that seemed to be a car park, a woman stepped out into the open air. She waved at us as if we were arriving at a party. Her long, mousy hair was tied back, an oversized cardigan and faded jeans were her casual attire. I actually wondered if she was a patient, if patient was the proper term; it seemed better than 'inmate'. I liked the term 'patient' in the way I liked to call Libby's problem a 'condition'.

I pulled up next to another car, as Libby seemed to slump further into her seat.

The woman came over to greet us, as I stepped out of the car. 'Hi there. I'm Ronnie. I'm one of the nurses and I'll be working with Libby initially.' She took my hand and held it with her two, in the same way Derek did; but it didn't feel as slimy when she did it. Her touch made me feel so welcome. I was guessing she was in her fifties, and I felt warmth around her that made me want to go with her. I knew instantly that Libby was going to be fine; the guilt that had been twisting through me started to subside.

We were doing the right thing.

But it seemed Libby didn't think so. She sat rigid in the front of the car, staring straight ahead, as if fear was paralysing her. I knew she wasn't taking in the sandstone building, the old mesh windows or the neatly trimmed bushes that surrounded the house.

'You coming, Lib? This is Ronnie; she's going to look after you.' Marianne was standing beside me, telling Ronnie how beautiful the place was. Ronnie was smiling, but her eyes were on Libby. I closed my door and walked around the front of the car. Opening the passenger door, I could see Libby was physically shaking. Her body was trembling, her face ashen, her hands clenched together, squeezed between her knees.

'Please don't let me go in there, Kat. I promise I'll stop.' Her bloodshot eyes stared at me as her head juddered slightly from the vibration of her body.

'Libby, this is for the best,' I said softly but firmly, although I was crumbling. My insides were falling apart as my little sister begged me. I had no option. Was she begging me now because she knew they wouldn't let her take anything? If she came home she knew where she could get her fix. She couldn't stop; she'd proved this.

'I can't go in there.' Every word shivered on her lips as tears coursed down her gaunt cheeks.

'Will you trust me?' It was all I could think of to say. Part of me wanted to pull her from the car, tell her to sort her life out; the other part wanted to drive away as fast as we could, and protect her vulnerability.

This wasn't easy. It wasn't as if we were sending her abroad on an expedition, encouraging her to enjoy her youth. This was the last straw. This was a final call for help. If Libby couldn't do this, couldn't achieve the goals we were putting in place for her, I couldn't bear to think of the future she was heading towards.

'Hi, Libby. My name is Ronnie.' Ronnie placed a hand on my shoulder. As I removed myself from my kneeling position, she stepped in to replace me. In essence, she was replacing my role too, but I knew she'd do a better job than I had. In fact, what had I done to help Libby, except become increasingly angry that she was being so self-centred? I'd never told her that's how I'd felt, but she'd probably picked up on the vibes. I'd told her I'd be there for her. I'd pray to Mum, promised her I'd look out for Libby.

Once again, I'd let them both down.

As Ronnie spoke softly to Libby about how lovely her room was, how the other residents were looking forward to meeting her, I felt useless.

It took about five minutes, but finally Libby slowly stepped from the car. She was so fragile, a shell of her vibrant former self.

My tears pleaded to be released as Ronnie offered her arm and Libby took it. I swallowed back the urge to push Ronnie out the way, let me step in, take over, insist that *I* could do this. *I* could help her. I *wanted* to help her. Forcing away this selfish impulse, I opened the boot to lift out her suitcase.

Marianne and I followed them both through the old wooden door that creaked as it opened. Inside we were faced with the grandness of a luxurious country hotel. Dark wooden polished floors spread across the entire space, and red carpet runners centred the walkways. An open fire heated a casual living space, soft fabric sofas surrounded the cosy area. Flowers had been professionally arranged, a sweet lavender smell enriched the homeliness and the enormous pictures on the high walls possessed an understated grandeur.

'Hi there, you must be Elizabeth.' Another woman who was dressed smartly in an A-line grey skirt and pink blouse came towards us, her hand held out towards Libby. I was pleased that Libby took it politely.

'It's Libby.' Her faint voice was barely audible.

'It's lovely to have you here, Libby. I'm Adrianne. I'm the administrator here. We'll confirm a few details and then Ronnie will show you around.'

We all circled the fire, sitting down on the sofas. Adrianne asked questions that Marianne had more than likely already answered before. Ronnie would nod in certain places, but she studied Libby quite frequently.

Once the boxes were ticked, we spent the next hour touring the stunning venue that Libby would soon become accustomed to. We were shown Libby's bedroom first. A single bed dressed with a flowered quilt was situated against the far wall, accompanied by a bedside table, a set of drawers and a wardrobe. Plain, simple and basic, but what else would be needed? It was explained that no televisions were allowed in the rooms, as they thought it was important that bedrooms were used for resting and sleeping. There was a television room, which all residents were allowed to use, when they weren't scheduled for other activities. The view from Libby's window was breath-taking; trees surrounded this secret hideaway and the perfect lawns enhanced the beauty. Two men were sitting on a bench, wrapped in thick coats, one wearing a hat and scarf. It occurred to me that by the time Libby came out, our thick winter coats wouldn't be needed. Time would pass as the season changed and hopefully Libby would be free.

Free from her evil world.

Ronnie showed us the rest of the house: the television room, rooms where one-to-one counselling took place, a room for group sessions, a lounge, the kitchen, the eating area and other rooms where residents could rest. Most were adorned with a large open fire, wood ready to burn. I wondered if they were for decoration only. I was surprised how quiet the home seemed. It was so peaceful and tranquil. I wasn't sure what I'd expected – people shouting at each other, withdrawal taking over their social graces but there was no such disruption. I could have stayed for a week or so myself.

After the tour of the lavish house, Ronnie sat us down near the entrance. The comfortable sofas embraced our bodies and our tired minds. If I'd been relaxed enough I could have easily curled up and dissolved into a deep sleep.

We listened as Ronnie explained that the first week would be very intense for Libby. It was advised that there should be no contact with anyone outside the clinic for the first week. I understood this and didn't make a fuss, but I hated the fact that I wouldn't be able to call her and ensure she was okay. Ronnie then explained about the daily routines which involved a variety of therapy sessions, group activities, lectures, discussions, walks in the grounds and relaxation therapies. She described how the support Libby would receive would be life-changing.

As I mentally took note of how Libby would be supported by understanding carers and people who had been through what she had been through, I felt certain that we were doing the right thing. I had to let her go. Ronnie told us there would be a chance for us to schedule two family therapy sessions, but we would arrange a date once Libby had settled into her first week. Visiting was only allowed on Sundays, but we would have to miss the first Sunday to allow Libby to find her feet.

So, it was sorted. She was officially booked in. Her new home. It would be fine. Libby would be fine. She needed these people.

We left Libby at the door with Ronnie, looking lost. Ronnie's arm securely around her shoulders.

A kiss goodbye, a wave of affection, a wish of good luck.

We left Libby in her tragic world.

12

So … I made it to the new mum's group.

Suzy, June, Marianne, Clare and Jane had all insisted, and Dr Knowles had commented before I left, 'It will do you good.' Once, I'd have seen this as a fantastic networking opportunity; marketing to new mums who definitely needed pampering. Now, it was a tiresome task that would drain me.

But I'd listened and finally I was sat in a room full of women who I didn't know. As I tried not to study them individually, I thought about how Libby felt when she was attending one of her focus groups. Did she feel this intimidated?

One of the main reasons I'd chosen to come was because I couldn't focus. Libby was in my every thought. I couldn't concentrate. I'd even mistakenly mixed up Rosie and Poppy's milk. Consequently, Rosie had cried all day in pain from merely having one five-ounce bottle of the wrong milk. She'd been hungry and thoroughly enjoyed sucking away on the tiny teat, but an hour or so later she cried endlessly. Her legs curled up to her middle as she winced in pain. Luckily June had helped with Poppy while I rocked Rosie. Bounced her around, rubbed her small, bloated stomach and massaged her back. It had been so exhausting, listening to her screams. At one point June took Poppy out for a walk. In the midst of Libby's crisis, I'd forgotten how tiring Rosie was. She'd become accustomed to her new milk, she'd become settled, she'd become a happier baby. The moment I'd mixed up the formulas the exhaustion hit me. June had later poured me a glass of wine, asking, 'How the hell did you cope for so long?'

I hadn't answered, because I didn't know.

I browsed around the room at the other new mums, and wondered if any of them were suffering in the way I was. Were they really enjoying this new chapter in their lives?

'My name is Brooke and this is Chelsea,' the girl sitting next to me, who looked about twenty-five-ish, was announcing to the other women, who were now staring at me.

'I'm Kat, and this is Rosie and Poppy.' I was last to introduce myself … because I was the last to arrive. I'd squeezed on the end of the chairs that were arranged in a neat semi-circle, hoping nobody would notice me.

'Twins … how do you cope?' One mum, who was dressed in tight jeans, her figure all of a size six, asked me.

'Oh, you just do,' I smiled, while wanting to scream, *do I look as if I'm coping?*

'God, I find it hard enough with one. I don't know how you do it!' Another mum with black, tied-back hair, wearing no make-up and a baggy cardigan, joined in, shaking her head.

I don't know how I do it, I thought, but didn't say. I was hoping the conversation would divert elsewhere.

'Ladies … it's lovely to see you all. We hold these groups because being a new mum can be a lonely place,' the health visitor, who'd introduced herself earlier as Sandra, told us. A few of the other mums nodded in agreement. 'We have six sessions, and generally you ladies can chat together but there'll always be a theme. This week, it's basically to get to know each other and talk about any concerns you may have. Next week we'll talk about weaning, then there'll be a session on choosing the best educational toys and so on …'

'I think Freddy needs weaning now,' one mum laughed. 'Honestly, sometimes I think he's going to pull my breast off.'

Really! Did she have to?

'Oh, I know. Harvey twists mine, I swear it's like sadism,' another mum said, laughing with her.

'It must be a boy thing,' Brooke joined the conversation, beaming down at Chelsea, who was dressed in a pink mesh dress that would have been more appropriate for a party, as were her pink sparkly shoes that were too big for her tiny feet. I'd not even thought about shoes for the girls; I wasn't even aware they were available for such small babies. 'I didn't do the breastfeeding thing.' The room fell silent as Brooke admitted her shocking sin to the group. I half-expected a chant to start up – 'Burn her at the stake!' – as the disapproving eyes fell upon her.

'It's not for everyone,' Sandra smiled warmly, obviously aware that the women were about to pounce.

'But surely, it's best to offer your child the best start in life,' Harvey's mum said to Brooke.

'I *have* offered my child the best start: she has a loving home.' Although she was young, Brooke was not going to let this woman walk all over her.

'But what about bonding with your baby?' another Mum piped up.

'We've bonded amazingly. She loves *The Real Housewives of New York*,' Brooke laughed. No-one cracked a smile. I wanted to leave.

'But it's not only about the bonding process, it's about building their immune system.' Harvey's mum sat rigidly upright in her chair.

'Do you think they would sell formula milk if it was bad for our babies?' Brooke asked. I assumed she'd had this argument before.

'As I said, everyone has to do what is best for them.' Sandra clapped her hands and smiled broadly, obviously trying to defuse the debate.

'Anyway, it means my boyfriend can get up in the night and feed her,' Brooke laughed again.

I really wanted to leave. But a few of the mums softened as they joined in:

'Oh, tell me about it! Since I stopped breastfeeding, we've been doing one night each. It's great.'

'Oh, you lucky thing, there'll be no way Glen will get up when I *stop* breastfeeding.' Harvey's mum accentuated the fact she *was* still breastfeeding, clearly trying to make most of us who were now using bottles, bad for not holding out as long as she had.

'God no, Jeff won't either.'

'Daryl has been amazing. I'm very lucky.' Brooke beamed.

'You *are* lucky. Roger wouldn't even know what a night feed was.'

'I don't think my hubby knows what a day feed is either.'

'I'm with you there.'

'What about you, Kat, does your husband, oh sorry, partner help?' They all turned to stare at me. The question was fired at me from a plump, short woman with frizzy red hair. Her cheeks were burning with rosacea, embarrassment or over-heating. My own cheeks felt as if they matched hers as I felt them glow fiercely. The words seemed to lock in my throat. I thought about lying, making up a fantasy figure. My perfect husband!

'We're not together.' I sounded more confident than I felt.

'Oh … I'm sorry.' The woman's cheeks flushed even more. The redness spreading across her face and neck.

'It's fine. We're fine.' More silence followed. So, not awkward, then. 'To be honest, it's easier, really; it means I don't have to look after him.' I had to make light of the situation, as they all stared at me in pity; me, the single Mum in the corner, who not only had one baby but two. How awful.

'I totally agree,' one of the mum's contributed.

'God yeah, it's as if they're just as helpless.'

'Is anyone else experiencing jealousy?'

'Oh, don't talk to me about jealousy.'

'My husband's been great, really loving.'

'Loving? Really? Have you ventured back into the bedroom yet?'

'You haven't?'

'Oh my God, the sex is great afterwards. I was so nervous but …'

It was time for me to leave. I'm not prudish – there are many times when Suzy and I have discussed our favourite positions and how long it's lasted and even the profound objects we have used – but I didn't need to hear this.

I'd thought this group was supposed to make me feel better - let's talk about sleepless nights, colic, babies' nappies; or even better, let's not talk about babies. Let's talk about shopping, pampering, favourite beauty products, favourite celebrities, favourite programmes, favourite drink … anything but men, breastfeeding, sex and babies.

But I was being unfair, because I didn't really want to talk to them about anything.

It wasn't them … it was me.

*

I'd been taking the tablets for three days. The first day I'd stared at the tablet as if it might eat my insides if I dared to touch it. I'd picked it up. Put it down. Picked it up. Put it down; before I finally succumbed. I did it because I wanted to feel better. I wasn't convinced it would work, but I had to try.

I had to try for my girls.

Don't get me wrong, I'm not one of those people who didn't believe in medication, that depression was all in one's head. I didn't latch onto the stigma depression created. I'd lived it. I'd seen it erode both Dad and Libby's bodies. I believed it was an illness, but I also believed that the therapies I used to use on my customers would have helped too. The problem I had at the moment was that I couldn't be bothered (or felt I had the time) to find a therapist who could help me in that way. The tablets seemed like the best answer, an easier way to crawl from my own mind. I needed easy, even if I wasn't sure they would work. Dad's had never worked. But then, we had been told numerous times that they wouldn't work with alcohol; not the amount Dad consumed anyway.

I don't know what I expected when the doctor told me it would take at least two to four weeks for me to feel any different. Citalopram 20mg a day, he'd started me on. If these didn't work we'd increase it slowly until I was starting to feel normal again. I'd not felt my normal self since falling pregnant. Had I had depression all the way through my pregnancy and not noticed? Suzy had thought so. She'd told me about prenatal depression: apparently, she'd read an article that showed it was more common than post-natal depression, and apparently women don't talk about it, as they're ashamed. All I knew was my life seemed to have taken a spiral downwards. Now I was at the bottom struggling to work my way to the top. 'Let's face it Kat, you were going through so much,' Suzy had said.

It didn't make me feel better. I felt guilty for feeling so lost, so lonely and not enjoying, what should be, a special time in my life.

*

I left the church where the new mum's group was being held, and, if anything I felt lonelier leaving than when I'd gone in. The sun was dazzling, stinging my eyes with the intensity of its brightness. Unfortunately, the temperature was still slightly lower, but the boldness of the sunny skies was making the statement that it would soon be warm. Spring would soon be upon us and hopefully Libby would be fixed. As I faced the burning sun, I prayed I would be right.

'Kat. Which way are you walking?' Brooke was behind me, her heels clicking against the pavement. Heels? I didn't understand. My back was still in pieces; heels were definitely out of the question. I was definitely not a yummy mummy. Frumpy mummy – I should set a trend.

'Oh … I'm just down here, not far.' I was only a five-minute walk away from the flat.

'Me too, I'll walk with you.' She was at my side, as the other mums started leaving behind us.

'See you next week,' one of them shouted. I waved politely. I think not.

'What a load of old hags,' Brooke said, shaking her head.

'I'm their age, I'll have you know,' I laughed, but slightly offended.

'Oh my God. Honestly …' she said in despair, shaking her head. 'Did you hear that woman going on about breastfeeding? I tell you, Kat, these are for my man.'

I smiled hesitantly, unable to answer. Actually, pleased she'd not announced *that* in the session.

'Then the whole sex thing, you know, me and Daryl were at it two weeks later.'

'Really?' Was that possible?

'I wasn't waiting around. You've got to keep 'em happy you know, or they'll move on.'

'I know.' She seemed oblivious to my sarcasm.

'So, are you going to go to the massaging class?'

'Probably not.' I'd signed up to the baby massaging, because everyone else had. I'd already stood out enough without them asking why I didn't want to go.

'It'll be fun. Please come. I won't get on with anyone else.'

'No pressure, then,' I smiled at her. Although she was loud and coarse, I liked her. I knew it was because she reminded me of Libby, outspoken, unrefined but innocent.

We chatted on the way home, or rather Brooke talked at me. She told me she'd started a psychology degree, (which surprised me – which was wrong: anything I had learnt as a beauty therapist is to never judge a book by its cover,) but she fell pregnant so decided to wait a few years; but she had every intention of going back. Daryl was older than her, by ten years. Her parents didn't approve, but then, when she'd fallen pregnant they'd apparently seen sense. I didn't contribute much to the conversation.

As we walked past the salon (I was still getting used to the 'Luscious Locks' signage that had replaced 'Soothing Salon') the door opened, and Clare rushed out to greet us.

'How did it go?' she asked eagerly.

'It was okay,' I offered.

'It was awful, they were dowdy earth mothers,' Brooke contributed.

'Really?' Clare observed Brooke, obviously weighing up the outspoken youngster.

'This is Brooke,' I told Clare, hoping she would take the distasteful expression off her face, 'And this is Clare. The girls' grandma.'

A deep frown appeared on Brooke's unblemished forehead, her mind clearly working busily. 'It wasn't so bad, but it's not my thing,' I told Clare, ignoring Brooke's confused expression.

'Oh, Kathryn, you really must try again,' she said desperately.

'Are you the Kathryn that used to own this salon?' Brooke asked, as if I was a celebrity.

'That would be me.'

'Oh, my sister-in-law was so upset when you closed down. She absolutely loved your salon. Angie Donnelly. Do you remember her?'

Mrs Donnelly! Who could forget? So much for her being upset – she left me! I didn't say as much. It was over, now.

'I remember her.'

'What a shame you had to close down.'

'One of those things,' I said lightly, although my heart was sinking fast.

'If your sister-in-law would like to come to my salon, there's a twenty-per-cent discount for new customers,' Clare said as I raised my eyebrows at her, hoping she would catch my warning.

'I'll let her know,' Brooke said, 'but I think she uses some top stylist in Leeds, or something. I keep telling her she has to take me, but Daryl doesn't earn as much as my brother. Still, I think he should make sure his little sister is pampered too!'

'I agree,' I smiled, not wanting to talk about Steve Donnelly.

'Anyway … I'd better go. Chelsea will need feeding soon.' Brooke patted down the pink frilly hat her baby was wearing. 'Promise you'll do the massaging class?'

Her relationship with Mrs Donnelly had suddenly dampened any friendship I thought I could have with the young girl. But I found myself telling her I would definitely go.

We watched her as her heels clicked against the pavement as she walked into the distance, her black leggings silhouetting her shapely legs, a chiffon top elegantly covering her pert behind and her black leather jacket fitting tightly at the waist.

I was struggling with my baby weight. Okay, we all know I was struggling with my weight beforehand. But if I was honest, I was actually smaller than I was before I'd got pregnant. Don't be hating me! It was stress, nothing else but stress. And lack of time. If I found the time to eat, it was a biscuit here and there. I'd lived off diet drinks that were full of caffeine. However, although I was now a size twelve instead of a fourteen, I was all flabby. If I *did* take the opportunity to make myself a sandwich or my favourite pasta dish or heat up a microwave meal, I looked six months pregnant again. I'm not jesting. I'd always suffered with the bloated effect after eating too many carbs, as many of us do; but these days my balloon-shaped stomach would expand within seconds.

And dare I venture onto the breast area? Well, okay, just quickly, then I'll try to say no more about the situation. Before the girls, they were pert; big but pert. Now, I couldn't even see my nipples. They faced so far south they often experienced gravel rash.

'Henry's here.' Clare's word dragged me from my thoughts, as I stared longingly at Brooke's behind.

'Henry?'

'He was passing. He hasn't seen the girls for a few weeks, so he called in.'

'He's upstairs?'

'June said he could wait.'

'We better get up there.' I didn't like visiting Clare's house any more. I was always worried I'd bump into Max and Gina. Clare saw the girls every day, so it never seemed a problem. I suppose I forgot they had a grandad too.

His car was parked around the side of the building. I unlocked the door to the flat before releasing both the girls, then twisted my arms around them both to ensure they were locked securely to my body before venturing up the flight of stairs. I needed to find somewhere else to live: this was ridiculous. And Henry's surprise visit annoyed me slightly. I understood he wanted to see the girls, but couldn't he ring and let me know? If I had my own place, all these random visits would stop.

The top door was shut, which was unusual as I generally left it open when I left the flat. I angled my elbow to push the handle down. It released as the door slowly opened.

Henry jumped to his feet in surprise, as June wiped her mouth and quickly pulled herself into a seated position.

No … please tell me that hadn't just happened.

13

He said, 'Kat, what a surprise'. And I said, it shouldn't be, I live here, and then he came over to the girls. June made a cup of tea and we all acted as if nothing had happened.'

'She's a dangerous woman. That's why I've not wanted Derek around her.' I wanted to laugh. Derek? June and Derek? I wasn't sure my imagination stretched that far.

'I don't know what to do,' I confessed to Marianne. 'Do I tell Clare?'

'No, I wouldn't.' Marianne shook her head, as she gazed across the familiar fields we'd passed just over a week ago. The exact words Suzy had used: 'It could be nothing,' although Suzy, like me, believed it *wasn't* nothing, but she'd said it would cause a whole load of upset and the only person who would be blamed would be me. I knew she was right, but it didn't help matters. I'd asked June what she was playing at; she gave me some fictitious story about having something in her eye. It was hard to imagine that they'd been messing around like teenagers. Could I really believe it? Wouldn't the eye story make more sense?

Max had picked the girls up, so we could visit Libby. I hadn't mentioned anything about the dropping incident as I had mentioned it several times previously; although I was dying to confirm that he wouldn't drop the girls on their heads. No, I'd been polite. I'd only made one comment: 'Please be careful,' as he'd left. He'd nodded, not amused; but seriously, did he think I'd forgotten about it? Did he think I'd *ever* forget about it? I was only being easy on him because of June's story and Clare insisting how upset he was, both women telling me, 'It could easily be you.'

Before he'd left he'd asked if everything was okay, '… you know, changing the day …' He was referring to the fact that I'd asked him to take the girls on Sunday instead of our usual Saturday agreement. He'd wanted me to tell him about my life. I wasn't ready to cross that border yet. 'Everything's fine.' I'd told him I was going out with Marianne for the day. Not a lie, but not the whole truth.

The truth stood before us; the height of the house seemed to have increased since our first visit. The grandeur of the magnificent home encircled us as we entered through the main wooden door. The reception area was as breath-taking as it was when we first arrived, the only difference being the vulnerable young person who was now part of the picture. Libby came towards us, a smile spreading across her face. It didn't reach her eyes, but the upward turn was a good start.

'Hi, sweetheart.' Marianne held her arms out as Libby leaned in for a hug.

My own arms embraced her too, but I couldn't speak, supressing the tears that were still attacking my cheeks two or three times a day.

'Hello, there.' Ronnie was walking towards us, her attire still casual, her plaited hair, paisley shirt and waistcoat showing she loved the sixties. I wondered if she'd taken drugs herself. She looked as if she possibly still could. 'Do you want to come with me?' We followed her out of the warm room where the fire blazed invitingly.

Ronnie had called me earlier in the week, wondering if we could have our first family session when we visited today. Libby had requested we have our first session sooner, rather than later.

I'd been slightly worried Libby was on the warpath, and when I asked her if everything was okay, she smiled at me vaguely, shrugging as we made our way through the arched corridors.

'In here.' Ronnie opened the door to one of the rooms we'd viewed initially. We sat on the chairs that surrounded the unlit fireplace, as if the focal point made a difference to the therapy. A plastic cup of water was placed in front of each seat. Fresh for the meeting, I hoped, not stale and left over from others.

Ronnie opened her pad, her pen at the ready. 'Libby has really settled in this week.' Libby nodded, biting her lip as she agreed with Ronnie. 'The first week is always the hardest. We always say, if any individual can withstand the first week, then it can only get better,' Ronnie laughed. Marianne and I politely laughed with her. 'As I explained previously, we are here to talk about Libby's illness, but the point of the family sessions is to understand how everyone feels and if there are any issues we need to embrace that will help Libby move forward.'

'Wonderful,' Marianne said, clasping her hands together then resting them between her knees, squeezing her fingers tight. I noticed she was shaking.

'Now, it's important to understand that we don't have all the answers. But if we can work through any issues that may prohibit Libby continuing to get better at home, we can discuss them today.'

My throat was suddenly dry. I drank the water that was on offer; thankfully it *was* fresh.

'So, Libby, is there anything you would like to discuss?'

'I want them to know how sorry I am.' She peered at us both, her fingers fumbling together.

'Good, is there anything you would like to say in response?'

'We know, we just want you to get better,' I offered.

'Excellent.' Ronnie made a quick note on her pad, then turned her body towards me. 'So, Kat, is there anything you would like to discuss?'

'Not really. We just want Libby to get better.'

'Marianne?'

'Mmm …' Marianne frowned at me. 'No, I don't think so. As Kat said, we want Libby well again.'

'I have something I need to say,' Libby said suddenly, which surprised me and clearly Marianne too, as her eyes widened flicking between Libby and me. Ronnie, however, didn't flinch. I wondered how many counselling sessions Libby had participated in that allowed her to be so vocal. 'I've stolen money.'

'We know about that, it's in the past,' Marianne waved a hand. 'From Clare.'

'What?' I'd obviously misheard her.

'It was only the once, I had every intention of putting it back.'

I swallowed away the lump that was suffocating my throat. I was fully aware Ronnie was watching my every move. I was gutted that Libby had steeped so low. But I was trying to understand why she'd done it? She'd been desperate. That's why she was here. And we were here because we were supporting her, not making her feel worse than she already did.

'How much?' I found myself asking.

'Fifty pounds.'

I rubbed my hand along my forehead, my finger and thumb tracing the sides of my face. The silence filled the room, the uncomfortable display of disloyalty driving between us once again.

'I can pay her back,' Marianne said.

'I'm sorry,' Libby said weakly.

'Kat, how do you feel about this?' Ronnie's softness reached me as she leaned towards me.

'I'm …' I shook my head and shrugged my shoulders, not daring to say how I really felt about it. That I was angry, but sad. How could I feel these two emotions so strongly, at the same time?

'Talk to Libby,' Ronnie encouraged.

'It's fine, we'll sort it,' I managed, not wanting to put any more pressure on her. 'Do you think she knows?' I had to know whether Clare had some inclination. I needed to know what I was dealing with.

'I don't think so.'

'We don't need to tell her,' Marianne said, her brow puckering. 'If she hasn't said anything, she hasn't noticed.'

The stilted silence was heavy. I stared at my feet, the inside of my mouth becoming increasingly sore as I chewed the soft skin.

'I'm so sorry,' Libby said, her lip quivered as her eyes filled with tears as she blinked nervously at me.

'It's fine, at least you've told us.' I couldn't believe I was being so sympathetic. At one stage I would have exploded. I was furious she'd stolen from Clare, it put me in a right predicament, but then Libby *must* have been desperate.

Leaning forward in my chair, I took her hand and looked at her, ensuring she met my eye. 'We want to help you.'

'I know and I'm sorry.' Libby kept her eyes down, as she wiped away a tear.

'Oh, please don't cry.' I reached over to her, hugging her. 'We want to help you, Lib,' I said the words again, hoping she truly understood.

'We'll sort Clare, don't you worry about that,' Marianne said. How she thought we'd sort Clare was unknown to me. Did we tell her? Did I slip fifty notes back in the till? I wanted to ask Libby when had she had the chance to steal the money, but it seemed irrelevant: it could have been at night, early hours of the morning or middle of the day, it didn't matter, she'd done it.

We spent the next hour discussing issues that involved Mum dying, Dad's depression, Marianne's role and how it all fitted together. Libby had obviously explained her family history in previous meetings, as Ronnie knew all about us. She knew the exact timeline of my life. There was no blame, no guilt to be given to any party. Libby seemed extremely happy with the way I'd handled things. 'I couldn't have asked for a better sister,' she'd said. I'd half-expected her to rip me apart, blame me for her problems, but she didn't. She'd attended so many counselling sessions in the last week, though, I wondered if they'd made her understand she had to take responsibility.

When the session was over, Ronnie thanked us for our time, and left us so that we could wander the grounds with Libby. Other residents were walking with their families. I was surprised by the normality of the people here. I'd also expected them all to be young, around Libby's age if not younger, their parents spending their university fund on rehab … but I was wrong. The age range was vast.

A couple in their fifties sat together on one of the benches. Libby said hello to them, and we followed suit. Libby explained it was the woman who had the problem; this was her third time in rehab.

Third time? Please God, this first time had better work for Libby.

She told us that they had two children in their teens who knew nothing of her addiction to prescription drugs; they thought she was away working while she rested in Pondergate Park. It was so sad.

A family passed us; two children, aged, I guessed, between ten and fifteen, accompanied the grown-ups. A man aided by a walking stick bowed his head solemnly at us. Libby told us that the lady was his daughter and the children were his grandchildren. He'd had years of abusing alcohol and a variety of drugs, generally prescription, whatever he could get his hands on. It was a different world. A world I wished we didn't have to be part of.

Libby wasn't overly chatty. She explained quite matter-of-factly who everyone was. But I was pleased she had some knowledge of them, because it meant she wasn't cocooning herself in her room. She told us briefly (with lots of prompting from Marianne and me) about the therapy sessions, the lectures she'd attended and the complementary therapies that had helped her relax. It sounded like a place I would have loved to have come to, except I didn't really want to talk to anyone. I was pleased, though, that Libby seemed settled, considering I'd not been able to get her out of the car when we'd arrived. I hoped this place would work.

After we'd kissed her goodbye, told her to stay strong and keep up the good work, Marianne and I were accosted by Ronnie as we were leaving. Her bright eyes and warm smile brought us into the aura of kindness that she presented.

'She's doing great, isn't she?'

'I'm really surprised, actually,' I agreed. I was surprised. Having Libby smile, granted not a huge smile, and have a conversation without snapping my head off was a massive step.

'Thank you for coming today, I can see how much you care about each other. It's wonderful to know she has a loving, supportive family for when she leaves.'

'We'll be here for her,' Marianne said proudly.

'That's good.' She clasped her hands together. 'We do offer one-to-one sessions for family members too.'

'We're fine, thanks,' I smiled. I didn't want counselling.

'Does Libby think we need them?' Marianne was clearly confused.

'I can't reveal what we discuss in her sessions, I'm just saying the service is there if you felt the need to use it.'

'I think it might be a good idea, Kat,' Marianne peered at me.

'I'm fine, but you feel free to go,' I continued to smile, hoping it was warm rather than as rigid as my body felt, claustrophobia taking over, as the air in my lungs struggled to find a way out. I didn't want to talk to anyone, especially someone who didn't know me.

'We'll chat about it,' Marianne smiled. *No, we won't*, I wanted to scream, struggling to contain my composure. I didn't want to talk … *I really didn't.*

'The offer is there.' Ronnie's hands were still clasped together.

'Thank you,' Marianne said. I struggled to speak.

We left Ronnie standing at the door, watching us walk across the gravelled car park. I felt her eyes burning into my back. Had she picked up on the fact that I wanted to shake Libby, shout and scream at her, bring her to her senses? But at the same time, I wanted to hug her close, keep her safe, soothe her and make all her pain go away.

'I'd prefer that you didn't tell Clare,' Marianne said as I started the engine.

'Oh, Marianne, I can't believe this.' I let out a huge sigh.

'We don't need her judging our family,' Marianne practically whispered.

'But I feel awful keeping it from her.' I ran a hand through my hair, feeling at a complete loss. I was sure Clare must know. But, then, how could she? Wouldn't she have said something? 'I could say that I borrow—'

'I'm sure if you can protect your aunty, you can protect your sister.' Marianne's words, although spoken softly, sliced through me.

She was right.

14

The boutique was quaint. The shabby-chic furniture embellished the luxury feel of the finely decorated shop. Suzy glided along the carpet, the mirrors reflecting how stunning she looked. It was a Caroline Castigliano dress, an exquisite lace fishtail gown, flaunting intricate embroidery across the delicate fabric. It feathered out from her knees, the strapless style highlighting her slender shoulders, the design fitting perfectly around her slim waist.

'So elegant.' Her mum clasped her hands together as she wiped away a stray tear.

'You look stunning, Suz.' Watching my friend embracing this next chapter of her life filled me with joy. Or was it fear? Would I be alone for ever? I wouldn't have said the words aloud at this time, but it wasn't only me that a new man would take on; it was the three of us. I found it a scary thought, so God help any potential partners!

'Do you think?' She bit her lip. 'Do you think Lawrence will like it?'

'He'll love it,' Suzy's mum said.

'Honestly, Suzy, it's perfect,' I encouraged, because it *was*. Plus, it was a bit late to change her mind; this was her first fitting, the dress was already paid for.

Debra, who owned the boutique, handed Suzy's mum a tissue. We'd all instantly fallen into Debra's grasp on our first visit. She had been warm, embracing the challenge of ensuring that Suzy's dress would be here within the short time frame Suzy had given her.

Some of the other bridal shops had given her the option of their sale rack and the off-the-shelf gowns that Suzy could take away there and then. Most told us, 'it takes at least sixteen weeks for the wedding gown to come in,' so there was no-way they could promise the dress would be ready on time. Debra had hinted at this too but had said she would do her best to make sure the dress Suzy wanted would be ready by her wedding date. That's all Suzy wanted; someone who would do their best for her. We had to give Debra her due: she'd pulled out all the stops and Suzy stood before us a figure of flawless perfection.

'We just need to pull you in at the top.' Debra pulled the dress tightly around Suzy's breasts, the gaps at the sides disappearing. 'He's a very lucky man.'

'Isn't he?' Suzy's mum boasted. Suzy rolled her eyes at me. I smiled, although totally agreeing with the other women. Suzy's long blonde hair fell around her shoulders, her pale skin soft, her bright blue eyes sparkling like the jewel on her hand. He *was* a lucky man. But I had no doubt he was fully aware of this.

I studied myself – frumpy and less glamorous than my friend. The silver satin dress pinched my waist, making my breasts bulge and ruffling the material into a shabby state. My oversized arms sat chubbily over my boob-fat, while my back had a crease across my spine. On top of that, I felt as if I'd squeezed into a size six, when in fact it was a size fourteen. I couldn't breathe. 'They are small fitting,' Debra had kindly told me as my lungs squashed together and called for help. Luckily, she told me there was enough material to let out an inch or so.

Had I been kidding myself I was fitting into my size twelve trousers? Size twelve *maternity* trousers, the horrible little voice in my head told me. Yes, I was still wearing my maternity trousers. They were comfortable. There was more room. It doesn't matter how I look at it, they are a size twelve and this thought makes me happy.

'So, let's see, the wedding is in six weeks, so if we schedule an appointment for four week's ' time ...' Debra walked over to a neatly organised desk. A diary was open in front of her. She counted the pages to the date she needed.

'Will two weeks before be enough time?' Suzy turned away from the mirror, her eyes following Debra. A bell sounded across the boutique, reminding me of the chime of the salon. It was these small triggers that hit me hard, but as always, I tried to ignore the heavy weight on my heart.

'It'll be fine. If we need to make any alterations, we can do them quite quickly. But generally, after the first fitting we don't need to make any changes, so hopefully you'll be able to take the dress home with you,' Debra told Suzy, as she walked across the room to open the door to her next customer.

'Oh, how exciting!' Suzy grinned, her hands caressing around the dress as her reflection stared back at her. Suddenly the smile was replaced with an anxious pout, a crease of concern furrowing across her forehead. 'You're sure he'll like it?'

'It's perfect, Suz, honestly, he'll love it,' I smiled, wanting to give her confidence a good kick. For someone who was so naturally beautiful, she really was so humble. But then, that's probably why I loved her.

It was the voices I heard first, those soft, manipulating tones grating on me before I even had the chance to turn around. The smile vanished from Gina's face, as she quickly bowed her head and whispered something to her mother, who instantly looked my way.

'Kathryn, how lovely to see you.' Paula's arms were stretched out as she came self-assuredly towards me, grabbing my chubby arms and kissing both cheeks before I had the chance to breathe. 'How are you?'

'Fine thanks.' I could barely hear my own voice.

'Shall we get changed?' Suzy grabbed my arm as we rushed into the changing room, glowering at her mother to come and help us.

'Trust this to happen when I'm busting at the seams,' I whispered.

'You look great,' Suzy said quietly, as she released the zip that allowed my flesh to bounce back to its usual shape.

'What's going on?' Her mum said, appearing seconds later, clearly confused.

'It's Gina and her mum,' I whispered, pointing to the curtain. Suddenly, Suzy's mum grabbed the curtain and peered back into the room.

'Mother!'

'They're still looking at dresses,' she said, not so quietly.

'SSSHHHH!' Suzy hissed, as loudly as her mother.

'Oh, this is a disaster,' I mumbled to myself.

'Sorry,' Suzy said, as her mother undid her buttons.

'Let's stay completely quiet until we get out of here,' I suggested.

Finally, we were all dressed. I'd hoped Gina would have left the shop by now, but no such luck. She was still working her way through the luxurious range of gowns. Debra had started filling the other changing room with a few of the dresses Gina had chosen.

'Can I say how lovely the babies are?' Paula was upon me as soon as I came out of the changing room.

No, you can't say, because you shouldn't have seen them. 'Thank you,' I managed.

'Where are they today?'

'With Marianne.' I didn't know if she knew who Marianne was, but I wasn't about to start explaining.

'Oh, it would have been lovely to have had a little cuddle,' she beamed as if talking about her own grandchildren. I tried to smile, my throat swelling and my heart started to beat rapidly. 'Little Rosie with her problems, isn't she a delight? Max was telling me what you've been through, backwards and forwards to the doctors and hospital, and then our Gina dropped the poor little mite—'

'*Gina* dropped her?' I couldn't hide my shock.

'It was an accident, as Max explained, but Gina cried for days. I told her these things happen and you would understand.'

I didn't. *Gina* dropped her? Paula was standing in front of me, unsuccessfully trying to block my view of Gina, who was coolly scanning one of the designer racks. Debra had disappeared back into the changing room with Suzy to confirm all the alterations. I wanted to run in there with them.

'Clare was saying that Maxwell was the same as Rosie, you know, with her milk problems.' Paula went on. 'It must have been so hard for you.'

'It has.'

'But they are both a delight. You must be so proud.'

'I am.' I glanced down at my hands, avoiding eye contact, not focusing on anything , feeling the sweat breaking out across my forehead.

'You know, Max and Gina are sorry, but when two people are meant to be together …' She lowered her voice and placed her hand on my arm. 'It's a tragic situation for you.'

'Suzy, I'm going to wait outside,' I raised my voice towards the changing area.

'I'm sorr—'

'It's fine, I just need some air.'

'Take care, Kathryn,' she shouted after me.

'You too.' I had no idea how I'd formed those words as I passed Gina, who didn't look at me as she continued to gently handle the silk and lace fabrics. I wondered if she was taking any notice of the stunning gowns.

The cool air outside stung against my burning cheeks, the breeze enveloping my hot face. Undoing my coat, I gulped some air, breathing through the nausea that should have stopped by now. I held on to the wall to aid me.

Why was she so involved in my babies' lives? I'd found it hard enough with Max and Gina playing happy families, but I'd accepted this was the way it had to be. But now her mother? This was too much. I needed to sit down with Max. But what would I say? I don't want Paula visiting while you have the girls? How ludicrous would that sound? Please don't leave the house or have any interaction with the outside world? Could I sound any more ridiculous? I think not!

Suzy and her mum joined me as I wiped away the tears. It was as if there was a valve inside me that wasn't working properly. If only I could ask a plumber to come and tighten it and stop all the leaks. Suzy wrapped her arms around me. 'Are you okay?'

'I'm fine, it was just a shock.'

'I bet it was.' Suzy's mum rubbed my back.

'Anyway, this day is about you, not my dramas.' I rubbed my wet face and stood up straight.

'Are you sure you're alright?' Suzy stared at me, her frown asking a hundred and one questions.

'I'm fine, honestly.'

'Come on, let's go and get a coffee,' Suzy's mum suggested.

We walked arm in arm in search of a coffee shop, Suzy's mum in the middle of us. The three of us together, we could have passed as a family if my dark mane didn't clash against Suzy and her mum's fairness. I know there are many families with a different array of hair colours, but their soft, natural beauty compared to my strong features made it obvious we didn't bear the same genes.

'I should have stayed away from here. We should have known she'd be looking in that shop,' Suzy said, as we took a seat in the first eatery we came to. I had known it was likely that we would bump into Gina in Stokesley, but I hadn't really thought about bumping into her in a bridal shop. They weren't getting married for two years: wasn't she being a little eager? But then, wouldn't I want to browse every bridal shop, no matter how far away my wedding date was. Probably. 'I'd avoided Northallerton for that reason,' Suzy continued.

'It wouldn't make a difference: we could have bumped into her anywhere,' I said as I took off my coat, placing it over the back of the seat.

'That's very true,' her mum agreed, as she scanned the menu. 'Ooohhh, I think I fancy a scone with cream and jam.'

'Sounds nice. I think I'll join you. What about you, Kat?'

'Oh, I'll just have a drink.'

'Oh, come on, I'm treating you girls.' Suzy's mum was adamant.

'Did you see that dress on my voluptuous hips?' I laughed.

'Don't be silly, you looked great,' Suzy's mum said. I appreciated her kind-hearted lies. 'Anyway, one scone won't make a difference.'

'Oh, if you insist,' I smiled. Although I wasn't hungry, I didn't want to offend her.

A lady approached us, a pen and paper in her hand, asking if she could take our order. Once Suzy's mum had informed her of our choices, Suzy made her excuses to go to the Ladies.

'I hope you don't think I'm speaking out of turn,' I said to Suzy's mum, who glanced at me, not saying a word. I knew Suzy would be upset if I said something, but being alone with her mum was too good an opportunity and I had to take it. 'But Suzy's mentioned about the wedding, how upset you are ...'

She peered at me, then down at the menu.

'It's just that ...' I stuttered, daring myself to go any further. 'Suzy's really upset ... you know, about the whole thing ... she can't have her wedding day without you there.' I'd started so I had to finish.

'Then she knows what to do.'

I was surprised by how cold her voice had become. 'But she can't really do that when her dad is paying for the wedding.'

'I can't bear that woman and I can't bear her playing happy families with my daughter on her wedding day.'

Suddenly I could see myself in thirty years' time. Sadness coursed through me. 'If anyone understands that, I do.' I smiled at her. 'But Suzy doesn't see her as family. She sees her as her dad's girlfriend, and that's how everyone else will see it.'

'Even her presence in the room drives me insane. He hasn't even been with her that long.' She was softer as she turned away.

'I understand that. But think about Suzy's feelings. I know how you feel. I can't bear the girls going to Max's, with Gina there playing Mummy for the day, and now her mum playing Grandma, but I do it for the girls. Not for Max, and definitely not for Gina.'

'Bill has said the same to me,' she said. Bill being her present husband. 'He said I'm not being fair on Suzy. But if they'd been together longer … a few years … I'd understand, but six months … she'll wear a flouncy outfit, everything will be hanging out. She'll be trying to play the part of doting stepmother.'

'She's only Suzy's age, isn't she?'

'They all try to play that part.' This was somewhat true. Suzy had backed off from many of them when they'd tried to become a powerful figure in her life. 'It's so hard. It always has been. Not for me, but for Suzy, with all the different women in her father's life. I've had to work so hard to make things stable.'

'But she understands that. She's really grounded.'

'Yes, she is.'

'That's because of you,' I said. She smiled at me. I wanted to touch her hand reassuringly, but I didn't want Suzy catching us. 'I suppose I felt the need to say something, because I also know what it's like not to have a choice about your mum being at your wedding. You can't do that to her.'

She suddenly looked sad, as if realisation dawned on her about my own situation, I sometimes found that even those who were around me when Mum died seemed to forget. Not intentionally. It was a long time ago, it wasn't on their minds when relationships were discussed, like it was mine.

'I said it in anger.' She shook her head and put the menu down, folding her hands over it. 'When she rang me to tell me the news that her father was giving her all this money, I felt so sad. Which I realise is awful, but the small amount we'd contributed seemed to fade into insignificance.'

'Don't be silly. Suzy would never think that.'

'He hasn't been there, and now he's stamping his mark with his money once again, telling her how her wedding should be and who to invite.'

'But none of that matters, because she doesn't want to get married if you're not there.'

'The scones look lush.' Suzy was suddenly back, sitting down, pulling in her chair and glancing at our faces.

'They do look lovely,' her mum said, looking back at the counter where a variety of scones and cakes were displayed.

'What are you two talking about?'

'Noth—'

'How gorgeous you look in your dress!' Suzy's mum was much better at recovery than me.

Suzy observed us both, clearly unconvinced.

I hadn't planned to tackle her mum about the wedding. Suzy had firmly told me not to, but I couldn't waste the chance to say something; a window that I could have either stared at or leapt through.

I'd chosen the latter and I hoped I hadn't made the wrong choice.

15

'I really don't appreciate being lied to.'

'I didn't lie, but I knew you'd be angrier if you knew it was Gina who dropped Rosie.' Max was shaking his head.

'Of course, I would be: she's a nurse, for God's sake.'

'It was an accident.'

'Would she say that to a parent at the hospital, when they sued her arse?'

'I understand you're upset, but so was she.'

'So, she should be, Max,' I said, sitting down on my sofa. 'Honestly, it's stressful enough without having to worry about them being safe in your care.'

'You're being dramatic.'

'Am I?'

'You know you are.'

'What about her mother … what part is she playing in this bloody mess?'

'What do you mean?'

'Oh, nothing,' I shook my head dismissively, not wanting to be the neurotic ex-girlfriend, but knowing I was failing in that objective.

'Kat, please, you have nothing to worry about. Gina couldn't believe she'd been so silly.'

'Honestly, I know accidents happen, Max, but you've got to understand why I'm so frustrated.'

'Of course, I do.' He sighed loudly, sat on the sofa and rubbed his hands through his thick blonde hair. 'I don't know how to make things better.'

We sat in silence, the girls lying in front of us on their play mat. Rosie was at last able to lie flat on her back, happier than she'd been in weeks. She was still sometimes a little sick but nowhere near as much as she had been. Poppy was forcing her head round to ensure she could see us. Her face was alight, her smile so full of love whenever Max walked in. I was surprised she remembered him. I know he called in once or twice a week, and they had their own time together, but still it amazed me that she had this little memory that was already storing details. Rosie wasn't as joyous. She would smile but generally she studied people. She was a thinker, not an unhappy baby (well, not any more).

'I'm trying my best,' Max said, staring at the babies.

'I know, but so am I.' I stared at him, at his tired face, his unshaven appearance, the skin around his eyes that was becoming darker every day.

'I wish we could all be amicable.' I didn't answer. 'I am sorry, Kat. For everything.'

'I'm not going back down that road.' I didn't want to analyse it with him. The silence stretched between us, every second filling the room with bitter tension.

'There's something else I have to tell you.'

'What?'

'I wasn't going to do it today, Gina wanted me to wait.' He became quiet again. 'She's pregnant.'

'Oh ...' I felt as if he'd slapped me, but I hoped it didn't show.

'I know. I was shocked too.'

'When is the baby due?' I managed.

'September.' The word 'Congratulations' stuck in my throat. I wanted to be the better person. I really did. I wanted to hug him, wish him all the best; but her pregnancy impacted on my little family. Where would the girls stand if Max had his own baby to contend with at home? 'And there's something else.'

'She's having puppies.' It just came out.

'She wants to get married before the baby comes.' Ignoring my bitchy comment, he looked at me. 'But we're going to make it a small affair.' He paused and looked at *our* girls. 'The thing is, we will be reducing numbers dramatically.'

'That's my invite in the bin, then.' I'd be going for the whole sewn-up-mouth op very soon, or I could enrol on a course: *Get help with your scorn - sarcasm is the lowest form of wit.*

'The thing is, Gina thinks – and, I agree – that the girls will be a bit young.'

'So ...?'

'So … we were thinking that maybe my mum could bring them to the church, but then maybe you could pick them up.'

'You don't want your daughters at your wedding?'

'It's not that I don't want them there, but they are too young to enjoy it. Other people will have to look after them. It seems unfair.'

'So they're an inconvenience now.'

'I knew you'd do this.'

'Do what?'

'Make it out as if I'm a bad father or something.'

'You said it.' It was a low shot, but I was furious. I was already upset with the whole 'Gina dropping Rosie episode' and now this!

'I'm going. Sometimes there's no talking to you.' He rose from his seat, his hands clenched. He leaned forward towards the play mat, lifting Poppy first, kissing her forehead. 'Daddy loves you,' he told her as he placed her back down, then he picked up Rosie and repeating the picture that would have any outsider's heart melting.

'I'll call you about the weekend.' He left, his back straight and his hands still knotted into a ball as he walked away from us, again.

He always got to choose when the conversation ended.

I sat cross-legged on the floor with the girls, stroking Poppy's head and rubbing Rosie's feet. A tear fell onto Poppy's pale pink cardigan. Although I didn't feel angry as he walked back to his own life, leaving us sitting on the periphery, there was an ache that swelled deep inside, like a torn muscle that was pulling. But I knew the tears weren't for me; they were for my girls.

I wished so much Max had stayed. I wished that we'd been able to work it out and be the family I'd so wanted us to be. I was a mother who was automatically doing the things she needed to do, and I felt sometimes that Max was a father who placed them at the bottom of his priorities. Maybe I was being unfair to Max, and to be honest I didn't want him and Gina to play the family game, especially on their wedding day. However, I knew that if I was getting married - not that there was much possibility of this happening in the near future, but if I was - I would have done my utmost to ensure the girls were with me, even if it meant hiring help for the day. I couldn't rationalise his decision, even if he could justify it.

The opening of the secret door made me jump to my feet, quickly wiping away the evidence that once again I was crumbling. Clare entered, her grin fixed; she'd already learnt the art of smiling for the customers. A client followed behind her, a black towel wrapped around her hair. I'd already sent June out so that I could talk to Max privately, but once again, Clare was barging into my home.

I couldn't bear it any longer.

I needed to move.

16

'But where would you move to?' Marianne was feeding Poppy, while I fed Rosie. Derek was standing in the corner, ironing. It made me smile, I didn't comment, but I bet Marianne thought she'd won the Lottery. I don't think Dad knew what an iron was.

'I'm thinking about Yarm.' I'd searched Rightmove for places to rent, all afternoon and evening after Clare had finally disappeared back downstairs.

'It's nice there.'

'I want somewhere I can walk with the girls, without having to bundle them in the car every five minutes. I'd move a bit further away, but Max would probably kick off, assuming he'd be bothered.' I was still chewed up about his wedding news. I'd tried all night to convince myself it was the girls I was upset for. Not me.

'Of course he'd be bothered and so would I,' Marianne smiled.

'Kat needs to live her own life like her sister.' Derek's well-spoken words hung in the air. I raised my eyebrows as Marianne's cheeks coloured a darker shade of pink, her eyes fixed on him.

'Don't worry, I'm not going anywhere,' I laughed, dissipating the tension as quickly as it had formed. 'I need somewhere that has enough space for me to set up a beauty room.'

'Oh, wonderful, you're going to start your business again?'

'Slowly; I was thinking evening appointments at first.'

'You know I'm happy to have the girls during the day. We want you to get back on your feet.' She glowered at Derek. 'Don't we, Derek?'

'Yes, pet, it's wonderful that you're becoming focused. We have the time, but we don't have the money.'

'Derek!'

'I'm only saying.' He looked at me. 'But Kat knows that God will help, he will lead you, pet.'

'Thanks.' I turned away from him.

'You should come to church with us,' Marianne smiled, her soft eyes drilling into me.

'I'm not sure it's for me.'

'The church is for everyone who is willing to embrace God.' Derek frowned as he pressed hard on a pair of trousers.

'If you are willing to let him into your heart, then—' Marianne started.

'I'm—'

'Maybe you should come with us on Sunday,' Marianne encouraged, not allowing me to speak, 'before we go and see Libby.'

'That's awkward, trying to get the girls sorted and things ...'

'I'm worried about you.' Marianne's gentle face tilted to the side, her eyes still fixed on me.

'Don't be. I'm fine.'

'I've been thinking about the counselling Ronnie offered us. I think it would do you good.'

I stroked Poppy's cheek. She seemed to misinterpret my own quietness, I could see she'd thought she'd upset me, or she would have continued to persuade me.

I had thought some more about counselling, but if I *did* decide on that route, then I wanted it to be on my own path. Not on Libby's.

We finished feeding the girls. Marianne helped me change their nappies and we placed them down on a pale-pink fleece blanket that Derek had laid out for them. We talked to Poppy and Rosie for a while, Marianne's playful, high-pitched voice coming towards them and backing off. Both the girls loved it, their little smiles beaming as she tickled their tummies and stroked their faces with one of their soft toys, playing a game of, 'It's coming to get you.' Their little arms stretched out, their legs curled up towards their tiny bodies. Rosie was a completely different baby from the tiny ball of pain I'd initially brought home.

'So, when is June thinking of going home?' She grinned at Rosie as she used the same playful voice.

'She hasn't really said,' I answered, as she continued to talk to Rosie. 'But … there's something she's suggested.'

'What?' Marianne continued to gaze at Rosie.

'The thing is … Libby may struggle when she comes out.' Marianne sat up to face me. 'June has offered for her to go and live in Devon, until she's feeling better.'

'I think it's a wonderful idea,' Derek said lightly. 'Once she's better we might be able to think about setting a date.' He looked down at the underpants he was ironing. Underpants? I didn't need to see that.

'A date?' I diverted my eyes to Marianne.

'We were hoping to get married this year,' Derek told me as he lifted up the underpants and placed them in a pile. Nice.

'Oh. Erm … congratulations,' I found myself stuttering. 'But you never said.'

'I don't like to make a fuss.'

'Because it's not happening yet.' Derek's briskness rattled through the room.

'So many things keep getting in the way. We will do it eventually.' Marianne fumbled with Poppy's soft monkey, whose arms and legs were longer than the body.

'It's because of Libby isn't it?'

'No, don't be silly.' Marianne stared at Derek, 'It's lots of things.'

'Like rehab,' Derek said quietly.

'Derek, please!'

'What is going on?' I directed the question at both of them.

'Nothing is going on. I just want Libby better so I can relax and enjoy my wedding day.'

'That's not strictly true.' Derek switched off the iron before he came to sit on the sofa. His stoutness, balding head and aura were powerful enough without his confident personality. 'Now, I have a lot of time for Libby, but rehab has cost a lot of money. It's used up a good chunk of our savings.'

'Savings that could have been used on your wedding,' I stated.

'Exactly, so what I'm trying to say, without being rude, is that I'm worried that Libby falls back into the trap once she's out of rehab.'

'Because it will cost you more money?'

'No.' Marianne scowled at Derek (it wasn't a real scowl, but as good as Marianne could pull off). 'Because we want her to be better.'

'Of course, it's nothing to do with the money, really. But it doesn't help,' Derek said. I knew he was lying, but I could appreciate his frustration.

'I understand.'

'Derek isn't trying to put Libby down or—'

'Marianne … Derek is right.' An ache in my chest pulled as I felt remorse for my sister's antics. 'But I'll be honest, I'm not sure if Libby living with June will help her.'

Marianne stared at the monkey she was still holding, her hands twitching around the soft toy. 'I think she'll feel we are pushing her away.' Marianne's sad eyes reached mine.

'Maybe Ronnie can help to explain,' Derek suggested.

I ran my hand through my thick dark mane, shaking my head. 'Derek I understand where you're coming from, and I'm also worried that she might fall back into her old life, but I'm not sure I can send her away, again.'

'There'll be less temptations for her if she moves away.' Derek was almost begging.

'Yarm, that's away—' I started.

'That's only a bus journey away from her old life.' Derek shook his head at Marianne. 'She needs a new start.'

'The thought of us sending her away as if we don't care …' Marianne's eyes filled with tears.

'I'm sorry, Derek, but I agree with Marianne,' I said, wishing I'd not started the conversation.

'I think you're being a little bit narrow-minded about this,' Derek said as he stood up. He grabbed the basket, which held the carefully placed ironed clothes, and left the room.

The next hour seemed to pass in slow motion. I kept waiting for a suitable chance to leave, a change of subject maybe, but it didn't seem to happen. Libby and June kept creeping into the conversation. I tried to venture onto the topic of weddings, but Marianne kept avoiding any direct answers by immediately talking to the babies. Finally, Poppy started to get restless. As she was a textbook baby, the only thing left for her to cry about was tiredness. I could have kissed her tiny body from head to foot as she gave me the excuse I needed to leave.

Marianne helped me put the girls in their car seats. As always, I was grateful for the extra pair of hands. The girls were snuggled in the back, facing the rear of the car, a mirror fixed to both their seats.

Marianne grabbed my hands, pulling me close to her.

'Listen, please don't be offended by Derek.'

'I'm not.'

'Sometimes he speaks out of turn.'

'Marianne, it's fine. I totally understand where he's coming from, even if I don't agree.'

She nodded, letting go of my hands, letting me walk around the other side of the car. 'You're sure you don't want me to call Ronnie about setting up a counselling session?' she stuttered, as if pushing herself to ask the question.

'I'm positive,' I smiled. I didn't want to offend her, but I had to do this my way.

As I drove away, I held my hand up so that Marianne could see it through the back window. She stood on the pavement, waving frantically as if we were going on a long-distance journey.

I knew I had to call Dr Knowles and make my own appointment. I *would* see a counsellor. I didn't know if I was doing the right thing, or if it would work; all I knew at the moment was that nothing seemed to be working. I had to give the tablets a chance, but I felt so frustrated and tired.

It was the bitterness of Suzy's mum that had pushed me forward. She was still so angry even though she'd remarried. She'd been with Bill for over ten years. Suzy spoke of him like a father. But there was a lingering resentment that her mother let eat away at her.

I couldn't be that woman. Somewhere deep inside, I didn't really think I would be: I thought I would get over it. I'd be able to face Max and Gina together. I'd be happy for them. But if I was honest with myself, every day seemed to hit me harder than the day before, every day I had to physically push myself to move. To breathe. I knew I had to keep functioning because if I didn't function my girls couldn't function either.

What if this cloud never lifted?

Because of that thought, I was willing to try anything.

17

The weather was improving, but it was so haphazard: one minute it was raining, next it was blazing sunshine and we'd even had snow, all in the same day. I walked with Brooke and June along the river towards the church. Each week the air was becoming warmer, items from our winter drawer slowly being discarded one by one. We'd all left our gloves at home; although I wished I hadn't, not for warmth purposes, but vanity. Brooke's perfectly manicured hands put my own bitten-down, unpainted nails to shame. I was the beauty expert, for God's sake. She'd be telling her aunty, 'She's let herself go.' In some respects, I suppose I had, but I didn't see it as, 'letting myself go': it was more about making my life easy.

I didn't have time to style my hair, so it was easier to put it up. I didn't think about my make-up too much; I still applied one layer of foundation, with a bit of blusher, but that was habit. Not applying one layer would be like going outside without my bra on, and trust me, that wasn't an option these days. But as for eyeshadow, eyeliner and mascara, which had been applied so delicately every day since I could remember, it wasn't happening. There were days when I had the chance to do one eye, and then I'd forget about the other one because Poppy or Rosie had decided to summon me, so then I looked like a clown. As for painting my nails: that thought makes me laugh. Time to paint nails? I'd probably fall asleep mid-application.

It was moments like these, when I was walking alongside Brooke, that I wished I'd been something else. Not a beauty therapist. I thought if I'd had a different career, I wouldn't have noticed how much I no longer beautified myself. Maybe I was wrong, but I assumed the pressure wouldn't have been so strong. Maybe I needed to change my profession. I tried to think of something else that I would love to do, but nothing grabbed me in the way beauty therapy did. I enjoyed pampering women. I loved the therapies. I would get a buzz from women feeling better after their treatments.

I missed it.

Maybe it wasn't counselling that I needed; it was my life back.

We entered the church hall, where familiar faces from the baby group smiled at us. Women were starting to form a huge circle.

'Place your bags by the walls, ladies, lay your baby on the towel in front of you,' a young woman, who I assumed was running the class, told us. Her pink shirt and smart grey trousers seemed a little overdressed for baby massaging. I wondered if this was her full-time job. I also wondered if she had children. If so, had she massaged her own babies? But I kept my thoughts to myself as I laid two towels out in front of me. June helped by unfastening the girls' pushchair straps. I'd been advised to bring another person to help me.

'It's about bonding,' Sandra had told me at the baby group. 'You won't get the same connection if you're trying to do two babies at once.'

So, no pressure then, which baby did I choose to bond with? I could pick up the techniques and do this at home alone, one baby after the other, but here in front of all the other mums, would they be judging me on my choice? 'I'll toss a coin,' I told June, who glanced at me quizzically. 'Heads, I massage Rosie. Tails, I massage Poppy.'

I threw the 10p piece into the air. It slipped from my hand and landed on the floor.

'Heads,' June clarified, picking up Poppy.

The other mums were chatting to each other, while Brooke had situated herself beside me. We removed Rosie and Poppy's clothing as the tutor, as she called herself, directed. No name, only 'I'm the baby massage tutor.'

She started to tell us about the oil that we would rub into our baby's skin, when Harvey's mum (I can't tell you her name, because I simply can't remember) rose from her place, lifted up Harvey, giggled and announced he needed feeding. She then sat herself at the front of the class, in front of twenty women, or so, lifted her top, undid a catch and let her breast hang down, adjusting Harvey's head as he took a few seconds to latch on. She then stared over at Brooke and smiled.

'Silly bitch, I think she's making a point,' Brooke whispered. I put my head down, concentrating on rubbing Rosie's tummy.

Brooke turned her focus back to Chelsea. Harvey's mum didn't come back down from the pedestal until the class had ended half an hour later. She swapped breasts mid-feed, not putting the other one away, with snide glances at Brooke and a smirk of defiance. I was waiting for an argument to break out. It hadn't been as relaxing as I'd hoped.

June was oblivious to the undercurrent. She talked to Poppy all the way through, asking if she liked it. I was a little annoyed with myself that I'd been so distracted.

Finally, we left the hall. Harvey's mum was chatting to another mum as we left, but made a point of glaring at us, as did the woman she was talking to.

'God, this is like playground stuff. I doubt I'll be coming back,' I told Brooke as we left the church. At the same time, I wanted to shout, 'I breastfed, don't be analysing me.'

'What is?' June was totally unaware of the dagger eyes and snarls that had taken place.

'I'm not letting that snooty bitch stop me,' Brooke said.

'Do you really want the hassle?' I asked Brooke, shaking my head.

'What hassle?' June scanned us both looking confused. 'What's going on? I really enjoyed that.'

'Breastfeeding politics,' Brooke said, as we walked into the village, away from the church where it felt as if a cult was forming.

I felt so thrilled to be away from Harvey's mum's stare. Poor Rosie couldn't have felt any bonding from my anxious hands. Plus, I was so pleased the tutor had given us a sheet with instructions, as I wasn't listening to a thing she said. I knew Harvey's mum wasn't pointing the daggers at me, but I also knew that through my association with Brooke I'd been categorised. I wanted to stand up to Harvey's mum and tell her it's all about choice. But I knew that would cause a huge debate (and confrontation) that I wasn't strong enough to face.

We chatted as we headed back towards the flat. I didn't enjoy the walk. But then I never really did. Even if I'd only popped to the shops, I would be pleased to be back in the flat. Although, I didn't feel the flat's joy or its homely warmth, as I used to experience when it was mine. I didn't have that sense of belonging any more.

Henry's car was waiting outside when we arrived back. June's cheeks coloured as she told me she would take the girls upstairs while I sorted the pushchair. Clare was upon us before Brooke had the chance to say her goodbyes.

'Henry's here,' she announced, flouncing from the salon.

'Yes, I've seen his car,' I said, messing with the latch on the pushchair to try and fold it down.

'I hope you don't mind, but I let him into the flat. He doesn't want to be sitting down here with all these women.'

'He was only here last week.'

'He was passing, and with us not seeing you much at our home …'

I nodded, noting her dismay. I supposed I should make the effort. But everything *was* an effort lately. And I didn't like Clare using my flat as if it was some kind of waiting room, or meeting area. But then, it wasn't mine.

'I was thinking, Kat, do you fancy coming over for a drink one night?' Brooke spoke into the small silence that had formed.

'Oh, sounds like a wonderful idea! You should Kathryn,' Clare encouraged.

'Er … yeah.' How did I get out of this one? I couldn't use the babysitting excuse because Clare would have offered, and I had a built-in babysitter with June; but I couldn't think of anything worse than going to Brooke's for a drink. What if Mrs D was there? 'Maybe for a few hours while the girls are sleeping,' I said. I could cope if it was only for a few hours, couldn't I? I'd have my excuse to leave readily available.

'Friday then?'

'Er … I just need to check if June can—'

'I can babysit. The girls can come and stay at our house. Give you a full night to yourself.'

'Oh … when Rosie is better.' I felt my heart beginning to pound, my security blanket being whipped from around me.

'I thought she was better,' Clare smiled, but her eyes drilled into me.

'She's getting there, but she's still a bit sickie,' I found myself stuttering, flustered that I had to make excuses for myself. I didn't want the girls to be away from me all night, not just yet anyway. I couldn't explain why I felt so strongly, and so on edge about them being out of my sight.

'Anyway, I'll go and see Henry,' I said, snapping the pushchair into place.

'I'll call you,' Brooke said before leaving.

Clare went back into the salon after saying her goodbyes, as I made my way to the door of the flat. I placed the pushchair behind the front door before venturing up the stairs.

The door into the flat was slightly ajar. I could hear voices whispering. I stood still, trying to grasp what they were saying, but they were too quiet. I opened the door, and walked in. They were both standing in the kitchen. They turned to look at me.

'I'm just putting the kettle on, Pet, would you like one?' June asked brightly.

'Hi, Henry, two visits in two weeks, you must be keen,' I smiled, as I took off my coat. June had placed a sleeping Rosie on the sofa, while Poppy lay on her play mat, searching around the room, trying to trace my voice.

'Had to come and see my girls,' he grinned, walking towards me.

I bet you did.

I tried to keep any expression from my face, but I knew I was grimacing. So I turned away from him, as he made himself comfortable on the sofa, not even acknowledging the girls.

I knew I had to put a stop to this before it even started.

<h1 style="text-align:center">18</h1>

Dr Knowles was studying my notes, clicking the end of his pen absentmindedly as he scrolled through the screen. Poppy and Rosie slept soundly in their pushchair. I willed them to stay that way.

'We can increase the tablets, see if there is any improvement,' he said, as he typed on the keyboard, mumbling to himself as he updated my notes and printed out a new prescription. He then turned to face me, a serious expression on his tired grey face. 'Have you thought any more about counselling?'

'Actually, yes I have.' I unravelled the scarf that was starting to contribute to my body's overheating. I'd tossed the counselling idea back and forth, one minute, believing it was the best way forward, the next minute dreading the prospect of unloading all my scary thoughts onto a stranger.

I'd survived so far; did I really need counselling?

'And … do you think it will help?' Dr Knowles pushed me for more.

'Do you?'

'I think so,' he nodded. I felt myself biting the inside of my mouth, as I struggled to respond. 'Did you ever have any bereavement counselling when you lost your mum?'

'No.' I shook my head.

'I think it would be a good idea.'

'But … I'm more concerned about now.'

'But many things that happen in our future are the result of the impact of our past lives.'

I nodded, although not sure he understood me. 'I think about her constantly, but it happened. I've moved on with my life. I'm not sure dragging up her death will help me. I thought counselling may help me cope with what is going on now.'

'It will help you and you don't have to talk about anything you don't want to,' he said gently. I felt myself biting the soft inside of my cheek again. I heard myself breathing loudly, exhaling into his stuffy room. 'Why don't you give it a try?'

'Apparently, I have access to Libby's counsellors,' I said, wanting to know if he would agree with my thoughts without actually asking him. He knew all about Libby: not only was it plastered all over her notes, but I'd told him everything on my own visits.

'But they're for Libby.'

'Apparently, we can see them as a family, or I could see someone individually.'

'I think you need to speak to someone about *you*.' He was looking directly at me, as if his eyes were searching my sole for answers. 'Someone who will solely concentrate on you. I don't want to disregard Libby and her problems; they are challenging. But I believe we need to set this route up for you, with your own counsellor.' I nodded again, not responding, pleased he *did* agree with my thoughts. 'I think you need counselling without any pressures, counselling that concentrates on *you*, without you worrying about other people.'

'Okay,' I managed. He wanted me to pour my heart out about my whole life, delve into the past and bring out the skeletons, without worrying about Libby. But Libby was part of my life, my shadow until the last year or so.

'So, shall I get the process started?'

'Yes,' I practically whispered, struggling to get the simple word out.

'Great,' he smiled. 'You'll receive a letter over the next few weeks with a date.'

'Thank you,' I said, although I didn't feel very grateful. I was still pessimistic that speaking to someone who didn't know me would work. I could air off to Suzy, Marianne, June or even Clare if I really needed to. These were the thoughts that had edged to and fro, scraping across my mind. But not only had what happened to Suzy's mum given me a need to crawl out of my cave of resentment and negative thinking, but my conversation with Libby was at the forefront of my mind: if counselling had helped her … it must be able to help me.

I'd spoken to her earlier. She'd seemed brighter, her tone an octave higher than it usually was. She'd not been over-chatty, or excitable – I think we had a long way to go before we reached that stage. But she'd sounded lighter, optimistic even. I'd not told her about my visits to the doctor, because I wanted her to stay focused on herself. Not that the Libby I knew would have cared, but still I didn't want to burden her when she was trying to pull herself round.

I had quizzed her about the counselling. 'Do you think it's helping?' I'd asked casually.

'At first, no. To be honest, they did my head in asking all these bloody questions about how I feel. But as the weeks have gone on, I've found it really helpful.'

'And you're starting to feel better?'

'Definitely.'

'You definitely think it's the counselling that has helped?'

'Combination of everything really … why?'

'I want to make sure you're getting better and everything is working out.'

'I am getting better,' Libby had said softly. 'I wish I could make up for the hurt I've caused.'

'You don't need to worry about that,' I'd told her. 'We're all here for you. We want you to get better. We want you to be free.'

'Thank you,' she said. 'Are you coming on Sunday?'

'Absolutely,' I told her before hanging up. 'I was going to bring the girls.'

'I'd love that.' I could hear the smile in her voice.

So I'd walked to the doctor's surgery, the Friday morning blending into all the other days of the week, knowing deep down, in the pit of my stomach where all the gut decisions are made, that this was the right thing to do.

However, as I walked back, the low blinding sun glaring painfully at me, I wondered why I felt unsettled. He'd mentioned bereavement counselling. Had it been offered to us, but Dad had refused? I could ask Marianne or June, but I didn't want them knowing I was talking to a counsellor. I didn't want them worrying about me. If I could keep hold of my brave exterior I knew I would survive.

I could carry on and everyone around me would think I was fine.

Coping mechanisms come in all shapes and sizes. A switch of the thinking can have us riding through each day, powerful human beings ready to fight any problems. What if the counselling didn't allow me to use my switch button? What if my defences came down and my mechanism didn't work?

I knew I couldn't analyse this anymore. I had to go for it.

I had to try and see if someone else, a stranger, could help me skip through each day instead of suffocating under the weight of anxiety that had me crawling through every second of every hour of every day.

19

'My head is banging, Brooke, I'm really sorry, maybe next week.' I felt terrible for lying. Not that it was a huge lie as such … my head *was* hurting, a little … but nothing a few paracetamols wouldn't sort.

When I'd arrived home from the doctor's, June was getting herself ready for a night out. She'd planned to go to a local bingo night. She'd seen a poster on the church wall, and said it would do her good.

'On your own?' I'd queried her motives.

'For God's sake, Kat, how do you think I survive down in Devon?' I'd not answered her. Quite truthfully, I was pleased she was going out; the flat to myself felt like bliss.

Max was due to pick the girls' up tomorrow. I was helping Suzy put together her wedding favours, so a nice relaxing night was exactly what I needed. A hot bath, some good old crap on the television and a nice glass of wine. Heaven.

June came out of Libby's bedroom, the room that she'd made her own over the last few weeks. Wearing a classic black dress, high-heeled diamante shoes, and a pale pink cardigan hung around her shoulders. Definitely overdressed for bingo.

'You look …. smart.' I chose my words carefully.

'I didn't want to overdress, you know, stand out from the crowd.'

'I think you'll find most people are in jeans.'

'Not at bingo,' she shook her head. 'In Devon it's the highlight of our week.' She helped herself to a glass of wine from the bottle I'd just opened.

Poppy and Rosie were in bed, their six-thirty bedtime becoming quite the norm. We were finally getting into a routine, a tiny part of my life becoming organised. I watched June gulp down the wine in three mouthfuls, as I wrapped a fleece blanket around myself, relishing the fact I was about to have a few hours to myself.

'Don't wait up for me.' She practically skipped towards the door.

'Will you be late?'

'Bingo can get quite exciting.'

'It'll be over by half nine,' I told her.

'You never know. Anyway you're shattered, you'll probably be asleep by then.' She opened the door. 'I've got my key.'

'June.' She stopped to face me, her foot already on the top step. 'Please be careful.' It was only a second, I mean literally two at the most, but she definitely paused. A fleeting thought undeniably passed through her mind. I could see her hesitate, but she smiled and continued down the steps.

*

'She didn't get in until after midnight,' I told Suzy, as I placed five different types of sweets in a soft, silver organza bag: a Black Jack, a Fruit Salad, a packet of Refreshers, a packet of Love Hearts and a lollipop, to be precise. Suzy had debated endlessly on favours, but I was pleased with her choice, loving all the sweets that were included. I would be collecting all the leftovers on the day.

'Maybe she made friends with people.' Suzy was carefully writing out the names of each guest with a glittery silver pen. A ribbon was threaded through the card and wrapped snuggly around the bag.

'Come on, Suz … you really believe that?'

'Not really, but you can't accuse her until you have proof.'

'But they were at it on my sofa.'

'You don't know that either.'

'Suzy, help me out here. I can't turn a blind eye to this.'

'If you go in all guns blazing it will cause an argument. And let's face it you could be wrong!'

'I just can't believe her.' I wrapped a ribbon and nametag around one of the bags. 'I don't trust her.'

'She might have changed. Perhaps you finding out about your dad has showed her how much it hurts.'

There was a slight pause between us. Although I wanted Suzy to be right, I wanted June to have changed, I couldn't believe it. Something was niggling deep inside. 'I'm worried she's going to take Libby,' I admitted.

'Take Libby where?'

'She suggested Libby could live with her for a while in Devon when she has finished in rehab. But she's probably running a brothel,' I jested, hoping my joke was nowhere near the truth.

'You never know,' Suzy smiled, shaking her head. She completed the card that said 'Gina', but put it aside, not allowing me to put the label onto the favour bag. Although I appreciated her protecting me, I leaned around her to pick it up.

'It's fine,' I said, before she had the chance to argue.

'Look, I've been meaning to thank you.'

'Thank me?' I raised my eyebrows, while placing several packets of sweets into one of the bags.

'For talking to my mum.'

'Now then, girls.' The front door opened, and Joe walked in, his grin warm and excitable like a small child's.

'Hiya, Joe.' Suzy stood up, embraced him and welcomed him into her home.

'How you doing, Kat?' He winked at me, a cheeky grin spreading across his face, his dimples accentuated.

'I'm good, thanks, Joe. You?'

'Yeah, sound,' he nodded. 'How's the babies?'

'Tiring, but gorgeous,' I forced myself to laugh. I hated both those question. How are you? I'm crap, but thanks for asking. How's the babies? They're good, thanks, but my life has completely turned around, it's upside down and backside first.

But I knew people would switch off. They didn't really care; it's one of those things we ask each other to be polite. I didn't doubt Joe was interested in the basics, but if I'd really started to reel off about Rosie's illnesses and the fact that I felt like a zombie, he'd become one himself. It was easier to simply pretend all was great. There were plenty of us doing it.

'Where's the big fella?'

'Upstairs, in the office. Go on up.'

He did as Suzy told him.

'He's home early, I thought they weren't going until the end of the week.' I was talking about Lawrence's stag do: a five-night break in Barcelona. Suzy had considered my feelings when arranging her hen night. Although I'd told her I would go anywhere, she'd insisted on a luxurious spa day, no overnight stay. I'd argued, but secretly I was pleased I wouldn't be away from the girls.

'He needs to sort things out with Max,' Suzy said.

'What do you mean?'

'Didn't I tell you? Since you guys split up Max and Joe haven't spoken much?'

'Really?' I lowered my voice. 'I thought everything was fine, especially with Lawrence having them both as his best men.'

'Nope,' Suzy shook her head. 'I think Max has tried but Joe's a bit reluctant.'

'He can't blame Max, though, surely.'

'He obviously does, but they'll work it out. It makes it a bit awkward for us though.' Suzy rolled her eyes.

'I'm sorry …' I found myself stroking her arm. 'Between the four of us, I promise we won't ruin your wedding.'

'I did say to Lawrence, when Mum started causing problems, that we should go away and get married in private,' she laughed, but I knew she was serious.

'I'm sorry I spoke to her, I know you—'

'Not at all. Whatever you said it worked.'

'I felt awful after. I thought I'd prob—'

'It's fine. You've done me a favour. I'm grateful you said something.' She stopped elegantly writing names and squinted at me, as if she was in pain. 'I have something to tell you.' A deep frown creased her usual flawless skin. 'Lawrence has done something quite bad.'

'Are you okay?' I was suddenly worried for her.

'I'm fine ...' she paused. 'It's not about us.'

'What is it?'

'He told Max last night.'

I stared at her shaking my head in bewilderment. 'Told Max what?'

'About Libby.'

'Aahh ... makes sense now.' My insides turned over, nausea rushed through me.

'What does?'

'His twenty questions when he picked the girls up this morning.' I tied a ribbon around the bag I was working on. 'He asked me where Libby was. He said he hadn't seen her for a while. I told him she was visiting a friend down south. I didn't think he believed me.'

'I'm sorry. Lawrence feels awful. He said they were just chatting and he assumed he would know.'

'Don't be silly, it's fine,' I shrugged, waving my hand at her. I didn't want Lawrence to feel bad, but a great heaviness was suddenly weighing down on me. Keeping that part of my life, a secret felt like the only thing to do. It wasn't because I was ashamed, although it wasn't something I would announce to the world; but I didn't want Libby to be judged, because when she did get through this – and I truly believed she would – opinions wouldn't shift so fast. I didn't want her to be labelled. I didn't want that cloud hanging over her. To be honest, Max, Gina and even Clare's opinion didn't really matter to me, but I knew that once Libby was better, they would matter to *her*. I knew I would have to broach the subject with Max once he brought the girls back home. Hopefully, he hadn't spread the news too far. Hopefully, he hadn't told Clare.

We worked our way through the fifty favours. Suzy was so grateful for my help, she hugged me five times before I left, followed by: 'I know you're not yourself, so it's much appreciated.' And: 'I know how tired you are, so honestly, I can't thank you enough.' And 'You're such a good friend, I don't know what I'd do without you.'

Her affection was quite overwhelming. I knew she was trying to tell me, 'I know you feel utterly crap and miserable, and I know favours are insignificant in the great scheme of things, but still, you've helped me and I appreciate that.' I suppose to some extent she was right. Did I care if some of the bags had one sweet in, three sweets in or more than the allocated five? No, I didn't care. I wouldn't lose any sleep over it, but I knew Suzy would. I cared about Suzy, so in essence it *did* matter. It mattered so enormously to her that I was a little envious, because I wanted such a trivial detail to matter to *me*.

I drove home, the pit of my stomach feeling the need to erupt. The urge to scream was overwhelming. My teeth clenched as a tear escaped. I was aware of the constant need to vent my frustration.

I'd tell Max that Lawrence was mistaken. I really didn't want Max knowing about this part of my life. It was nothing to do with him anymore. If anything, I should be annoyed that he was quizzing me. But the reality of the situation sent shivers down my spine. I knew why he was quizzing, why he needed to know what was going on. For the same reason I'd want to know – for our girls.

If I'd known he was allowing our girls to be under the same roof as someone using drugs and excessive amounts of alcohol, I'd be telling him to get himself a good solicitor.

20

'So we've booked it for the week before Suzy and Lawrence's,' Max was telling me as he held Poppy, who locked onto his every word: even though she'd spent the afternoon with him, she was mesmerised.

'Don't you think that's stealing their thunder?'

'I agree, that is a bit off,' June told him as she pulled on her coat. She made it so obvious she loved getting a dig in where she could. She could barely speak to him most of the time.

'Where are you going?' I asked her. She was stylishly dressed, in her dark jeans and a crisp white shirt. Her modish brown leather jacket and knee-high boots completed the trendy outfit, while taking a few years off her age.

'I'm meeting a friend from bingo. We're going out for tea.'

'You've not been in the village five minutes and you have more of a social life than me.'

'That's your fault - keeping yourself huddled in here is not good.' She raised her eyebrows at me. 'Anyhow, I'll be back later.' She left after kissing the girls and me goodbye.

'I don't think Lawrence and Suzy mind. They haven't said anything. They were pleased,' Max said when June had left.

'They're not the type of people to tell you if they *did* mind.' I shook my head. 'Honestly, what would it take to think about someone else?'

'Don't start with me, Kat. I'm not in the mood.' He turned away, his jaw tight.

I thought it best not to provoke him. His bad mood could have stemmed from a variety of reasons, but I didn't want it to be about Libby.

It was the knock on the door and twist of the key that broke the silence, as Clare came in. 'Oh hello, Maxwell. I didn't see your car,' she said abruptly.

'It's round the other side.'

'Avoiding me, are we?' she asked brusquely. Max ignored her; he was obviously avoiding her, as he had plenty of other times. 'I've just come to say goodbye to my girls.' She leaned forward to kiss Poppy's head. Poppy was snuggled in Max's arms, still gazing at her father adoringly. Rosie was sitting in her bouncy chair, which she was slowly becoming used to. Clare peered over the brightly coloured toys that hung randomly, and kissed her forehead. ''Night 'night, sweetheart,' she whispered.

'You don't need me for anything tomorrow?' she asked me.

'No, I'm fine.'

'Great, I'll call in on Monday morning,' she said, before she kissed Max's cheek and left through the not-so-secret door.

'Does she do that every day?' Max had waited until we could hear her footsteps disappear down the staircase before he spoke.

'Morning, night and often a few times during the day,' I smiled.

'How do you cope?'

'You have to,' I laughed, my artificial self on show again. Max knew me, though. He didn't smile. I kept forgetting how much he'd learned about me in our six months together. 'I've not told your mum yet, but I'm thinking about moving.'

'Where to?'

'Maybe Yarm ... I'm not sure; I've not even been to look at anything yet.'

'Can you afford it?'

'What business is that of yours?'

'None, I suppose ... but ...'

'You're worried I'll come after you for more money?'

'No, don't be silly, I just want to make sure you and the girls will be—'

'We'll be fine Max.'

'I know, but …' he put Poppy down on the play mat and picked up Rosie, giving each of his girls an equal share of his affection. He didn't usually stay this long when he was just dropping them back home. He eyed me carefully. 'I'm here for you … if you need any help.'

'Thanks.' I forced myself to be polite. I didn't need his help. He wanted to be the conqueror, the knight, forgetting what he'd done to cause this situation.

'I need to talk to you about something,' he rocked Rosie in his arms, who looked as if she would fall asleep. She wasn't in awe of Max as much as Poppy.

'What?' The words stuck in my throat. I knew what was coming next. I knew why he was delaying leaving.

'It's about Libby.'

'What about her?'

'Lawrence told me she's in a rehab clinic.'

'She is,' I said coolly, wanting to lie, but knowing there was no point hiding it from him.

'Don't you think we need to talk about it?'

'Not really,' I shook my head.

'I'm worried about the girls, Kat.'

'There is nothing to worry about. Do you think I'd put them in danger?'

'No, but—'

'There's nothing to worry about, then.' I turned away, pretending to rummage for something in the kitchen. I didn't want to make eye contact with him. 'Libby is getting better. She's had a rough time, but she would never hurt the girls.'

'I'm not saying she would, but what about the people she's in with?'

'What do you think I'm doing, running a drug den or something?'

'No, but I'm saying—'

'Max, I get it, but there is nothing to worry about. If I was concerned I would tell you. I wouldn't put Rosie and Poppy in any danger.'

'I know—'

'It's fine.' I walked past him into my bedroom, still pretending to be busy. It felt easier being on the move when he was around me. I caught a glimpse of my messy hair in the bedroom mirror. My pale, plain face looked horrifying; the make-up I'd applied earlier in the day had slowly disappeared. My old black tracksuit, which I'd jumped into when I'd arrived home from Suzy's, was i

n need of replacing. I bet Max thought he'd had a lucky escape.

'Obviously I'm concerned.'

'There's nothing to be concerned about.' I came back from the bedroom.

Darkness fell across his face. He gave a slight bow of his head, as if he realised he wasn't going to get any further with me, though I knew he didn't believe my reassurances. 'I better be off, then.' He put Rosie back in the chair. Her little lip protruded, quivering as her vocal cords prepared to make themselves heard across the tiny village. 'Oh, sweetheart, I'm sorry, Daddy has to go.' He looked lost: the opposing desires to rush off back to his other life or stay and take care of his child competing forcefully.

'It's okay, darling, come here,' I fussed, as I lifted Rosie from the chair. Once again, I took over the situation that he could flee from.

'I'll call when I'm back from Barcelona.'

'Have fun,' I hoped I sounded causal.

He left me to soothe Rosie, who soon fell asleep in my arms. I settled her in her cot. The babies' whole routine was up in the air; it was too late in the day for Rosie to nap, so she was bound to be awake late into the night now. But once she'd decided she needed a sleep, it was pointless trying to keep her awake. Poppy was still happily lying on the play mat, trying to roll over onto her front, huffing, squeezing and panting with her efforts. I sat down beside her, encouraging her to turn, but then the smell hit me. Her noises had been more sinister.

'Oh Pops, that's not good.' I grabbed the changing bag that I kept behind the sofa. It was everywhere.

Somehow she'd managed to squeeze it out of the nappy into a wonderful design up her back. 'Oh bloody hell,' I mumbled, as I lifted, wiped and changed her. 'Daddy always seems to miss this bit, doesn't he?' Her eyes gleamed at me. Pure love. Pure happiness.

When do we start to transfer our own thoughts, feelings and emotions onto these innocent beings? When do our beliefs become their beliefs? When do they decide they do actually have their own minds? I didn't want my unhappiness to become *their* unhappiness. My life experiences had marked me, but I didn't want my girls to be tarnished before they had the chance to think for themselves.

Once I'd changed Poppy into a white babygro, her dirty clothes aside, ready for another wash load, I picked her up. As I held her close, and she grabbed my hair, my tears fell. I *had* to be stronger than this.

I so wished I could protect their innocence for ever. Keep them safe for all eternity.

21

The journey to see Libby was painful and uncomfortable. There was still an unbreakable tension between June and Marianne that could send shivers down my spine. Their inability to be polite or accept each other was utterly frustrating.

I knew it was down to Marianne more than June. But I also knew that June didn't care enough to make amends. I'd suggested she take Marianne out for lunch, clear the air, told her Mum wouldn't have wanted this; but she'd shrugged me away. I'd have to accept it was a relationship that wasn't going to improve. Pity I was stuck in the middle of it, though.

We drove into the grounds that still took my breath away. June gasped as we drove along the smooth road. 'Wow,' I heard her mumble from the back seat, where she was squashed between the girls' car seats. There was little room for her. The long drive had allowed the girls to sleep, though, and June had only murmured once that she was aching.

We all climbed from the car, stretching our legs in the radiant sunshine, June bending her legs as if she was about to start a marathon run. It was agreed that Marianne would squeeze into the back on the way home. Marianne who was usually the most accommodating person ever, had clearly been put out, but, it was June's tactless comment that had Marianne seething: 'Let's face it, you are bigger than me, so I can sit in the back on the way home too.' After this comment, Marianne's cheeks flushed, 'I'll be perfectly fine thank you,' she replied through gritted teeth. I knew Marianne was determined to sit in the back, even if we had to call the fire brigade to get her out when we got home.

The girls started to stir as I lifted them into their pushchair. Soon it would be feeding time and they would start hollering. 'This is amazing,' June gasped as we approached the house taking in its beauty and its magnificent architecture. Max would love this place, I thought fleetingly.

Adrianne greeted us as soon as we went in. The fire was burning ferociously, spreading a welcoming warmth. Marianne unfastened her coat. Adrianne told us she'd go and find Libby while we settled on the sumptuous sofas. I quickly emptied my bag; too quickly, as nappies, bibs, wipes and other baby paraphernalia fell to the floor. Grabbing the bottle bag, I handed it to June as I hurriedly pushed all the other bits back into the bag. I remembered when I used to carry only lip-gloss, mascara and blusher. They were a must. But old essentials had been replaced by new ones.

Marianne was lifting Rosie from the pram. June, obviously not letting her take over, started to coo over Poppy, as she undid the straps, lifting her delicately into the air before snuggling her into her arms. I handed them both a bottle, taking pleasure in handing over the job to someone else, for a change.

'Hi.' Libby came around the corner. My breath caught in my chest, as her appearance took us all by surprise.

'Libby, sweetheart, you look great,' Marianne said. She was unable to hug Libby because she was holding Poppy, but she lifted her cheek for Libby to kiss.

June followed suit. 'You look fantastic.'

'You do look so much better,' I smiled, as I pulled Libby towards me. She was still thin, her jeans baggy on her hips, her white jumper hanging shapelessly around her skinny figure; but something had come alive. Her eyes were focused, lively, welcoming.

She was in there.

'I'm feeling much better,' she said, a genuine smile emerging. Something I hadn't seen in a long time.

Warmth engulfed me, as I watched my sister lean towards her nieces and kiss their tiny faces. A surge of happiness nearly choked me.

We spent a few hours with Libby as we walked the grounds, showed June the beautiful rooms and generally enjoyed the splendour of Libby's temporary home. Our small talk was uplifting, surfacing above the issues that were facing all of us.

We fed Poppy and Rosie again before leaving, in the hope that they would sleep all the way home. The long journey was tiresome; but it was worth it. The two weeks that Libby had been there had already started to transform her. As we waved her goodbye, I wiped away the tears and stifled the urge to turn back and take her with us.

It was for the best, of course it was; but as we left her alone, guilt flooded through me as it always did when we said our goodbyes.

22

The week had passed by quickly. I'd avoided being invited to Brooke's. I'd been interrupted rudely by Clare, twice daily, customers in tow at every other visit. I'd visited Marianne when Derek was out. He seemed to have this urge to talk about Libby; if he wasn't praying for her, he was telling me how disappointed he would be if the rehab centre didn't work, that he thought Libby moving to Devon with June was the best option. I wanted her home with me. June had made excuses most evenings to be out; she had lots of meetings with her friends from the bingo. They'd even set up a reading group, she'd told me.

I didn't believe her.

'I felt awful,' Suzy was saying as I poured us each a glass of wine. 'She was sobbing her heart out. You'd think he'd left her.'

'Did you tell her to get a grip?'

'Of course not. Remember what you were like when you were pregnant?'

'But Max was cheating … with her,' I said, handing her the chilled glass.

The Saturday evening had been eventful. June had scurried out the door, all glammed up. It had taken a while to settle the girls. Suzy had arrived expecting a relaxing night, but ended up rocking Poppy to sleep. She'd been busy enough. Lawrence had left for his stag-do two days earlier, while Suzy had been sorting last-minute wedding arrangements. She'd also had to soothe a hormonal, neurotic Gina.

'She was really upset,' Suzy said as she savoured the wine, when we'd finally settled the girls. 'Mmm … lush.'

'He's on a stag-do for God's sake. Leave him be.'

'I know, but she can't get hold of him. She's worried. I think he's being unfair.'

'Have you spoken to Lawrence?'

'Lots of times. I've told him Max needs to ring Gina, but Lawrence said he's out of it most of the time.'

'I'm so pleased I'm away from it all.'

'Are you?' Suzy sipped her wine again, licking her lips as I considered her meaning. Not quite understanding what she was getting at. 'Don't you miss Max?'

'No.' I shook my head. She stared at me a moment longer. 'Yes, sometimes,' I admitted.

'Would you go back to him?'

'No!' I *did* mean that. 'I wish it hadn't happened, but it has and I can't change things.'

'But it's so hard, doing all this on your own.'

'I wish I had an extra pair of hands, and sometimes I wish they were Max's. But I couldn't go back. I'd never trust him. Anyway, it's not as if it's an option.'

The sound of stirring from the bedroom caused me to stop drinking. I felt my eyes narrow as I glanced at Suzy, disappointment running through me. All I ask for, Rosie and Poppy, is a few hours with my friend. Would you please allow me that? I begged silently, as I waited for the stirring sounds to turn into a yell. But they ceased and I felt my shoulders relax. I took a sip of wine, allowing the cool drink to ease my body and mind. Within seconds, though, the stirring had started again, and this time it turned into a scream.

I quickly jumped up, hoping the screech wouldn't wake the other baby. Too late; both the girls were yelling, their screams blaring through the flat. Suzy was seconds behind me. She lifted Poppy as I rescued Rosie, our relaxing girlie night disturbed before we'd got started. Poppy settled straight back down, but Rosie seemed to be struggling, so I rocked her around the lounge, a routine I thought we were getting out of.

As Suzy and I chatted, I thought back to her words about me missing Max. Although, I didn't rate Gina, or her fake innocent persona, her 'feel sorry for me' approach to life, I really hoped he wouldn't let her down.

Finally getting Rosie down to sleep, I sat back down on the sofa next to Suzy, enjoying the wine once again. The knock on the front door surprised us. I wasn't expecting anyone. June had a key, unless she'd forgotten it.

I quietly went downstairs, avoiding the places that I knew would creak under my feet. I squinted through the peephole – which I'd had fitted when I'd first started the salon, to avoid any customers who thought they could invade my personal space – to see Libby's face staring back at me.

23

I'd paid the taxi man the eighty pounds it had cost to bring Libby home. I'd guiltily taken the money from the girls' savings. Money that had been given to them as gifts from birth; money that I'd hidden from Libby. As I fumbled for the box where I hid their wealth, I'd made sure she couldn't see me.

She sat casually on the sofa. Her short dark hair was sleek, healthier than it had looked in months. She'd applied make-up, her jeans and jumper fitted her nicely. She was still thin, but there was more colour in her cheeks.

'What is going on?' I asked, stumbling up the stairs.

'I felt better. They said I've improved.'

'I don't understand.' I was panicking.

'When you all came to see me last Sunday, I wanted to come home with you.'

'I wanted that too Lib, but this won't help. You need to finish the programme.'

'I didn't see the point of wasting Marianne's money, so I thought I would come back home.'

'What does Ronnie think?'

'Yes, she's fine. I can leave whenever.'

'But you have another three weeks left. You're only halfway through.'

'I don't need it, Kat. Honestly, I feel really strong.' She stood up, walked across the lounge towards the kitchen. 'Would you like a cup of tea?'

Suzy had been sitting quietly. I realised she'd hidden the wine. I shot her a look, shaking my head, fear running through my body.

'Cup of tea, Suz?' Libby asked casually.

'Erm … no, thanks,' Suzy managed.

'Libby, I'm not happy about this,' I began.

'Oh, please don't start with me. I thought it would be a nice surprise.'

'Why didn't you wait until tomorrow? We could have brought you home with us.' This all felt so wrong; and yet she looked healthier than she'd looked in weeks, months … years, in fact. She sounded fine. I couldn't remember the last time she'd asked me if I wanted a drink, or if she could do something for me.

'I wanted to surprise you.'

'What, with an eighty quid bill?' I couldn't help myself.

'Sorry about that, I didn't really think.' She smiled and scrunched up her nose, her face the picture of innocence. The problem was she never *did* think. She never thought about anyone but herself.

I already had the number logged into my phone. I spoke to Libby several times a week, so I had it to hand at all times. 'Hi, is Ronnie still on duty please?'

'Oh, come on, Kat. You can't be serious?' Libby glared at me. I ignored her.

'Can I ask who's calling?' The lady at the other end of the phone asked.

'It's Kat Neasham.'

'Yes, two seconds.' I assumed it was Adrianne. She'd spoken softly until I'd said my name, but then her voice became two decibels higher and she began stuttering as if she was deciding which move to make.

'Hi, Kat. I'm assuming Libby's made it home?' It was Ronnie.

'Yes. What is going on?' I asked, looking at Libby, who was shaking her head at me in disbelief.

'We seemed to be making good progress, but I've been called in because she's left. She ordered herself a taxi, Adrianne tried to stop her … but as Libby told her, we can't stop her from leaving.'

'I don't understand.'

'She told Adrianne she was better, she didn't need to be here anymore and she wanted to discharge herself.'

'And Adrianne let her?'

'Kat, this isn't a prison, everyone is here of their own free will. Adrianne called me straight away, but by the time I arrived, Libby had left.'

'How do I get her back there?' I looked away from Libby, not wanting to see the disappointment in her eyes.

'If she'll talk to me, I can—'

'She's here.' My arm stretched towards her, the phone hanging between us.

'I don't want to talk to her.'

'You *have* to talk to her.'

'I can't.'

'Libby …'

She breathed out deeply, her hand shaking as she reluctantly took the phone from me. Each breath that escaped her was shallow, seemingly hard to control, as she whispered the word, 'Hello.'

'I feel fine, though.'

'I'm not sure that's working out.'

'I've talked enough.'

'Honestly, I think I'll be better here.'

'I'll call you if I'm struggling.' She handed the phone back to me.

My insides felt as if they were on fire, my heart was pounding, vibrating through my body, as I took the phone back. 'Ronnie?'

'I'm sorry, Kat, but I can't force her to come back.'

'What should I do?' I was hoping Ronnie detected my panic, but not Libby.

'I'd advise Libby goes back to the programme she was on. She'll need a lot of on-going support. We're here if you need us.'

'Thank you.' I could barely speak, words of appreciation not fitting this situation. I hung up the phone, staring at Libby who peered at me from above her mug, her eyes sad, a troubled young soul struggling inside.

'Are you sure you're doing the right thing?' Suzy finally found her voice.

'I promise I'm better.' Libby stared at us both, her eyes pleading with us to believe her.

My heart beating even faster, fear, disappointment and fury raging through me.

I wondered how many girlie nights I'd taken for granted. How many times I'd sat with Suzy, and enjoyed her company but not really appreciated it.

As this night had turned into a complete disaster, I wondered if I'd ever get those nights back.

24

'Libby, it's already paid for.' Marianne told her as we sat on the sofa.

'Can't you ask for your money back?' Libby suggested.

'No—'

'She signed the contract that wouldn't allow any refunds to be given,' Derek interrupted, shaking his head at Libby. 'I told her to pay weekly, but for some reason she trusted you'd stay there.'

'But I'm better now,' Libby said feebly.

'After all the lies you've told, the stealing, the deceit, you really expect us to believe you?' Derek stood up as he spoke.

'Derek calm down,' I said. Although I somewhat agreed with him, I had to protect Libby. 'Libby has said sorry for those things.'

'Sorry isn't good enough.' He thrust his hands into his pockets. 'We all know where this is going to lead.'

'I promise, I won't go back down that road.' Tears welled in Libby's eyes as she looked at me desperately.

'You won't be able to stop yourself.' He walked towards the door. 'I want that money repaying or—'

'Derek—' Marianne tried to stop him.

'No.' He turned to her. 'I've kept quiet for too long now. This girl is running rings round you. You offered a way out and she's thrown it back in your face. I am happy to help anyone who will help themselves. This is ridiculous.' He slammed the door as he left the room, making both Poppy and Rosie flinch. I tensed as I silently begged for them to stay asleep.

Libby let a tear escape as Marianne came to sit the other side of her. 'I'm sorry,' Libby choked, as she took Marianne's hand. 'I promise I'll pay you back somehow.'

'Look, why don't we talk about you going back there?' Marianne asked tenderly.

'No, please don't send me back,' Libby practically begged.

'Why?' I shook my head at her. 'You were enjoying it.'

'But I want to be free.'

'You were free there,' I said. 'When was the last time you felt free here?'

'It's all the restrictions.'

'But they will help you get better.'

'They have.' Libby's eyes were pleading. 'I don't think I need another three weeks.'

'I don't think it will do you any harm,' I said.

'I agree,' Marianne nodded.

'I can't.' Libby shook her head.

'Did something happen?' Marianne asked, concern stamped across her face.

'No,' Libby said, far too quickly. Tears filled her eyes. She blinked, rubbing them away.

'Are you sure?' I asked softly.

'I just wanted to come home,' she snivelled.

I glanced at Marianne, who met my gaze. I wondered if she was thinking what I was thinking: Libby was lying. Something had happened.

'We'll have to get you enrolled back on the programme,' Marianne said.

'I could go and live with June in Devon.' Libby broached the subject that I'd not mentioned to her, so June obviously had.

'No,' Marianne said abruptly, startling both Libby and me as we both gaped at her. 'I'm not sure that's a good idea,' she said, her tone softer after a brief silence.

'Has June asked you?' I queried.

'Yes.'

I felt anger rise through me, biting my lip to stop myself exploding. How dare she?

'Like she said, there's nothing for me here. She said she could help me,' Libby told us.

'I'd prefer you stayed here with us.' I agreed with Marianne, not wanting to let Libby out of my sight now she was back.

'There's so much going on here, you can't keep an eye on me twenty-four seven. We've already tried and it hasn't worked. In Devon, I could start a new programme. June could help me.' She spoke as if repeating every word June had said to her.

I wondered how long June had been whispering in her ear. Had she been ringing her while she was in rehab? Was this why Libby thought it was okay to leave?

'You could live with us,' Marianne said, clearly very unhappy with Libby's plan.

'No, that's a bad idea. Derek is so angry,' Libby said.

'He'll be fine.'

'No, you need to be building a life with him,' I told Marianne.

'I'm getting in the way,' Libby pleaded.

'You're not,' Marianne said.

'You're not in the way.' I rubbed Libby's leg as I spoke, desperate for her not to feel so low, or be so hard on herself. But so bloody frustrated with her at the same time.

'But June has plenty of space. I'll be away from all the temptations that are here.' June had definitely been talking in her ear: these weren't Libby's words. Another tear escaped, as she said, 'I've made such a mess of things. It's best I set up a new life somewhere else.'

I swallowed away the lump that was forming in my throat. 'But I don't want you to go.' I said anxiously. I so wanted to make her better with a wave of a magic wand.

'If you want to help me, you'll let me go.'

There was silence as I sat with the two women I loved more than anything. I wanted to slap Libby but then hug her. Why did she have to make this so bloody difficult?

'I s'pose it doesn't have to be for ever,' Marianne said finally.

'I can come back when I feel strong enough.' Libby bit her lip and let the tears escape.

I cuddled her as she wept. We all sat in silence as I soothed her. Marianne wiped away her own tears.

I tried to smile through mine. I'd miss Libby: God, I really didn't want to let her go. But I *had* to let her go. I couldn't allow her to fall back into the vicious, evil trap that had encompassed all our lives. People became better. Many people worked their way through their addictions. Libby had to be one of them. Her words penetrating through me: 'If you want to help me …'

I had said I would never let go of the rope, but the tiny threads that held the rope together were disentangling. I couldn't let them snap.

Moving in with June was probably Libby's best option. Away from this place. Away from the people who would drag her back down.

But, I found myself silently apologising to Mum.

25

The next morning, I'd chased Marcoway, Libby's old programme, who'd agreed it would be best for Libby to go back in and register. They could then refer her to a programme in Devon. Rosie had a hospital appointment, her first check-up with a consultant, so June had agreed to take Libby.

Marianne had a fete day at church so couldn't have Poppy for me while I took Rosie to her appointment. Clare was training on some new products, and obviously, Max was working, so Poppy had to join us on our little jaunt.

In fairness, both the girls were brilliant. They loved being out, which was sad – because I hated it. I'd started to feel I'd be happiest as a recluse, though I was slightly worried that when we did move from the flat, the constant visits that were really getting me down would stop completely. That sounded bliss at the moment, but when and if I ever felt better, maybe the loneliness would become too much.

But I couldn't think about that now. Once Libby was sorted, my next step was to find somewhere else to live.

We sat in the crowded waiting area, where children who I assumed were aged two to four years eyed one another carefully before slowly letting go of their inhibitions and started to interact with each other, or play side by side. How would Poppy and Rosie play when they developed into small people with individual personalities? Judging by their characters at present, I thought Poppy would be the easy-going one, while Rosie would be more demanding.

Was it my fault she was so needy? The textbooks would tell me, yes. I'd succumbed to her every cry, never allowing her to be alone to experience her own pain. I'd let her fall asleep on my chest, rocked her to sleep in the pushchair and hugged her close in the hope that her agony would pass. Had my doing so not helped her become an independent baby?

And I'd never really let Poppy cry either because it would be as if I was openly admitting I loved one child more than the other. And I didn't; it was just that one was needier than the other.

The love I felt was too tremendous, too powerful to comprehend sometimes. I'd often gaze at the girls and wondered how I could even think about wanting my old life back.

An hour had passed by the time Rosie's name was called, and I'd begun to worry that they'd be wanting their next feed. Luckily, they slept. I was so grateful. I remember the days when I was thankful for good wine and good food ... how times change.

People kindly made way for me as I manoeuvred apologetically past them with my huge pram. At last we got out of the busy waiting room and into the corridor, where I found room three and opened the door.

A male doctor of Chinese origin greeted me. It took him two minutes to ask me questions about Rosie's allergy and how she was taking to the new milk. It took me all of thirty seconds to tell him that she was a lot happier but she was still quite sick. Nowhere near as bad as she used to be, but still I thought it was worth mentioning. Although she was putting on a bit of weight, I was concerned it wasn't enough. Compared to Poppy, with her chunky arms, legs and chubby cheeks, she looked feeble.

I was surprised by his calm nature, his ability to communicate with me as a mother, rather than reeling off bullet points from textbooks. As I explained how I'd read somewhere (well, Suzy had told me) that a woman had been advised to give her baby, who suffered with reflux, baby rice at three months old, he agreed this would be fine. Simply agreed: there was no concern, no disregarding me as if I was the worst mother ever for suggesting such a thing. He simply typed into his computer, updated my notes and told me this would be fine. 'Slowly at first, once a day, increase next week, then in a few weeks move to more solid foods.'

This was the only advice he gave me. Since Rosie had been diagnosed, most of the doctors, nurses and specialists had treated me with respect, listening to my views rather than dismissing me as a neurotic first-time mum who had no idea what she was talking about.

As we left his room I felt a fleeting sense of relief, which was soon wiped away as we walked straight into Harvey's mum. 'Oh … hello,' she smiled; or winced – I couldn't tell.

'Hi,' I forced myself to say.

'Do you have problems too?' she asked. Oh, many! She didn't let me answer as she threw herself into her own self-obsessed world. 'Harvey is lactose intolerant.'

'Poor thing.'

'It has been a nightmare, especially with breastfeeding. I have to watch my diet; any little thing can have him in so much pain.'

'I've found it easier to feed Rosie rice milk.'

'Each to their own,' she said disapprovingly, her mouth turned downwards.

'I did try breastfeeding, but it didn't work out really.' I felt awkward, my cheeks started to burn with embarrassment as I felt the need to justify my actions to this woman as if I was standing in a courtroom.

'It's hard work, I must admit,' she said quietly, as if relieving herself of a big secret. 'I'm hoping to get some milk for Harvey. I really want to keep going with the breast, but I'm sure he can't be getting the correct nutritional value.'

'Hopefully, the doctors will be able to help.'

'I hope so. To be honest, he's feeding so much at the moment, I'm exhausted, because I've cut so much out of my diet.'

'I hope you get sorted. They've advised I can start feeding Rosie baby rice,' I blurted out before I could stop myself, noting I must go for surgery to get my mouth sewn up.

'Oh …' She seemed bewildered. 'Isn't that a bit soon?'

'Yes, but she's still quite sick, so—'

'Oh, I don't like that idea.'

'If it's best for Rosie—'

'How could it possibly be best?' She said it so politely I wondered if I'd misheard her.

'Mmm …' I was stuttering. 'If the consultant thinks it's okay, I'm sure it is.'

'I'd get a second opinion.' She eyed me knowingly, as if she was letting me in on a big secret. I didn't want a second opinion, I was happy with the first. But I didn't say so as I watched this woman judge me. This woman who knew nothing of my life. 'We should meet,' she said suddenly, waving a hand in my direction. 'Just me and you.' Not Brooke. I knew the words were on the tip of her tongue.

'Yes. That's a nice idea,' I lied.

'Here's my number.' She pulled a business card from her bag. 'PA and Virtual Secretary' peered at me in purple italics. Nancy Nott scrawled underneath. *Nancy Nott … was that her real name? Sounded more like a stage name.* 'Call me. Must dash, our consultant will be waiting.'

'See you soon.' I let out a huge sigh as soon as she'd disappeared.

Baby-group politics, here we come.

*

We drove into the village, with my stomach doing double-flips as it always did when we approached the salon and the flat, and the lead weight descending on me again.

I steered my car into my regular car parking space – and noticed Henry's car parked in the side street. The same place Max parked when he was avoiding Clare.

My heart was racing. Did I drive away? Ignore that this was happening? Did I barge in and catch them at it? Oh my God, what should I do?

'Help!' I shouted into the air. Rosie jumped, her dreams disturbed, her hands rigid. Then they slowly relaxed again, while Poppy slept oblivious.

The banging on the window nearly sent me through the roof. I turned to see Mrs D grinning full force at me, waving. If the window was down she'd have been right in my face she was so close. I waited until she stepped back, then I slowly pressed the button for the window to open.

'Oh Kathryn, look at you.' Her hands were on my cheeks, pinching them as if I was a small child. Her teeth were so bright I thought I might have to reach for my sunglasses. 'Come on, get out. Let's look at you.' She waved me out of the car. Yes, she actually physically waved me out; and for some strange, unknown reason, I followed. I followed as if she was the boss of me. I removed myself from the car and stood in front of her, allowing her to examine my uncoordinated state: my not-so-tight but comfy jeans, my oversized t-shirt and gigantic cardigan. I stood there, letting her eye me up and down.

'Mrs Donnelly—'

'Ange! I've told you,' she grinned, hitting my arm playfully.

'You look great as always.'

'Hi, Kat, we were going for a walk.' Brooke was standing at the back of the car, holding her phone and typing fast with her thumb on the keypad.

'Brooke said she met you at the mum's group. It's such a small world.'

'It's a small village,' I smiled, hoping she hadn't noticed the sarcasm.

'Brooke was telling me you girls are going to have a girlie night.' Mrs D stared at me. Was it a question?

'Maybe … we did talk … I think … yes.'

'Excellent, when?'

'What?' I stuttered.

'When are you having this night?'

'Ange, we haven't put anything in,' Brooke drawled as if she was bored, still not looking up from her phone. 'Kat was ill last week.'

'Headache,' I confirmed.

'Let's put a night in now,' Mrs D ordered.

I'm busy every night – for ever. The words, I swear, were on the tip of my tongue, hanging out to dry.

'Friday or Saturday's good for me,' Brooke mumbled.

'Will you get off that phone?' Mrs D chastised her, then shook her head at me, obviously unimpressed. 'Bloody Facebook. How the hell did they survive in the olden days? So how about Friday?'

'I'll see if I can get a babysitter and let you know.'

'I can babysit any time Kathryn.' Clare was suddenly in the conversation, walking briskly towards us. I wondered how long she'd been hovering. 'Honestly, how many times have I told you to simply ask?'

'I didn't see you there.' I faced Clare, glaring at her, willing her to read my call to get me out of this dreadful situation; but her senses were oblivious to my needs.

'See, there we go.' Mrs D clapped her perfectly manicured hands. 'It's a date.'

'Excellent.' I hoped I grinned, but it felt more like a grimace. 'So, what time, Brooke?'

'Whenever.' She finally glanced at me. 'What's best for you?'

'Eight?' I suggested, already trying to think of another excuse as to why I couldn't go.

'Fab, as long as you're feeling better.' Brooke studied me, eyebrows raised. I realised I'd obviously offended her with my fake headache.

'Hopefully,' I smiled. She relaxed and showed me the same white teeth as Mrs D.

This would be awful. We'd talk about celebrities I'd never heard of, dinner parties Mrs D had given, how wonderful her Stevie was … it would be hell.

'I've so much to tell you about …' Mrs D winked and nodded, not so discreetly, in the direction of Melanie's salon. I smiled politely. And we'd talk about Melanie and Mandy … it would definitely be hell.

We watched the two women walk away. They were more like sisters than sisters-in-law. Her Stevie had definitely modelled his wife on his sister: the likeness was eerie.

'Here, let me help you with the girls,' Clare said authoritatively, opening the car door on the passenger side. 'Henry's upstairs waiting for you.'

Oh. Did she already know he was here? His car was parked so discreetly, I wondered if she'd just picked up on it now.

'Okay.' Clare lifted Poppy from her seat while I lifted Rosie. Her eyes flickered. I tried to rock her slightly, praying she would go back to sleep. She didn't. Oh, for the love of … I tried not to swear, feeling the urgency to get into the flat before Clare.

My heart was beating a little faster and my palms felt sweaty as I tried to unlock the door while holding a wailing Rosie. The door opened. Either Clare knew something was going on or she was being a little insensitive, because she almost pushed me away from the entrance in order to get ahead of me.

'This little one needs to lie down,' she said as she practically leapt up each step. 'Oh …' was her deflated response when she reached the top of the stairs. Seconds behind her, I nearly knocked her flying.

June and Henry were sitting on the sofa, drinking coffee, seemingly engaging in pleasant conversation. When we barged in, they looked at each other before peering at us in apparent surprise.

'Is everything okay?' June didn't move. Her high boot crossed over her knee was swinging casually. Henry was a safe distance away from her.

'Yes, fine,' Clare said as she walked into my bedroom, I assumed to place Poppy in her cot: I didn't bother asking because it seemed to be a free-for-all in here at the moment.

'Could you hold Rosie for me?' I handed my screaming child to June before she had the chance to answer. 'I've got to make the girls their bottles.'

Henry moved closer to June, touching Rosie's cheek with his finger. She became silent as she stared up at her grandad. This surprised me, as Rosie wasn't the easiest child to make happy. She yelled at strangers who dared to stick their head in the pram. Maybe she could sense some good from Henry.

The silence was intriguing … I really thought there was something going on between June and Henry. I'd thought June's nights out had really been about meeting Henry, not bingo. But as they sat there looking casually unconcerned, I wondered if I could have been wrong.

My worry was Clare. She knew … or she thought she knew.

26

It was decided that June and Libby would travel back to Devon at the end of the week. This would give them enough time to get their things together. In the meantime, Libby quietly settled back into the flat. June had taken up residence on the sofa, offering Libby her room back, who didn't argue about getting her own bed back.

It was strange having them both in the flat. It had only been two days, but already claustrophobia was crushing me. The flat was overcrowded to say the least, but the lack of privacy and personal space didn't seem to faze Libby or June.

'God, how do you move in here?' Max asked when he paid an unexpected visit on his way back from Barcelona.

'With great difficulty.'

'I can take the girls for a few days, until—'

'Thanks, but we're fine.'

'The offer is there,' he shrugged. 'Can I go and see them?'

I nodded. I'd explained, when I'd opened the door to him, it was late, and they were sleeping, but he said he needed to see their little faces, if I didn't mind. I didn't mind, and although I wanted Max to be a good father, it would sting a little that he wasn't here with us all the time. But, there was no going back for us, and I hated the regret that would wash over me.

'Hello, gorgeous girls,' I heard him whisper as I stood near the door. My heart swelled as I heard his tiny murmurs. I pulled myself away and busied myself in the kitchen, not allowing myself to be tortured by his kind words.

'So, how was Barcelona?' I asked, when he walked back into the room. I removed towels from the tumble dryer, folding them neatly onto the kitchen side.

'Good, I think,' he laughed. 'From what I can remember anyway.'

'Didn't want to say but you look a bit weary,' I smiled.

'Thanks. I haven't slept much.' He ran his hand through his thick hair. 'I haven't been home yet.'

'Gina won't be happy.'

'She doesn't know I'm here.'

'Max!'

'I'm going to be so busy over the next few days with work, so I'll probably not get the chance to call in before the weekend,' he said defensively. 'If I'd told her I was coming, it would have caused a world war.' I carried on folding the towels, not answering. I didn't want to get involved in his relationship with Gina. I also didn't want to side with her by admitting I'd be a little upset if I was her. And, I didn't want to be the cause of any arguments. 'I hear Libby is back,' he said.

'News travels fast.'

'You know what my mum's like,' he smiled. I raised my eyebrows and shook my head. 'How is she doing?' he asked softly, his concern throwing me.

'She's getting there,' I said, not wanting to get into this with him.

'Where is she?' he asked causally, but I knew he was wondering whether she was out with her 'dodgy friends'.

'She's in her room. Sleeping or listening to music. She hasn't left the flat unless she's with one of us.' He looked at me as if he was trying to work out if I was telling the truth. 'Have you spoken to Gina?' I changed the subject: onto one that I'd just tried to avoid, but at least it was away from Libby.

'Yeah, before we got on the flight back.'

'Is she alright?'

'Yeah, why?' He sounded defensive.

'No reason.' I held my hands up. 'Suzy said she was upset because she couldn't get hold of you, that's all.' I wasn't trying to stir things, but I just couldn't help myself.

'She'll be okay,' he shrugged. Then he seemed to drop his guard as he told me, 'Got a bit of an ear-bashing, actually. I thought it would add fuel to the fire if I said I was coming here.' I didn't say anything, suddenly wishing I'd not asked. 'Hormones …' Max said.

'I remember it like it was yesterday.' I walked past him, placing a pile of towels in my room, which at the moment had the most space. There was a silence while I put them away.

'Anyway, I best be off. She'll be tracking me.' Max's comment was flippant, and I wanted to curse him for being so disrespectful to Gina. Not that I had any respect for her, but to attack her in front of me was unfair. My silence seemed to worry him, 'Are we still on for Saturday for the girls?' he asked quietly.

'Yeah, see you then.' I wondered what he was playing at. He was probably hung-over, tired and somewhat exhausted, I told myself as I listened to his steps echoing down the stairs.

As the front door opened, the bitter night wind carried screams from outside into the flat. I instinctively ran to the top of the stairs. Was someone hurt?

I saw Max rushing into the cold night air, the front door left open to swing in the gale. Leaping down the staircase, holding the wall as my slippers seemed to slide from underneath me, I lost my balance and fell, banging my back against each step, swearing loudly.

'Kat, what's going on?' Libby was at the top, peering down at me. 'Jesus, are you alright?'

'I'm fine. Something is going on outside.'

'What?'

I didn't answer her, the pain searing through my spine and backside making me wince.

'Oh, shit,' I said louder than I meant to.

A dark figure was blocking the front of Henry's car. The streetlight shining across the glistening road showed the fear in June's face as she peered helplessly out at the menacing person who had no intention of letting her get out of the car safely.

27

'Mum, come inside. Let's calm down.' Max held Clare by her arms.

'She needs to get out and talk to me,' Clare rasped, as if she was possessed. I wondered if she'd been drinking.

'No, you need to sort this out with Dad, not her.'

'Come on, Clare. Let's go home and talk.' Henry was standing by the side of the car, the glow of the orange streetlight highlighting his flushed face.

'I'm not going anywhere with you,' Clare growled.

Should I step in? Should I shut the door? Should I disown June? Should I drag her from the car?

Libby was by my side, wrapping her dressing gown tightly around her waist. 'Oh hell,' she said lightly, with a laugh. How could she find this funny?

'Mum, please. Look Kat will put the kettle on.' Will I? Max was unusually calm.

'Max, why don't you take your mum home?' I suggested.

'I'm not going anywhere until she gets out of that car.' Clare roared.

I ordered Libby to hold the door as I walked out into the chilly night, the breeze stinging my legs through my flannel pyjamas. I shivered as I walked over to Clare. My heart racing as I took hold of her hands, which were clenched into tight knots. Our eyes met. A surge of anxiety ran through me. She didn't look like herself. She could probably murder June at this instant, and plead insanity.

'Clare,' I spoke quietly, trying to calm her. But her eyes diverted past me, staring straight at June. 'Clare, I think it's best you go home—'

146

'You do?' She spoke with such harshness, that I felt the need to take a step back.

'I think you need to sort this out with Henry,' I said. There was no way I could get June out of the car while Clare was still here; although part of me thought I *should* unleash Clare onto her, to make her think twice about wrecking marriages in future.

'It doesn't work,' she suddenly shouted, staring past me again, glowering intensely at June, who looked petrified. 'It doesn't work.' Her screams filled the air, then she started to cry, her body collapsing. Max caught her before she hit the rocky concrete. Crumbling to her knees, she begged for someone to help her. Henry came towards her, his hand upon her back. 'Come on, pet,' he said, as she swung her arm backwards, thumping against his leg.

'Leave me alone,' she sobbed, as Max pulled her to him.

'Come on, Mum. You can come home with me.'

'I'm sorry.' She gazed at Max, her hand reaching out to his tired face as she stroked the side of his cheek. 'I'm so sorry.'

He didn't speak as he lifted her up and helped her to his car.

'Let me know how she is.' I was trembling as I spoke. Clare's exterior mask had been broken. Cracked in half. Worse: smashed to pieces.

Max nodded, as he stepped into his car and drove his mother away.

I watched as his lights disappeared into the quiet village. Clare's wails hadn't attracted too much attention. There'd been a twitch of a curtain, but no-one had tried to interfere. I was hoping for Clare's sake no-one had recognised her.

'I'm sorry Kat—' Henry started.

'I think you should leave.' I walked to the passenger side of the car. June had finally unlocked it and was stepping into the icy air.

'Sorry ...' he bowed his head, resembling a schoolboy who'd been caught red-handed.

'I need to talk to Henry for a second,' June told me.

I stared at her, barely able to conceal my disgust. I stayed where I was as she walked around me. She glanced back at me. 'Privately …'

I could have slapped her. My body was shaking as I walked towards Libby, who was still holding open the front door. 'You wait for her,' I said to Libby through gritted teeth. Libby nodded.

I went quietly upstairs, trying not to wake the girls. Both had continued to sleep soundly throughout the whole commotion. I could hear June and Libby whispering urgently to each other at the bottom of the stairs, then the door was closed, and they came upstairs. June entered first, her face pale, her usual glamour replaced by the faded look of an older woman. Her elegant style was gone. All I could see was a lonely, insecure, selfish being, who was desperate to be loved. No matter what it took.

'Is this how you treated Mum?' I spat at her, blood rushing furiously through me.

'No, your mum has nothing to do with this.' She shook her head, taking off her coat.

'It looks to me like she does. Is it that you're jealous?' June didn't answer me as she placed her coat over the sofa. 'These women are so much better than you, so you have to have what they have.' I was being harsh, but my argument was for Mum, not Clare. June still didn't answer as she sat down on the sofa, her eyes not meeting mine as she ran her hands through her fine wisps of hair.

'Kat, I think it's best to leave it,' Libby said softly.

'Leave it?' If the girls had not been sleeping, I would have been screaming. My aunty and sister living in their own bubbles, destroying lives as their decisions whipped away happiness of others. I silently paced back and forth, the image of Clare's crushed form torturing me. Is that what Mum had been like?

I sat down on the sofa opposite June, running my hands across my dry, tired face, shaking my head. Finding the strength to look at her, I asked 'Is this it, then?'

'Is what it?' she snapped back at me, infuriating me further.

'You and Henry … you're going to ruin *their* marriage now.'

'He doesn't want me.' Her words threw me. 'He wants to work things out with Clare.'

Libby and I looked at each other. No-one spoke. A deafening silence filled the room. I stood up, and went to fill the kettle. The sounds of the water boiling seemingly louder than usual. Libby sat down next to June. I watched the two women and wished I was alone.

I made us all a hot drink. 'Where do we go from here?' I asked, sitting down opposite them both.

'I think we should leave tomorrow.' June had softened, but I could see the bitterness creeping in. 'Henry has made it perfectly clear I was his playmate. It seems he's had plenty of them.'

<h1 style="text-align:center">28</h1>

The brown envelope stood out amongst the pile that was scattered across the floor at the bottom of the stairs; another part I'd grown to hate about living in the flat, as the postman used to hand all my post (personal and professional) through to the salon. I'd soon put a stop to that when Clare seemed to inspect every single letter that arrived.

The stairs felt an effort today, more than usual. I'd hardly slept, again. I'd left June to sleep on the sofa, Libby to gather her own thoughts in her room, as I'd battled with the anguish of where my loyalties lie. I felt as if I was being tested. Maybe by Mum. Was she trying to show me what type of person June really was? Was she telling me Libby shouldn't be moving with her? It could have been a test for June. Would Libby living with her, give her a focus? All these frustrating questions. I didn't see the point in asking June as I doubt she knew the answer.

She was huddled beneath a quilt, not stirring as the girls and I busied around her. Poppy and Rosie were lying happily on the play mat after being fed and changed. My own state was something not to be desired. I'd decided I would make the most of June and Libby's last morning by having a peaceful shower. Alone.

I opened the brown enveloped. My girls were stirring in the background; their soft babbles comforting. As I pulled the thin white letter from the envelope, my shoulders tensed, as I read confirmation of the time and date I would meet my counsellor. As I stared at the crisp white paper and the neatly printed words, I'd fought the urge to rip the letter up and put it in the bin.

I could do this on my own. Couldn't I?

There were days when I could see the light, see hope, see a future full of my dreams. But most days I was wading through, pushing my body to take the next step. Forcing myself to the finishing line, where I could collapse into bed. Sleep. Get up and start again, although I didn't really want to. It was for that reason, that I folded the letter neatly, and placed it in my handbag after marking in my diary the letter 'C'.

Maybe I should refer June: she seemed to need it more than I did.

My mobile vibrated, bouncing around the sofa where I'd carelessly left it. Max's name flashed at me. I'd removed his photo many months ago, but sometimes even his name caused a flick of fury, or hurt. But today I grabbed it before I missed him. 'Hi,' I said quietly, walking towards the kitchen so as not to wake June.

'Hi.'

'How is she?'

'She's still sleeping. She didn't go to bed until late. I gave her some sleeping tablets.'

'Is that safe?'

'Yeah, they're fine she's had them before. She needed something.'

'Is there anything I can do?' *Like shoot my aunty*, I nearly said but thought better of it.

'Would you mind telling the staff in the salon that she's ill?'

'No worries. Of course, I can.' I hated setting foot in the place, but I couldn't let Clare down, feeling somewhat responsible for this mess. I quickly squinted at the clock. Eight-thirty: there'd be no-one on show for another half an hour.

'It's not the first time,' Max sighed.

'I gathered.' Remembering what June had said.

'He's had loads of affairs. But I do wish he'd chosen someone other than your aunty.'

'Me and you both.'

'The last time was meant to be the *last*. The salon was a gift.'

'A gift?'

'She'd threatened to leave him, but he promised to get counselling. He can't live without her.' I listened, as Max revealed a part of his family history that I'd never picked up on. As he spoke, I remembered their anniversary party, when a friend had shouted out, 'You're not wrong there,' when Henry had said Clare was the reason their marriage worked. 'When the salon opportunity came along, he'd encouraged her,' Max continued, 'In fact, it was actually his idea. He told her he would do anything to make her happy. He told her he would never cheat again. But he's said that every single time.'

'Do you think he's got problems?'

'Many?' Max laughed, surprising me. 'The problem is, I told Mum that if he did it again, I wanted nothing to do with it. She knows what he's like and I think she can do better on her own.'

'What will you do?' I was surprised Max had kept this from me, although I'd had many other things on my mind at the time Clare was taking over the salon. But she'd been vibrant, full of life, so excited about this new opportunity. Had it been a lie?

'I don't know.' Max sighed deeply into the handset. 'But I can't leave her to it.'

'Good,' I was relieved. 'Because she needs you.'

'I know.'

'Max …' Gina's voice boomed in the background.

'I'm on the phone,' he shouted briskly, away from the handset.

A silence followed. I wondered where she was. Was she listening? Did she know he was talking to me? Suddenly, I felt like the other woman. I didn't like it. 'I'll let you go,' I said quickly.

'No, it's fine. She's fine,' he sighed. 'Aarrghh, do you know? She's not fine,' he stated, obviously stressed. I didn't want to hear this. I didn't want to be caught in the middle of them. He was being unfair. My silence, I thought, would show him I wasn't interested, I wasn't pursuing this line of questioning. 'I had to tell her I was at yours last night.' He wasn't getting the hint. I hoped he'd phrased it better than he just had to me. 'She wanted to know why I would want to see my sleeping babies. She thinks it's about you.'

'Max, you shouldn't be telling me this.' I tried not to sound curt.

'But maybe she's right.'

'It's her, isn't it?' I could hear Gina's words thumping towards me as I quickly hung up the phone.

What the hell …?

Suddenly I felt a surge of anger towards him. Who the hell did he think he was? How dare he think it's okay to relieve such feelings? Such emotions? Anger washed through me as my phone vibrated again, Max's name flashing irritably. I ignored it as Libby emerged from her room. Her dark bob was hanging scruffily around her thin cheeks, her pyjamas were hanging off her. Her thinness was so much more apparent when she was constantly with me.

'What time is it?' she asked groggily. Opening the fridge, she squinted as the light illuminated her scrawny features.

'About eight-thirty.'

'Got any fresh orange?' she asked, yawning.

'Not unless it's in there.'

'There's fuck-all in here. You need to go shopping,' she said, as she closed the fridge door.

'S'cuse me if I haven't had time to make sure the fridge is packed for you bloody lot.'

She held her hands up. 'It was only an observation.' She walked into the living room, sitting down on the floor, leaning her back against the sofa. There was no room to sit on it, with June's body scrawled on one end, the rest covered with clothes, towels and an assortment of accessories that didn't belong.

As Libby played with the remote control, I suddenly couldn't wait for them to leave. Guilt then hit me as I realised it was Max who had riled me, but it was Libby who nearly got the blunt end of my tongue, questioning me about my fridge etiquette. She'd never bloody contributed to any of the food. In fact, she'd never contributed to anything financially. She merely drained those around her of their money. But I refused to bite at her. I knew I would only feel guilty once she'd left. I felt guilty enough about her leaving with June. Even as she switched the television on, inconsiderately disturbing June and making the girls jump, I fought with the mixed emotions that I knew she needed to go. It was mayhem while she was here. But why didn't that shift the guilt?

If she stayed with me in the flat she'd be like a shadow, or I'd be like hers. But I knew we couldn't go on this way. She needed one-to-one support, and I was struggling to support myself at the moment, let alone bring Libby into the mix. I also knew she would soon deviate, she'd soon find those old friends when my life became too boring and stale for her. I couldn't assist her every step. I wanted her to get better, make a life for herself. Not become the absent shell our father had become. Living with June could work. They could support each other. Maybe June needed support as much as Libby.

'What time is it?' June ruffled the covers, turning to face us, her usual pristine image tainted.

'Eight-thirty-ish,' Libby mumbled, the remote pointing at the television as she flicked through the channels.

'My head hurts,' June said, dramatically placing her hand across her forehead. 'Have you any headache tablets, Kat?'

'Yes.' I rummaged in the cupboard where all my medicines were kept. Most, except the paracetamols, were hardly ever used. Finding the blue and white packet, I pushed two tablets from the foil packet, poured her a glass of water and handed them to her. She thanked me sheepishly.

'I'm going to go and have a shower; can you keep an eye on the girls?' I'd tried to *tell* them rather than ask, but still I found myself practically begging.

'No probs,' Libby mumbled, glued to the television.

'Of course, pet.' June waved me away.

I was in the bathroom, the door shut before they had the chance to change their mind. I let the water flow around me, the drops prickling my skin as they cleansed my pores. I took the opportunity to wash my hair, delighting in the freshness, savouring the extra minutes I could have to myself rather than rushing back to the girls, or placing them on the bathroom floor next to me, singing to them, making them giggle as I tried quickly to wash.

As the hot water surrounded my body, I thought of Max. What had he meant? He couldn't do this to me. It was unfair. I wanted him so badly sometimes, but I couldn't go there. I couldn't allow myself to show him any weakness.

He was being unfair.

Maybe he couldn't handle pregnant women? He'd soon fled when my hormones were raging.

It wasn't me he wanted; it was the ideal world. This was what I told myself on those nights when I longed for him to be next to me. It wasn't Max, I longed for, though. It was the fantasy that many people dream about. The perfect family. The happiness that surrounded the actors and actresses on many of the adverts that were thrown at us. The smiling faces, the laughter … these people didn't have bills to pay, they didn't have to worry about nappy changes, routines, weaning. They didn't have schedules or deadlines to live by. That's what they made us believe, anyway.

There was no going back for me and Max. He'd burnt his bridges. It was unfair for him to think otherwise. Wasn't it?

He'd probably had a drink. Really? At eight-thirty in the morning? I doubt it. So where the hell was this coming from?

If he was seriously thinking about me and him, I'd have to put a stop to his presumptions before they got out of hand.

29

Marianne had asked if we could go for lunch before June and Libby left. She'd included June in the invitation, but June had declined: 'I've got lots to pack.' *That* I didn't doubt, I had no idea where her money came from, but June did like to shop. I had been getting a little worried we couldn't squeeze her wardrobe in, let alone her to go with it.

I too wanted to refuse the summons, a little worried that Derek's sullen attitude would upset Libby. Although I agreed with him, I didn't see the point in making the situation worse. What did he hope to achieve by being hostile to her? His nagging would not make her see sense. She needed evidence, she needed to see the effects of her behaviour. Not be talked at, righteously. Blamed.

'Please be on your best behaviour,' I told her as we pulled up outside Derek's house. She raised her eyebrows, shaking her head, as if I was silly for suggesting she wouldn't be. I observed the home that had quickly become Marianne's. Admittedly, I'd thought I'd feel sad when she left Dad's old house, but I hadn't. A new start was what Marianne needed. She'd moved out a few weeks after me. It had been a simple, quiet move. It took a few hours to move her suitcase and a few belongings. No fuss as she simply became part of Derek's home.

'Hello, hello …' Marianne had opened the door as Libby and I trundled down the garden path, both holding a car seat which in turn held an ever-growing baby. The baby bag across my shoulders, replaced any handbag I had before. I'd laugh at myself now about, how I used to match my handbag with my shoes, or outfit.

Yes, I missed that part of my life. But I'd get it back … someday … apparently.

'Hello, girls, it's lovely to see you all.' Derek was jovial as he took the seat from Libby, Poppy gurgling from inside it.

'And you,' I answered. Libby smiled politely. I leaned forward, kissing Marianne and then Derek on the cheek, hoping Libby would do the same; but she didn't.

'Come through.' Derek led the way as we followed him into the lounge. His house was full of old, traditional, warm colours: dark reds, deep greens, royal blues and creams, which contrasted seamlessly, filling the house with warmth. The patterned Axminster carpet led the way across the hallway and flowed up the staircase. It was a similar layout to Dad's house, except larger and immaculate. There was no ripped wallpaper hanging from walls, or rickety staircases with missing spindles. It was neat, uncluttered … refined.

Derek had laid the pink blankets out for the girls. Although I found him hard to connect with, I appreciated his efforts. Marianne unclipped Poppy from her seat as I released Rosie and we placed them both on the soft fleece.

'Would you like a drink?' Derek offered, looking at us both. I was dying to ask for a glass of wine but knew it was unfair to Libby, so we both agreed to a soft drink.

'How's Clare?' Marianne asked when Derek had left the room.

'I think she'll be okay. Apparently this isn't the first time.' I'd rung and explained to Marianne all that we'd found out in the last twenty-four hours about Henry and his promiscuous behaviour.

'Poor Clare.' Marianne shook her head.

We chatted generally for the next fifteen minutes while Derek busied himself in the kitchen. Libby joined in where she could; not overly, but she listened and participated, which I was pleased about. Marianne fed Poppy and I fed Rosie before dinner was served. I hoped they'd sleep while we ate. I had noticed Libby hadn't had much interaction with the girls. At the moment I put this down to her state of mind, but a part of me was saddened that she seemed to distance herself from them. But I'd thought it best not to push things. She had enough on her mind.

As I watched her, I'd hoped she'd be back soon. I hoped this trip would make her better, and not worse.

Derek was soon calling us to take a seat. The dining room had a dark oak table that seated six padded chairs. A buffet-style lunch greeted us.

I'd placed the girls back in their car seats. Poppy smiled and happily explored her surroundings. Rosie on the other hand had different ideas. Her cries started as soon as the straps encased her. As I carried her into the dining room, she stopped crying, but as soon as I put her down, her wails began to fill the room. I tried to rock her with my foot, but to no avail.

Derek tried to say grace as Rosie's unhappiness increased. I waited for him to finish before freeing her from the chair. As we tucked into the delectable spread Derek had surprised us with, I rocked Rosie quietly in my arms. She stared at my face as her eyes flickered, her tiny body needing to sleep as her active mind fought against it.

'Do you want me to try?' Marianne suggested, wiping away the crumbs from her mouth after eating a cheese cracker.

'I think she's nearly there,' I whispered. The silence between us seemed to be helping her fall asleep. Poppy was already sleeping. Marianne had gently rocked her car seat with her foot - not that she'd needed it.

'We'll stay quiet until she's sleeping,' Marianne smiled.

'Suits me,' Libby said quietly; in fact so quietly I was surprised that it seemed to resonate into the air and hang above us. I glared at her. She grimaced as if she hadn't really meant to say it aloud.

'That's the problem with you, isn't it?' Derek suddenly bellowed across the table. Rosie flinched, her little lip quivered. 'It's whatever suits *you.*'

'Derek!' Marianne sat straight.

'No.' He shook his head. Rosie began to cry loudly. 'I won't be quiet. It's about time there were some home truths around here.' Libby paled as he glared at her. Rosie's howls filling the air, I felt myself becoming hot as I tried to rock her harder. But this made her worse. 'Do you know how much money we've spent on you?' Derek demanded.

'I never asked you to,' Libby said defensively.

'No, you didn't. But we offered and you accepted.' Derek was now pointing at her. 'You have thrown it all back in our face. You sit there with this high-and-mighty air, as if the world owes you something. Well, young lady, it doesn't.'

'Derek—' Marianne was now pleading.

'Suits you to sit quiet, does it? After everything everyone has done for you? You should—'

'Derek, stop!' Marianne raised her voice. Rosie's yells were reaching the ceiling, as I stood to rock her. 'I won't have this. I won't have you speaking to her this way.'

'She needs to know—'

'No. No, she doesn't.' Marianne's eyes filled, her lips trembling as she pushed herself from the table. 'I can't take this from you anymore.' She manoeuvred past me, holding my elbows, to avoid sending me flying.

'Marianne,' I urged.

'I need to be alone,' she said, fleeing the room.

'See, what you've done,' Derek accused, glaring at Libby.

'I want to go.' Libby stood up, pushing her chair forcefully back.

'Yes, you run away. That's the answer to everything, isn't it?'

'You're being unfair, Derek,' I found myself saying above Rosie's screams.

'No I'm not,' Derek said, his hands coming together as if he was praying. 'The problem we have here is that everyone pussy-foots around her. She needs to know the truth. She needs to know how much she's hurting everyone. How much everyone has tried to help her and how she has pushed it back in their face.'

'Please take me home, Kat,' Libby said quietly. To my surprise she picked up Poppy's car seat, and walked out of the room. I quickly placed Rosie into her seat, her shrieks hurting my ears, as I tried to lock the catch, my hands shaking. I wanted to cry.

'I'm sorry about all the food,' I said to Derek, as I lifted a bawling Rosie in her car seat. Derek waved his hand at me, as if dismissing me from the room. 'Sorry,' I said again, before walking into the hallway.

'I even did salmon …' I heard him mumbling to himself.

The front door was open, awaiting my exit. Libby was standing by the car, Marianne was putting an arm around her. 'I'm sorry, Kat,' Marianne said to me as I walked towards them.

I unlocked the car door. 'Are you okay?' I asked her.

'I'm fine.' She shook her head, the tears brimming. 'I told him to make this special; I didn't know when I'd see you again,' she said to Libby.

'I'm sorry I can't make things better,' Libby said quietly. I secured both the girls into the back. Rosie's cries ceasing as she gazed out of the window.

As I silently hugged Marianne, she let the tears fall.

'I'm sorry,' Libby whispered, and before stepping into the passenger seat she blew Marianne a kiss. Marianne smiled, clenching her fist to her chest.

'Are you okay?' I asked her again, knowing that she wasn't.

'I can't take this from him anymore.'

The perfect relationship I thought she had with Derek was flawed. I'd not worried about Marianne; I'd thought she was living a happier life, comparing her life to the one she'd had with Dad. Before Dad. But did that mean that anything better would make her happy? Not necessarily.

'He's understandably upset,' I told her. I didn't want her blaming Derek. Although I thought he had been very harsh, I understood he was at the end of his tether with it all. Libby wasn't his daughter and he'd probably done more for her than most people had. He'd cared. He'd wanted Libby to get help and he felt she was throwing it back in his face. He was bound to be upset. *I* was upset, and she was my flesh and blood.

'Sometimes he won't listen,' Marianne sniffled.

'But he cares for you. It's you he's thinking about; that's where the anger comes from.'

'But still, he should keep it to himself.' Marianne wiped her eyes, as I rubbed her arm. 'I told him before you arrived; no matter what's happened, I begged for him to be nice. Let it go over his head. It could be our last dinner together for many months.' Months? I was thinking weeks! 'He's let me down.'

'But he didn't do it out of malice.' I knew where Derek was coming from although I didn't agree with his outburst. I knew he had so much pent-up frustration. What surprised me more than anything was his lack of forgiveness, especially for a man who lived by God's rules. 'Look, I'll call you later. You go in there, make peace with him. You don't need to be falling out over this.'

'Thank you, Kat.'

'Don't thank me.'

'I do. Thank you for not judging him.' She kissed my cheek.

I bit my lip as I fought the urge to say, Oh, I'm judging. But I wanted quiet. I wanted everyone to be calm. We'd been through so much turmoil I wanted it to stop. I needed peace. My head was too busy for any more troubles.

We left Marianne on the side of the road, waving us slowly away. Libby stared out of the window. I waited for a sarcastic comment. A clever innuendo. As she lifted her hand to her cheek, wiping away the tears that were escaping, I realised she had none to give. I placed my hand on her leg. Without looking at me she laid her thin long fingers on top of mine.

'I'm sorry,' she said quietly.

'It's going to be okay,' I said, focusing on the road ahead. Focusing on the journey ahead. Our journey. The journey that would hopefully get us to the destination we all wanted to arrive at.

Hopefully, some good would come out of Derek's outburst. But it probably wasn't his words that would bring Libby to her senses: it was Marianne's sorrow.

Because that sorrow was proof that she was harming not only herself, but all of us around her.

30

'Call me when you arrive,' I said, as June put the suitcases into the back of her car.

She slammed the boot and walked towards me, her arms stretched out. 'I'm sorry, Kat,' she said, as we hugged. 'I came here to help and I've made a mess of things.'

'Things will sort themselves,' I said smiling, fighting back the urge to tell her, yes, you're right … one huge mess … but don't worry, I'll pick up the pieces.

Libby hugged me, pulling me close to her delicate frame. 'I'm sorry too.'

'Oh, let's stop with all the apologising,' I laughed, trying to make light of this upsetting situation. I was gutted that Libby was leaving us, peed off that they had to rush off so soon because of June's insensitivity to others. I wanted to squeeze Libby but I was frightened I would break every bone in her body. 'Please do me one big favour.'

'Anything,' June said eagerly.

'Look after each other,' I smiled, my throat swelling, tears stinging.

'We will,' June said, hugging me again. Libby nodded gravely.

'You best go, it'll be midnight by the time you get there.' I forced back the tears.

Libby pulled me close again. 'I'll miss you,' she whispered gently into my ear.

'I'll miss you too. Hopefully it won't be long before you want to come back,' I said softly.

'I promise I'll get better,' she said, wiping away a stray tear. 'Then I'll be here for you.'

I smiled at my sister who suddenly seemed to understand, suddenly seemed to get it. I just hoped she could keep her promise.

They got into the car. The sound of the engine roared into the brisk air, loud in the quiet village. Backing onto the main road, they reversed away from me. I walked slowly towards them, telling myself to stand still. Don't chase them. Let them go. They need to go.

The horn echoed into the cloudy afternoon skies, as they drove away from me. Onto another journey; another path.

I knew this was the right thing to do. For Libby. For June. For me.

I had little strength as it was. I had to fight my way through each day. Now I could concentrate on turning my world back around. Aiming forward instead of feeling as if I was taking two steps back. There were two little people who needed me more than my sister and my aunty.

It was time for *us*. It was time for *me*. But I wished I could take away the pounding misery that stabbed at me. No matter how many times I told myself this was for the best, it was the guilt that I'd let her go that throbbed. Striking me constantly. Twisting around every part of my body. Although I told myself I couldn't have stopped Libby leaving, I wondered if I'd tried hard enough.

As I went back into the flat, where the girls were sleeping soundly in their cot, I told myself again: I was no good to Libby at the moment. I couldn't help her. I had to start accepting this.

31

There was no getting out of it. Brooke had hounded me all week. Mrs D also had my number, texting a few times to ensure I was still on for Friday night. Clare, even in the midst of her heartache, told me she really wanted to babysit. 'It will take my mind off things,' she practically begged. Alcohol helps too, I'd wanted to say. Which was kind-of bad when I'd sent my sister off to other lands for that reason.

So, for no other purpose but to please everyone else, I was now sitting on Brooke's huge, elaborate sofa. Her very expensive-looking sofa; the cream and gold swirls elegantly embroidered into the thick plush cushions, gold tassels hanging from the armrests and gold-plated legs shining beneath as if holding up a masterpiece. I felt uncomfortable sitting on such finery, and couldn't help but imagine how the fine fabric would look in a few years. Tassels ripped to shreds by tiny fingers as Chelsea swung like Tarzan. The clean, cream material grubby, the gold feet peeling from being endlessly bashed with toys. Still, this didn't make me feel any better as I scrutinised the immaculate room. Cream carpets, glass ornaments and burning candles. There was no sign of babies in this house. Maybe Chelsea wasn't allowed in this room.

'Ange should be with us soon,' Brooke said, handing me a glass of chilled wine. Taking the crystal glass, I hoped I didn't drop it. She placed a gold coaster on the glass table in front of me. There was a knock on the front door. 'Sounds like she's here.'

I could hear their voices mumbling in the hallway as I quickly drank a huge gulp of wine. It chilled my chest. I wanted more.

Forget about the girls waking in the night, I needed to get through this evening.

'Hi, Kathryn, I'm so pleased you could make it.' Mrs D walked towards me, arms outstretched. I stood up, because it would have been rude not to. She pulled me close, kissing each cheek. 'Oh, thank you, Brooke,' she said taking the filled crystal glass from Brooke's hand, 'Where's Daryl?'

'He's in the bedroom, he'll be through in a bit,' Brooke said, sitting on one of the one-seater chairs that could have fitted two people. I thought this was meant to be a girlie night. I drank more wine, trying to relax. Blend in. Bit difficult when they both looked as if they were going for a night out: make-up perfect, hair styled, not a strand out of place and both wearing sequins. Sequins! Not that there was anything wrong with sequins, but this was a night in. Brooke may have dressed in a more casual style, with black slacks and a loose black top, but still, it had sequins across the neckline. Mrs D had an array of sequins across her short red skirt, her low-cut black top and even on her tights. Both were wearing red lipstick, which marked the rim of the embellished glass. I felt frumpy to say the least, in my comfortable jeans, black baggy jumper and no lipstick. Not even gloss. And I'd worn flats. I'd left them at the front door, discovering I had a hole in my sock. Odd socks: one was black, and the other had faded, and not that I noticed earlier but the faded one had a small pattern on the toes, I might as well have dressed in the dark. I decided it was best to drink more wine.

The next few hours passed slowly, each minute feeling like an hour. Daryl had joined us, sitting on the sofa next to me. I wasn't sure if it was the alcohol that was quickly working its way through my brain cells or if he was staring at me provocatively, with a lick of his lips or a little wink. At one point he told a funny story (or, he thought it was funny, me not so) and his hand progressed over the sofa and landed on my thigh. No-one else took any notice. Brooke didn't even bat an eyelid. So I thought it was probably me. Maybe he was a very friendly guy.

As the conversation moved from shopping in Paris and New York to how shopping on the internet was so much more easier for Brooke now she had Chelsea, I didn't contribute much; I couldn't remember the last time I'd actually enjoyed shopping. And I couldn't remember the last time I'd shopped for *me*. And I'd never shopped in Paris or New York. They could have been speaking in a foreign language as they reeled off names I'd never heard of. And little did I care. I tried hard to keep my eyes open.

It was around the fifth glass of wine, I think – it all became a blur after the second (they were large glasses and I'd not had this much in a while) – that Mrs D suddenly burst into tears. 'He's at it again,' she announced dramatically.

'Oh Ange, you know he's not going to change,' Brooke said, getting out of her seat and walking towards her sister-in-law.

'He's promised, though.' She sobbed into her glass, drinking and crying at the same time. 'Another IVF treatment failed.'

'I wondered why you were drinking.' Brooke was kneeling next to her. I was silent. I didn't know what to say.

'I give up,' Mrs D sobbed. 'He's shagging some slut from work. She works in the offices. Of course she bloody does, that's why she got the job there in the first fucking place, so she could steal my husband.'

'I'm sure that's not the case,' I said gently, thinking I was helping; but when they both glared at me, I decided staying quiet was the best option.

'Three treatments have failed now.'

'Do you know what's wrong?' I asked before I could stop myself. You should already know by now about my problem; I was waiting for the op to get my mouth sewn up.

'I can't have babies ...' Mrs D shook her head at me as if I was stupid. My silence obviously made her feel guilty as she said a little more gently, 'We don't know why. It doesn't seem either of us has a problem; it's just one of those things. We're not compatible, or something ...' She gulped down the last of her wine. Brooke automatically filled it from the bottle that sat in a wine chiller in the middle of the table. She then leaned forward to top mine up, and I couldn't have been more grateful.

'It will happen,' Brooke told her adamantly, as if she could see into the future.

I couldn't understand why they were having this conversation, why she wanted a baby with a man who was constantly cheating on her. I fought back the urge to say this, although the alcohol begged me to. My lax mind was swimming as I really thought this was a debate worth having, and I found myself saying, 'You should leave him.'

Mrs D gaped solemnly at her glass, as Brooke glared at me and curtly said, 'No. They're having a few problems. Nothing that can't be worked out.'

'No, a leopard never changes its pots ...' I mumbled, hiccupped and laughed. 'Spots.' It seemed the last glass of wine had not only mashed up my thoughts, but had stopped the connection between brain and mouth.

'She's right, Brooke,' Mrs D started to sob into her glass, 'He'll never change. All I want is his babies.'

'Why do you want his babies?' I was in full flow.

'So she can keep his money,' Daryl said, winking at me again.

'Ooohhh ... I see ... makes sense.' I leaned back on the sofa, the one that I'd felt so uneasy sitting on originally. Now I wrapped myself in its softness, I'd even managed to secure my legs underneath me. Really made myself at home.

'It's not that Daryl,' Brooke barked at him.

'I love him,' Mrs D wailed dramatically.

'How can you?' I was perplexed and I couldn't keep my drunken confusion to myself. 'He obviously doesn't love you ...' Brooke glared at me. 'I mean, in the way that he should.'

'You said he loves me in his own way.' Mrs D looked at me. Did I? 'In the salon that day, when I found out Stevie was cheating with your friend.'

'My friend?' I shook my head, feeling suddenly hot. 'No, *your* friend ... Diane or something ...'

'It was your friend too.'

'I don't know Diane, or whatever she's—'

'No, not Diane. *Your* friend,' Mrs D said blankly.

'I don't know what you're talking about.' My cheeks were starting to burn, sweat forming at the back of my neck, as I flipped my legs round in front of me, suddenly wishing I hadn't drunk so much.

'That girl you were with, in the restaurant … Sarah … Simone … Sharon … S- something or other.'

'Suzy.' I blurted.

'That's her.'

'I think it's best I leave.' I needed to be out. Away from her. If not, I might have thrown up all over Brooke's immaculate floors.

'I'm not blaming you,' Mrs D said, looking at me as I lifted myself from the sofa.

'But I don't know what you're talking about,' I said again, hoping the more I said it, the more she would believe me.

'Come on, Kat, he told me all about it. I know it was her that wrote the letter about the baby.'

'You do? I don't know what you mean,' I said quickly, my legs beginning to shake.

'It was obviously a lie because there is no baby … is there?'

'She had a miscarriage,' I snapped, cursing myself: I'd inadvertently admitted it had been Suzy. My head was spinning, lies were truths, truths were lies … I wasn't really sure what was real. Although I felt as if I was sobering up pretty quickly, I still felt wobbly. 'She didn't know who he was,' I said, sounding stronger than I felt, but feeling an injustice towards Suzy that needed to be rectified.

'I know.' She sipped her wine, mascara leaving track marks down her cheeks. 'Michael …'

'Yes,' I said quietly, as I sat back down on the sofa. 'I'm sorry.'

'It's not your fault,' she shrugged. 'It's not your friend's either.'

'She didn't mean to send the letter.'

'I'd have done worse,' she smiled. The vulnerable woman who'd broken her heart in my treatment room was back. Her image was stripped back, once again. I felt so sorry for her.

'Why didn't you say anything?'

'I didn't know at the time.' She shook her head. 'It was a few weeks later, when I found out about another string of girls. It came out in an argument.'

'Maybe he needs counselling,' Brooke suggested.

'What, cos he can't keep his dick in his pants?' Mrs D laughed. 'It happens, doesn't it?'

'Women throw themselves at him and he can't say no.'

'Suzy didn't throw herself at him.' I found myself defending my best friend.

'I'm not saying she did … but …'

'Suzy doesn't need to throw herself at men.' I sounded like a petulant child, but I wasn't having her throwing accusations, sticking up for her dishonest husband.

A silence filled the room. A stillness. I felt uncomfortable and had the sudden urge to leave. Now. My chest seemed to tighten around my heart, anxiety rising. I needed to be out of here. 'I'm going to go. I'm not feeling too good.'

'I haven't upset you, have I?' Mrs D seemed full of remorse. I pitied her. Why was she bothered about my feelings when she had so much more going on?

'No, I'm fine. Too much wine.' I tried to laugh, but it fell flat. The conversation had hit a serious peak; there was no room for hilarity.

'Let Daryl walk you home,' Brooke suggested.

'I'll be fine.'

'Please, I insist. I know we live in a quiet village, but you never know who is lurking,' Daryl said, as he rose from the sofa.

You're lurking, matey. I wanted to say to him. Winking, touching and licking those lips. I'd be lucky if I made it home safe with him as my bodyguard; it was him I needed protecting from.

Quickly I thanked both Brooke and Mrs D for inviting me.

'We must do it again, very soon,' Brooke said.

I nodded, not letting myself speak, worried I'd say, *No, please let's not!*

As we went out into the chilly air, I felt embarrassed I'd left in such a rush, but I couldn't sit there any longer. What I didn't understand was why Mrs D was doing it to herself, humiliating herself. Was it really about the money?

As if reading my thoughts, Daryl said, 'It's all about the money.'

'Really, you think so?' I didn't really want to engage in conversation with him, finding his sliminess insufferable; but it would have been rude to ignore him.

'Yes, of course it is. If she leaves him now she has nothing.'

'I'm sure she'll get quite a bit from him. She's entitled to half of everything, surely.'

'But that will soon run out. A child will mean he supports her for many, many years into the future.'

'No, she's not that shallow.'

'It's not about being shallow. It's about survival.'

'I'm sure she could survive on half of what he's worth for many years,' I said. 'She could get a job.'

'Like that's going to happen,' he laughed.

I didn't answer. I suddenly wished I'd not been so catty about her, especially not to Daryl. As we walked along the path, the street lights beaming, paving our way. The only sound was the swiftly flowing river and the rustling of the leaves. The noise of the river echoed into the dark skies, swirling around rocks, bashing against the roots of the trees as it surged along. The leaves battled against each other, whispering and hissing as we made our way through the old country village.

The stars twinkled, covering the sky like sparkling jewels scattered across a blanket. The moon, which wasn't quite full, seemed to smile down on us. It was a perfect night to wrap up warm, choose the brightest star and make a special wish. I maybe would have done just that, had I not been with Daryl.

Maybe I was being unfair. I'd probably got him completely wrong. He might have a twitch, he wasn't winking, poor guy. He probably had trouble with his eyesight. The licking-of-the-lips thing could have been the crisps, excess salt around his mouth, stuck on his unshaven skin. The touching: he was merely being friendly, making me feel welcome in his home.

We reached the door to the flat, I fumbled for the key inside my bag, 'Brooke really likes you.'

'She's lovely too,' I said distractedly. Found it. I grabbed hold of the plastic key-ring that held a picture of Poppy and Rosie. Fumbling to unlock the door, I'd either not sobered up enough, or someone had moved the keyhole.

'Let me help you,' Daryl breathed into my ear, taking the key as he smoothly ran his hand over mine.

'I've got it.' It dropped to the floor. 'Oh, shit.'

We both leaned down, his hands brushing against mine as he reached the key before I did. He tried to meet my eye, but I stood up. This was awkward. What was he doing? He put the key in the lock, turning it for me, before stopping and looking at me. I stepped back, his closeness intimidating.

'You know, you should come round again.'

'Yes, will do,' I laughed, sounding half-hysterical: I was desperate to be away from him. Really wanting to be inside my flat, alone.

'Good, we'd like that.' He winked again. Then he opened the door for me. I held out my hand flat, in the hope that he would drop the key straight into my palm, none of this creepiness. But no, he still managed to place his hand on top of mine. I pulled it away.

'Thanks for getting me home.'

'Anytime.' Another wink. That was no twitch. As I turned to step through the door, he touched my backside. It was a moment, a quick brush with the palm of his hand, but he definitely touched my arse. I practically jumped through the door, shivering with revulsion.

'Bye,' I said quickly. Closing him out.

Oh my God, did that just happen? I couldn't have drunk so much I was imagining these things.

I made my way up the stairs. I thought I was being quiet, but I kept bouncing off the wall. Clare appeared at the top of the stairs, opening the door for me, her finger to her lips. 'Ssshhh!' she said.

'Sorry,' I mumbled, reaching the top and making my way to my bedroom.

I quickly checked my sleeping girls, kissed my hand and pressed it against their foreheads, hoping my toxic fumes didn't harm them. I kicked off my shoes, then made my way back into the lounge. Clare was boiling the kettle in the kitchen, as I flopped on the sofa.

'You're home early,' she said, as my eyes started to close.

'Am I?'

'It's only ten-thirty.'

'Is it?' I was surprised. I'd not checked, but I'd thought it was nearer midnight. It felt as if it should be way after. The evening had dragged, but this was good, as it meant I could squeeze a few more hours' sleep in.

'Did you have a good night?'

'They're not real.'

'What do you mean?' Clare asked, sitting down on the other end of the sofa, oblivious (or being polite) to my intoxication.

'You know, they are like rubber people.' Was I slurring?

'Rubber people …' She smiled.

'Yeah, like, all plastic on the outside. They have these smiles plastered on their faces, but inside they're all wobbly.'

'Are we not all like that?' Clare asked quietly. Probably the wrong time to have this conversation, as I felt far too tired (and drunk) to analyse feelings. 'I know I am,' Clare added, obviously wanting to have this conversation. Now.

I tried to sit up, focus on her as she poured boiling water into two cups. 'I am too,' I managed. My mouth dry, I licked my lips.

'I've gone back to Henry.'

'Really?' I said, although I knew she would. I tried to resist the urge to tell her, 'You're just like Mrs D,' hoping my mouth wouldn't run away on its own; it had done enough of that already tonight.

'I've said I'll give it one last try.' She handed me a cup of steaming coffee, the smell turning my stomach. I took the cup, not wanting to be impolite. 'It's been many torturous years, but I think things will come together.'

'What has changed?'

'I stayed at Max's for a night. I think that frightened him.'

I bit my lip, resisting the urge to tell her she was mad.

'I've never left him before,' she said. I tried so hard to listen. My eyes were fighting to close. I really wanted to sleep. 'I think it shocked him.'

'You'd be fine on your own, you know.'

'I'm not as young as you, Kat. I can't start again.'

'It's not about age …' I struggled to find the best words, tell her she was worth so much more. My sloshed brain wasn't computing. We fell silent and I forced my eyes to stay open.

'I'm pleased June has gone,' she said suddenly.

'Of course.' A nervous laugh slipped out: but I was taken aback that she would want to talk to me about her.

'I think it will do Libby good to be away from here,' she said. I'd never spoken to her about Libby, so didn't really want to venture into unknown territory. Not without a sober mind, anyway. 'I know about everything …'

'You do?' Not really sure what she knew, really wishing I'd *not* downed that last glass of wine, or two.

'About the money.'

'Oh …' Now I was wishing I'd downed two *more* glasses of wine, then I would be too far gone to have this discussion.

'So you knew Libby had stolen from me?' she asked me softly. I could feel myself tense as I wondered if this was a trick question; but then I felt my head dozing, as if it didn't belong to me. The strategic part of my brain that might have helped me out of this situation wasn't working. 'I knew money had gone missing, at first I thought it was one of my salon girls. In fact, I quite rudely interrogated them.'

'But how do you know it *was* Libby?'

'Well, not only have you practically admitted it, I wasn't completely sure until Max told me about her rehabilitation. Plus there was that hooded man I saw her talking to, I put two and two together.'

I wanted to argue that it wasn't Libby, but had I practically admitted it was her? I suppose my long 'Oh …' didn't help. And I knew Max would tell her. I should have lied to him. It wasn't as if he hadn't lied to me enough. God Damn him.

I got up from the sofa, taking my coffee with me. I needed some water. My throat felt as if it would close up, while my tongue seemed to stick to the roof of my mouth. 'I'm sorry, I'll pay you back.' Giving up on the idea of trying to prove Libby's innocence.

'No, I don't expect you to.' I poured myself a glass of water, really hoping the cold chill would help to revive my exhausted soul. 'But I want you to know I'm here. I know it's been hard for you, and I don't think Libby and June helped.' She paused. I didn't say anything. 'You've got to take care of yourself.'

As if on cue one of the girls stirred. I begged silently for an escalation of tears: not my usual prayer for silence. It was Rosie: I could tell by the sudden burst of emotion. I thanked her silently for getting me out of this conversation.

'I'll check her,' Clare said, rising quickly from the sofa.

I let her, as I sat back down, the water helping to refresh my dehydrated body. A sigh escaped me, as I let the cushions envelop me. I was enjoying the serene feeling that I was floating. It wasn't so much my body that was enjoying each muscle slowly becoming untangled, but my mind was unravelling, and it felt like bliss. There was no tension, no jumbled thoughts, no worries, no cares. I felt peaceful as I stretched out across the cushions. Soon I fell into a deep sleep.

32

I could hear the sounds in the distance, people mumbling, things being moved. Chatter. Gurgles. I tried to turn away from the noise. My head didn't just hurt, it was caving in. Pressure was squeezing the soft tissues, every bone ached and my neck throbbed. The noises became closer.

I was slavering, a long line dribbling down the side of my mouth. I quickly wiped it away, as I opened my eyes to find Max and Clare talking quietly to one another while placing nappies into the baby bag.

'Morning,' Clare chirped as I regained a seated position. I pushed my hair down, running my hands over my face as if this would magically make me look wonderful.

'Hi …' I croaked. 'What's happening?'

'It's Saturday.'

'Did I fall asleep?' I peered around the flat, but tried so hard to look composed. 'Did you stay?' Clare was still dressed in the same attire she had on yesterday.

'I thought it best. You didn't seem in any fit state to look after the girls.'

My back stiffened. 'I only had a few.'

How dare she? In front of Max, too.

'I know, but you're exhausted,' she said gently. 'I thought it would do you good to sleep through rather than be woken up.'

'If they *could* have woken you,' Max added sarcastically, his tone completely different to the other night on the phone.

'I was fine,' I snapped. 'Jesus, do I have to become teetotal now I'm a parent?'

They both fell silent. I guessed the answer was, yes.

'I didn't drink when Max was younger,' Clare said. I didn't speak, feeling my insides stir, roll from side to side. Blood boiled through me; I wanted to explode, and throw up. Clare busied herself with creased vests and babygros. She must have grabbed a handful from the huge ironing pile that was currently squashed into the corner of my bedroom. 'Do you have any that are ironed?' she asked.

'No.' I felt about two inches tall, as I watched them organise the girls' belongings, Clare's obvious disapproval seeping towards me. I wanted to scream. I lifted myself from the sofa. My head swayed and my body felt weak, but I fought through the urge to flop back down again. They would not see me crash.

'I'll iron them.' I held my hand out. She handed me the crumpled baby outfits. Either ignoring my annoyance or acting totally oblivious to it, she walked back into my bedroom. I didn't ask why, or what she was looking for, because I had no energy. I was trying to keep my cool.

Poppy and Rosie were lying on the play mat. I quickly bent down and kissed them on their foreheads. They both gave me a huge, warm smile, their tiny faces alight at seeing mine. I could feel Max watching me as I straightened up. All I wanted was to lie on the floor, cuddle up next to them, and go back to sleep; but I fought off the heaviness, the feeling that I was carrying a big strapping load on my back. I walked into the kitchen, avoiding eye contact with Max. I took out the iron from underneath the sink and a towel that I kept in a crowded drawer, and set up my makeshift ironing board on the kitchen worktop.

'Oh, Kathryn, we really do need to get you organised,' Clare said coming back out of my bedroom with a handful of baby clothes.

'I'm fine.' I tried not to grit my teeth so hard.

'Look at all this! You'd think June would have helped,' Clare added, mumbling to herself. I could feel Max staring at me, but I refused to look at him. I needed them to leave.

The clothes were ironed. The bottles were ready and the bag was full of the girls' belongings. I'd decided against them feeding

Rosie baby rice. She'd only tried it a few times, and although she'd thoroughly enjoyed it I didn't want any disasters. The girls were strapped into the car seats. Max carried Rosie and I carried Poppy outside. The breeze chilled us, as we walked towards his car. Gina was sitting upright, her face composed, her eyes meeting mine. She never usually came with him.

'Look Max, I wasn't that drunk last night,' I mumbled, before we reached the car. I could remember everything and I hadn't been sick, so I couldn't have been that bad. Could I?

'You don't need to explain to me,' Max smiled. I wondered what Clare had told him.

'I know, but she makes me feel as if I'm the worse mother ever,' I confessed.

'We both know that's not true.' We were at the side of the car, where Gina couldn't see us. He stared tensely at me.

'You better be off.' I broke his gaze. I didn't want to play his games. I only wanted him to know I hadn't been that drunk. I didn't want him thinking I was a drunken mother or discussing my flaws with Gina, although it was probably too late for that.

I kissed Rosie's soft cheeks before he opened the car door and locked her into place. I could hear Gina mumbling something but I didn't catch it. Whatever it was, Max ignored her. I handed him Poppy, then bent to kiss her chubby delectable skin. She gave me her biggest smile. I grinned. 'See you soon, sweetheart.'

'Back around four or five,' he confirmed as I started to walk away.

'Great, see you then.' I gave a little wave and turned away, not wanting to meet Gina's eye. I could feel her gaze burning into my back. It took all my willpower not to go back over to her. Who the hell did she think she was? As if I was the other woman. I wished I'd never got mixed up in their bloody love life. If I'd had any inkling that something would happen between them, I'd have never started with Max. But if we all went around worrying about exes, bloody hell, none of us would ever have a relationship.

No-one would ever move on. I didn't want Gina to see me as a threat. Because I certainly didn't feel like one.

I didn't want to be Max's other woman. I'd wanted to be his *only* woman.

Back in the flat I found that Clare had tidied around. She was putting away things that didn't need putting away. Moving bits that didn't need moving. 'Shouldn't you be going downstairs?' I asked.

'I thought I'd give you a head start on tidying up.'

'I think I need a shower and change first.'

'You go and freshen up, and I'll make the place more liveable.' I could have screamed. I lived in a two-bed flat with two small babies; there was no space to make things liveable. We simply worked with what we had. Considering June and Libby had now gone, I had a lot more space, but she could surely let me do it in my own time. In my own way.

'Great.' I heard myself agreeing. I didn't see the point in arguing. I was fully aware though of the need to find somewhere else to live.

Sooner rather than later.

Or I would definitely end up in St John's.

33

It was here. The day I'd been dreading. I'd toyed with the idea of cancelling it. I'd spoken to Suzy, who was the only one I'd confessed to. She'd told me to try it: 'If you don't like it, if you feel it doesn't help, then you don't have to go back.'

I wish I could tell you what scared me most. It could have been revealing all my personal thoughts. Reliving my past. Talking to a stranger about my most in-depth feelings, when I was generally a private person. Even when I was running the salon, the secrets I heard, the tales that were told, none of them were mine. I'd listened. Now, I was putting myself in place of one of my customers except I wouldn't be pampered at the same time. I'd be judged and analysed.

Was I ready to take such a huge step?

But it was a bit late to analyse that now. I was sitting opposite the woman, who'd introduced herself as Rhonda. I guessed she was a few years older than me. She was dressed in tight, stonewashed jeans, knee-length boots and a light-blue cashmere jumper. Her casual attire, I supposed, was to make me feel comfortable. I'd half-expected to lay down on a chaise longue, someone scribbling notes behind me.

There were three chairs; did it matter which one I chose? Would she judge me because I sat on the red chair rather than the blue? Wasn't it a psychologist's job to worry about things like that? This poor woman had probably placed the chairs where they would fit in the room, and the uncoordinated colours were more likely to do with the lack of budget rather than deeper insight into a patient's psyche.

I could feel my hands shaking, my heart beating loudly against my chest, pulsating throughout my body.

'Dr Knowles has referred you,' she said. Was it question? I smiled, nodding politely. 'I see you've recently had two baby girls.' Was that a question too?

I wondered if nodding could get me through this. She asked a few questions about Poppy and Rosie, nothing too probing, general things such as their sleep patterns, feeding, temperaments etc. Also, how I must be finding it hard with two babies. The usual chit-chat – or *was* it chit-chat? Was she noting everything I said?

As we comfortably settled into an informal conversation, I realised I had to stop trying to work out when I thought she was analysing me. If I didn't open up, instead of worrying what she thought of me, there was no point in me being here.

'Do you feel the medication has helped?' she asked

'Not at first, but over the last few days I've started to feel a lot calmer. Not as irritated.'

We were soon falling into an in-depth conversation about my irritability. As I talked, and she probed, I found myself opening up the past few months of my life. How tired and exhausted I'd felt since the girls arrived. How Max seemed to pick and choose when he came and went. How people kept barging into my home. How I felt I had no space to think. No place to rest.

I told her the details of mine and Max's relationship, the quickness of the pregnancy, the speed with which he soon moved back to Gina. She asked me small questions, such as, 'What would you like from Max now?' Questions I'd not asked myself. I wanted nothing from Max, except that he be a good father. We talked about the dynamics of our relationship. She simply bobbed her head in agreement, or stopped me when she thought I needed to think clearly.

I aired thoughts about Rosie's milk allergy and reflux; was I to blame for this? She asked me how I could be.

'Could I have done something different? Did something about my pregnancy affect her?' I stressed.

'But surely it would have affected Poppy too?' she said, and then she continued to make me feel better by telling me that I'd helped her since she was born. I'd done everything I could when I knew she had a problem. No-one could ask more than that.

I was so comfortable with all this information flowing from me – as if a button had been switched on, a barrier had been let down – that I even touched on my thoughts about Libby. How I felt so guilty that I'd let her down.

Rhonda listened carefully, and then finally asked me, 'Does she blame you?'

'She's never said so,' I told her. 'She's never directly pointed her finger my way. But how could she not blame me? I'd felt it when we visited her at Pondergate Park. The way Ronnie had looked at me, I could read it in her eyes. She thought I was to blame too.' I let out feelings I'd not told anyone.

Rhonda smiled. 'I doubt that Ronnie blamed you. Have you considered that *you* blamed you, and you were looking for confirmation elsewhere?'

I didn't say anything. I'd never really seen it that way. Maybe Ronnie had looked at me with sadness. Had she wanted to help us all? Rhonda checked her watch and pushed the files together. 'It seems our session has to end for today,' she said softly. I wondered if this was a trained voice, an actress, or whether she genuinely was this nice. 'How do you feel?'

'Fine.'

'I think we've progressed quite quickly.' She started to write on a piece of paper. 'Next week, same time?'

'Mmm ... yes ... if it's a problem, can I call to change it?' I was wondering whether I'd be able to get babysitting sorted.

'Yes, of course.'

I walked away from the building, feeling a little lighter. My shoulders seemed to have relaxed. I felt as if I was floating. It was a calmness, a tranquil state that I could soon get used to.

What had surprised me most about the whole hour was that there was no judging. Not once did Rhonda point her finger at me. She didn't blame me and I never got the feeling she was trying to over-analyse me. There was no look in her eyes, no deeper meaning, there were no hidden messages.

Marianne had come to the flat to look after the girls. As I walked back to my car, which was only five minutes away, it felt strange not to be pushing a pram: not having the babies to make small-talk with. I wasn't even aware I did it until they weren't there. I'd talk to them about our stroll. 'Listen to the birds, girls,' or, 'Ooohhh, it's a bit nippy today.' Until I'd gone out without them, I hadn't realised how much I relied on them to keep me company.

As I crossed the car park, avoiding holes in the bumpy tarmac, kicking small stones underneath my shoes, I breathed in the fresh air, enjoying the rustle of the trees and the birds singing. I felt as if a tiny element of peace had been instilled.

This could work.

I had no-one else to air my thoughts to, no-one else who wanted to listen to me rant to them for five minutes, let alone an hour. I had Suzy, of course, but I doubt she really wanted to listen to me drone on: she did it because that's what friends do. She wanted my life to turn around, she wanted me to be happy. All she heard at the moment was my guilt, my torment and my misery.

But, as I got into my car and drove home to my family, I knew we were going to be fine. We were going to be okay.

And when I could see straight, when I could focus, when my mind didn't seem as cluttered and the future looked brighter, *then* I could concentrate on Libby. I could help her.

I arrived at the tiny village and a smile spread across my face. I could feel my cheeks bloom as I let this positivity take me. It felt so refreshing.

As I entered the flat, feeling more optimistic than I had in months – in fact, maybe a whole year, I heard a voice that made the smile disappear and replaced the good feelings with utter dread.

Melanie. What the hell was she doing in the flat?

34

Her stomach was extended. A thick grey woollen jumper was stretched across it. It looked like a football shoved up her front. She rubbed the ball, as if feeling uneasy that I was staring at her roundness.

'Hi, Kat,' she said nervously. Probably worried I'd throw her down the stairs.

'Hello,' I said curtly. The audacity, that she could sit in my home, smiling at me as if we were long lost friends, took my breath away.

'Would you like a cup of tea?' Marianne asked me, breaking the tension.

'Please.' I noted Melanie was already holding a cup. She'd already settled in. How long had she been here? I hoped Marianne hadn't made her feel too welcome. Polite, yes. Comfortable, absolutely not.

'I was passing by, so thought I'd call and see how you were.'

'I'm fine.' I bit back the urge to say, *only friends call in, and you are no longer my friend.*

'You look great,' she said, her eyes glistening, as if she was holding back tears.

No I didn't. She was obviously trying to be nice. I struggled to say anything back to her. As awful as it sounds, I found it hard to mention the visible bump. If I was to recognise such a vital detail in her life, it would be like saying, 'It's okay. We're okay.' And we weren't.

I removed my coat and placed it over the arm of the chair. Poppy gave me her biggest smile as she realised I was in the room, her tiny body bouncing in her chair. Rosie was lying on the play mat, her eyes glued to something Marianne had put on the television. Vibrantly coloured characters jumped across the screen, screeching to each other and mumbling nonsense. I couldn't even figure out what the characters were, but Rosie seemed content. I didn't disturb her: if I kissed her head, or drew attention to the fact that I was in the room, she'd soon lose interest in the TV and demand my attention.

'I know you don't want to see me.' Melanie was shaking, tremors pulsating through her words. 'I had to give it one last try.' She let a tear fall, and quickly wiped it away.

'I don't mean to be rude, Melanie, but I don't know what you want from me.' I spoke calmly. Calmer than I felt.

'I don't want anything. I don't expect anything.' Her lip quivered.

'Then why are you here?'

'I've left the salon.'

'Oh.' That *did* surprise me. Although I was dying to know the gossip on that front, I refused to ask.

'Mandy was a nightmare. Sophie left after only a few weeks.'

'Really?' I tried not to sound so interested, but furtively hoped she'd tell me more. Marianne handed me a cup of hot tea. I blew the top, rippling the surface of the milky liquid. Marianne walked back into the kitchen, then started to wash bottles and other pots that I could have sworn were clean and were waiting to be put away. She was clearly finding things to do so that she could avoid being part of this.

'Sophie went to work in the town centre, I think.'

'You didn't stay in touch?' Why was I bothered?

'No.' Melanie shook her head. 'Mandy was quite rude to her. I think she blamed me for letting Mandy bring her in. She didn't say so; you know Sophie, she was too quiet. She rang up one day and said she wasn't coming back.'

'Sounds familiar.' Sarcasm radiated from me.

Melanie bit her bottom lip. 'I am sorry for everything. If I could turn back time, I would.'

'Mel, without sounding too callous, we can't. So we have to get on with it.' I tried to say it as kindly as possible, but I knew I sounded as if I was lecturing her. Why I cared what she thought was beyond me. But as she sat forlorn with her pitiful eyes, her sad expression, her desperation, I suddenly felt sorry for her. She looked lost.

'We're moving away.' She held back the tears and smiled at me. 'Bobby's got a job in Surrey. I'm going to wait until the baby is born, and then set-up on my own. I'm going to try mobile first. I'm not sure I can handle having a shop again.'

'Lots of overheads,' I agreed: a non-committal answer.

'You know, Kat, I am truly sorry.' Melanie released the pent-up distress she had obviously been holding on to. An almighty sob escaped her, making Poppy jump. Rosie was still glued to the television and had not noticed anything remotely different about her surroundings. Melanie held her hands to her face as she let the tears fall, trying to wipe them away. Marianne's brow wrinkled as she tipped her head to the side, her eyes wide, willing me to do something. What? Throw her out, perhaps. I didn't want her emotional overload in here. Why should I try to make her feel better? She hadn't been there for me when I'd needed her the most.

But I felt my calmer side taking over, as my hands went around her shoulders, patting her gently. 'Come on, don't get upset.'

'I've hurt you so much,' she sobbed, and sniffed at the same time, wiping her hands across her black leggings, leaving a snotty smudge. 'You did so much for me. I let you down. I let myself down.'

'Sometimes we make decisions, and it's the best decision for us at the time.'

'I really wish I hadn't done it, then you wouldn't have lost everything and I wouldn't have lost you.'

'I've come to realise that some things happen for a reason.' I wondered if my counsellor had carried out some hypnotherapy on me without my knowledge.

'What could my reason possibly be?' she cried. 'I was selfish.'

'Sometimes we have to be selfish,' I heard myself saying, wondering where I'd conjured this up from. 'If Mandy had been the nicest person ever, you probably wouldn't be sitting here now, you'd have made the best decision for you.'

'But she wouldn't have set up on her own if she was a nice person, and I should have seen that. I feel as bad as her for following her.'

I smiled at her comment, remembering how I'd always thought Melanie was worse than Mandy. I thought it best not to say that. 'I don't blame Mandy for wanting to have her own business and run her own salon. I wanted that too. It doesn't make her horrible for wanting to set-up on her own. What annoyed me was, she took *my* business. She could have set up miles away, even in the next village. She purposely targeted all my clients, and I wasn't in a position to fight her.'

'I'm sorry.'

'Look, Melanie, you're moving away now. You need to move on.'

'But I need you to know I am truly, utterly sorry. If there was one thing—'

'It's happened.' I released my arm from her shoulder. I noticed Melanie's hands were no longer pristine. We used to keep our nails short, but our hands were always impeccably manicured. The amount of creams we used kept them soft and supple. Her hands didn't look as dry as mine, but they soon would be. I had the urge to tell her to look after her hands, look after herself. But I didn't. It seemed so superficial, compared to what we were both trying to say.

I was proud of myself for being so calm. Maybe the medication was finally working. The coil that seemed to have wound around my lungs, heart and other vital organs seemed to be slackening. Not fully. I didn't want to shout from the rooftops, skip through the village while picking flowers. But I was on my way.

Melanie stayed for another ten minutes. I forced myself to ask when her baby was due. She explained she was six months pregnant. So she must have just found out when she last came to see me in the salon. In fact, it would have been only months after they opened the salon. I bet Mandy wasn't happy about that.

I didn't analyse Mandy with her, because I didn't want to. I had no idea what went through that's woman's mind. I imagined thick blackness, as if the emotional part of her brain, the part that enabled us to be socially competent, didn't exist. Her whole mind, I believed, was tattooed with her name. It was all about her. Whoever she trampled on along her journey was not her problem.

I showed Melanie to the door, feeling deflated, the lightness I'd experienced on my walk home, was replaced by complete fatigue. 'Thank you, Kat,' she said, as she hugged me. I embraced her graciously. 'Please stay in touch.'

'I will.' I knew I wouldn't.

She climbed into the car I'd not noticed when I'd arrived home. A new car, a bigger car, obviously preparing for her baby. I closed the flat door, knowing that, that would be the last time I would see Melanie. But I was pleased we'd had some kind of closure. I was pleased she'd driven away with a smile on her face. It felt nice to release her from my dark thoughts. I'd never forget, but I couldn't let the anger chew away at me.

Since moving back into the flat, I'd been swallowed by the feeling of dread. I hated venturing out on my own, even when the girls were in tow. It was suffocating, often terrifying, to feel so afraid, but not be able to pinpoint what it was exactly that I was fearful of. Anxious I'd bump into Mandy or Melanie? Probably. It was the possibility of confrontation, or the awkwardness even if we didn't speak. It was apprehension that had sapped my confidence to move forward.

Now Melanie would be gone for good. There was no way she'd come back to this village again. She'd have no reason to. But even that thought didn't settle me. Mandy was still a two-minute walk away, even if I did my utmost to avoid her dazzling salon.

I'd blamed my wanting to move on the constant interruptions, the comings and goings, the unscheduled visits; but although all of that *did* bother me, immensely, it was their salon that had been festering at the back of my mind. I wanted to be able to walk into the street without looking over my shoulder, wondering who I might bump into, wondering which way was the best way to walk to avoid hostility. Sometimes it wasn't even the hostility, it was the inquisition I'd receive if I bumped into an old client.

I felt trapped. In these four walls. In this community.

Although Melanie's visit had helped, although I'd never thought I'd say that, I still needed to feel free.

*

Later Suzy called in. She seemed harassed. Her usual pale, calm features were tense, her jawline taut as she gave Poppy and Rosie a kiss. I'd just bathed them, which was another palaver that would have me sweating cobs. It was best to do Poppy first, as she didn't scream as much. In fact, she loved kicking her toes in the warm water. Rosie, on the other hand – my sensitive soul – hated it. She could bear it for all of thirty seconds before launching into high-pitched squeals. I'd quickly wrap her in a towel, dry her down, fight to put on the nappy, squeeze her legs into a babygro and then breathe. She usually gave in once she was clothed. Not one for being naked.

'You alright?' I asked Suzy as she slumped onto my sofa.

'Yeah …' Suzy said solemnly, but smiled as I handed her a cup of green tea. No, I wasn't having one.

'Come on, what's wrong?' I picked up Rosie, bottle in hand. I always fed Rosie first at this time of the evening, as I knew Poppy would entertain herself for longer.

'Do you want me to feed Poppy?'

'Good idea,' I said. 'Actually, feed Rosie.' I handed Suzy my baby girl. The bottle was attached to Rosie's mouth as she sucked furiously: there was no way she would let go of it as we swapped.

'So, what's the matter?' I walked round to the kitchen grabbing Poppy's bottle.

'It's all a bit too much. I wished we gone away and got married. Or maybe I wish we weren't getting married.'

'Why? Who's upset you? I thought things were sorted with your mum.'

'It is. Mum has been great since, but Dad has split up with his floozie, so I've got to hope and pray he doesn't meet someone else before then.' I picked up Poppy, whose lips searched until she locked onto the bottle, utter contentment filling her as she murmured with pleasure. 'Lawrence and I had a huge argument last night.'

'About what?'

'The table plan.'

'What?' I stifled a laugh.

'We never argue; but now, where we sit our bloody guests, half of who I'll probably never see for another year or so after, is causing us big problems.' I listened rather than advising: Suzy clearly needed to vent. 'Lately all we seem to do is bicker. We never had a cross word before we were planning the wedding. Everything was always calm between us, and now it seems all we discuss is suits, cravats, cake-tasting and why his bloody family find it so hard to reply to a frigging invitation.'

'Ask him to chase them.'

'I have. He passed the job to his mother. So now it looks as if I'm a snotty cow getting my mother-in-law to do it because I'm pissed off, or something.'

'No-one will see it like that.'

'I'm sure half his family don't like me. That's probably why they haven't replied; they don't want to come.'

'If they don't like you, it's because they're jealous.' I didn't know how they couldn't love Suzy, let alone dislike her.

'Thank you,' she laughed, her usual sparkling eyes dull; the smile not quite reaching them.

'Look, I'm sure you guys are just stressed because you've been really busy organising everything,' I said, trying to make her feel better. 'Remember the stories I would hear in the salon? I'm surprised anyone gets married.'

'My head is all over at the moment. I feel like telling him to shove the whole marriage up his arse.'

'Let's calm down, and think logically here,' I ordered. 'Do you love Lawrence?'

'Yes. Of course I do.'

'And you want to spend the rest of your life with him?'

'Yes. But I could have done it without a ring on my finger and all this stress.' She lifted Rosie, rubbing her back, enabling her to burb mid-bottle. Poppy would down the whole lot before she released any wind. 'Bloody hell, we're only having a small do, how do people organise big weddings?'

'So it's the wedding that's causing all this frustration and all this stress. It's not Lawrence. Once the wedding is over, you guys can go off traipsing hills or whatever it is you do for fun.'

'S'pose.'

'I think you and Lawrence need to have a nice meal, somewhere romantic, and wedding talk is *not* allowed. Plus, we've got your hen-day in a few weeks. That will help calm you just before the wedding.'

'You're right. Thank you,' she smiled. 'Will do us good. Lawrence is stressed out with Max and Joe, apparently the tension is quite bad.'

'Well, I have another story ...' I rattled off my version of events: Max with his innuendos, Gina with her claws and me pretending to be blasé about the whole situation.

'Would you go back?'

'No way.' I shook my head.

She considered me questioningly. 'You wouldn't even think about it?'

'Not for a second.'

'Lawrence thinks he's made a mistake.'

'It's amazing how so many people are making mistakes, but at my bloody expense.' I explained about Melanie's earlier visit, wanting to get away from the subject of Max now that she was interrogating me.

Suzy's interpretation of the whole sorry event was the fact that Melanie was easily led. She also thought, as she'd told me before, that Mandy would have taken my clients and set up on her own even without Melanie.

'But if Mel had stayed, we'd have had more chance of surviving.' I told Suzy, as I'd told her many times before. But I couldn't keep going over old ground; it was making me tired. It was stopping me from moving forward.

Suzy stayed for a few hours, helping me put the girls to bed. I updated her on the 'mummy group' situation, how Brooke's other half thought it was okay to touch my behind, wink and practically lick me. She thought this hilarious.

I admitted the attention was quite flattering for someone who felt frumpy, frail and dishevelled most of the time; okay, all of the time. Even if it wasn't the best kind of attention, it was nice to be noticed.

We laughed our way through the evening, and it felt so exhilarating. Endorphins were being released, tension was moving away from my tight shoulders, my body was falling into a relaxed, settled state.

Later, when I fell into bed, I let the happiness take me; it might not be there in the morning. If I'd not been so exhausted, I'd have tried to keep myself awake a little longer, to enjoy the serenity.

I remembered how Dad used to have good and bad days. The good days soon became few and far between. But Libby's bad days seemed to hit us instantly. Overnight her life seemed to have become full of badness. Although it didn't happen that way, by the time I'd realised, it was too late. But hopefully, I'd stopped myself from falling into that pit.

I wrapped the covers around me, letting my dreams take me, succumbing to the heaviness of my head, floating into a world of dreams.

Feeling better than I'd felt in a long time.

As I'd suspected, the next morning didn't feel as joyous, but maybe that was because both the girls had woken at the same time. 3.37 a.m.

I'd tried to settle them. I'd tried to leave them: the 'controlled crying technique', or whatever those textbooks call it. But, I had no willpower. If I persisted, I'd get there, that's what the experts said. But I couldn't listen to both my girls crying endlessly. It was as if they were competing to see who had the loudest screams. It was hell.

If I'd only had one baby to contend with I'd have even put her in my bed. Shock! Horror! Yes, I would be the parent who would have children in my bed until they were thirty. Because apparently, once they're in, they don't leave. Ever. But the fact of the matter was, I had two babies and no room in my bed. I was worried one would fall out because I couldn't secure them enough. So, with the no-space issue, I'd tried singing. They screamed more. I'd tried dummies, but they both hated them. Rosie sounded as if she would choke (I think she was going to be a dramatic child). Poppy spat it out. There was no messing; she simply didn't want it. So, after I'd fed them, which was totally out of our routine – but I swear I'd have tried anything – they still weren't happy. Rocking them both in my arms, I'd worn the carpet thin in my room.

It was understandable that I felt fragile. The relief that my new life was coming together had been cast away into the night, washed away as every minute turned into hours. By the time I'd climbed back into bed, they'd woken for their morning feed.

Due to the fact that as the sun rose, I found it hard to squeeze two words together, let alone a full sentence, I thought it best we stop at home. I could laze. I might even put a sofa against the door that Clare was always unexpectedly popping through. Although, I played with the idea, but I knew there was no point. She'd bang on the door, or shout my name until I opened it, or she'd run around to the outside door and ring the bell endlessly; and if all else failed she'd call the police. That was all I needed: the crime squad turning up, bashing down my door with their battering ram while I lay on the couch, still in pyjamas with a cup of tea.

So, because of this pressure, I showered once the girls had settled for a morning nap, which was earlier than their usual 10 a.m. snooze. I could easily have climbed back into bed, my mouth furry, my eyes sore; but I forced myself to shower, clean, be fresh. I yearned to feel as steady as I'd felt yesterday, but it didn't work. So I pulled on my baggy black tracksuit, which within a few hours would have slack, shapeless knees, and this marked the start of our lazy day.

But it didn't turn out to be so lazy, really. I spoke with Libby and June, who were both lively, cheery and sounded as if they were having some form of a girlie holiday. I fought back the jealousy that had risen. I should have left Libby here and *I* should have gone. I needed a break. I scolded myself for being so ridiculous. This was good. This was progress. It had only been a day or so, and Libby sounded so invigorated. June had also sounded jovial; but then, that was normal, really, she never seemed miserable.

June had asked me how Henry was. I'd coldly told her I had no idea, but I knew that Clare was deeply upset. This had silenced her for all of a second, before she switched the subject to rocky cliffs and beautiful seas and how they'd been for wonderful walks on the beach.

After speaking with them, feeling slightly better that Libby seemed so upbeat, I worked my way through three hours' worth of ironing over a six-hour period; between feeds, nappy-changing, playing … but I got there in the end.

I'd wanted to leave it out for Clare, so she would be impressed that I had finally completed the task she'd noticed I'd failed miserably at. But we'd not had our usual morning visit. I'd hoped everything was okay. Admittedly, it pleased me that we'd actually had a full morning to ourselves: a full day, actually; but I'd done the ironing and I wanted it to be recognised. I'd not slept or blocked off the door with the sofa … typically she didn't bloody come up. I'd felt like texting her, but that was encouragement. That was like saying, 'Why the hell haven't you visited? We love your visits.'

She did finally trudge up the stairs, before she was leaving. Her usual air of superiority seemed to have burst a little. She looked tired, pale, her skin dry and aged. The lines and saggy skin underneath her eyes seemed more apparent than ever. Looking vulnerable and distracted, she kissed the girls.

'I can't stop,' she said hurriedly. 'Sorry I've not called earlier, it's been a busy day.'

'Don't worry.'

'Anyway, I best be off.'

'Clare.' I stopped her before she darted down the stairs, her whirlwind mini-visit unusual. Uncharacteristically hassled and agitated, she held the door handle and turned to look at me. 'You seem distracted …'

'I'm fine,' she nodded unconvincingly. 'Lots to do. Must dash.' She was gone.

It was one of the strangest moments. I wondered if I'd upset her. I couldn't think what I'd done. I was also a little put out that I'd not had the chance to mention the ironing. Not even the chance to say, 'Yes, I've been busy too, got all that ironing done.' But knowing the Clare we all knew, she probably wouldn't have praised me, she'd have said something like, 'About time, you really do need to get yourself organised, Kathryn.'

Once she had disappeared, the doorbell rang. Max. He'd said he would be calling in to see the girls.

I let him in. He followed me up the stairs. I'd purposely stayed in my old tracksuit, not applied my make-up and left my hair to fall scruffily around my face. I didn't want him to find me attractive. Our whole situation was complicated enough without him creating more difficulties.

He cooed over the girls as soon as he walked in. Rubbing his nose against theirs. Poppy's excitement was apparent: as her eyes lit up, her hands reached towards his bristly unshaven skin, her smile spread across her tiny round face. Even as he gave his full attention to Rosie, Poppy's eyes followed him, not allowing him out of her sight. Rosie acknowledged him with a smile; not over-enthused, but she made an effort.

He chatted to them about their day. Poppy pursed her lips, trying so hard to join in his conversation, making little noises that always made my insides turn to marshmallow, suffocated with the love I felt for them. Rosie made me smile as she listened intently, not giving anything away. That's my girl, I thought.

'So how's work been?' I tried to sound as casual as possible, staying on a neutral subject that couldn't possibly pose any risks.

'Busy.'

'That's good. Think of the money.'

'I know, but I might be losing a contract, which could cause me major problems.'

'Oh … is there anything you can do to save it?'

'I'm working on a few things,' he said. 'But it's hard. Gina wants me at home all the time. She wants me to help out with the wedding and I haven't got time.'

'There's a lot of work involved.'

'I know, but she's the one who wanted to bring it forward.' He leaned his hands against the kitchen worktop. 'I'd rather have waited until the baby was born, maybe a few years.'

'Did you tell her this?' Why was I asking questions? I didn't want to talk about his relationship with Gina.

'Many times.' He raised his eyebrows, his forehead showing more lines than it usually did. His face seemed to have paled into that of a stressed, tired, older man. 'We can't have a honeymoon, as I haven't got time; but still she wanted this whole huge wedding. It's bloody a farce.'

'Maybe it's best to talk to her rather than to me.'

'That's the thing. I can talk to you better than I can talk to her.'

'Max, let's not go there.'

'I think I've made a mistake.' He blurted the words out fast; they seemed to hurtle towards me. The silence between us compounded as Rosie started to become irritated, needing some attention, her little whines seemed to echo in the stillness.

I shook my head and started to walk past him, but he gently grabbed my arm and twisted me round to face him. My heart was racing. I wanted to slap him but at the same time have him take me. Take me? I didn't want him.

'We could make this work.'

I could feel his hot breath on my cheek. I removed his hand from my arm, hoping he couldn't see that I was shaking. Finding the part in me that knew this was wrong, I said, 'No. No, we can't Max,' and walked towards Rosie, glad that she was giving me a distraction.

'We could. Of course we could,' he said desperately.

'I can't.' I picked up Rosie and turned to face him. 'You're having another baby with another woman. What the hell are you playing at?' I felt the burning inside rising throughout my body, fury building as the anger I'd felt over the past year threatened to boil over.

'I don't know,' he said despairingly. 'It's as if everything has happened so fast. I turned to Gina when I felt alone.'

'So you're turning back to *me* now?' I shook my head. 'Max, you can't do this. It's been so hard.'

'I know it's been hard.' He ran his hand distractedly through his thick curls.

'It still is, Max.'

'That's why we should sit down and talk about things properly. We didn't do that. We got caught in the web, you were so tired being pregnant, then there was all that with your salon, my work was busy, we weren't communicating properly and things fell apart, when they didn't have to.'

'I think you should leave.' I spoke quietly. My head was pounding.

What was he doing? We were sorted. I didn't want him. I didn't love him. I'd told myself all of these things. I'd moved on from him. Hadn't I? It wasn't Max I wanted. It was the ideal family unit that he'd taken away from us. It wasn't that easy to put it back together.

'Please, let's talk—'

'There's nothing to talk about.' I tried to keep my voice low, but the intensity of my confusion, and indignation was startling Rosie. 'You made your choice, Max.'

'But I've made the wrong choice.' He came towards me, placing his hands on my shoulders as I cradled Rosie. I thought my heart would pop out of my chest, 'This is one big mess because we were both stressed. Every night I'm driving home and I wish I was coming home to you and the girls. I've missed out on so much of their lives already, and I don't want to miss out on any more.'

'It's not going to happen.'

'I know I hurt you, but we could work through it.'

'Are you insane?' Rosie flinched. 'What is it, Max, that you can't seem to handle?'

'What do you mean?'

'You don't want us, you—'

'I do.'

'You don't. You don't want the hassle of Gina being pregnant and a wedding to sort out. Have you considered her feelings in all of this?' Why I was bothered about her was beyond me, but still I felt sorry for her. 'So you come and live back with us, which isn't going to happen, but in theory, say you did. Gina would be devastated. The wedding will be cancelled—'

'That would bother you?'

'Of course, it would be horrendous for her,' I snapped. Rosie's lip quivered, I rocked her quickly. 'She's having your baby. What happens when this baby is born? You'll be bored with us.'

'I won't get bored.'

'You will … it's all about nappy-changing, feeding and sleepless nights.'

'I could help with it all.'

'You couldn't bear me exhausted and snappy when I was pregnant. Trust me, this is ten times worse.'

'But you're so different now. Admittedly, you were a bit fraught in the beginning, but you've chilled so much over the last few weeks.'

'Maybe I'm getting used to my life, but still that doesn't mean you'd enjoy it.' The medication must be working, if the change in me was noticeable; but I wasn't about to admit this to Max.

'But I look at you, you're so …' He breathed deeply, sitting down on the sofa that for once was clear of junk. 'I don't know … you seem in a place that is happy. I want to be part of it, again.'

'Max, you're being irrational.' I sat down across the room, opposite him.

'I wish we'd stayed together.' I didn't answer him, because I too wished we had. I'd forced myself into believing this was the right decision for us. It was meant to be this way. I couldn't let myself think any other way: it was pointless. It would drive me crazy. 'I really think we could make this work,' he said.

'I don't.' I shook my head at him, chewing on the soft inside of my lip. 'I think you should leave, now.'

'But—'

'Now.'

36

ax had left quite swiftly when he realised I wasn't softening. Not on the outside anyway.

Once I'd put the girls to bed, I'd slung myself onto the sofa and watched a few soaps, trying to stay awake for as long as I could, knowing I wouldn't be getting a full night's sleep if I was to dream-feed the girls too early. But embracing the cushions, loving the fact I had the whole sofa to myself with no clothes or other people's baggage cluttering up my personal space, I found my eyes struggling to stay focused.

It wasn't until both girls had been happily fed, their snores and snuffles blending into a rhythmic pattern, that my eyes decided they'd like to be wedged open. My mind thought it would be a good time to become active, bouncing thoughts around like effervescent bubbles. I didn't want to be with Max. I told myself this, over and over. I'd accepted that our relationship wasn't meant to be. I told myself endlessly that it had happened for one reason, one reason only - for the girls; they were meant to be here. They were my precious family and Max didn't play a part in that.

Of course I'd dreamed of us staying together. I'd tortured myself thinking about the amazing family we'd have been: all happily eating breakfast together, waving him off from the doorstep as he went off to work, smiling and singing. When he arrived home, his tea would be made, the girls would be pristine, everyone would be smiling, full of joy and happiness. We'd bath the girls together, feed them together and put them to bed together. We'd finish our evenings, gazing into each other's eyes, freshly laundered sheets greeting us as we wrapped ourselves in each other's arms.

Nowhere near reality, I know, but I wondered if *he* was thinking in those terms.

Oh, I had no idea what he really wanted, or why he thought coming back would be the answer to his prayers. Why I cared was bothering me more than anything.

It was hard doing it on my own. I often felt lonely. Yes, I had everyone around me, but they were on the outside. Even though the flat often felt like a motorway at peak times, it was as if I was in a bubble, watching it all happen.

It would have been nice to have someone to share my life with, have someone to tell the little things to. I had Suzy who I could ring at the drop of a hat, but to have someone here constantly, someone for me ... It would be easy to say that person should be Max, because he was the father of my children. But what about the connection Max and I had? It had gone, hadn't it?

I had to think about what was best for me. It wasn't Max. Was it?

My thoughts went round in circles. After lying for more than two hours, thinking and worrying. I forced my tired body from the warm sheets, pushed my feet into my worn slippers, pulled on my fleece dressing gown and made myself a Horlicks.

I cursed him for doing this to me.

Cursed myself for allowing him to.

*

Marianne had agreed to come to baby massaging with me. Although I'd tried so hard to get out of it, Brooke had refused to listen to my excuses. 'I'm a bit tired ... the girls haven't slept ... my head aches,' I'd pleaded. She wasn't having it. I did think about confessing all. 'Your boyfriend's a sleaze and I feel guilty being around you.' But I thought better of it.

So, feebly, I went. As we walked along the gravel paths towards the church community centre, I felt a little lighter knowing that I wouldn't bump into Melanie, but a little apprehensive that Mandy could be lurking somewhere. We chatted about nothing in particular.

I wanted to avoid any subject that might involve Brooke's world. I found it hard to ask if Mrs D was okay. Not only would I have to call her 'Ange' but I'd have to bring up that strange night. I was worried Brooke would mention Daryl. What if he'd told her that I'd come on to him, telling his side of the story before I told her mine?

Max was also still on my mind. I'd tried to push him aside, focus on the fact he'd left me for another woman when I was pregnant. He'd wandered. He didn't stay to fight. All of that mattered. He couldn't come knocking now things were tough on his side of the fence.

With technology today, you'd think someone would have designed a headset that could hack into our thoughts, so that I could have pressed the delete button and make him disappear from my head.

'Kat, how lovely to see you again.' Harvey's mum was in front of us, blocking the entrance to the centre.

'Hi Nancy.'

'How's little Rosie getting along with her baby rice?'

'Great. What about Harvey?' I asked, feeling Brooke's eyes boring into me. 'Did you get sorted?'

'Yes, thank you. They gave me some milk, but I'll stick with breastfeeding for a few more weeks.' She smiled at Brooke, who gave a smile that looked more like a wince.

'I really hope he gets sorted,' I said, trying to finish the conversation, move her along.

'Rosie has been so much more settled. Hasn't she, Kat?' Marianne joined in.

'Yes, so hopefully Harvey will settle, too,' I said. Now move along.

'We should get together, we have so much in common. Especially with you trying breastfeeding. It didn't work for my friend. She told the nurses she couldn't do it. But at least she tried.' Nancy directed her answer at Brooke, who glared at her. Devil eyes, piercing into her. I imagined Brooke wanting to turn her into flames.

'I'm really busy at the moment. I'm looking at moving and things are up in the air … but yes, we should.' I hoped it wasn't obvious I was trying to avoid her, as I'd waffled about something that wasn't actually happening, yet.

'You've got my number. Call me.' She raised her hand, spreading her fingers so her little finger touched her mouth, her thumb touched her ear: a sign for using the telephone.

'Will do,' I said, forcing a smile.

She walked into the centre.

I felt Brooke's enflamed eyes burning through me. 'What?' I shrugged.

'You know what!' she whispered furiously. 'Why do you have her number?'

'I bumped into her in the hospital, and she gave me a business card.'

'She was acting like you two were best buddies,' she snapped at me.

My blood boiled as I peered at the youngster who'd desperately tried to befriend me over the last few weeks, who had forced her way into my life. I'd had no choice but to let her in, because every time I said no she would worm her way in until she got a yes.

'Brooke, although we are friends, I can pick and choose my other friends,' I said calmly and quietly; not wanting to embarrass her, but she needed to know we were not in school now.

'So you'd rather be friends with her than me.' Brooke placed her hand on her hip, staring at me with all the indignation she could conjure up. I heard Marianne stifle a laugh as she released Poppy from the pram after we'd parked up in the pushchair station. Luckily Nancy Nott had already gone through, pram too. She didn't do parking her pram in the appropriate place. 'It might get stolen,' I'd overheard her say to one of the other mum's.

'Are you serious?' I asked Brooke, who appeared to be furious.

'Yes, I am. She's not a nice person. I can't believe you'd rather be friends with someone like that.' Brooke's eyes started to glisten, her lip quivering. I glanced at Marianne, who raised her eyebrows quickly. Was this really happening?

'I haven't said I would rather be friends with her.' I didn't want Brooke making a scene. This was embarrassing. 'I was saying, if I was, then it wouldn't affect you in any way.'

'But why would you want to be friends with her? She's horrid.'

'I haven't said that I do.' I tried to stay calm, fighting the urge to tell her I didn't have to explain myself to her, and walk straight back out again. 'Look, you need to calm down. We are friends; that's all that matters.'

She wiped away a stray tear that had left a smudge of black mascara down her cheek. 'I'm sorry. I'm so emotional lately. I don't think Ange is helping, she's all over the place. I know my brother is a twat, but I love him. I can't help but stick up for him … and then me and Daryl are not connecting like we used to … I'm being silly.'

'Come on, let's get in here and relax.' I patted her arm, not feeling close enough to her to wrap my arms around her. I didn't want to discuss Mrs D, Daryl or Brooke's emotional state.

The class seemed to pass by slowly. There were a few stare-offs between Brooke and Nancy Nott, a bit like a western. They just needed a gun and a hat and we could have sorted this out once and for all.

Marianne loved the oils, rubbing them into Rosie's skin. Rosie responded with absolute pleasure. Poppy was quiet and taking in the surroundings, wriggling as I tried to massage her legs and press on her tiny feet, her toes stretching in delight.

I was glad when the class ended. There was no way I could do this again. I could massage the girls at home. I didn't need this six-week course. It was causing me more angst, and that wasn't supposed to be the objective.

We walked home, our small talk dwindling. Brooke was obviously not her usual light-hearted self. A barrier had been put up. I didn't have the energy or the interest to overcome it. Marianne chatted all the way back, filling in the silences. She was such a diplomat, but then, she'd been doing it for years. She didn't once mention Libby or June, which pleased me, as Brooke knew nothing of my personal life. I'd like to keep it that way.

I expected Clare to pounce on us as we approached the salon, but she didn't. I couldn't see her inside; not that I tried to look too closely. I hated going into the place, so avoided it as much as possible. I did hope she was okay, though.

Brooke continued to walk on, not stopping for her usual chit-chat or begging me to arrange a girlie night. She merely gave a little wave and said, 'I'll see you later.' I let her go. I had no desire to save a friendship that wasn't really a friendship but a drain on my energy.

'She's a little demanding, isn't she?' Marianne exclaimed.

'She's got a lot going on.' I found myself sticking up for her.

'But still …'

'I know.' I smiled, liking the opinionated Marianne. Her ability to speak her mind, not be influenced by those around her, was quite comforting. The way she'd stood up to Derek had in some way satisfied me; not in a sordid, cruel way, but it was good to see her confidence growing. She was no longer the doormat she'd been for many years.

A man was waiting outside the flat door as we turned the corner. He was average build, I'd say around five feet ten. He was dressed in jeans, trainers and a black North Face jacket. His shaven head and bulky figure were overpowering as he walked along the path, back and forth, kicking stones in front of his feet. He looked as if the weight of the world was upon his shoulders.

Marianne put her hand on my arm as we slowed. Obviously her mind was also spilling over with thoughts of drug dealers, loan sharks and whoever else Libby had been involved with.

He noticed us. We stopped.

He lifted his head, his eyes desperate, as he said politely, 'Hi there, I'm looking for Libby Neasham.'

37

'She's not here,' I told him, wanting to run into the flat, but worried that if I took the key out of my pocket he'd grab it. 'Do you know where I can find her?' He seemed harassed.

'Who are you?' Marianne was cool.

'Matt.' He held his hands up. 'Sorry, I should have introduced myself. I'm from Pondergate Park. I was one of Libby's counsellors.'

'Why are you here?' I could feel the frown creasing my forehead. 'Have you come to try and encourage her to come back?'

'No … no, I haven't.'

'So why *are* you here then?' I asked him again.

'Look, here's my card. Would you mind passing my details on to her? She'll know what it's about.' I took the card. 'Thanks very much.' He met my eyes, before bowing his head as he shoved his hands into the pockets of his jacket and started to walk away. 'Sorry to have bothered you.'

Inside the flat, I could feel unease pricking at me like thorns. A vice-like grip had taken hold of my stomach, twisting it into an uncomfortable ball.

I picked up the phone and pressed the numbers quickly. 'Can I speak to Ronnie please?' Marianne was watching me as she put the girls on the play mat. She knew I didn't believe for one second that the strange man worked at Pondergate Park. The business card could have been a fake.

After giving my name, I heard some scuffling around and then I was placed on hold. The soothing classical music being played into my ear did nothing to dispel my tension.

'Hello, Kat, how can I help you?' Ronnie asked kindly. I explained about 'Matt' and how I was a little concerned he'd told me he worked for Pondergate Park. She was silent for all of five seconds, but it felt much longer before she confirmed, 'He is a counsellor.'

'So why is he here?'

'I think it's best you talk to Libby.'

'I'm asking *you*.' I tried not to snap but I needed answers. I had nightmare images running through my mind. Was he supplying her drugs? Secretly giving her drink?

'Look, there is an ongoing investigation, so I can't say too much.' Ronnie sighed, but still remained soft and calm.

'Investigation?'

What was she talking about? The seriousness of her words stunned me.

'Yes. Investigation.'

'I assume it's him being investigated.'

'I can't say.'

'What is he being investigated about?'

'Kat, I can't tell you any details.'

'Of course you can if my sister is involved.'

'I can't.'

'Did he hurt her?'

'No,' Ronnie said quickly, obviously realising even the smallest of statements could get her into trouble. 'Look, I can't say anything … confidentiality, you know …' She still spoke gently, but slightly more firmly, as if she'd seen this conversation coming. She'd probably practised all that she would tell me. Which was nothing. 'You need to speak to Libby.'

'I will,' I said, and hung up the phone, not waiting for her to say her goodbyes.

'What is going on?' Marianne was holding toys out for the girls, distractedly playing a little game with them.

'I don't know.' I bit my lip as I urgently dialled Libby's number. 'Come on, answer.' My feet were tapping an impatient rhythm on the wooden floor. I was greeted with her answer-machine message, so I hung up. I couldn't leave a calm message; I knew I would sound like a panicked neurotic. 'I don't know what to do.' I breathed out heavily.

'Libby will call back,' Marianne said, still holding the long-legged monkeys out to the girls, who gurgled in satisfaction. 'What did Ronnie say?'

I explained the bitty conversation that had got me nowhere, except into a further confused state. Marianne frowned, clearly perturbed.

My phone beeped, signalling that a message had arrived.

'Sorry about earlier, things r bit difficult at mo, don't want 2 lose u as friend, Brooke x'

My body seemed to sag with disappointment. Not just because it wasn't Libby, but because I had enough trauma in my own world without having to listen to Brooke's. I wanted to ignore her text.

But still, I replied, 'No worries, I'm here if u need to talk x'

'Have you tried June?' Marianne asked.

'Good idea.' Why hadn't I thought of that? I searched for her number, dialled then listened to the phone ringing endlessly until June's answer machine acknowledged my call. I hung up and tried the house phone. Still nothing.

'They'll call back. Try not to worry.'

'Thank u, why don't we do another girlie nite, without Ange, she can really bring the mood down x'

'Shit.' Brooke's reply had me cursing. 'Sorry,' I said to Marianne, who may have been exposed to my foul language when we were younger, but not since I'd grown up and started respecting her.

'Don't be silly. Who is texting you?'

'Brooke, about another girlie night.' Irritation was running through me. 'I wish Libby would answer.'

'You need to calm down.' Marianne raised her eyebrows. 'Libby will call back.'

'What if she knows what is going on? If she thinks we know something? What if she's too scared to call me back?'

'Kat—'

'What if she's avoiding me?'

'You're not thinking straight.' Marianne lifted herself from the floor, the girls still gurgling in the background. 'Libby will call you back. Ronnie told you he didn't hurt her, so I'm sure she'll tell us the full story.' She sat down beside me. 'Organise to go to Brooke's house, I can babysit the girls.'

'What, so her creepy boyfriend can come on to me?'

'What?' Marianne shook her head in obvious confusion.

I found myself letting out a laugh: the whole situation sounded ludicrous, even as I explained to Marianne about Daryl's antics, I still felt that I must have been wrong somewhere. 'So I need an excuse *not* to go. But how do I let her down?'

'Tell her you're busy over the next few weeks.'

'Busy? What, changing nappies? I think she'll know I'm putting her off.'

'Tell her you can't get a babysitter. I don't mind looking after our gorgeous girls, but she doesn't need to know that.'

'I'll probably bump into Clare while I'm with Brooke, and she'll offer.'

'It's up to you. Don't go because you feel you should.'

'But *you* would go?'

'Years ago … maybe,' Marianne shrugged.

Rosie was fidgeting, starting to whine I assumed she realised Marianne wasn't coming back to play. 'They'll be hungry,' I said getting to my feet. 'It's okay, Mummy's doing it.' I spoke lightly, wishing I felt so buoyant.

'Come here you two.' Marianne was on her hands and knees crawling across the floor, happily chatting to them both in baby-talk as she smothered them with her love.

My mobile rang, interrupting me from preparing the two bottles. Running across the floor as if I was in a 100m sprint, I hit the answer button accidently before realising it was Brooke, and not Libby. I cringed at Marianne, who held her hands up in despair.

'Hello,' I murmured.

'Hi, Kat, I wondered if you got my message.'

'I did. I was about to feed the girls.'

'We really need to do a girlie night, I feel awful I was so off with you but that woman really winds me up, who the hell does she think she is?' She didn't stop for breath as she blurted her rage at me.

'You should just ignore her.' I rolled my eyes at Marianne.

'I know.'

'Brooke, I'll have to call—'

'I really need a girlie night. When are you free?'

'I'll have to check babysitting.'

'You know Marianne and Clare will help out, how about tomorrow night?'

'I can't.'

'The night after?'

'Okay, I'll check one of them can babysit.' I found myself saying, before she could reel off 'the night after' so many times, we'd get through a full year. I thought about asking her to come to me, but at least in her house I could choose when to leave. Here, she'd probably stay over.

'Okay, text me.' Yes, demanding one, I refrained from saying before we hung up.

'So you're going, then?' Marianne smiled.

'Honestly, she's so bloody insistent.' I continued making the bottles, the girls surprisingly patient, although Marianne had a lot to do with that. 'Can you babysit on Thursday night?'

'Of course I can.'

'Great, thank you.'

'I'm happy to have the girls at ours overnight.'

'I know.' I continued to make the bottles, ignoring the pressure that had risen inside, ready to erupt like a bubbling volcano. 'But, if you don't mind coming here—'

'I don't mind at all,' Marianne said. I could feel her eyes burning into me. 'I was thinking, though, it would be practice for when we have them overnight for Suzy's wedding.'

'Maybe in a few weeks.'

'Her wedding is in a few weeks.'

'We'll work something out.' I handed her a bottle and she picked up Poppy, I could feel her eyes tracing over me, seemingly debating whether she should continue this conversation or leave it. Leave it. I was still so nervous about the girls sleeping out, but I knew I would have to get over it. But I'd think about that later.

I turned my thoughts back to Libby. Why wasn't she answering her phone? What could she be doing that was so important? What could she and June *both* be doing that was so important? Was June leading her astray? I knew it had been a bad idea for her to go and stay with June. But how could I have stopped her? She was old enough to make her own decisions. She was no longer a minor although I still found it hard to pull back. I wanted to smother her in cotton wool, every inch of her fragile, skinny body.

Night fell. Marianne had left the girls and me alone. The silence had become overbearing, so I'd switched on the television in the hope that the background noise would distract me from checking my phone every five minutes. I'd tried a few times to call Libby and June but still no answer. What the hell were they doing? God, I hoped they were okay.

The urge to sleep finally took over, after I'd wandered anxiously around the flat for what felt like hours. I kept looking out of the window, as if Libby might turn up at any moment. But the only thing I was faced with was the sight of the sleeping village.

38

I lay in the hot bath, letting the water lap round my baggy skin. My belly now looked more like a pale wobbly jelly than the firm island that had been my pregnancy bump. I really wished I could lose the flabbiness. I could hear Suzy's words: 'There's only you who can do something about it.'

The bathroom door was open so I could listen out for the girls, who were having their morning nap. I'd had a restless night, but unusually it wasn't the girls who'd caused it. For once the girls had slept brilliantly and I hadn't. Which is bloody typical! I'd still had no word back from Libby, and was so worried. All kinds of thoughts were running through my mind, from her and June being kidnapped to Libby being in a gutter overdosed somewhere.

I'd decided a bath might help ease my tense, aching muscles. I wished I could bathe my mind. I'd thought I was starting to feel a little happier. Settled. The medication seemed to be kicking in. I still wasn't ready to open the champagne, or throw a party; although one party I had to think about was a christening for the girls. Both Derek and Marianne had commented on how lovely it would be to have one. And how we could use their church.

It wasn't that I didn't want to christen the girls, although it was slightly hypocritical when I was still confused about the powers that be. I had to have some faith, or where was Mum now? But then, if He did exist, why did He let her die? I would probably still be searching for answers on my own deathbed. It wasn't so much the religious aspect that was putting me off having a christening, it was the celebration afterwards. Yes, we didn't have to have one. We could simply get the girls blessed at the church and come home.

But Clare and Max would take over. I couldn't handle that.

Maybe this was something we could look at later. I had no plans to put them into a Church school. That was another thing to think about – schools! They couldn't even walk yet. There was a long list for the local nursery. It was discussed at the baby group. But again, this was something else I'd pushed to the back of my mind, figuring *when* we move I'll start searching for schools then, and hope I'm not too late!

No-one tells you these things, no-one sits you down and tells you all the little things you need to worry about. Even bullying. It was a bit early to be thinking about bullying, but there had been an incident on the news: a teenager had committed suicide, and it came to light that she was being bullied. I told myself that my girls would be fine; they had each other. But what if they were completely different? What if they didn't actually like each other? What if one was more popular than the other?

I'd tried so far in their short lives to make things equal, but what if by some twist of fate this didn't continue throughout childhood? As in Libby's case, there wasn't really anything I could do about it. Except keep them shut away from the world. Home-school them, maybe?

My wild thoughts were wandering too far into the future. I noticed my skin was becoming wrinkled and the water had cooled. As I raised myself out of the bath, I heard the secret door opening.

Clare? She'd been up earlier. What was she doing?

'Hello,' I shouted.

'Hello.' At Clare's response I grabbed the towel and quickly wrapped it around my saggy body. Shit. I couldn't go out like this. I had hairy legs! I'd only quickly shaved under my arms, as I didn't want the spindly hairs peeping out from my T-shirt and scaring people away.

I popped my head around the door. There she was, not with one customer but two!

I forced a smile, 'Hi, I was having a bath.'

'It's 10a.m.!' Clare exclaimed, looking at her watch.

'Only a quickie while the girls slept,' I said weakly.

'You wouldn't mind if I show these ladies the girls?' It sounded like a question, but it wasn't: she was already half-way across the flat. I smiled at the women, who followed her rather apologetically. I recognised them as old customers, but they hadn't been regulars.

The towel tightly wrapped around my body, I hid behind the bathroom door, not allowing my bushy legs to be on show, in case the women thought they were two shaggy dogs.

I could hear the three ladies whispering. Please don't wake my girls. At least let me get dressed first.

About a minute later, although it felt like thirty, they reappeared. The three of them tiptoed across the flat, as if they hadn't already disturbed us, and disappeared through what had been my secret door. I wished I could magic it away.

I breathed a deep sigh of relief, quickly walking to my bedroom in case one of them decided to come back up. I pulled on my dressing gown swiftly.

The girls were still sleeping soundly, so I got out my laptop and logged on, and typed … 'houses to rent'.

One of the houses seemed spacious from the photos. I didn't look at the dimensions, not like Max would have done, checking every inch of the space he had to play with. It was in a nice location, on the outskirts of Yarm. So I made an appointment to view the property that afternoon. The woman, who was lovely and was obviously trying to get this month's quota in for her bonus, was very persistent. I got up from the sofa, pushing away any doubts that might have me changing my mind. Although this was what I wanted, making the appointment made it real. A trickle of excitement, or nerves, ran through me.

'Change is good,' I told myself. 'This is progress.' I tried to encourage myself. I really wanted to be out of this flat. I really needed to do this.

Two hours later, the girls and I were ready. Kitted out in their tiny pink coats, pink leggings, hats and mitts, they looked adorable. I, on the other hand, looked as if I'd been dragged through a hedge. I couldn't get the hang of this: getting the girls and me ready on time. How the hell do other mums do it?

My mobile rang as we were leaving the flat. I started to panic. I'd tried to contact Libby again this morning, but still there was no answer. Holding the car seats tight, I rushed forward, awkwardly trying to open the car door, catching my nail, cursing, then cursing myself for cursing in front of the girls; worried their first word would be, 'Fuck!'

I was mid-way through strapping the girls into the back seat when the phone stopped. 'Shit!' I shouted. 'Sorry, girls.'

Flicking through the screen, I could see it was Libby I'd missed.

'Shit,' I said again, quickly getting into the driver's side. I plugged in the hands-free set, started the engine and drove down the lane, listening as the ringing droned into my ear.

'Hello,' she answered within two rings.

'Where have you been?' I was louder and harsher than I'd intended to be.

'Sorry, we went out to the cinema and then got a bite to eat after. It was too late to ring you by the time we got back.'

'What about this morning?'

'We were in bed. You rang at eight-thirty. That's, like, the middle of the night.'

'It's halfway through the day for most people,' I snapped, trying to focus on the road. 'I've been worried sick.'

'Sorry. June thought it would be nice to get out and have some fun. I didn't think I needed to live to a schedule while I was down here.'

'You don't …' I sighed, not wanting this to turn into an argument. 'Look, a man came to see you.'

'What man?' she asked quickly.

'Matt.' She was silent. I could just about hear her low breathing, over the hum of the car engine. 'He left his card.'

'What did he say?'

'He wanted to see you.'

'So, what did you say?'

'You need to tell me what's going on.' I could feel the irritation rise through me again, I didn't want to play her games: he said this, I said that.

'Nothing is going on,' she retorted.

'I've spoken to Ronnie—'

'What?' she practically screamed at me.

'I didn't believe him, Libby.'

'For fuck's sake, Kat!' Her outburst shocked me. 'I've got to go. I'll call you later.'

'But—'

She was gone. The dead line hummed into the earpiece. I threw the phone onto the passenger seat.

What the hell was she playing at?

I drove along the country roads, trees hanging graciously overhead the narrow lanes. With every ounce of willpower I possessed, I forced my attention onto the visit ahead, trying to push Libby to the back of my mind.

I parked at the side of the road, as there was a car on the paved driveway. The semi-detached house, which was probably built in the 1970s, had a large, inviting bay window. There were two windows on the second floor, one of which was three times bigger than the other. The curtains were pulled back neatly, staged for my arrival: I knew the house had been vacant for a few months, which was the reason they'd reduced the monthly rent. The garage was attached to the house but further down the drive, which had been my motivation for viewing: the owners had insulated the garage and it was used as an office. Perfect for my beauty room.

A woman in a light-grey suit greeted me, her skirt flaring at the knee, the smart cut of her blouse elegantly showing off her slim neck. Once again, I felt like a tramp.

I really needed to sort myself out, especially if I was going to start working in beauty again. If I handed this woman a business card, she'd run a mile if she thought this was the best I could do.

'Ms Neasham? I'm Lynn from Brickwork Homes. Did you find it okay?' she asked, smiling warmly.

I put my arm under the handle of Rosie's car seat and awkwardly shook the hand she offered. 'Please call me Kat. Yes I did, thank you.' I smiled politely, taking hold of the car seat properly, before Rosie landed on her head.

I followed her into the place that someone had once called their home, a strong smell of lavender assailing my nostrils. We walked from the vestibule into the living room, where vivid orange and yellow swirls adorned the walls and the red carpet was threadbare.

'Oohh, that's a bit …' I shuddered.

'I know, that's why we're having trouble renting it.' She held her folders against her chest.

'Would they allow the new tenant to decorate?'

'I'd have to ask them. No-one has shown any interest in the place yet.' She shrugged her shoulders. She walked on through another door, which had damaged wooden panels. Placing the girls, still fastened securely in their seats, onto the lounge floor, I checked the front door was locked before I followed her round. She launched into a sales pitch about the Yale lock, and how safe it was.

'How long has it been up for rent?' I asked as we left the hideously coloured lounge, wondering if the owners took drugs.

'About six months.'

'Really?'

'It's the décor. The thing is, if people only want to rent for six months or a year, they don't want to spend money decorating. Especially with the choice that's out there at the moment. We'll look upstairs first, then I'll show you the kitchen because that leads to the converted garage.'

'Do you have any others with a converted garage?'

'No.' She turned to face me in the poky dark hallway. 'Actually, the conversion hasn't helped. Most people want a garage.'

She started to walk upstairs. The carpet underneath her high-heels was blue and worn, the tattered walkway giving way to the house's history. A strange feeling rose inside: would the girls and I leave a trail of our homeliness? The white walls needed a revamp. I imagined a new lick of paint, and all of our photos on display.

'Has it not had many viewings?' I asked as we reached the first floor.

'We've had a few more enquiries since we removed the front room and bathroom photos from the website,' she said smiling as she opened the bathroom door.

Everything was green. Green bath, toilet and sink. There was no shower cubicle, but there was a shower head attached to the bath taps. Despite the colour, it was pristine. If anything the fixtures looked brand new. The newly painted mint-green walls displayed stickers of dolphins, and the small green tiles that surrounded the bath were embellished with images of seashells. It wasn't to my taste but it was spotless; which helped, as replacing a bathroom wasn't in my budget. The two back bedrooms also looked as if they'd been recently decorated: simply, with magnolia paint and a new cream carpet that dared me to enter with my shoes on.

Back downstairs, Lynn showed me the open-plan kitchen diner, which was clean, fresh and spacious. White cupboards, lino flooring and white walls. It was basic, but I was quite pleased the owners hadn't put their own stamp on it. Lynn then showed me the room that had compelled me to book this viewing.

A door from the kitchen led into the garage. The room was quite dim, until Lynn switched on the spotlights that had been inserted into the ceiling. The room came to life: smooth flawless white walls, laminate flooring, a window onto the back garden and another door on the other side of the room, giving access to the outside. Perfect. It was as if this room had been built for me. I couldn't have designed it better if I'd tried. The room had been better cared for than the house.

'I want it on one condition,' I said quickly, turning to Lynn, whose eyes opened wide, her mouth slightly ajar.

'What?' She composed herself, her beaming smile back in place.

'I can redecorate the living room and the stairs.'

'I'm sure it won't be a problem, but I'll have to call the owners when I get back to the office.'

'Great.'

'We do have other properties that don't need any work.' She seemed shocked that I wanted this house.

'No, this is what I need.' I took in the room that would hopefully become my new workspace. 'This is perfect.'

*

I drove away and realised I was smiling. A warm feeling ran through me. This step felt so big, but so right.

Our new life.

My phone rang on the journey back to the flat. I recognised the number as the agent's and quickly plugged in my earphones, catching the call before it diverted.

'Kat? It's Lynn from Brickwork Homes.'

'Hi,' I said nervously, fearing her next words.

'They're happy for you to do this.'

'Fantastic!'

'So when are you thinking of moving in?'

'Oh …' my mind seemed to cloud; I couldn't think straight. 'I'd not really thought about it.'

'Oh.' Lynn sounded confused. 'Do you need it by a certain date? People generally move in on the first of the month, if you're not in a hurry.'

'Mmm… yes … great … April, then … the first of April.'

'Great. I'll need you to call at the office to complete the paperwork. Do you have an email address? I'll send over the details we need from you.'

I reeled off my email. A little flutter of excitement gripped me at the thought of setting up a new email for my new business. My new business in my new room. The next chapter of my life was about to begin, and I was excited about the change. I couldn't remember the last time I felt like this.

'Can you pop in tomorrow?'

'Yes, no problem.'

'Ten o'clock?'

'Great.'

I was going to have my own home. It had felt so perfect, as if it was meant for us. I could see Poppy and Rosie there for their first few years at least. I could see us walking down the high street, where no-one knew us. No-one knew our names, let alone our history. It would be our fresh start.

The only niggling worry that was spoiling the excitement was Clare.

How the hell do I tell her?

40

First thing the next morning, after feeding and changing the girls, and after receiving a voicemail to tell me my counselling session was cancelled but would go ahead next week, I drove excitedly, and nervously, over to Brickworks Estate Agents. They needed me to drop my identification documents off, and pay the bond and first month's rent. Paying such a lump sum made me realise I really needed to look at building my client base again, before my bank balance dwindled to nothing. Scrawling my signature over the contract that would ensure the girls and I had a roof over our heads for the next year felt liberating. I held onto that feeling of being free, rather than the knot of apprehension that pulled tight around my insides.

When we arrived back at the flat, I realised I was humming. I felt a happiness that I hoped I could build on. A happiness that would stay with me. As I filled the kettle with hot water, my phone rang. It was June. Libby had apparently had a restless, sleepless night. Welcome to my world.

'They started a relationship ...' June whispered, as if relaying interesting gossip.

'What do you mean?'

'A RE-LA-TION-SHIP!' She spelt it out to me as if I was foreign, or stupid.

'Like sexual?'

'Uh-huh.' I could imagine her shaking her head disapprovingly. Double standards.

'So where do we go from here?' I was confused. If he'd been her counsellor, how the hell was this allowed? Ronnie words, *'investigation'* flashed in my mind.

'Libby spoke with him last night. He's on the verge of losing his job because of it all. Apparently, one of the other members caught them—'

'What, at it?'

'Unfortunately, yes.'

'Oh my God!'

'I know. Libby was mortified. They suspended Matt, but she had to leave. She says she couldn't face the rest of the staff.'

'Oh my God!'

'Can you say anything else?'

'No, I can't.' I couldn't think straight. I wondered if it was possible for Libby to do anything in her life without causing a drama. Although, part of me was relieved that this had nothing to do with him supplying her with drugs or alcohol, this was still not a good scenario.

'Look, she thinks she's really fallen for this guy ...' she paused. 'I've told her he can come and stay with us.'

'What!'

'It's the best solution, Kat. There is no point keeping two people apart who want to be together.'

'She needs to get better, June.' I felt my heart racing, as anger welled. 'You said you would look after her.'

'He's a counsellor.'

'Not while he's with her.' My voice was raised. Rosie's eyelids flickered, and her lip quivered.

'He'll help her.'

'She needs to find out who she is on her own.'

'We're not all like you, Kat.' Her stony response was as hard as the brick I felt she'd thrown at me.

'What's that supposed to mean?' I managed through my tightened airways.

'Oh ... nothing ... I think Libby—'

'No,' I interrupted. 'What do you mean?' I wanted to leave it. But, I couldn't.

'You seem to cope ... you get on with it.'

'Because I have to.'

'Because you're strong.'

'I've had to be strong.' I felt my temper rising, ready to erupt. I breathed deeply, trying to supress the turmoil of emotion, but it flared into overspill. 'Where were you?'

'What do—'

'Where the hell were you when Mum died?'

'I've explained why—'

'You know, if you'd loved us so much you'd have stayed. You'd have fought for us. You'd not have left us in that demented house. You have the cheek to say that we're not all like me. I am as I am, because I've had to be—'

'Kat—'

'No, you listen. I've done my best with what I had.' Tears pricked, the lump in my throat swelled.

'I know that,' she said softly.

'So don't make this out as if I'm so cold-hearted that I simply move on from situations.' I wiped away a stray tear with the back of my hand. How dare she?

'I didn't mean that …' June stuttered. 'I just meant, I thought Matt coming would help Libby. He's a counsellor, she has feelings for him. He's not going to lead her down the wrong path.'

'But it's someone else she'll start relying on.'

'She needs that.'

'She needs to be on her own.' Why wasn't she getting this? 'If he leaves her, for whatever reason, what do you think will happen?'

'I think you're worrying too much about this.'

'I have to, June. If he hurts her, she will go downhill. She needs space.'

'I think it's too late, though.'

'Why?'

'He's on his way.'

*

After I'd told her, 'If this goes wrong, I will blame you,' we ended the conversation. I was still simmering with fury. It was as if she lived in this make-believe world of fairy tales and romance, where everything would have a happy ending. But she must've known from her own life that this wasn't the case. I couldn't believe how stupid she was being. I had to fight the urge to jump in the car and drive down there. Sort things out in the way I'd always had to. I knew I should have stood my ground when it came to Libby leaving.

It was at this moment that I understood why Marianne couldn't forgive and move on with June. She'd probably seen plenty of this behaviour: not looking at the consequences, absorbed in a delusional world. The whole affair with Henry, I'd had to forgive, or not think about too much. I'd not told Clare this, obviously, but I'd felt somewhat sorry for June. I'd seen it as a cry for help, loneliness. Henry was probably there when she needed the attention. And as Max had said, this wasn't the first time. Playing on her vulnerability, he'd lured her in. I'd showed my disappointment, though I'd not truly blamed her. But involving Libby in her fantasy world was too much. I didn't want Libby getting hurt any more than she already had.

I thought about her words: 'It's the best solution, Kat. There is no point keeping two people apart who want to be together.' Was she really referring to herself? But she hadn't been talking about Dad, surely. It was Libby and me that June had wanted. It was us she'd come back for. Wasn't that how the story went?

Maybe she'd had endless affairs in Devon. A secret life.

It wouldn't surprise me. I was worried she'd spin Libby into her illusory, whimsical world of dreams, and the only person who would get hurt was Libby.

I couldn't find the words to tell Marianne, when she turned up to babysit the girls, so I could have my delightful evening at Brooke's. It felt easier to keep it to myself until I knew if Matt had arrived. There was no point worrying Marianne, because that's all she would do.

*

When I turned up at Brooke's house, candles were lit around the lounge. Flickering, dancing shadows flitted round the plain cream walls. A grand portrait photo, displayed in a heavy gold frame, exhibited Chelsea as if she was a prize possession. A pink headband around the wisps of blonde hair, and a dress that would have suited a pageant queen, made me cringe. I wondered if her lips were really so rosy, or if Brooke had actually put make-up on her.

Brooke gave me a glass of wine. She'd dressed down this evening: well, down for her. Still in black, but a velour jogging suit, that looked expensive. Her hair was arranged elegantly strands falling sexily around her high cheekbones. I'd dressed in black trousers and a loose black top I'd found at the back of my wardrobe.

'Daryl's putting Chelsea to bed.'

'He's good,' I smiled, then wished I hadn't paid him a compliment.

'He is,' she agreed. 'He's such a good person, but like most men he demands so much.'

'Show me one that doesn't,' I joked, swigging a large mouthful of wine. This would be a long night. I needed to change the subject, or leave. 'I've been looking at a place in Yarm.'

'You're moving?' She looked shocked.

'Mmm … yes,' I mumbled. 'It's only down the road, you can still visit.' Oh God, what was I saying? The night, once again, was already going from bad to worse.

'Why are you moving? I thought you loved it here.'

'Many reasons, really, but I'm looking at starting my beauty business back up.'

'But you could still do that with the salon. Clare would let you wouldn't she?'

'She probably would, but I need to be away from Melanie and Mandy's salon.'

'But Melanie's not there anymore.'

'You know about that?'

'Everyone knows about that.' Brooke took a sip of her wine, running her tongue across her top lip as it glistened from the residue. 'Mandy's losing customers every day. Ange doesn't use her any more. I think Mandy was rude to one of her customers when Ange was there, or something like that.'

'So where does she go?'

'I'm not sure. She keeps batting around a few, she can't settle.'

'Hello there, Kat.' Daryl purred, walking into the room. A tight-fitted white T-shirt showed off his well-defined muscles. His chest boasting from underneath the constricted fabric and his arms bulging. In any other setting, he might have turned heads twice. In this scene, I wanted to run. Away. Fast.

I managed to nod, but no words came out. I quickly guzzled a good two mouthfuls of wine. I thought this was meant to be a girlie night. A girlie night that Brooke so desperately wanted.

'I'll go and get the crisps and dips,' Brooke said, standing up from the sofa, running her hand across Daryl's sculptured chest as she passed him. He winked. Oh, that god-awful, unnerving wink. She let out a giggle, and left the room. Leaving him me alone … with him.

'How are you this evening?' he asked, strutting towards me, then sitting down beside me.

Why *me*? Sit over there. Slurping another mouthful of wine, he stared at me, waiting for an answer. 'I'm good, thanks,' I finally allowed myself to say.

He cocked his head to the side, his forefinger suddenly stroking my thigh. 'I've not been able to stop thinking about you.'

'Oh, there's nothing to think about.' I let out a light laugh, moving slightly away from him. My heart was sprinting. My wine rippled as my hands trembled.

As he edged his way towards me, the fierce desire in his eyes was burning and his warm breath was upon my neck.

'I want you,' he groaned quietly. 'Relax, Brooke won't mind.'

The part of me that could find the strength to move, made me shove my hand against his chest, meeting the rock of his muscles.

I slid from the sofa, the floor feeling the weight of my backside. My wine spilled out from the glass, slopping down my front, splattering wet blotches across my trousers and Brooke's carpet. And even as this nightmare was happening, as the liquid absorbed into her thick cream carpet I was thankful I wasn't drinking red.

'Don't be scared, just enjoy it,' Daryl urged, exhaling huskily. I think he thought he was being sexy, but he sounded asthmatic. 'Come. Sit with me.' His wolf-like eyes seemed to undress me with his intense stare, as he patted the sofa next to him.

'Go on, Kat.' Brooke appeared suddenly from the kitchen. She'd removed an outer layer of clothing, a vest top accentuating her big bosoms, which were squashed together in an undersized bra, forming a deep cleavage.

'I think I'd better leave.' I scrambled to my feet, holding the coffee table to keep my balance.

'Don't leave,' Daryl purred, his hand running across his open legs.

'Oh, Kat, I'm sorry,' Brooke said desperately. I wrestled with my coat, tripping over the edge of the sofa as I tried to leave.

'Please stay,' Brooke begged, following me, panic showing in her face.

'That's not a good idea,' I said hastily, sweat bursting from my every pore.

'The other night, we thought you might be interested. Letting Daryl walk you home, touch you.'

'Touch me?'

'You know.'

'He felt my arse!' I was outraged.

'I'm sorry, we read the wrong signals. I thought with you coming back round you were probably interested, and ... you're on your own.'

'You didn't give me much choice, you practically begged me round here. Luring me into this ...' Whatever I said would have insulted her. Although her behaviour was way out of line, I could see her vulnerability and wondered if she really wanted to play these games, or if it was all Daryl's ideas. I wasn't staying to find out. 'I've got to go.'

'Call me …' I heard her small voice disappear behind the front door as I slammed it shut.

I ran for my life, the wind urging me on through the village, the river swarming turbulently beside me, the trees rustling and hissing overhead. My feet padding heavily against the pavement, my coat swishing against the strong marching actions of my arms. Ricocheting breaths against my ears, inside my head was the vibration of short sharp breaths.

I finally made it to the flat. My chest was burning, the stitch in my side felt like a needle. Not wanting Marianne to see me in this state. I leaned against the wall, composing myself, trying to catch my breath.

'What the hell was that?' I said to myself, shaking my head in horror at what had just happened. Had Brooke been grooming me?

The thought sent a sudden shiver of amusement through me. I heard the roar of my own laughter. My chest began to ache as more laughter poured out of me. Great bouts of glee erupted.

Suddenly, the sadness of the whole situation pierced my hilarity, as I slid down the wall, resting my head in my hands, my laughter turned into tears of sadness.

41

I missed the several calls from Brooke the following morning. After her fifth attempt, I turned the phone off. I couldn't face talking to her. I was embarrassed. For myself as much as them. Was this what they did? Look for the sad, lonely, single mums who looked so desperate they'd jump at the chance of a threesome? I presumed that's what they had in mind.

I had no intention of finding out.

I followed my usual morning routine: feeding and changing the girls, then showering while they slept (not daring to relax in the bath again), but every step this morning was an effort. I felt weak and lethargic. This was definitely going to be another day indoors.

I tried to relive the excitement I'd felt when I'd looked around the house we'd soon be moving to. But nothing was budging the stale, pulsating raft of torn emotions. I felt hurt. Used. I'd thought she needed friends and I'd put myself out there.

I climbed into my jogging suit, the one that was for the flat only. Suddenly the door resounded under the loud hammering of a fist. The girls still had ten minutes' sleep left. There was no way I was letting anyone wake them, so I quickly went to answer the door.

Brooke looked pale, and the dark shadows under her eyes showed she'd not slept well. Her hair had obviously not seen a brush, let alone a mirror. 'I'm sorry, Kat, you're not answering my calls and I had to see you.'

'I've had my phone switched off all morning.' Half a lie is okay, isn't it?

'I'm so sorry about last night—'

'Let's forget it.' Really wishing I could.

'I feel awful.' Her lip quivered as a sob escaped. 'I haven't got many friends, and when I found you I thought it was great. We're so alike.' Are we? 'Now I've messed it all up.'

'No.' I sighed deeply. It took less energy to forgive her than it did to fight. I found myself bringing her in for a hug. Feeling sorry for her. 'No. It was a mistake, that's all.' Her body was trembling against mine, soft gulps of air caught with the tears that poured dramatically from her. 'Come on. Come up for a coffee.'

'Thank you.' She wiped her hand across her wet nose. Sniffling up the excess residue, trying to wipe her shiny wet cheeks with her palms.

Inside the flat after we'd had a cup of tea, Brooke helped to feed Poppy while I fed Rosie. Little Chelsea lay asleep in her car seat, which Brooke had detached from the pushchair. The pushchair that was now blocking my front door: another reason to move.

'Daryl puts so much pressure on me,' Brook said sadly as she looked at Poppy.

'In what way?'

'He always wants to try something different. There's no normal sex, it's always backside first, upside down, objects, people, or jumping off bloody wardrobes.' Brooke shook her head. I didn't know what to say. 'When we first met it had been exciting, you know?' *No. I didn't know!* 'It had been fun, but lately it's too much. I'm knackered.'

'Understandably.' Finally, a subject I could relate to.

'We've had threesomes before …' And back to a subject I couldn't relate to. 'He usually finds someone who is up for it. He thought you were prime material.'

Prime material – what the hell did that mean?

'He thought you were definitely up for it,' she continued. I was lost for words, as I didn't want to insult her any more, I think my sharp exit last night had shown the fact, I absolutely *was not* up for it. 'I want him to just want me. Only me.' Her eyes filled as she blinked the tears away. Not having a free hand to wipe them, she leaned forward and wiped them on the sleeve of her chiffon top, her arm expertly not moving the bottle away from Poppy's mouth.

'Have you talked to him about it?' I asked softly.

'No,' she said, shaking her head, 'There's no point, I know he'll go off cheating, otherwise. They always say you marry your dad. I didn't. I married my brother. He's always at it somewhere, but he'd be lost without Ange. That's why I was trying to convince her the other night that he couldn't live without her.'

'But how is that fair on Mrs Don … Ange?' Now at a complete loss.

'It's not,' Brooke snivelled, 'but she's there for the money. It works for them.'

'She didn't look as if it was working for her the other night.'

'She's always like that when she's had a drink. It's nothing to do with our Steve, it's because she wants a baby.'

I nodded, as if understanding, when I truly didn't. I really didn't understand how Mrs D could stay with a man who cheated on her all the time. It seemed obvious that, as Daryl had said, it was for the money; but still this made no sense to me. It didn't feel appropriate to bring this up with Brooke, though.

Suddenly the key turned in the secret door, and as if they were listening outside, Clare and Mrs D walked straight in.

'What's this about you moving?' Clare asked me abruptly.

'W-w-what?' I found myself stuttering.

'Moving?' Clare was obviously very put out. Her eyes were wide.

I didn't know where to look. I felt as if I'd been caught out in an illegal act. My chest felt as if it had hit the floor. My throat dry, as I tried to focus on how to answer.

'Brooke was telling me about you setting up a salon in your new house. I was passing and popped in to see when it was happening, I'm desperate for you to come back.' Mrs D announced.

'Sorry,' mimed Brooke, obviously seeing the look of horror on my face as I grasped at different excuses, wondering which one to use.

'It's for the best, Clare,' I said, finally finding my voice, deciding lying was not an option. I knew we had to talk this out, but I'd been trying to think of a way that wouldn't hurt her. I would have to think pretty quickly now. 'I need more space.'

'But you have more space now Libby and June have gone,' Clare said indignantly.

'But Libby will be coming back.'

'I'm really upset you haven't told me.' Clare was clearly hurt and quite angry. Her cheeks were flushed, her jaw line was tight, as her eyes seemed to burn through me.

'I'm sorry. I was going to—'

'I'll leave Mrs Donnelly with you,' Clare interrupted, quickly shutting the door before I had the chance to say anything.

'Oh, she's not very happy, is she?' Mrs D seemed to be mocking Clare.

I felt my own cheeks burn as guilt grabbed at me. I was unsure how to handle this. Mrs D sat down next to Brooke, who was obviously aware of the tense atmosphere.

'I best go after her,' I mumbled.

'I'd wait until she's calmed down,' Mrs D said. Was she right? I didn't want to make a scene downstairs. 'Anyway, when are you moving?' More questions distracted me from chasing Clare.

As I explained my plans to Mrs D, she didn't seem to notice my anguish. She asked questions and clapped her hands in excitement. Excitement for herself, not for me. While she asked about treatments, slated Mandy and generally centred the whole conversation around herself, I fought the urge to cry.

I felt terrible. Clare had offered me the flat rent-free. It was as if I was throwing it back in her face. She'd know that I was moving because I couldn't bear her walking in every five minutes. She'd know I was making up excuses. She'd be devastated that

I hadn't come to talk to her about it. But I hadn't wanted to make demands. I knew how generous she'd been: who lives rent-free these days? Who has that opportunity? I'd felt so grateful to her, but I needed to move on.

And it wasn't only her. It was being in this gorgeous, picturesque village, that I adored so much, but now I felt so out of place.

I hoped Clare would understand when I spoke to her.

42

Even without everything else that was going on, I'd found this week quite testing anyway; but then, I always had. This particular week of the year would always have me on edge, wondering what other mothers were planning with their daughters. Wondering what I would have planned on Mother's Day with my own mum. Perhaps it would get easier when the girls were older and they wanted to make an effort on Mother's Day (in hope that they would).

I'd never bought Marianne a card on Mother's Day. Even last year I'd avoided her. She'd always been Dad's girlfriend: she wasn't like a mum to me. Whereas now it was completely different. I couldn't bring myself to buy her a card that stated 'To my mother', but I had found myself searching for a 'someone special' card. Something that would show I cared, without betraying Mum. So after finding the perfect card (the perfect title: 'You mean the world to me', that had a perfect poem inside) I'd purchased two bunches of flowers from the local florist.

Marianne's bunch of flowers was an array of white oriental lilies, elegantly arranged in a glass vase. Clare's on the other hand were a lot more elaborate. I'd felt the need to buy her a peace-offering gift. Not so much an apology, I couldn't apologise for needing my own space, but the way she'd found out wasn't the best. I would apologise for not telling her first. She'd not only stormed out of the flat, but stormed out of the salon, and wouldn't answer my calls. I hadn't bought Clare a selection of blue hyacinths, with white, pink and mauve tulips to outdo Marianne's simple but elegant arrangement: I'd picked both women's favourite flowers. I'd thought about offering Clare a peace lily, thinking the name of the plant would be ideal; but considering she thought lilies should only appear at funerals, I didn't think that would help to fix our relationship.

I pulled up onto Clare's drive, relieved that Max wasn't there. My plan was working so far: calling at Clare's early so she would be in and Max wouldn't have arrived yet - assuming he was seeing Clare on Mother's Day.

The girls were sleeping in the back and I didn't want to wake them, so I kept the engine running as I carefully pulled the flowers from the car front footwell.

I knocked on the door quietly, not daring to knock too loudly in case I sounded too demanding. No-one answered, at first, then Henry finally appeared. His eyes lit up when he saw me. 'Kat, dear, come on in.'

'I can't … the girls …' I pointed towards the car.

'Bring them in.' He waved his hand in mid-air. I wondered if he was being polite or if he was overanxious, as this was our first encounter since his shenanigans with June had been revealed.

'They're asleep and I'm going to Marianne's,' I smiled, not wanting him to think I was making excuses not to be in his company. 'Is Clare home?'

'Yes, I'll go and get her.'

'Thank you.'

As I watched him wander down their wooden hallway, I had a sudden memory of Gina bumping into the wall as she'd emerged from the toilet. That night had been a game for Gina and Max. He'd already been seeing her, using Dave as a decoy, because they'd fallen out. No wonder she'd been so drunk. I was surprised she hadn't told me the truth. In fact, if anything, she'd lied: she told me Max had wanted me, and that hadn't been the case.

How could they both have played such an awful trick? How could they have been so devious? It made me feel stupid. But that was over now, I shouldn't be worrying about them. Thoughts of Lampford Hall entered my mind, as I pushed them away, knowing I'd be angry by the time I spoke to Clare, which hadn't been my intention.

Clare emerged looking tired, dressed in black linen trousers and a black top, representing someone who was in mourning. Her hair perfected, as always, but her make-up not fully covering the lines like it normally did. Had I hurt her that much?

I held out the flowers, in the hope they would soften her. She smiled wearily, as I said, 'I just wanted you to know I really do appreciate that you've let me and the girls live in the flat, but I'm not happy in the village anymore.'

'These are lovely, thank you,' she said, taking the huge bunch of flowers from me, smelling them as if she was about to taste a new wine. 'They are gorgeous, but you really didn't have to.'

'I wanted to. I'm sorry you found out the way you did.'

'Admittedly, that hurt.'

'I was going to tell you.' I didn't tell her I'd struggled to tell her in case she thought it was her fault. Because it *was* partly her fault, but I didn't think she needed to know this.

'I understand you need some space, but I wish you'd told me rather than letting me hear it second-hand.'

'I know. I'm sorry.'

'So when do you move?'

'Beginning of April.'

'That soon?'

'Apparently it's best to move at the beginning of the month, or something like that. Helps with the rent payments.' I shrugged, not really wanting to talk to her about this.

'If you need any help packing, or babysitting, you know where I am.'

'Thank you.'

'Are you not coming in?'

'No, we're off to Marianne's.'

'Well, thank you for these, they are much appreciated.' She leaned forward and hugged me close, a ten-second hug that felt like ten minutes, as if she didn't want to let me go.

As we drove away, I felt relieved she'd made that easy. I suppose I was more worried about telling her because I was 'biting the hand that fed me' as the saying goes. But I'd not really thought how it would affect her in terms of the girls. At the moment she could see them every day; twice, three times and more if she wanted to. When we moved, there would be limitations: she would have to ring first when she wanted to visit and how would she fit this in with running the business? I couldn't stay in the flat, though, just to please Clare. I needed to move on with my own life or I'd be there for ever.

When we arrived at Marianne's, Derek came out to greet us. He helped unlatch the girls from the car, then took Poppy in her car seat towards the house, while I followed with Rosie. Bag over my shoulder, the vase of flowers clamped in one hand and car seat swinging from my other arm, I was getting pretty good at piling myself up and still having a hand free.

Marianne smiled from the doorway, as always beaming whenever she saw us. 'Happy Mother's Day,' she said as she kissed my cheek.

'Thank you,' I responded. 'These are for you.'

I handed her the vase of lilies. She took them, and I could see her swallow and blink, then she hugged me again. 'Thank you,' she choked. Then a tear escaped.' Oh sorry, look at me.'

'I hope that's a snivel because you like them,' I jested, wanting to remove the awkwardness between us, the unspoken *but you've never done this before.*

'I love them … you shouldn't have.' She wiped away a tear.

'I wanted to.'

'Thank you,' she said again.

'You're more than welcome.'

We went into the living room, where Derek had already taken Poppy out of her car seat. Happily she rolled around on the pink fleece blanket, giggling as Derek talked to her. Marianne took Rosie out, giving her a sloppy kiss, and putting her down next to Poppy. Derek gave a surprise gasp as Rosie gawped up at him, stared intently, gave a little smile and then tried to roll over.

'I'll put the kettle on,' Marianne said, leaving the room.

'So how are you?' Derek turned and asked me quite seriously.

'I'm fine,' I smiled, hoping the smile met my eyes.

'It's hard work.'

'I know.' You don't need to tell me.

'We have a parent and baby group at the church, maybe you'd like to attend.'

'Oh, I'm already in a group.' It was the only thing I could think of to say. I didn't want to attend any more groups. I'd met enough loony people at the last one.

'I'm sure joining some more groups will help you get through the hard years.'

'Maybe,' I shrugged, refraining from asking if the group would help me with sleepless nights, feeding and changing.

'I'm sure Marianne would go along with you.'

'Go where?' Marianne popped her head back in.

'To the parent and baby group at the church,' Derek said.

'Of course, I would.'

I half-nodded and hoped I hadn't grimaced, not wanting to offend Derek I decided it best not to answer.

Derek turned to the girls and started to talk gibberish again. I smiled along with him. Marianne appeared with a tray of teas and biscuits. She then handed me a pink envelope with the word 'Mummy' scrolled across the front.

'What's this?' I asked, placing my cup of steaming tea down on the table.

'It's for you,' Marianne said as she sipped from her own cup, her eyes alight.

Ripping open the envelope I pulled out the card that read, 'To our Mummy on Mother's Day'. Inside Marianne had written both the girls names. I hugged her, unable to speak, emotion sweeping over me. 'Thank you,' I swallowed. I was so touched that Marianne had thought to do this. I'd thought Max might have made an effort; but then why should he? We weren't together. The way he was going on at the moment, though, I'd thought he might have tried with something. But then what would Gina have said about that, had she found out?

'I spoke with Libby this morning.' Marianne dipped a biscuit into her tea.

'How was she?' I put the card back in the envelope, looking forward to putting it up when I got back to the flat.

'She seems to be fine. She said her and June were getting on great—'

'Which doesn't surprise me.'

'You didn't tell me June had invited that Matt guy.'

'I was trying to forget it was happening.'

'He might help Libby,' Marianne said as she munched on her soggy biscuit.

'I think she needs to get through this on her own at first.'

'I agree,' Derek said, taking a chocolate biscuit from the plate.

'I don't think June would dare fail you.'

'It's Libby she'd be failing,' I responded.

'It's both of you.' Marianne paused. 'I know we didn't want her to go, but after speaking to Libby I've got a good feeling about this.'

'I hope you're right,' I said, thinking how lovely it would be to have Libby back in the new house with me, drug-free. I hadn't told her about the house yet, but I was hoping it would help her set a goal. A target to reach. I missed her. Not that I'd seen much of her when she was living with Marianne, but not being able to see her whenever I wanted was harder than I'd thought it would be. It had been hard enough when she was in rehab, but at least we could see her every week, and I knew they were keeping an eye on her. She was there for a reason.

I was worried June would forget this reason. I was worried she would go off and lead her own little life, as I'd come to realise it didn't take much to distract her. But hopefully she was keeping Libby safe. I hoped Matt's presence wasn't so he could babysit Libby while June headed off to bingo, or wherever else she frequented on an evening.

I just had to hope and pray that Marianne was right.

<h1 style="text-align:center">43</h1>

The next week seemed to pass in a blur. I started to pack up the flat in between feeding, changing and other baby jobs that seemed to take over my life. I tried not to show too much excitement in front of Clare who seemed very low. I didn't know if she was more upset with me or with Henry, and I didn't like to ask. She was distant and subdued.

I'd accompanied Suzy and her mum to the final dress-fitting. Our dresses fitted perfectly, which was great. Although it wasn't even my wedding, I was starting to feel nervous. But everything had gone to plan (up to now). Suzy's mum had taken the dresses to her house, to make sure Lawrence didn't even get a glimpse and because we'd planned on getting ready at Suzy's mum's on the morning.

As I waited for Rhonda in the waiting room, I wished she'd cancelled this week's counselling session also. The thing was, I felt fine at the moment. I didn't need to talk about anything; the tablets had really kicked in. I was starting to feel happy, and positive about my life. But I was signed up now, and would have felt guilty if I hadn't gone.

I examined the room. The floor was covered in brown carpet tiles and the walls painted a musty, creamy colour that looked dirty and in need of a good old refurbish. It was so depressing in here. Vibrant colours and pictures would have lifted the room's aura: but I wondered if a counsellor had influenced the decor, not wanting anyone to feel too cheerful, as this would distract from how they were really feeling. As I analysed the need for an interior designer in this dreary place, other random thoughts passed through my mind. One being Suzy's hen day.

Suzy's spa day would be on Sunday. I couldn't wait to get her there: I'd never seen her so wound up. She'd randomly come out, mid conversation, about things she really needed to think about doing. To be honest, I'd be quite pleased when the wedding was all over, I guessed Suzy would be, too. I should have handed her my counselling session today. She'd have enjoyed reeling off all the things that were driving her insane at the moment.

But my biggest worry was tomorrow – Max and Gina's wedding. I told Rhonda this once she'd let me into the room.

'So what's the plan for tomorrow?' she asked, relaxing back in her chair. Was she interested in how I felt about the wedding, or was she just being nosey?

I explained to her I would feel extremely uncomfortable standing outside Lampford Hall watching Max and Gina getting married. It wasn't only the fact it was *Lampford Hall*, or the fact that I'd be standing on the edge like a spare part while people stared, pointed and gossiped about me being the mother. It was also the worry about the girls: what if they were sick down their dresses before they arrived? What if Clare missed their feeding time? I was going to try and schedule their feeds around the 2 p.m. wedding, but that wasn't their routine. The other thing that was narking me about the whole thing was that Max hadn't offered to buy them nice dresses. I'd asked him what he'd like them to wear, in the hope he'd delve into his pockets and also help me choose but he'd merely said, 'Something smart.'

'What does *something smart* 'mean?' I asked Rhonda, as if she should know.

'Why didn't you ask Max outright if he could help?'

'It's his wedding. He should have decided what he wanted them to wear. If I don't put them in something really nice, Gina will think I'm doing it to spoil the photos.'

Rhonda simply nodded. I wasn't sure if she agreed with me or not. She had trained eyes, if that was possible, but they were so intent, listening to every word but not once could I read what she was thinking.

'Anyway, I've bought them some lovely cream dresses, which Max will probably think are over the top.'

Rhonda nodded again. 'I'm sure he'll be pleased you've made the effort.'

'This is the other thing …' I launched into the story of how Max had suddenly told me he wanted me back. I couldn't believe how comfortable I felt talking to Rhonda. It was wonderful being able to say all these things to her and know they would go no further. And I'd thought I didn't need this session.

After my spiel Rhonda asked me, 'How do you feel about getting back with Max?'

'There is no way I'm going back there. I love the idea of us being a family, but it's a fantasy now. There is no going back. I *couldn't* go back.'

Rhonda chewed the end of her pen. She seemed to be thinking for a second, then she suddenly changed the line of conversation and asked, 'How was Mother's Day?'

'Not as bad as I'd expected,' I confessed. I'd told Rhonda on the previous session that I was dreading the day.

'That's good,' she said, smiling.

I explained what had happened with Clare and that I'd spent some time with Marianne, and that I'd coped, whereas every other year I'd always found something to do to keep me occupied. One year I'd even opened the salon on Mother's Day, but that was a killer: mothers and daughters laughing together as they had their treatments. I'd cried all night and a few days after.

It brought it home to me what I was missing. So I'd never opened on Mother's Day again.

'Hopefully each year will become easier,' Rhonda said, scribbling in her notepad.

The session ended, and Rhonda showed me to the door. I had the urge to hug her. The only person who'd heard such in-depth thoughts was Suzy, and I always hugged her.

I felt slightly drained, although settled. Speaking to someone who didn't really know me was actually therapeutic, but the amount of personal anguish that seemed to spin off my tongue was exhausting.

I wondered if she'd wanted me to open up more about Mum when she'd asked the Mother's Day question.

Maybe I was ready to do that next time.

Later, in my flat, my comfy tracksuit on, the girls asleep, I lay on the sofa with a chilled glass of wine. The coolness helping me to relax. Exhaustion swept over my body, but my mind ticked over.

It was Max's number flashing from my mobile that distracted me. I answered, although something told me to leave it.

How I wished I had as when I answered he said, 'I'm giving you one last chance and I promise I'll call off the wedding …'

44

Clare and Henry were early. Blustering around the flat like a whirlwind, I soon had the girls dressed, their bag packed and an agreement made that we'd all meet up at Lampford Park in a few hours. It would take me an hour to get there, so I would literally be getting ready and immediately following them.

As I shut the front door I was pleased that neither of the girls, had thrown up all over their cream frilly dresses. 'Please get them there clean,' I prayed.

A text from Brooke was waiting for me when I came back into the room, asking me if I'd like to meet later. No, I didn't *like* to. I had enough going on today without seeing an insane friend. Could I even call her a friend? Acquaintance, maybe.

My focus for today was to get to and from Lampford Hall without having some kind of mental breakdown. Not only having to stand and watch Max and Gina smiling happily, but Max's words were echoing in my head as if he was just speaking them.

'You'll regret this,' he'd told me. 'We're meant to be together Kat.' I'd not been able to speak. I'd wanted to scream at him. How dare he do this? How dare he do this the night before his wedding? 'We had so many good times, so many laughs. Can you remember the time—'

'I don't reminisce about us anymore Max, it was a long time ago.' I stopped him as talking about memories would make my heart pull. I purposely didn't think about our memories.

'But what about the time—'

'Max, seriously, you can't do this.' I wouldn't allow this to happen.

'I want you Kat.'

'But I don't want you.' I lied. 'Look Max, I've got to go.' I hung-up. I hadn't slept too well after that.

I hoped the photographs would be over by the time I arrived, so I could take the girls and leave swiftly. I didn't want to be the centre of attention, or a part of their wedding. If I could have got Clare and Henry to meet me down the road I would have done. Preferably a pub, so I could drink away the twisted knot that had tightened every part of my insides.

But, swallowing my fear, I showered, dressed - with the TV on as a distraction - and forced myself to smile. They would not see how much this was getting to me. Especially Gina, whose sweet innocence had been such a lie. The thought of her really enjoying watching me standing in the shadows, being the audience to her big day, made me frustrated. I wanted to tell her about Max calling me, but I knew she wouldn't believe me. She'd think I was trying to ruin her big day. And Max, who had shown his true colours, would deny all.

Just stop! Stop! Stop! Stop!

I'd drive myself insane if I carried on with these thoughts. I didn't want Max. No matter what happened, even if he left Gina, he *could not* come back to me. I *would not* let him come back.

I'd not worried about what I'd wear today, but suddenly, as I searched through my wardrobe, I realised that none of my clothes were right for this occasion.

But what type of occasion was it? I wasn't a guest, so I couldn't turn up in a glamorous outfit. If I went too casual, everyone would be thinking, no wonder Max left her for Gina.

In my panic, I started to freak out as I pulled trousers, jeans, tops, dresses and skirts from my wardrobe and drawers – many things I'd not seen since I'd fallen pregnant – but nothing seemed suitable.

'What is suitable?' I asked aloud, hoping for some kind of epiphany. And as if the universe was listening to my thoughts, reacting to my desires, my phone beeped. A text from Suzy to see what time I'd be there; she'd meet me outside.

It felt strange Suzy being part of their day. She'd not wanted to go. She'd begged Lawrence, who was their best man to let her stay at home. She would fake an illness if it got her off the hook. Lawrence wasn't over keen himself on going to the wedding, Suzy had told me, he didn't particularly like Gina. I wondered if he'd always felt like this in the past, or was it because I was on the scene? Did it matter?

'struggling with outfit! Do I go casual, dressy or middle. Skirt, dress, leggings, jeans or trousers – help!'

My phone rang within seconds of me sending the text.

'Hiya,' I flapped.

'Casual, definitely casual,' Suzy said quietly, practically whispering. I wondered who was in earshot. I hoped Max and Gina weren't; I didn't want them knowing about my outfit crisis. They'd know I was bothered. And as we know, I absolutely wasn't …

'Like, jeans casual?'

'Jeans and your suit jacket?'

'Suit jacket?' Was that casual these days?

'Yes, suit jacket. Do you still have that pale-pink sparkly top? That always made you look great.'

'Not sure I have it any more. It was a pre-pregnancy top.'

'If not, something sparkly but casual,' Suzy ordered, obviously loving this little mission.

'With my boots?'

'*No, no, no*! Heels.'

'I have heeled boots.'

'No. Shoes. High-heeled shoes. You have some gorgeous ones. Get them out.'

'I thought you said casual.' My mind searched through the boxes of glamorous heels I'd hidden away since falling pregnant.

'This is your new, natural, casual look,' Suzy laughed.

'You think?'

'Got to go, Gina's heading my way. See you soon.' She'd put the phone down before I'd had the chance to say goodbye.

'Right … heels,' I said to myself, as I headed towards my bedroom. I searched through the boxes of sparkly heels that I'd once worn at any given opportunity: shopping, meals out, cinema, I'd worn them for fun! Yes, I'd worn heels for fun. Now, I didn't get what was fun about them. Achy feet, pulled carves … maybe I had to reinvent myself. My old, worn, beige UGGs seemed to stare at me, lonely in the corner of my room. I was tempted, but Suzy was still out there: she knew what was going on in the fashion world. Even her work attire, which was a tracksuit, was designer.

'Skinny jeans, not those comfy things you've been wearing xxx'

Suzy ordered over text message. Oh dear, not my comfy jeans – could I fit into my skinny jeans?

'It's only for this morning. We'll get *you* back on when we get back,' I said to my comfy jogging bottoms as I laid them on the bed, desperate to put them on now. After pulling out more clothes, I was actually quite pleased, a little excited. It was like having a whole new wardrobe. Clothes that had not seen the light of day in over a year appeared brand new.

I found the t-shirt Suzy was talking about. I racked my brains to see if I'd worn it when I was with Max. Would that matter? Would it spoil my look? Why was I bothered? I knew it wasn't Max I was trying to impress, or even Gina. It was their hundred and odd guests. I felt as if I was about to perform a dance at the West End. All eyes on me; no-one should ever outdo the bride, but I knew I was doing exactly that, by just being there.

In any other circumstances I would have enjoyed (only a little) out-doing Gina, but today she would look the best she would ever look; while I, little old me, was still trying to get rid of baby fat and baggy eyes. To top it all off I was going to attempt to walk in four-inch heels across a rocky path, as if I was walking a tightrope; but I had to appear natural. 'Waddling duck' sprang to mind.

I emptied the 'old make-up' bag; you know, the one with all the special goodies that enhanced rather than merely covered. Using my old techniques, I made myself up, then realised why I didn't do this every day: it took far too bloody long. Jesus, I'd be lucky if I finished applying by the end of the day with Poppy and Rosie in the background. How the hell did I do this every day before they were born?

As happy as I could be with my causal, natural style, that had taken two hours to prepare, I left the flat, feeling apprehensive. Actually my medication had definitely helped in lowering my anxiety levels, which worried me somewhat: what state would I have been in without them?

The car seemed to take me automatically towards Lampford Park. The weekend I'd bought my first car, Libby and I drove this way. Although I was only twelve when we'd taken that awful previous journey, I knew it that day with Libby, as if it was imprinted on my brain. Today felt the same: not only the roads, but the same feeling of uncertainty.

I'd hoped that day, with Libby, for some form of closure. But it hadn't happened. We'd walked around the grounds with trepidation. I hadn't enjoyed the scenery and Libby had seemed pained, as if memories she'd deeply hidden had come to the forefront of her mind. She'd said it felt creepy, which was exactly how I'd felt. I'd thought we'd feel love, warmth, and close to Mum, but all I'd felt was a strange feeling of resentment. If we'd not been here that fateful day, Mum might still be with us. If Dad hadn't cheated on Mum with June, would they have made such an effort for a family day out?

Lampford Hall had a lot to answer for, and I wasn't looking forward to visiting the place again.

An hour later I drove the car along the wide extravagant drive, the trees romantically shadowing the grey stone driveway, the sunlight breaking through the mass of spring leaves. My heart was beating fast. My hands shook as they grasped the steering wheel. I was worried it would jump from my hands, and veer me off course.

'Calm …' I told myself, exhaling deeply. 'You can do this.' I quickly sent Suzy a text to say I'd arrived, in the hope she'd help get me in and out at quick speed.

A crowd of overdressed people were congregated at the back of the hall, which was visible from the side of the road. People sat on the stone wall, chatting, laughing. Most were holding a glass of champagne. I remembered how we'd sat on the grass enjoying a picnic with Mum and Dad, just down from the terrace. How Mum had told stories about the fairies who lived inside.

I hoped Max and Gina's guests didn't recognise me, or my car, as I followed the driveway that curved around the side of the old building, leading to the car park at the front of the hall. For the first time this morning, I considered the weather, realising that the sun was shining and the rain had held off for their day. Usually I hoped for nice weather when couples were getting married, but I couldn't help but be a little disappointed that Gina's hair and dress hadn't been ruined by a monsoon. That's awful, isn't it? I wouldn't say it aloud to anyone.

I drove the car into the car park, really wanting to be invisible, discreetly parking in a corner so that no-one would know I'd arrived. I could imagine that Poppy and Rosie had received enormous amounts of attention from Max and Gina's guests, so my arrival would send more gossip rippling through the wedding party.

As I tottered across the stony path, fighting hard - but losing the battle - to look casual, I reached a smooth pavement that allowed me to walk more gracefully. I hoped Clare didn't say how lovely I looked. I wasn't meant to look as if I'd made an effort: I was *always* this chic.

Suzy greeted me at the huge old doors, heaving one of them open with her back. Glass of champagne in hand, I resisted the urge to grab it from her to relax me. She was wearing a cream chiffon dress, which accentuated her tiny waist and floated elegantly to her knees. Her long, shiny blonde hair curled voguishly around her shoulders, sweeping down her back. She could have been a model in a glossy magazine.

'I've told Clare you're here,' Suzy said, hugging me. 'Very good choice … I like, a lot.' She nodded approvingly at my outfit.

'It would be better if I could walk in these bloody shoes.'

'Kat?' A voice I recognised but couldn't quite place caught my attention.

'Nancy?'

'I didn't realise Poppy and Rosie were Max's,' she exclaimed loudly, as she walked towards me. Other guests stared and examined me: she's here, the mother of his children! Let the Chinese whispers begin!

'Yes …' I didn't know what else to say.

'They look gorgeous. As soon as Max's mum brought them into the church, I was looking all over for you …' she whispered. She lowered her voice further, scanning the room as she spoke, obviously trying to be discreet but failing miserably. 'Then I realised.'

'So you know Max?' I asked. But if that was the case, wouldn't I have met her? Especially if she was at his wedding.

'No, no … obviously I do now, but Gina's a friend.'

'Oh …' I tried to smile. 'How lovely,' I found myself saying, although I failed to see what was so lovely about it. This woman, who seemed to enjoy a good bit of gossip, knew my life story. Probably not in the way I knew it: in the elaborate, poor-Gina way, that Gina had probably told it.

'And you must be …?' Nancy stared directly at Suzy, in an overconfident way that made me cringe.

'Suzy.' Suzy held out her hand, Nancy took it and they shook politely. 'My fiancé is the best man,' Suzy said, proudly.

'Lawrence?' Nancy's eyes widened. 'You've done alright there!'

'He's lovely,' Suzy said, glancing quickly at me as if needing an escape.

'Max has told me so much about him, all those expeditions they've done together. Apparently you're doing one of those Ironman things. Oh, you've got more guts than me. I couldn't run a bath,' she laughed. We laughed with her.

'Yes, we're making it part of our honeymoon,' Suzy told her politely.

'Honeymoon?' Nancy was clearly baffled. 'You must be made for each other if you want to do such hideous things together,' Nancy laughed again, clearly a bit tipsy.

'I'll take that as a compliment,' Suzy laughed with her.

'Well, I think you make a lovely pair,' Nancy said genuinely. 'Now I really must dash, my husband will wonder where I've disappeared to. He doesn't really know anyone, you see. It was lovely to see you, Kat. We really must get together.'

'Yes we must. That would be lovely,' I lied, as she hugged us both as if we were old friends and walked off.

'She seems nice,' Suzy said, as we walked towards the reception area, where I'd said I'd meet Clare. I'd refused to enter the wedding crowd and be either stared at like a caged animal, or lurched upon like a celebrity.

'Mmm … in small doses, maybe,' I smiled.

'Kat …' it was Max's voice that made me turn next. He looked fantastic. I held my breath, as I tried to push back those thoughts. He was dressed in top hat and tails, the deep-blue cravat bringing out the blue of his eyes. 'The girls have been fantastic.'

I forced myself to smile and say, 'Great.'

'Stealing the limelight, I think,' he laughed.

'Gina won't like that.' I wanted to retract the remark as soon as it was out.

'She's loved every minute, having them here,' Max said joyfully, ignoring my sarcasm.

'Good. So are they ready to leave?'

'Yeah, Mum was handing them around for cuddles.' Max seemed happy. He seemed so full of energy, so full of life. I wondered if I'd dreamt his phone call: had it really happened? Maybe it was the ambience of the day, because I was sure the calls had happened. The days were a bit of a daze at the moment, but I wasn't that far gone. But I wasn't here to judge but to pick up the girls, which didn't seem to be happening as quickly as I would have liked. 'Come through for a drink,' Max said, waving his hand towards the door.

'No. Honestly, I'm fine waiting here.'

'Come on,' Max insisted.

'I'm fine.' I was harsher than I wanted to be.

'I'll wait with her here,' Suzy interrupted. She knew my fear of being unleashed onto their nosy guests.

'I'll go and hurry Mum along.' Max walked off through a set of double doors that stretched high to the ceiling. A bridesmaid in a long, dark-blue dress passed him, her hair in a tight bun, which was very traditional but elegant. They exchanged words, then laughed. He then went on his way, the bridesmaid not taking any notice of me, which I was pleased about.

Lawrence then swaggered from the room. He looked as charming as Max. His classic outfit suited his tall, lean figure.

'Kat! Don't you look gorgeous!' Lawrence put one arm out to me, bringing me in for a hug, his other hand holding a glass of frothy beer.

'Casual,' I laughed.

'Very natural,' Lawrence winked, obviously having heard second-hand from Suzy about my dress-code dilemma. 'The girls have been fantastic. No tears.'

'Good to hear,' I smiled. It wasn't really. I'd wanted them to scream throughout the vows. Perhaps I was being harsh. I hadn't really wanted them to cause commotion, but a little bit of bother to mar the wedding would have felt like justice. Awful, I know, but I couldn't help it. I suppose I felt a little resentment that Max hadn't wanted them to spend the whole day with him. Not that they would be aware, of course, but I was. And they would be when they were older. Or was that one of those things I'd have to keep to myself? I knew I should be the better person, the good parent, and let them believe the sun shone out of their father's arse. But I wouldn't be doing it for Max; I'd be doing it for my girls.

Lawrence released me, then draped his arm around Suzy's shoulders. Towering over her, he affectionately kissed the top of her head. 'This'll be us next week.'

'I know,' Suzy's eyes lit up and she grinned as she glanced up at him.

'I can't wait,' I said, and I realised I meant it. I actually felt a flutter of excitement. It felt nice to feel exhilarated about something, rather than everything blending into a nothingness.

'And tomorrow,' Suzy said eagerly, her eyes gleaming.

'Now that I definitely can't wait for,' I agreed.

'I think I should be allowed to come. I could do with a good old massage,' Lawrence said, stretching his neck for effect.

'What, like I was allowed to come to Barcelona?' Suzy nudged him in the ribs.

'You didn't ask,' Lawrence joked. Suzy raised her eyebrows and shook her head. 'Nah, you girls deserve a good old chill-out, especially you Kat.'

'Tell me about it,' I smiled, wanting to be on Suzy's hen spa-day *now*. Today. Away from here.

'Kathryn, dear.' Clare walked from the room, pushing Poppy and Rosie in their pushchair. I half-expected Gina to follow, but I knew she would avoid me today. She probably didn't want me here as much as I didn't want to be here.

'You look great,' I said to Clare, because she did.

'Thank you,' she said, smiling proudly. Her blue satin skirt suit rested just below her knee, her hat was elaborately covered in feathers and she had matched the colour of the bridesmaids. Now, not that I know much about wedding etiquette, but I'd had mothers of the bride in the salon who'd been searching endlessly for an outfit that complemented the bridesmaids. Clare wasn't the mother of the bride. I wondered how Paula felt about this.

'How's my girls?' I said to Rosie and Poppy who were beaming at me. Poppy's legs kicked out in excitement. I loved this. I loved being greeted with such enthusiasm. Every time I popped to the loo, you'd think I'd been gone hours. I'd been told to relish this, as it soon faded when they were older.

'They've been absolute darlings,' Clare said.

'Good. Clean outfits?'

'Rosie was a little bit sick, but nothing we couldn't handle.'

'Excellent. We'd better be off and let you guys enjoy the rest of your day.' The girls in my grasp I wanted to run from the place. Maybe not in these heels, though.

'They've had …' Clare started to reel off the times they were fed and changed. She then went on to recap the day's events: who had held the babies, who had fussed them, who had avoided them (apparently some young cousin, who was a 'layabout, anyway'). Finally, fifteen minutes later, she let me escape.

Max walked me to the car, which surprised me. I wasn't sure how Gina would feel about her new husband escorting his ex. But then, he was showing me off the premises, so she would probably be quite pleased.

'Thanks for this morning,' Max said, steering the pushchair across the gravelled drive. 'It's much appreciated.'

'You're welcome.' I was concentrating so hard on not breaking my ankle, while trying not to walk as if I'd crapped myself, that I wasn't really listening to what he was saying.

'As I said last night, I would have cancelled this for you.'

So it was real. Now I was listening. 'It wouldn't have worked between us Max.'

'I just wish … I wish …' He shook his head as we arrived at my car. 'I wish I could turn it all back.'

'Max, the inevitable happened. If it wasn't Gina it would have been something or someone else.'

'I was a prat.'

'You said it,' I laughed.

'I am truly sorry.' His lip seemed to quiver as he came towards me, his mouth, moving slowly towards mine. I placed my hand on his chest, swallowing hard, my heart racing as I shook my head.

'This is wrong,' I whispered. My heart was pounding. I would have kissed him, I would have loved to have felt his softness upon my lips; but it wasn't that simple. It was hurtful and disastrous. I was actually considering Gina as he stared intently at me. He was being monstrously unfair. And I didn't want him. I'd never be able to trust him.

'But I've made a mistake.'

'Bit late for that now. It's your bloody wedding day, Max,' I shook my head. 'This is so unfair on Gina. You can't do this.'

'Max …' Gina's voice echoed across the car park. How long had she been stood there?

'Coming,' Max said quickly, his eyes searching for her as he tried to focus on his new wife.

She looked beautiful. Her ivory dress accentuated her breasts, and the silky fabric flowed around her small, neat bump. Her black curls hung loosely around her petite features. Compared to my robust figure she was a vision.

Max helped me put the girls in the car. Although, I told him it was fine, he insisted. I felt uncomfortable as Gina watched us, her eyes boring into our every movement. I had this sudden urge to hug him close. But I didn't. I knew he had to get on with his life, walk back to the woman he'd said his vows to that very morning and live his life with her.

As I drove from the car park, Gina watched me but then focused on Max. From my rear-view mirror I saw Max wrap her in his arms, his hand moving across her back. To the outside world they were the perfect bride and groom.

I shook my head, suddenly feeling sad. Sad for Max. Sad for Gina. She had no idea what type of man she'd married. I don't think Max wanted me. I don't think he knew what he wanted.

It occurred to me as I drove away that I'd had a lucky escape. Max was, maybe, like his father. Although I had his children, I didn't need to wear the ring.

The girls were my gift, they were here for a reason. And as Lampford Park retreated further into the distance, I was suddenly overwhelmed with a feeling of joy.

Satisfaction. Excitement. My life was on the way up.

I didn't need Max. I didn't *want* Max. Gina was welcome to him. She'd soon find out the hard way.

All I needed was the two bundles that gurgled happily in the back of my car.

45

The pool rippled gently as if we were in foreign, sun-drenched lands. The underwater lights reflected a green glow across the water. The calmness that surrounded us was soothing.

Sitting cosily in the corner of the waters was, Suzy, her mum and me. She'd decided to keep it low-key. She had several groups of friends she could have invited, an endless list of girlfriends but she felt it was too much hassle. She'd said, 'If I invite one, I have to invite them all.' Secretly I was pleased. Not because I wanted Suzy to myself, but because this was bliss: not having to make an effort with anyone, not having to pretend to be something I wasn't, and, if the truth be known, not having to hide my fatty bits.

'Is our first treatment after lunch?' Suzy's mum stretched her back, letting the water envelop her body.

'Yes, facial first, then our nails,' Suzy said, as she gazed up at the white ceiling. Studying the spotlights that were reflecting off the calm waters.

'I'm going to try out the sauna. You girls coming?' Suzy's mum was out of the water, wrapping herself in a large, pristine white towel.

'Maybe in a bit,' Suzy said, which also pleased me: we had things to talk about.

Her mum padded lightly across the porcelain tiles, towards a door that indicated 'Spa Rooms'.

'So, tell me, tell me, tell me,' I whispered impatiently, once she was out of earshot.

'Oh, Kat, she became extremely drunk as the night wore on, and she seemed to stick to me,' Suzy groaned. She'd divulged by text before we got here that she *had* to tell me about Nancy Nott, but not in front of her mother. So I'd been desperate to hear the news, realising she would have called me earlier had she been alone.

'Did she embarrass herself?' I cringed.

'Not openly to the whole wedding party, but she did reveal some interesting information.'

'What?' I practically screamed, bursting to know.

'She started to advise me that I had to make sure Lawrence was the one for me—'

'Cheeky sod!'

'No, not like Lawrence was wrong for me, but that I had to make sure he was 'the one". She aired quotes marks in the air, water dripping from her elbows, as she raised her eyebrows, 'Because if he wasn't I might regret it, like she has.'

'What?'

'She then went on to tell me how her sex life was crap with her hubby, and she'd played about a bit.'

'No!'

'Yes!'

'Nancy Nott?'

'Nancy Nott,' Suzy nodded knowingly. 'She said that when they got married he'd never had as much of a sex drive as her, but she thought they'd settle and she'd entice him.'

'A bit daft, if she couldn't entice *before* they were married.'

'I know. She said, it got worse. Anyway, she started to tell me that she'd recently finished with a lover because his wife found out, and she'd actually been considering leaving her husband for this guy. Guess who it was?'

'Who?'

'Guess?'

'Max?' I gasped.

'Noooo!' Suzy shook her head, as if I'd said the most ridiculous thing ever. 'Steve Donnelly.'

'Noooo!' I repeated her exaggerated expression.

'Yep … and Mrs D knows all about it.'

'Aw, poor Mrs D.' I suddenly felt sad for her.

'Poor nothing, she needs to get her arse out of that relationship,' Suzy exclaimed.

'I know, but I think she's at a loss,' I sighed.

'Anyway, it was all a bit of a disaster. It went on for about six months, apparently.'

'Poor Nancy,' I sympathised.

'No, poor Nancy's husband,' Suzy raised her eyebrows at me. 'He was so lovely, so attentive to her all day and night. Really lovely man.'

'Who was?' Suzy's mum was suddenly above us, climbing carefully back into the still waters.

'Oh, some guy from the wedding yesterday …' Suzy said vaguely, shaking her head discreetly at me. I wondered if Suzy had told Nancy about her encounter with Steve, but I very much doubted that she would have. I didn't even know if Lawrence knew about it. It wasn't really up for discussion.

'You were quick,' I noted, as Suzy's mum splashed water across her burning red cheeks.

'The sauna's a bit too hot.'

We lazed in the pool for a bit longer before Suzy and I ventured into the luxurious steam rooms, which included an aromatherapy and salt vapour heat room. We then relished the outdoor heated pool and hot tub, which did as it said on the packet: gave us a completely refreshing, revitalising experience.

By the end of the day we were completely drained, but in the nicest way. I felt as if every thought had evaporated from my harried mind, and all I wanted to do was sleep. Marianne had offered to have the girls all day and night. I was nervous, yes, a little apprehensive; but as she said, they would be doing it next week when I was at Suzy's wedding, so this would be a practice run.

But when I'd arrived home, I was unsettled. I'd not seen them all day. Usually if this was the case, Max would be bringing them home. So I quickly rang Marianne to confirm what I already knew: they were fine. She'd taken them out in their pushchair, they'd had their sleep and feeds at their scheduled times and both Marianne and Derek were thoroughly enjoying their time with them. Before hanging up I made sure Marianne didn't want me to come and get them because she was too tired, but she ordered me to go and get a glass of wine and chill out. Marianne using the word 'chill' made me smile. She'd had Libby living there too long.

So I did as she ordered and opened the bottle that was gleaming at me from the fridge practically calling out my name. I'd had a glass of champagne with Suzy for lunch, but hadn't wanted to drink much more, as it was at the back of my mind that I might need to drive later to get the girls. But Marianne was adamant that wouldn't be happening. So I poured the dry white wine into a big goblet, listening as it swished against the sides, and enjoyed the cool chill, 'Lush.' I announced, holding my glass to the air.

The doctor had said to be careful with alcohol: 'It's a depressant, and your medication can increase the effects of depression.' I'd laughed, because although I used to enjoy a glass (or maybe a bottle) every Thursday, Friday and Saturday night, plus the odd night throughout the week before the girls were born, drinking that much now wasn't as much fun as it used to be. The fuzzy head didn't help with 2 a.m. feeds. But tonight, I could enjoy. I could relax. I could sleep through.

Oh how lovely, I was going to sleep through the night; an undisturbed night's sleep. I felt as if I'd won the lottery.

The knock on the door disturbed me as I refilled my second glass. I thought about hiding away, turning off the lights and pretending I wasn't home; but that was too obvious, as the person who was banging furiously obviously knew I was home.

I walked quietly down the staircase, suddenly worried. Who would be disturbing me at 8 p.m.? Who would be so demanding without calling first? Was it one of Libby's friends? Did she owe money?

I peered through the keyhole, and was surprised to see a tight-faced Clare.

46

'I can't do it anymore,' she said. There were no tears, no remorse. She was totally matter-of-fact. So looked tired, though, dark rings showing underneath her eyes. 'So that's why I've decided I'm going to move in here.'

'Here? In the flat?'

'Yes. When you've gone, obviously. I'm not moving in with you,' she laughed. 'Unless you wanted me to, of course.'

'Not sure what Max and Gina would have to say about that,' I spluttered, spilling my wine down my front as I choked on a mouthful. Resisting the urge to say, *of course I don't, you're one of the reasons I'm moving.*

'You know, Kathryn, I'm not sure what is going on with Maxwell at the moment.'

'What do you mean?'

'He doesn't seem happy.'

'I'm sure he is. He's always busy with work.' I drank more wine.

'He's lost some kind of spark, and quite honestly I don't think he should have married Gina.'

'I'm not sure you should be talking to me about this,' I said. Although I so wanted to hear more of her thoughts on this subject, it felt wrong.

'When you two got together, he fought for me to like you. I don't know why he went back to her. I don't think she'll make him truly happy.'

'I'm sure she will,' I lied.

'Admittedly, I love Gina. I was devastated when they split-up, but seeing how happy he was with you. It doesn't make any sense.'

I didn't want to get into this with Clare. I was trying to move forward with my life. Max, for some reason was still trying to find his path. He'd said he wanted to come back. He probably liked the fact that I was beginning to come back to my old self. But it was too late. It was too late for me and Max. There was nothing left between us, except two precious beings. I couldn't relay all this to Clare though.

I refilled her glass as she'd downed the first in seconds. 'He's probably just like his father,' she said. I didn't answer; agreeing was bad. Slagging off her husband and son was not a good way to go with this. 'He's been everywhere. You name it, he's fucked it.'

I spat out my drink in shock, my face covered in sprayed spit and wine. The swearing was *so* unlike her, although *fuck* sounded like an elegant, high-class word when she said it.

'He's been with his secretary, the neighbour, some tart from the golf club …'

'Why have you stayed for so long?' I found myself daring to ask.

'I had nowhere to go,' Clare shrugged. 'He always begs to come back, promises he'll never do it again. I was scared of being alone. But now, I have nothing left to give.'

'Are you sure you can't work this out?' Why I was asking this question was beyond me. I wanted her to leave, free herself. But she seemed so vulnerable, I wondered if she would cope.

'I don't want to.' She shook her head, sipping more wine. 'I avoided him at Max's wedding. He's an embarrassment … slobbering over Gina's friends.' I didn't answer. Nothing I could have said felt appropriate. 'He's like that wherever we go, when he's had too much bloody alcohol. I don't want to do it anymore. I have the salon now. I can move on with my life without him.'

I remembered how Max had said the salon had been a gift, because of Henry's infidelity. 'Without wanting to influence you, I think you're doing the right thing.'

'You do?' She raised her eyebrows at me.

'You've got to be true to yourself,' I said. Henry didn't deserve her.

'Do you know, Kathryn, I've cried endlessly over the last twenty years. I have no tears left.'

'That's understandable,' I said gently.

'I think June was the final straw.' As she spoke, she stared at the television, which wasn't switched on. 'I suppose I could cope with the other women to some extent as I didn't have to see them in my life every day, but this was too much to cope with.'

'I'm sorry,' I whispered.

'It's not your fault. It's being here, seeing you and the girls every day, knowing that he'd easily jumped into bed with your aunty, it's a reminder that he can't stop. He's at home probably planning his next betrayal.'

'I doubt he plans these things,' I murmured.

'That's what he says,' she laughed. 'It just happens, apparently. But most of us don't go around having sex with anything that walks.' She stunned me again, her blunt talk so out of character, I wondered if she'd had a drink before she got here. 'I've tried, Kathryn, God, I've tried,' she said, after a pause. 'We went to marriage counselling for years, but it didn't work. He started an affair between bloody sessions.'

'Do you think he has a problem?'

'Only one that involves his ego,' Clare smiled. 'I would have done anything for that man. Anything. But something snapped at Max and Gina's wedding, watching him preying on all the women. I knew I had to leave. All of this is happening for a reason: the salon, you moving out.'

I totally understood her. I wanted to applaud her for taking such a big step. I knew she was making the right decision. As was I, to stay away from her son.

It would be me that would be sitting and crying to my daughters in many years to come, when Max had cheated too many times. Maybe I was being cruel, maybe Max was nothing like his father. However, he hadn't proved to be much *more* than his father. Would he bounce between me and Gina for ever? When things became too tough at our end would he wander back to Gina? She'd always be in our lives: she was having his baby. He'd have to have weekly visits there, in the way he did here. While I was on the visiting end, I felt in control.

As Clare finished the second glass of wine, I knew things would get better for both of us.

47

'So, I was thinking: once I move, maybe you could come back up this way. There's plenty of room, you'll have your own space. It's away from the crowd, and we could enrol you on a different programme, or back on the old one, but I think you'll love it,' I said to Libby, who seemed to go silent on me. Only a few seconds, but it was noticeable.

'Actually … I'm enjoying it here.'

'What do you mean?'

'I mean, I think I'm going to stay.'

'Oh!' I felt punctured, like a deflated balloon. 'For how long?'

'It's nothing against you Kat, honestly, but things are working out here.' She ignored my question. It occurred to me that this could be for the foreseeable future. For ever.

'With Matt, you mean?' I couldn't help but unleash the sarcasm. I missed her. I was worried about her. We'd never spent such a long time apart, and it felt strange.

'Matt is here, yes, but he's helping me,' Libby said softly. A strange combination: Libby and soft. 'I've met some great people here, and I've got a little job.'

'Really?'

'Yeah, working in a café on the seafront. It gets me out. And the people are lovely.'

'Are you still attending your programme?'

'Yes, stop worrying. I feel great, Kat,' Libby laughed. 'Things are working out.'

'But … but …'

'Stop worrying.'

'But I feel as if I've let you down,' I admitted to her.

'You have not let me down,' she said adamantly. 'If anything, *I've* let *you* down. You've always been there, Kat. Always.'

'But you're staying there …'

'Look, you've helped me come to a place where I can move on and grow.'

'But you could have grown here.'

'Maybe I could, but I don't feel as if there's anything there for me anymore.' Thanks! I wanted to exclaim; and as if reading my thoughts, she added, 'Obviously there's you and the girls, but I don't know … being here … it's different. I feel as if I can rebuild a life without anyone knowing my past. I'm not judged here.'

'I understand that.' I choked away the tears, understanding exactly where she was coming from.

'June's happy for me to stay with her. Matt has already picked up a job down here—'

'Did he get a reference?' I felt the need to know.

'Yes. A good one. He's working with young offenders, and contributing to the rent.'

'That's good,' I said, because I suppose it was.

'I've been thinking about enrolling on a counselling course.'

'Oh … what about the teaching course?'

'I'm not sure if that's what I want to do. I'd like to help people who have been through what I've been through.'

'Sounds like a good idea,' I said, a little unconvinced that this wasn't one of her plans to distract me from questioning her.

'I always think that if you're getting help from a professional, it's nice to talk to someone who has experienced some form of turbulence. You know what I mean?'

'Are you saying Matt has had some kind of *turbulence*?' Had she connected with Matt because he'd had issues? Did she think this made him a good counsellor?

'Yes,' she admitted, quite strongly. 'He used to be an alcoholic.' Oh, bloody great! 'But he's been clean for ten years.'

'Ten years?' The guy who had knocked on my door couldn't have been over thirty.

'He started drinking when he was eleven—'

'Eleven!?' She must have had to hold the phone away from her ear.

'He was placed in care, and one thing led to another. Anyway, he stopped drinking when he was nineteen and hasn't touched a drop since.'

'Good for him.' I found myself saying. I didn't want to judge Matt's background but it did make me feel uneasy.

'He's really lovely,' Libby said. 'I'd love for you guys to meet properly, I think you'd really like him.'

'Not going to be easy while you're down there,' I said.

'I know, but I'll come up and visit, and you can bring the girls this way. Marianne was talking about coming in a few weeks. Why don't you come with her?'

'If I wasn't moving I'd have jumped at the chance, but there's so much to do here.'

'As soon as you're sorted, we'll arrange for you to come down and you can see how chilled life is here.'

She made me smile, using the same words Marianne had used days before. 'Sounds like a plan,' I said.

'Kat … I *am* happy here,' Libby said, after a pause.

'Good.' I was close to tears.

'You do know I'm thankful for all you've done for me.'

'No need to thank me,' I snivelled. It was too late, the tears were out.

'Don't cry.'

'I'm sorry.'

'Kat, I love you, I couldn't ask for a better sister.' I couldn't remember the last time Libby had said those words.

'I love you too, but stop, cos I'll be blubbering my way through the rest of the day.'

'You've done more for me than I deserve.'

'I haven't.'

'You have.' Libby sounded so strong, so grown-up. 'Most people would have wiped their hands of me.'

'But I kicked you out of my flat,' I sobbed.

'And so you should have!' Libby said indignantly. 'I also know that if I hadn't gone to Marianne's you would have taken me back, you wouldn't have seen me on the streets.'

'Yeah, I would have.' I tried to jest, make light of my upset as I smiled through the tears.

'I'm lucky to have you in my life, but I need you to do one last thing for me.'

'What? Anything.'

'Let me go.'

*

Marianne had gone on at me about the baby group at their church so much that I'd felt rude trying to get out of it. So finally I'd given in, but then, Brooke had decided to attend with me, and so had Mrs D, who, apparently, was bored at home. She'd also thought that being around babies might help get her womb in tune. Personally, I'd thought this was a bad idea. One of my clients from the salon had been trying for a baby for years. After many failed IVF treatments, she couldn't bear to be around babies. When her best friend had fallen pregnant, it upset her so much she ceased talking to her. I imagined Mrs D might go home after this, open a bottle of wine or two and sob her way into the night.

Marianne was waiting for us (well me, I'd not had a chance to tell her I had company), outside the church. I drove swiftly into a parking space, Brooke and Mrs D pulling in beside me. I freed myself from my seatbelt. I could see Brooke was already out, and chatting to Marianne.

'Hi, Marianne. Brooke and Ange decided to join me.' I stopped myself from referring to her as Mrs D. I hoped it was only Marianne who saw my raised eyebrows.

'Great, more the merrier,' Marianne smiled warmly.

Once we'd put Rosie, Poppy and Chelsea into their prams, we followed Marianne around the side of the church to the hall at the back. Mrs D excused herself to go to the ladies as we headed into the room, which was already busy and extremely noisy.

Toys littered the hall from one end to the other. Mothers sat on plastic chairs or cross-legged on the floor. I noticed two men chatting, who I presumed where fathers, I wondered if Max would ever take our girls to a group like this. I could imagine he could think of nothing worse; but then, neither could I before my babies arrived.

Children around the age of two were either playing, or fighting over a toy they so desperately 'needed'. The noise levels were higher than I'd thought they'd be. It was a bit different to the massaging sessions. But really, was I delusional to think it might have been calm? Was there such a thing as peaceful kids?

We headed to the corner of the hall, where a soft area had been kitted out for babies. There were two mums sitting and chatting, deep in conversation about how much they missed their sleep.

'Kat?' I turned to follow the voice that had echoed behind me.

'Nancy.' I hoped my smile seemed genuine, Suzy's revelation about Nancy's affair flashing in my mind like a huge red warning light.

'What are you doing here?'

I indicated Marianne with a gesture of my hand. 'Marianne does a lot for the church. She suggested I come.' I didn't want to explain who Marianne was as that would have Nancy asking more questions about my life: she knew too much already.

'Hello Nancy,' Brooke grinned, 'Kat invited us to come with her.' *No I didn't! You invited yourself!* It was on the tip of my tongue, but suddenly feeling childish, I held back.

'I come here all the time. I have a few friends who live this way, so it's …' Nancy trailed off as she spotted Mrs D, whose eyes seemed to be alight with fire, glaring at her.

'Nancy,' Mrs D said coldly, appearing from behind us.

'I'd better get back to my friends. I'll catch you later,' Nancy said, the colour draining from her cheeks. As quickly as she'd approached us she turned and practically fled across the hall.

'That bitch,' Mrs D sneered.

'Ladies, come on,' Marianne said calmly.

'Who is she?' Brooke asked.

'Steve had an affair with her, but she knew he was married. She's married her-bloody-self. I'm not even convinced that baby isn't Steve's.' Mrs D suddenly admitted, as she glared at Nancy who seemed to shrivel into a chair, as if feeling the burn from the stare.

'I think we should leave,' I said, my heart racing. How many times do I have to be with these people where I want to leave their company?

'I'm not going anywhere. I'm not having some tart drive me and Chelsea out of here.'

'Girls, let's get settled down here,' Marianne urged, clearly desperate to diffuse any confrontation before it even started.

Reluctantly I released the catch from the pushchair, lifting Poppy and Rosie from the fleece blanket that covered their seat, their warmth soft against my skin as I kissed each one of them, before putting them on the activity play mat.

'I'll go and get drinks. I know the ladies who are serving,' Marianne said, taking orders from us all for teas and coffees. Mrs D sat down on the edge of the baby area but continued to scowl across the busy room, quietly observing Nancy and her friends.

'Will you stop staring,' Brooke ordered Mrs D, as she and Chelsea joined us.

'That bitch wanted Steve,' Mrs D said. The two women who had been exchanging sleepless nights' notes glanced at each other, their eyebrows raised. 'She begged him to leave me for her. I wanted him to do a DNA on her child but he wouldn't. Apparently she didn't want to either. If he wasn't going to leave me then she said she would stay with her husband, who is totally oblivious to any of this.'

'You should have told her husband,' Brooke said firmly.

'Why hurt him?'

'I'd want to know,' Brooke said adamantly.

I didn't want to join in this conversation. I didn't want to be here.

'I didn't want to cause any more upset,' Mrs D said quietly.

The two women who were eavesdropping looked away quickly, leaned over to their babies taking hold of their tiny hands, obviously realising I'd noticed them being nosy.

'Oh, shit,' Brooke grimaced, her stare focused on Mrs D. 'Here comes trouble.' The intrigued women next to us whipped their heads around, as my eyes met the gaze of a tall, broad woman approaching Mrs D, who was now standing with her hands on her hips, ready for the confrontation.

'What is your problem?' the angry-looking woman asked quietly.

'I'll tell you what my fucking problem is.' Mrs D pointed across the hall, her voice echoing across the high-ceilings, as she announced very loudly, 'That tart, Nancy Nott. Yes, everybody, Nancy Nott was shagging my husband. She's not even sure that child—'

'Ange,' I said softly, flying from the soft play area as if I was Superwoman. My hands on Mrs D's shoulders, the aggressive woman was taken aback, shaking her head as she peered around at Nancy, who was crimson. 'Calm down. You don't want to do this.'

Mothers grabbed their children, some of whom started to cry, clearly petrified.

'Shagging!' The voice of a young child rang out round the hall, followed by gasps from indignant mothers. Then, as if enjoying the gasps, the child who was playing with bricks, oblivious to the stares around him started to sing, 'Shagging … shagging… shagging…' and actually started to have a wiggle as he kneeled on his feet. Yet, the Mother didn't step forward to claim the child (probably too embarrassed to admit ownership) as a deathly silence fell around the 'shagging' melody.

Marianne, wide-eyed and red-faced, stared over from the serving counter, where coffees, teas and orange juice were being dished out. You'd think the two open-mouthed women behind her had seen a ghost.

'Let's go,' I mumbled.

'Sorry, but it's not fair, that women like that …' Mrs D started to cry.

'Come on,' I said softly. My arm around her, I pulled her close, suddenly feeling sorry for her. I thought *I* was emotionally unstable, but Mrs D gave the phrase a whole new meaning. Being with that creep of a husband of hers didn't help. I didn't particularly want to make best friends with Mrs D, but I suddenly felt as if I needed to protect her. Her vulnerability had been shown to me so many times. I didn't want these women staring and laughing, thinking she was crazy, even if a small part of me thought she was. I wanted her to hold her head high and be proud of who she was. She would never be able to do that while she stayed with this man. It was all a façade.

We quickly grabbed the babies, the two women who had been eavesdropping smiling pitifully at us as we tried our hardest to make a quick exit, with everybody watching us.

Marianne was behind us as we left the hall 'I'm sorry.' I whispered. Brooke and Mrs D were ahead of us, talking intensely.

'It's not your fault.' Marianne patted my shoulder.

'So embarrassing,' I spoke quietly, not wanting Mrs D to hear.

'Ah, it's only Hilda and Brenda. It'll give them something to chat about at the next meeting. They've never seen such excitement!' Marianne smiled.

'Honestly,' I shook my head. 'There seems to be some kind of uproar wherever I go with these two.'

'Poor woman.'

'Mmm … I know what you mean,' I sighed. 'I want to give her a shake, but she keeps hanging on. He won't leave her, so she thinks that's a good enough reason to stay.'

'Love is blind, as they say.'

We reached the cars. Brooke had already transferred Chelsea into her seat, as if she wanted to be as far away from here as possible.

'I'm sorry, Kat and Marianne, I've totally—' Mrs D said, as we caught up with her.

'Don't you worry,' Marianne brought her in for a hug.

'Please apologise to your—' Mrs D began.

'It's fine, there's no need. Now come on, you need to be strong.'

'Thank you.' Mrs D looked at Marianne as if in awe of her.

'I'll call you Kat,' Brooke said.

I nodded, scared to say anything in case the words, 'Don't!' popped out.

Mrs D climbed into the passenger side of Brooke's car. The engine started, within seconds gravel flew into the air, as she raced away as if they were in the Grand Prix.

I kissed Marianne's cheek. 'Thank you,' I said.

'I didn't even get to give my girls a cuddle,' she said to Poppy and Rosie rather than to me as she peered down at them. Both girls seemed to be watching the clouds that were merging into various shapes overhead. She helped me get the girls into the car, as we chatted about Mrs D and how I thought she should leave Steve. Marianne, as always seeing the good in everyone, said it probably wasn't that easy, that sometimes things were not as simple as they seemed.

As I drove away, Marianne waving fanatically at me, like she always did, I thought about what had just happened.

So much hurt. And from one man.

I thought about Max and Henry. If I decided to succumb to Max's charms and make a go of it with him, would this be me? Would I turn into Mrs D? Clare? Would I smile my way through endless affairs, so the girls could have their father there?

I couldn't do it. Not only did I think I deserved better, but our girls deserved better too.

I thought about what Suzy had with Lawrence; and that's what I wanted. Lawrence adored Suzy, and vice versa. Why should I settle for anything less?

I *couldn't* settle for anything less. So, although the afternoon had been embarrassing, and I doubted I'd show my face there again, it had proved to me, once again, I was making the right decision by staying away from Max.

/

48

The musky, stale smell was still the same as on my previous visit, and I had to restrain myself from grabbing one of the paper feedback slips that hung untidily over a perspex holder, and filling it in, telling them to redecorate, or at least get an air freshener.

I flicked through *Homes and Gardens*, inspired by what I could do with my new home. As if I had the cash for such extravagance.

I felt comfortable in the room I'd first entered with trepidation. My foot swung casually, as I waited for Rhonda to call my name.

'Kat?' That wasn't Rhonda! I looked up to see a tired Nancy, peering down on me.

'Oh … hello,' I stuttered.

'You come here too?'

'Mmm …' I thought about lying, telling her I was waiting for someone: I wasn't crazy. I didn't need a therapist. Grab your bag and run! 'Yes,' I found myself saying.

'I've been seeing Samir for years.' She sat down next to me. 'I did stop for a while, but I had to come back after all the Steve business …'

I found myself nodding, not knowing what to say to her. Quite frankly I would have been happy never to bump into her again, after the commotion two days ago.

'I'm sorry about what happened at the baby group.'

'No need to apologise to me,' I said coolly.

'How do you know Ange Donnelly?' she asked after an awkward silence.

'She's Brooke's sister-in-law. Steve Donnelly is Brooke's brother.'

'Oh.'

'Kat,' Rhonda called from her office.

'I best go,' I smiled, relieved I was being dragged away from this woman who seemed to cause a drama wherever she went. Why did I attract these people?

'Kat.' Nancy stopped me. I turned to face her. 'Maybe we could go for a coffee after our sessions?'

A hundred and one excuses flew through my mind, from needing to be back for the girls to the fact I had a very contagious disease, 'Today's not a good day,' I managed.

'I really could do with chatting with someone after my session. I always like to analyse what I've said, or what I should have said, or shouldn't have said. Samir tells me this is one of the things I have to stop doing. But it would be great, just a quick drink. But I understand if you're too busy.' She was practically pleading with me. She might as well have got down on her hands and knees and begged. The confident out-spoken woman who I'd first met at the baby group was no longer there.

I looked at this desperate woman and suddenly felt sorry for her. Surely she had plenty of friends to talk to, why would she want to talk to me? And I found myself saying, 'Okay. I'll meet you outside in an hour.'

'Excellent,' she beamed.

Inside Rhonda's room, the hum of the radiator was soothing as I sat down opposite her. She huddled herself in an oversized black cardigan, wiping her nose with a tissue, apologising to me for being full of cold. I wished she'd cancelled the appointment. If I caught her bloody cold, the girls might catch it too. Did she know how much hassle that would cause me? However, I kept my thoughts to myself. This place was meant to relax me, not have my blood pressure rising.

'How have you been?' Rhonda managed, through her thick, snotty throat.

'Fine. Loads better.' In fact, I'm quite happy to leave now. Don't need to take your germs with me, thanks.

'Last time, we touched on your mum.' She watched me for a reaction. 'Would you like to talk about her today?'

'What do you want to know?'

'It's not about what I want to know, it's more about how you feel about her not being here.'

'Gutted.' I let out a bitter laugh. I hoped I hadn't sounded sarcastic, but how else did she expect me to feel.

'Let's go back to before she died. Let's talk about your relationship.'

This was the start of an hour-long session, as I explained how I remembered Mum: her laughter, her stories, how she was always there. How I had never considered for one minute that she wouldn't be. How if I could regress to those years, I'd tell her every minute of every day how much I loved her.

I told Rhonda my life history from the time Mum died, describing all the dramatics that had happened since: from the time Marianne arrived swiftly on the scene, through the years to Dad's death, June turning up and Derek's entry into our chaotic family dynamics. Rhonda asked constantly, 'How do you feel about that?'

Once the hour had passed, I felt even more drained than the last time; and unlike then, I had no sense of relief. My head was pounding, my eyes were sore and my body wanted to collapse into the nearest bed.

Nancy was waiting for me eagerly. 'There's a small coffee shop around the corner ... fancy it?'

I didn't no. Not at all. 'Lovely, yes,' I said. I wanted to go home, snuggle down with my girls, open a bottle of Pinot and sleep.

The coffee shop was a short walk away. As we headed along the path, we chatted awkwardly about the weather to fill in the silences. 'It can't make up its mind up. One minute we could have our shorts on, the next our snowsuits,' Nancy laughed. I agreed, muttering a few trite comments in return.

We arrived, ordered our drinks and went to a table in the corner. She seemed to want to be out of earshot, as she skimmed around the café, noticing the three people who were not interested in us. A man and woman were in deep conversation, while an older guy sipped a coffee and read his morning paper. They'd not even noticed us.

I was just wondering what Nancy and I would find to talk about when we'd already struggled to make conversation on the way here, when she suddenly announced: 'We're getting divorced.'

Well! That's one way to break the ice! 'I'm sorry to hear that,' I said, not knowing what else to say.

'It's been a long time coming. I don't love him anymore.'

'You must do what is best for you.' I found myself giving her the same advice I'd given Clare. The advice I was drilling into myself.

'I just felt I needed to explain that I'm not a bitch who went out to get someone else's husband. I loved him … I love him.'

'No need to explain anything to me.' I sipped on my frothy cappuccino, enjoying the milky texture but really wanting to be out of here.

'I didn't realise you knew Steve's wife.'

'Sort-of,' I said.

'I do feel bad towards her, but it all happened so quickly.' I remembered how Suzy had felt the same. 'I thought he loved me.' Suzy had thought this too. 'He told me he did, but when she found out, he told me it had to end. But I couldn't let him go. Anyway, we continued our affair. I thought if he stayed with me a bit longer he'd soon leave her, but she has some kind of hold over him.'

I didn't dare let my views be known about either party. I couldn't tell her she was delusional, that I knew exactly what sort of man Steve was. What did this man have that was attracting these women? What powerful magnetism, that hid his true colours?

'I admitted the affair to Glen last night. He was devastated, but said he knew.'

'How did he know?' I felt I had to say something.

'He said I've been distant for years. He knew there was someone else.' She sipped her drink. 'I thought *she* would have told Glen when she found out.'

'I don't think she wanted to hurt him.' By *she* I assumed she meant Mrs D.

'Like I have, you mean?'

'No, I didn't mean that.' Yes, I probably did!

'I suppose I should be thankful to her,' Nancy shrugged. She sipped her drink, again, then licked away the white, foamy moustache. She looked tired, her eyes sad … lost, even. 'The problem is, Harvey could be Steve's.'

'Really?' I exclaimed, as if I'd not heard this at the baby group from Mrs D, as had the other twenty women in the room.

'I know. It's awful.' Nancy shook her head. 'Now Glen wants a DNA test.'

I thought about how this would affect Mrs D. She'd be devastated. Especially with her and Steve trying for a baby. For him to have one with another woman … it didn't bear thinking about. At the same time, why was I bothered? How come I'd got embroiled in this drama?

'What will you do?' I asked after a brief silence.

'We'll have to do the test, and hope for the best.'

'Which is?'

'I don't know.' Nancy shook her head again. I knew by the look in her eye that she probably hoped it was Steve's. Even if they weren't together, she would then have a hold over him.

We chatted a while longer, and for some reason I found myself liking her a bit more. She suddenly seemed real. Yes, she'd been having an affair with a married man, which was totally against my rules in life; but she'd fallen in love. She'd stupidly and blindly fallen in love. Although I wanted to slap her, I remembered how I'd not considered taking Max back, but deeply I *had* analysed it. I wanted the fairy-tale dream.

Love did that; it made things rosy. Glossed over the bad. Made forgiveness so much easier.

As I watched this broken woman in front of me, her life in tatters, her marriage in pieces, the man she loved never to be hers, I knew she'd been brought into my life for a reason. All these things happening around me were warning signs. They were telling me something. They were shouting at me from the heavens.

Was it Mum's doing?

I would never know, but what I did know, as I sat opposite this fragile woman, was that I didn't want to be like her. I didn't want to yearn for something that wasn't real. I didn't want to be with Max worrying about who he would be seeing next or whether it was me he truly loved. So we had two babies together, we'd always be in touch, but we didn't need to be together.

Two gorgeous babies who were now my focus and my reason for being.

I was heading to a calmer place. My life was becoming peaceful. I was content. But it was an awful shame it was taking the tangled lives of those around me to show me how happy I really was.

49

My stomach was churning with excitement when I met Lynn from Brickwork Homes at the house. The house I would soon be moving into.

I'd decided it was best to decorate before we moved in. Paint fumes and the mess wouldn't really fit in with two babies. I'd checked with Clare that she was okay to wait for me to paint my new home before she moved into the flat. She could wait. She'd told Henry that she would be leaving him. They were currently living in separate parts of the house, avoiding each other. Quite frankly, I didn't ask too much as I didn't want to be part of it. I'd be there for Clare, as I told her, but I didn't need to know the gory details.

Once Lynn had left, I scanned the living room, envisaging how I would decorate it. Exhilaration bubbled, as I sang to the girls, wiggling my backside in a jiggle. They giggled from their car seats. I wondered when the time would come when they would no longer appreciate my clowning.

I heard the sounds of a car pulling up outside. Knowing it would be Suzy, I opened the front door to let her in. Lawrence strolled up the path, his long legs taking one step to Suzy's two.

She handed me a gold gift bag that was stuffed with red tissue paper, 'For you.'

'This is great,' Lawrence said eagerly. He leaned forward, kissing my cheek as I let him in. I loved his support.

'Aw thank you, you didn't have to buy me anything,' I said, eagerly pulling the paper out of the bag, followed by a piece of rope that created a figure 8, attached to the rope was a gold coin.

'It's a mystic knot,' Suzy explained quickly. I hope she hadn't seen the confusion on my face. 'It's a Feng Shui symbol. It brings never-ending good fortune and a happy life.'

'Aw thank you Suz,' I said again.

'It works best when you put it in the Southwest or Southeast part of the house.'

'Great, when I figure out where that is I'll make sure it's on show,' I laughed. 'Thank you so much,' I grinned.

'This is a great new beginning for you,' Suzy smiled.

'I hope you're right,' I said. We hugged tightly. 'Is Joe not with you?' I glanced over her shoulder.

'He's following,' Suzy said, staring over my shoulder, trying to get a peek of the lounge.

'Does he know where he's going?'

'Yeah, he's got a friend who lives around here,' Lawrence said, as they both headed straight into the lounge.

'Aw, Kat, it's really spacious,' Suzy smiled.

'Once Joe decorates and helps me put my own stamp on it, it'll be great,' I said, closing the front door.

Suzy had rung me to say that Joe was a dab hand at painting and decorating and had offered to do it for me. He had a week off before he had to venture back to work, so he was happy to help out. Max had been extremely put out when I'd told him, offering to also help. 'Joe knows nothing about interior design ...' he'd said disdainfully, sounding foolish.

'He's wallpapering. I've chosen the paper. He doesn't need to know anything about interior design.'

'Why don't you let me help you choose the colours?'

'No thanks, I'm quite capable.' We'd left the conversation. I didn't want Max's help. I didn't want his stamp anywhere on this house. I wanted to make it my own without any reminders of him.

Joe arrived five minutes later. He was dressed in a tracksuit, his hair gelled as always, his cheeky smirk showing off his boyish dimples.

'This will be easy enough,' he said, after browsing around the house. He felt the texture of the yellow and orange flowered wallpaper, as if this would give him further confirmation on the time it would take. 'A week … tops.'

I showed him the black and silver wallpaper I wanted across one wall in the living room. As Max had always said, 'Black makes a room look smaller,' I'd decided to go for it. Not because I wanted the room to look smaller, but I felt the need to do something Max didn't agree with. Make it my own. It was a colour I'd never have chosen before, but it felt liberating to do something different. I was thinking outside my box, breaking down barriers. It felt so good.

It was Marianne and Derek who interrupted the conversation as we stood in my empty lounge. 'Hello,' she shouted as they knocked and walked in.

'Hi, come on in.'

'Oh dear, not sure about the colours in here,' Marianne said, flinching.

'We need our sunglasses!' Derek exclaimed.

'I'll soon sort that,' Joe assured them as he winked at me.

I felt a shiver run down my spine. It was only a slight glance my way, but his eyes sparkled. Was he flirting?

No … no … no. I wasn't going there. He wasn't my type.

'I'm sorry I can't offer you a drink, I have nothing in yet,' I smiled.

Marianne hugged me, 'I'm really proud of you.'

'Me too,' Suzy smiled.

'Thanks,' I said coyly, feeling my cheeks flush at the praise.

As we stood in my new home, embracing the damp unlived in smell, the old air freshener had lost its fragrance, but still I wasn't put off, as I knew this was the start of a new life for me and my girls.

It felt so exciting.

50

I threaded the ribbon through each tiny hole, my fingers nimbly ensuring the back of the dress seamlessly blended with the front. I pulled at the silky ribbons, gently tightening every inch of fabric, ensuring the smoothness of Suzy's silhouette.

'Do you think Lawrence will like it?' she asked nervously, for what felt like the hundredth time, as she gazed into the full-length mirror, her hands moving across the delicate lace material. She looked stunning.

'How could he not?' I placed my hands on her shoulders, meeting her gaze in our reflections.

'Look at us.' Suzy breathed out deeply.

'I know,' I smiled. 'You've met an amazing guy. It's so perfect, Suz.'

'I couldn't be happier,' she said. Her pure white skin was as smooth as porcelain. Her creamy white hair, was pushed back loosely off her face. Curls lay gently around her shoulders. The diamond choker sparkled, flickers of dazzling light reflecting from the mirror.

The knock on the bedroom door distracted us from our moment of bonding. Suzy's mum popped her head in, her hand on her chest as she entered, her eyes filling with tears. 'Oh Suzy sweetheart,' she gasped. 'And Kat. Oh, girls. You both look stunning.'

'Thank you,' I said, gazing down at my silver satin dress, pleased I'd actually lost a few pounds, as it gave me room to breathe.

'Do you think Lawrence—'

'Yessss!' her mum and I said in unison.

'I'm so nervous.'

'You'll be fine.' Suzy's mum came towards her, hugging her close before kissing her gently on the cheek. 'Lawrence is a very lucky man.'

'I'll second that,' a man's voice boomed from the hallway. 'Can I come in?'

'Yes, Dad, we're all decent,' Suzy called. Her father opened the door. His tall, broad figure filled the doorway as he gazed at Suzy, tears springing into his eyes.

'Do I scrub up alright then, Dad?' Suzy joked, placing her hand on her hip, posing for the man she so wanted to make proud.

'You look beautiful, darling.' Her father sniffed, coughing into his fist as if to compose himself. 'The car is waiting, we'd better get this show on the road.'

Suzy drew a deep breath, 'Let's go.'

*

The day moved forward without a blemish or flaw. We arrived fashionably five minutes late, delighting in the gasps that followed Suzy down the aisle. There wasn't a dry eye in the church when she and Lawrence declared their love to each other. We were surrounded by laughter and love. The music … the atmosphere … the whole thing was perfect. It was how it was meant to be.

Suzy and Lawrence gave me hope. They made me understand the meaning of true love. With all that had gone on around me lately, I had started to feel there was no such thing. Not that I was being cynical, but I wondered if it was possible for two people to be so in love they didn't need anyone else. Suzy and Lawrence were proof that it *was*.

At the reception afterwards, my mind wandered to Marianne. She seemed to have something special with Derek. They had a connection that had to be admired. She was happy in her own way. I knew she thought he was too forceful with Libby, but someone had to be.

'They're good together, aren't they?' Joe sat down beside me, interrupting my thoughts. He removed his cravat, and his top buttons were undone, a few hairs were protruding from his shirt.

'Very,' I agreed, as we watched Lawrence and Suzy laugh throughout their first dance. Their secret whispers and shared love were endearing and captivating. Their guests watched them, while they focused only on each other.

'I see you've managed to successfully avoid Max and Gina all day.' Joe's dimples emphasised his boyish grin.

'Have you been watching me?' I smiled.

'I may have been.' He grinned, a glint in his eye. I tried to ignore the fact my heart was beating a little bit faster. 'I can't believe they didn't invite Poppy and Rosie to their wedding all day.' Joe suddenly all serious, was staring at me.

'Did you go to their wedding?' I'd not seen him there; but then, I hadn't exactly mingled with their guests.

'Yeah.' He relaxed back in the chair. 'I wasn't best man with Lawrence, though. Apparently it would have made Gina uncomfortable.'

'Can't see why,' I smiled.

'I don't think she really wanted me there, but Max ... you know ... he was a good friend,' Joe said, and I noted the past tense.

'Do you still love her?'

'No.' He shook his head adamantly. 'No, I'm not even sure I did. It was quite quick, quite full-on. Too much too soon, I reckon.'

'Shame.' I remembered how I'd been told Gina had thought this, not Joe; but I didn't say so.

'Not really. She was quite high maintenance,' Joe laughed. 'Lovely girl, but demanding.'

I didn't bother asking why he'd been prepared to marry her, then; as I didn't care to know. The less I knew about Gina, the easier my life was.

'You two look cosy.' Max was suddenly in front of us, hardly able to stand, slurring his words as he grabbed the table and luckily landed in a chair. 'It's a good do, isn't it?'

'Yes, great.' I was pleased the music was loud, so no-one could hear Max's drunken shouting.

'Well, Joe, are you working your way onto another of my girls now?' Max slurred.

'Max!' I exclaimed.

'If he comes on to you, you know it's only because I've been there.' Max waved his finger in mid-air down my body.

'Oh, for God's—'

'Max, you're out of order.' Joe snapped. 'Kat doesn't deserve to be spoken to in that way. You owe her an apology.'

'Oooohhhh,' Max laughed. 'Check you, being all manly.'

'Joe, leave it, he's drunk.' I placed my hand on Joe's arm.

'Max, I think it's best you go and sleep this off,' Joe said calmly, though his jaw was tense as he glared at his friend. He stood up, holding out his hand for mine. 'Come on, let's go and get a drink.'

Instinctively I took the offer. Not so much because I wanted to be with Joe, but I wanted to be away from Max.

'That's it, go and find a corner to shag in!' Max shouted. 'Do one for me, for old times' sake, mate. She's a better shag than Gina—'

It happened in seconds: the crash, the screams, as Joe's fist connected with Max's jaw. Max went flying off the chair, landing heavily on his back. He staggered clumsily to his feet and launched himself at Joe. The beautifully dressed table, which Suzy had spent hours planning, now saw the two grown men sprawled across it as they grabbed for each other. It suddenly collapsed under their weight, throwing them on to the floor.

Lawrence ran up, pulled Max from Joe, and then grabbed their chests and pushed them forcefully apart. As abruptly as it started, it stopped. Both men seemed to calm instantly, the realisation that this was Lawrence's big day clearly dawning upon them both.

Joe patted Lawrence's shoulder. 'Sorry mate.'

Gina appeared at Max's side, wiping away the blood that was dripping from his mouth. Suzy was at my side, rubbing my arm, checking I wasn't hurt. I told her I was fine.

Joe then turned and walked towards me. 'Should we get that drink now?'

<h1 style="text-align:center">51</h1>

The following week was strange …

I'd told Suzy how the fight had started. She thought it was great, and wished she'd been the one to offer the first punch; especially when I'd told her what Max had said. He'd obviously been extremely drunk, as he told me the following day. His grovelling was so pathetic. I was embarrassed for him. He'd confirmed for me in a few sentences that I definitely did not want to be with him ever, ever again. But I didn't want to fall out with him and make life difficult. I felt entirely indifferent to him. As long as he was there for the girls, we'd all get along okay. We'd do it for their sake and that suited me.

It was lovely to feel so contented.

A session with Rhonda had us exploring elements of my relationship with Mum; how I'd been turned into a fragile teenager, how I felt sad for not telling her how much I loved her. How I wished every day that I could turn the clock back. Rhonda told me we would work on this. She said my feelings were perfectly natural. She was going to help me work on moving past the hurt, and focus on living in the future rather than the past. I'd told her I felt as if I was actually getting there, so any help could only improve things.

I was so excited about this. The clouds that had hung over me for so long were lifting.

Marianne and Derek had a few days away in Devon. Marianne wanted to see how Libby was getting along, after I'd told her Libby's plans. I'd been desperate to join them, but decided I'd venture to see her in a few months, when I'd moved into my new house and Libby had hopefully progressed a little further;

although I half-expected her to be dragged back by her hair, if Marianne and Derek discovered she'd told me a pack of lies. But I was being unfair: this could be a fresh start for Libby, exactly what she needed.

Joe spent most of the week at the new house, decorating it in the exact way I'd asked. Not deviating, not telling me his opinion or asking me to rethink the colours I was choosing, in the way Max would have done. He apologised profusely for the punch-up but said he couldn't stand back and let Max be so disrespectful. I thanked him for his support, because it was nice that he'd defended me, although I couldn't help wondering if he'd been looking for an excuse to lay into Max. But I didn't push him. I appreciated his help, and we had a good laugh while he turned the house into my new home.

Brooke and Mrs D had ventured over.

'We have to see the new place.'

Brooke had informed me in a text message. I hoped they could back off a little once I'd moved. But it seemed that for now they were hanging onto me for dear life. Mrs D was desperate to know when I would be opening the beauty room. She couldn't wait to tell all her friends I was working again.

'That Mandy girl, she'll get the shock of her life when I get started,' she'd told me. I wondered what had happened that had offended Mrs D so badly. It could have been anything: 'a bad wax', 'the wrong music in the therapy room', 'making me wait two minutes'.

I knew customers like Mrs D, and I appreciated them. I'm not sure Mandy had. It was women like her who were my bread and butter. Mrs D, admittedly, wasn't someone I wanted to share my deepest, darkest secrets with, but she was one of the reasons I could continue my business. She was one of the reasons I could do what I enjoyed most. That being the case, I'd be the ear she needed, the shoulder she'd cry on; and I'd never let women like Mrs D leave the comfort of my salon again. I'd protect my customers. I'd make women like Mrs D and Brooke feel as if they were the most important women alive.

And I'd love it, just as I used to.

52

'I think this calls for a celebration,' Joe said, bringing out a bottle of champagne from his holdall.

'Ooohhh, man after my own heart,' Clare laughed.

'I'll get the glasses,' Marianne offered, walking into the kitchen.

'The box on the side next to the microwave,' I shouted through, before she could confuse herself with the mass of cardboard that surrounded her.

'Found them!' Marianne called back.

Poppy and Rosie lay watching us on the play mat. I'd ensured that in the move it was kept out, knowing I'd need to distract them once everything had landed in the house. I couldn't believe how much stuff I had.

Marianne and Derek had arrived back from Devon this morning and we'd loaded Derek's car with boxes, clothes and anything else we could squeeze into the crevices. Clare had turned up extremely early. I think she was desperate for me to move, so she could move in. She'd told me her removal van was hired for the following week.

Between Clare and I we loaded up both our cars and managed Poppy and Rosie between us. Max was away on business so he couldn't help with the girls, and I wasn't prepared to ask Gina. We'd agreed that Max would have the girls overnight when he came back from his trip. I'd managed through two nights alone, and actually enjoyed the sleep. I was a little apprehensive about them staying with Max and Gina, but he'd promised if there were any hospital trips, sickness, or any minor or major events then they would inform me.

Marianne brought through five mismatched glasses. 'I'll get you some new glasses as a moving-in present,' she said, as she placed them on one of the boxes in the lounge.

'I'm sure we could think of something a bit more useful,' Derek laughed. I wanted to agree with him, but didn't want to sound as if I was expecting gifts.

Joe poured the champagne into the glasses, the bubbles fizzed, and Clare had a little cheer when he'd finished. She grabbed a glass. 'To Kathryn!' She held her glass in the air, then quickly savoured the taste as the alcohol touched her lips, her eyes shut, as she murmured her appreciation.

I clinked my glass against Joe's. He winked at me; something he was doing often lately. And every time he did, it sent a small tingle through my body, but I decided it was best to avoid that type of complication.

'A huge thank-you to Joe for making this place look amazing,' I said.

'To Joe,' they all chimed.

'No problem,' Joe grinned. He looked so young with his tight T-shirt clinging to his masculine body. He had worked non-stop. He'd really put himself out for me. He'd helped to hire a van, to save me removal costs. Between him and Derek (undoubtedly mostly Joe: Derek did what his older body would allow, Joe taking most of the strain) they'd managed to get my furniture into the new home. I couldn't have thanked him enough.

'I'd best be off,' Clare announced after finishing her drink.

'I'll show you out,' I offered after she'd said her goodbyes to everyone.

'It's a lovely home, Kathryn,' she said when we were outside. The sun beat down across the front lawn, I'd have to cut that soon. I was so excited that I had a garden. I remembered the time, long ago, when Clare had judged me for not having such a privilege. And now she was moving into that very place. And I knew she'd be happier there than she'd been in years.

'Thank you,' I smiled. 'And, thank you for all your help today.'

'It's been a pleasure,' she grinned. 'I just can't wait to get into the flat myself now.'

'How are you doing?' I asked tentatively.

'You know … I'm absolutely fine.'

'Really?'

'Yes. I'm really fine,' she nodded, confirming her answer. 'I've not felt this free in quite some time.'

'But what does Henry think about this?'

'He wants to make it work but it's too late for that. He's had plenty of opportunities, plenty of chances.'

'But maybe if he realises how serious you are about moving out, maybe—'

'I don't *want* to work it out. It's over.' She shook her head. 'It ended years ago. Many years ago. I no longer love him, Kathryn. All of this is happening for a reason. For once I'm going to follow my own path, instead of his.'

'You know I'm always here,' I smiled.

'Thank you,' she said, hugging me. Her fragrance still sweetly hanging although we'd not stopped lifting boxes and other debris I'd managed to acquire over the years.

'Thank you, too.'

'For what?'

'For being there for me,' I smiled.

'Always.' She hugged me again before walking away. Her stride was purposeful. She was on a mission, and I couldn't help but admire her for it.

Back in the house, Joe, Marianne and Derek were chatting easily. Marianne had picked up Rosie, who was asleep in her arms. Joe was holding Poppy, who was staring intently at him, her eyes wide as she studied him.

'Clare's moving into the flat, then eh?' Joe asked me.

'Sorry, I thought it was common knowledge,' Marianne said apologetically.

'I'm not sure who knows. Max hasn't discussed it with me, so probably best we don't mention anything.' I smiled at Joe.

'Secret's safe with me.' He winked again, sending my stomach lurching. I wished he'd stop doing that. 'Now, little Poppy, although I could hold you all day, I've got to get this van back.'

'I'll have a snuggle,' Derek offered, relieving him of Poppy.

Joe picked up his bag and hauled it over his shoulder. 'It was lovely to meet you both,' he said to Marianne and Derek, who both agreed it had been a pleasure to meet *him*.

'Thanks for everything. And the champagne, very sweet,' I said.

I walked to the front door with him, outside he breathed in the fresh air. He then turned to me quickly, asking 'I was thinking, how about we go out for a proper drink? Together? Alone?'

'Mmm …'

'No strings,' he stuttered. His self-assured charm withered beneath his cute dimples.

I didn't do cute. I'd never gone for cute men. But there was something endearing about Joe.

'Yeah, why not?' I found myself saying. Maybe I could change the type of man I'd always gone for. It wasn't as if they'd proven successful in the past.

'Saturday?'

'Sounds good.' This would be a very good distraction as Max and Gina would be enjoying their sleepover time with the girls. I'd probably not tell Max my plans.

Once Joe had left, I shut the front door, feeling a little apprehensive about the date we'd arranged.

A date! I was going on a date!

I wished Suzy was here. She'd said I could ring her at any time, even if we were countries apart. But we were in completely different time zones. I'd probably wake her. I couldn't even think straight, to work out what time it would be. I'd text her later. She'd tell me what people wore on dates these days.

'So, how was Libby?' I asked Marianne and Derek. I'd been dying to ask all day, but hadn't wanted to broach the subject with either Clare or Joe in earshot.

'She's absolutely great,' Marianne beamed.

'Really?' I glanced at Derek, needing further confirmation: Marianne often liked to look on the bright side rather than the realistic side.

'She looks fantastic,' Derek agreed.

'You think it's worked then?'

'Up to now,' Marianne said. 'She seems to be back on track. And Matt is lovely.'

'You don't think he could make her worse?' I wasn't sure what I meant by that, but I was still worried that Libby had influences around her that could send her off track. 'It's only been a few weeks!'

'I think he's probably the best thing that has happened to her,' Marianne smiled.

'Oh, well, that's great,' I said. 'Let's hope he doesn't leave her and she goes downhill.'

'I don't think it would matter,' Derek said.

'What do you mean?'

'She seemed content. At peace. Obviously she's getting the support from her programme, but she was like a different person.' Derek seemed genuine.

'I hope so,' I said.

It occurred to me he didn't know Libby before the drugs and alcohol. So I truly hoped he was right, had he seen the sister I thought I'd lost. I was desperate, even more so now, to see her. I no longer felt as if I should be the one to make her better; that I was the only one who could help her. She'd found her own happiness, her own harmony. I was sure she still had a way to go. But it sounded as if she was on her way.

She'd travelled a journey. She'd lost her way. But hadn't I?

Hadn't I been fighting to find the perfect road? In the process we'd both come to a crossroads and we needed to find the right way. But now we were both on track. It felt so right. Even though Libby was hundreds of miles away, I felt connected to her. She knew, as did I, that we didn't have to take the same route, we didn't have to travel in the same way, we didn't even have to arrive at the same destination. But we had each other. No matter how far away she was, I would always be there.

'We have news.' Derek smiled, his eyes shining as he gazed at Marianne, who blushed. 'We've set a date.'

'To get married?' I asked excitedly. Marianne smiled shyly. 'That's wonderful news!' I actually meant it. I truly felt complete, overwhelming joy.

'We're going to wait until next year, though,' Marianne said.

'Why? Money?' I grimaced.

'No. We want the girls to be flower girls, so we thought we'd wait until they are walking,' Derek said firmly.

I felt a lump form in my throat. I struggled to keep it back, complete happiness filling me.

As we finished the champagne, chatting about the type of wedding Marianne would want, how she envisaged her day (quiet but spectacular: a mixture of Marianne and Derek, I think), I knew I'd overcome my hardest times.

I could only look forward to what life had in store for me. All those who had hurt me, challenged me or mentally beaten me down had made me stronger. Nothing could compare to the love I had around me, the love that I would use to push myself forward.

Life has a way of throwing us obstacles. It's how we deal with these challenges that makes us the people we are.

If three years ago someone had told me I'd lose my salon, I'd be setting up a new business in a converted garage, I'd be a single parent to twin girls - I would not have changed a thing.

I'd take this road again. Over and over.

I love my chaotic life.

-THE END-

ACKNOWLEDGEMENTS

Thank you Simon for being an amazing support, even when I was driving you crazy. Thank you for listening, discussing ideas, your advice and helping me develop along my chosen path.

Alexia and Gabriella, I am so proud of you both. You amaze me daily. I love you more than you will ever know.

Huge thank you to the late Jenny Drewery, you were an awesome editor. So sad not to be working with you on any other projects; R.I.P you lovely inspirational lady.

A massive thank you to Betsy and the wonderful team at Bombshell Books for your support and guidance. Thank you for allowing me to follow my passion and make my dreams a reality.